POKÉMON™
ADVENTURES
GOLD & SILVER

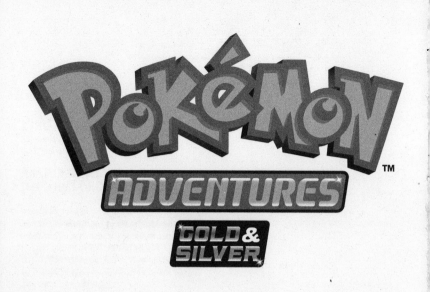

Pokémon ADVENTURES
Volume 12
Perfect Square Edition

Story by **HIDENORI KUSAKA**
Art by **SATOSHI YAMAMOTO**

© 2011 Pokémon.
© 1995-2011 Nintendo/Creatures Inc./GAME FREAK inc.
TM, ®, and character names are trademarks of Nintendo.
POCKET MONSTERS SPECIAL Vol. 12
by Hidenori KUSAKA, Satoshi YAMAMOTO
© 1997 Hidenori KUSAKA, Satoshi YAMAMOTO
All rights reserved.
Original Japanese edition published by SHOGAKUKAN.
English translation rights in the United States of America, Canada, the
United Kingdom, Ireland, Australia and New Zealand arranged with SHOGAKUKAN.

English Adaptation/Gerard Jones
Translation/HC Language Solutions
Touch-up & Lettering/Annaliese Christman
Design/Sam Elzway
Editor/Annette Roman

Printed in the U.S.A.

Published by VIZ Media, LLC
P.O. Box 77010
San Francisco, CA 94107

10 9 8 7
First printing, April 2011
Seventh printing, August 2016

www.perfectsquare.com   www.viz.com

PARENTAL ADVISORY
POKÉMON ADVENTURES
is rated A and is suitable
for readers of all ages.
ratings.viz.com

POKÉMON™ ADVENTURES

GOLD & SILVER

12 VOLUME TWELVE

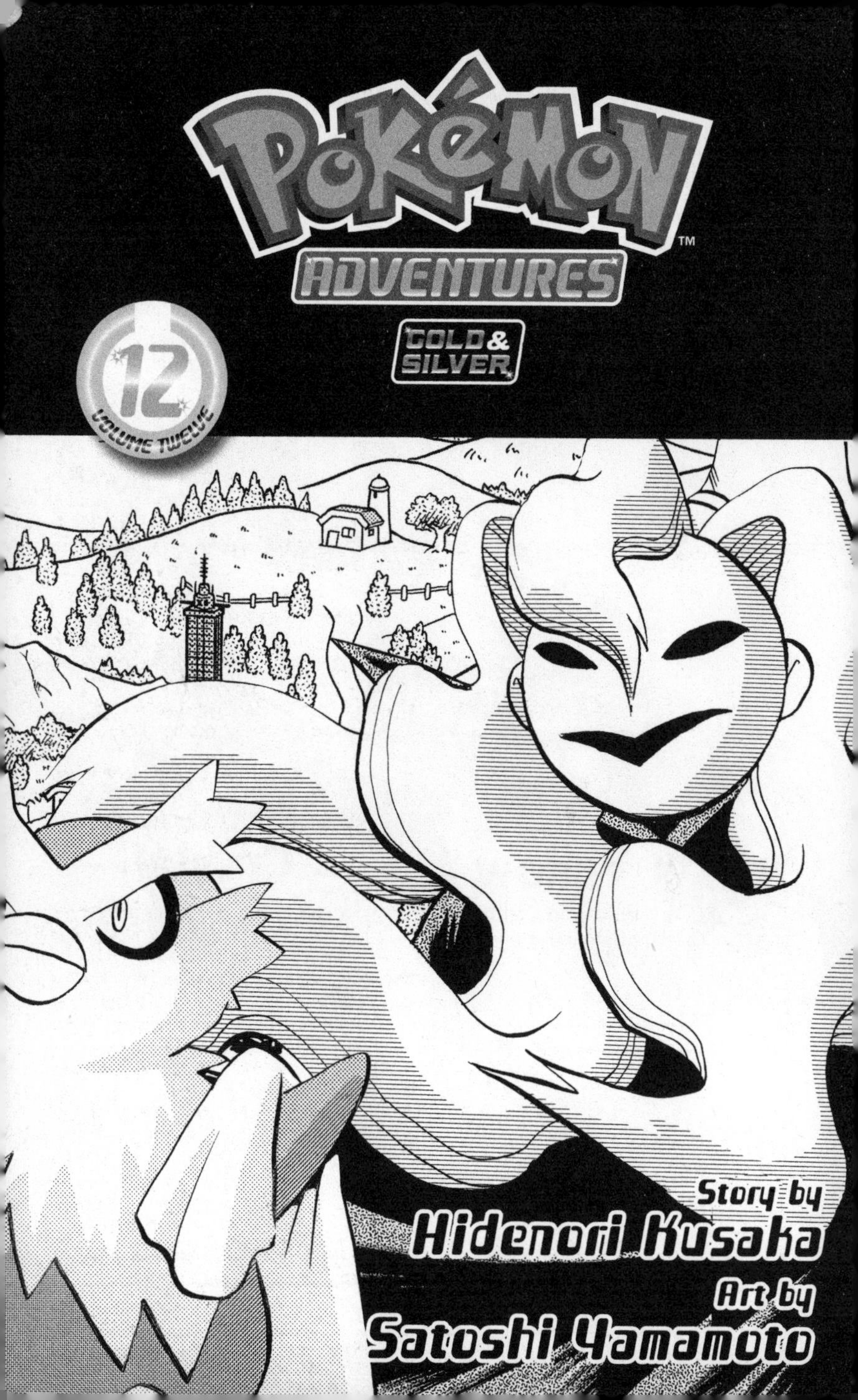
Story by
Hidenori Kusaka
Art by
Satoshi Yamamoto

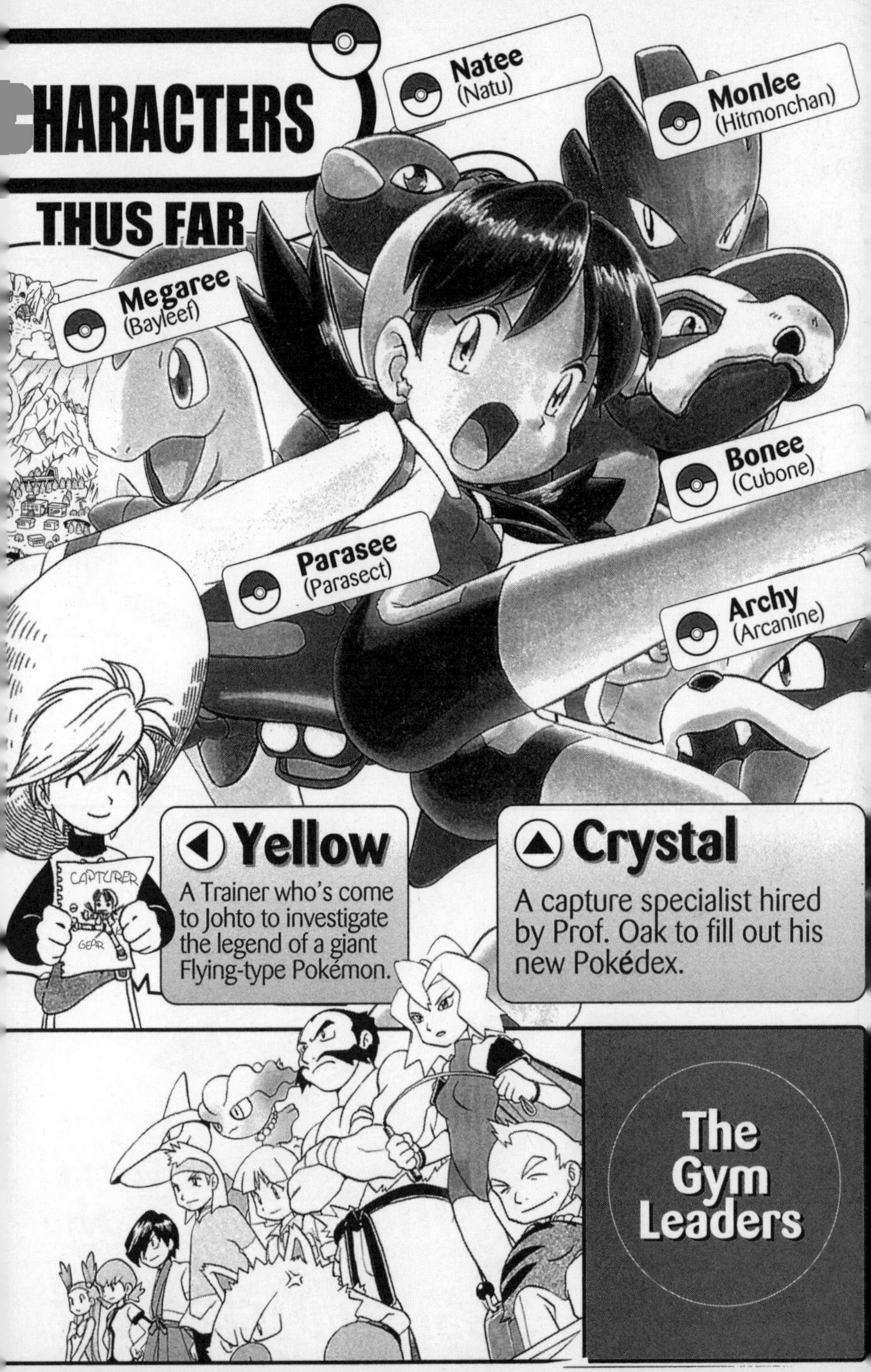
CHARACTERS THUS FAR
Natee (Natu)
Monlee (Hitmonchan)
Megaree (Bayleef)
Bonee (Cubone)
Parasee (Parasect)
Archy (Arcanine)
Crystal
A capture specialist hired by Prof. Oak to fill out his new Pokédex.
Yellow
A Trainer who's come to Johto to investigate the legend of a giant Flying-type Pokémon.
CAPTURER
GEAR
The Gym Leaders

MAIN

THE JOURNEY

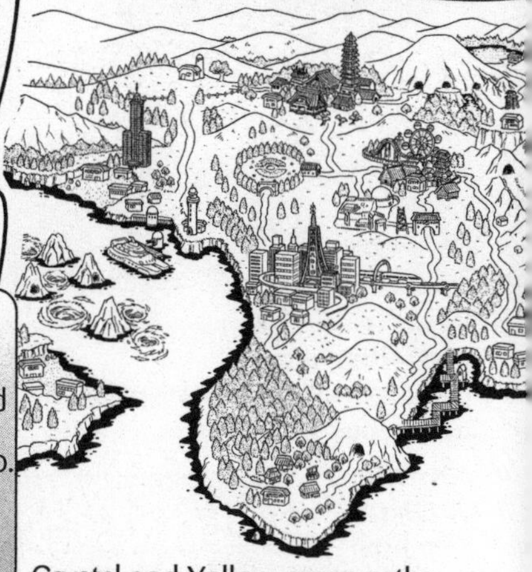

Crystal and Yellow cross paths on a ship near the Whirl Islands archipelago…and are promptly caught in a terrible vortex! Meanwhile, Gold and Silver—who disappeared at the Lake of Rage—pop up on one of the archipelago's islands!

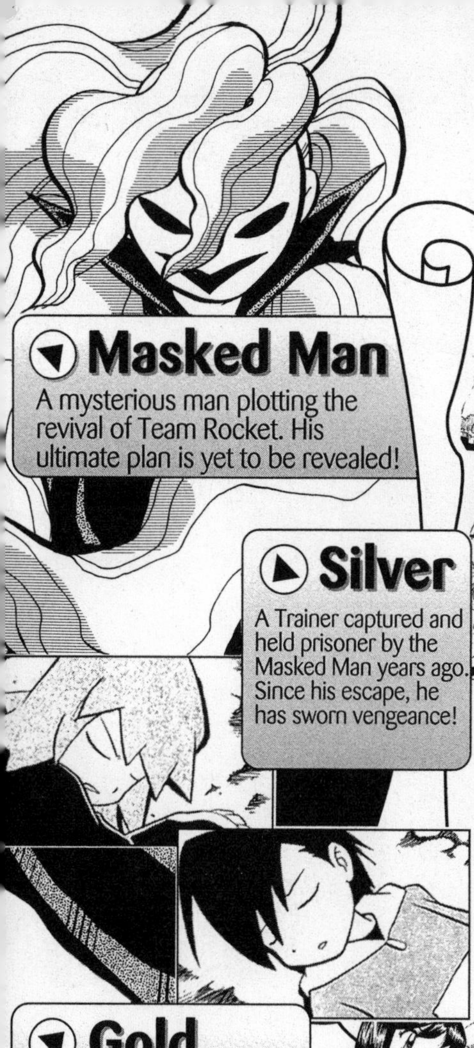

Masked Man

A mysterious man plotting the revival of Team Rocket. His ultimate plan is yet to be revealed!

Silver

A Trainer captured and held prisoner by the Masked Man years ago. Since his escape, he has sworn vengeance!

Gold

A Trainer who is a bit rough around the edges but has a heart of gold. Joined Silver in his battle against the Masked Man…and lost.

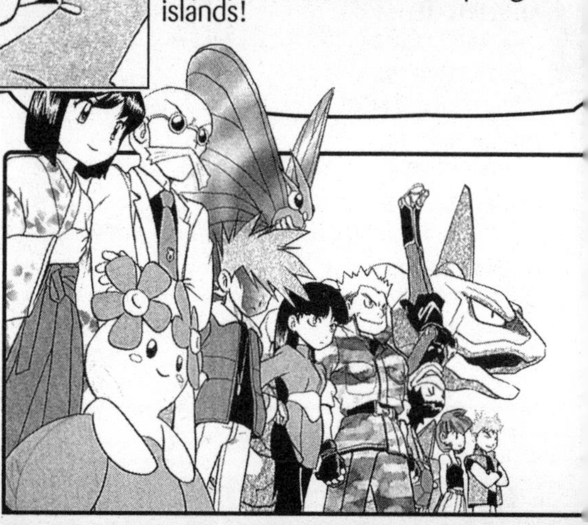

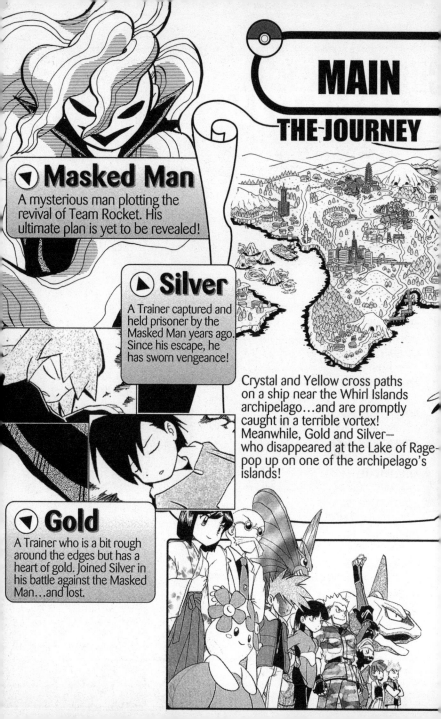

CONTENTS

ENTEI

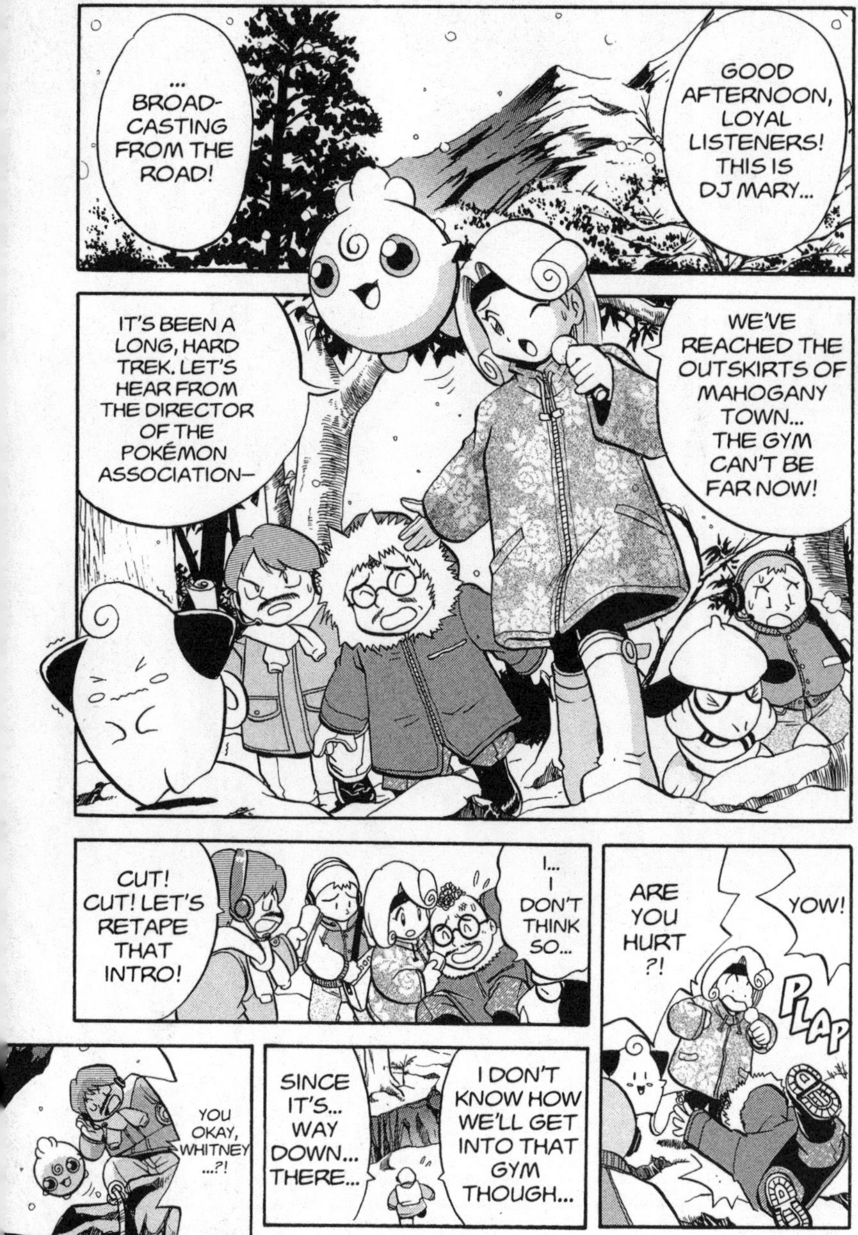
GOOD AFTERNOON, LOYAL LISTENERS! THIS IS DJ MARY...
... BROAD-CASTING FROM THE ROAD!
WE'VE REACHED THE OUTSKIRTS OF MAHOGANY TOWN... THE GYM CAN'T BE FAR NOW!
IT'S BEEN A LONG, HARD TREK. LET'S HEAR FROM THE DIRECTOR OF THE POKÉMON ASSOCIATION—
YOW!
ARE YOU HURT ?!
PLAP
I... I DON'T THINK SO...
CUT! CUT! LET'S RETAPE THAT INTRO!
I DON'T KNOW HOW WE'LL GET INTO THAT GYM THOUGH...
SINCE IT'S... WAY DOWN... THERE...
YOU OKAY, WHITNEY ...?!

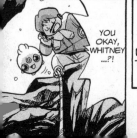

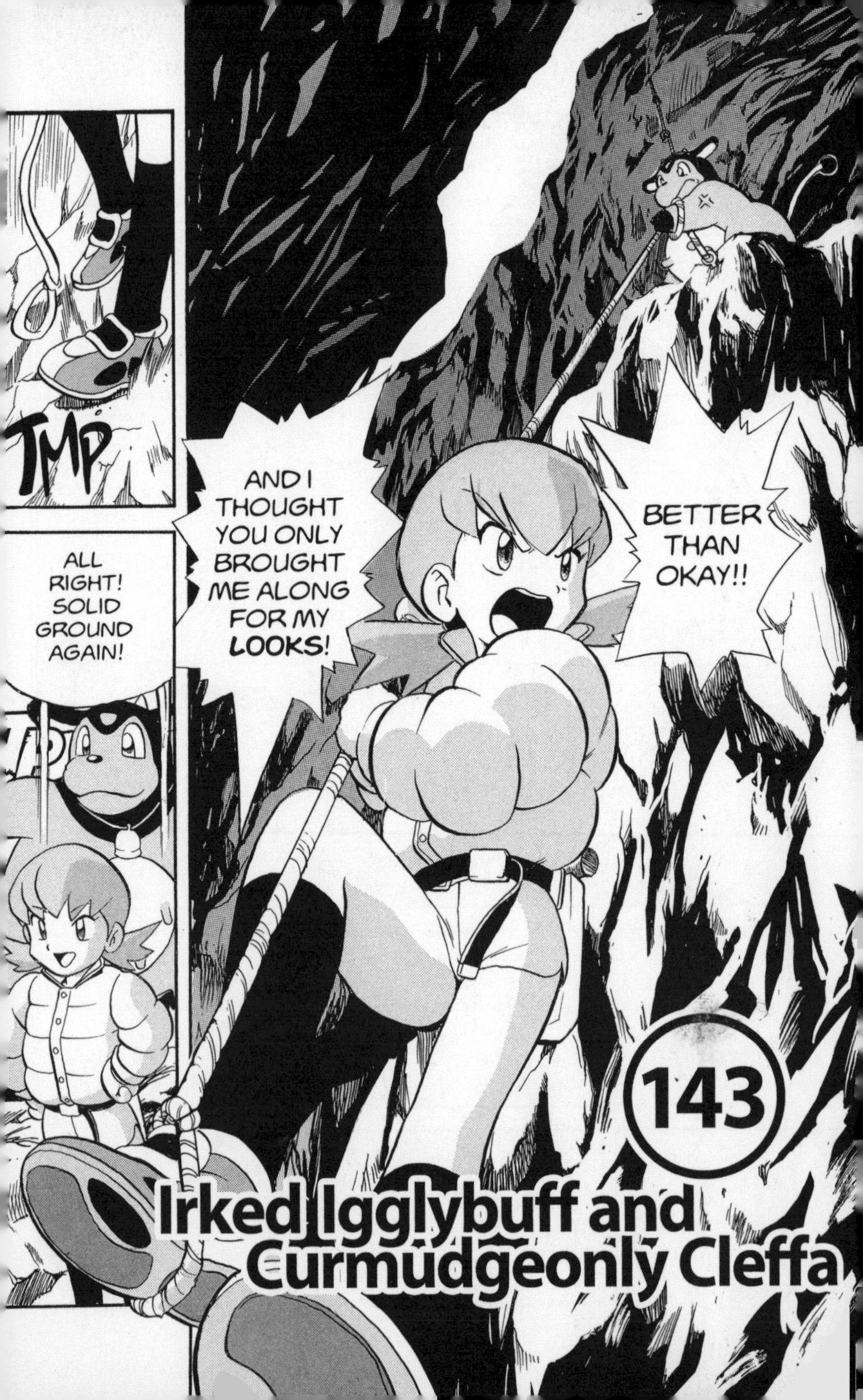
BETTER THAN OKAY!!
AND I THOUGHT YOU ONLY BROUGHT ME ALONG FOR MY **LOOKS**!
143
Irked Igglybuff and Curmudgeonly Cleffa
TMP
ALL RIGHT! SOLID GROUND AGAIN!

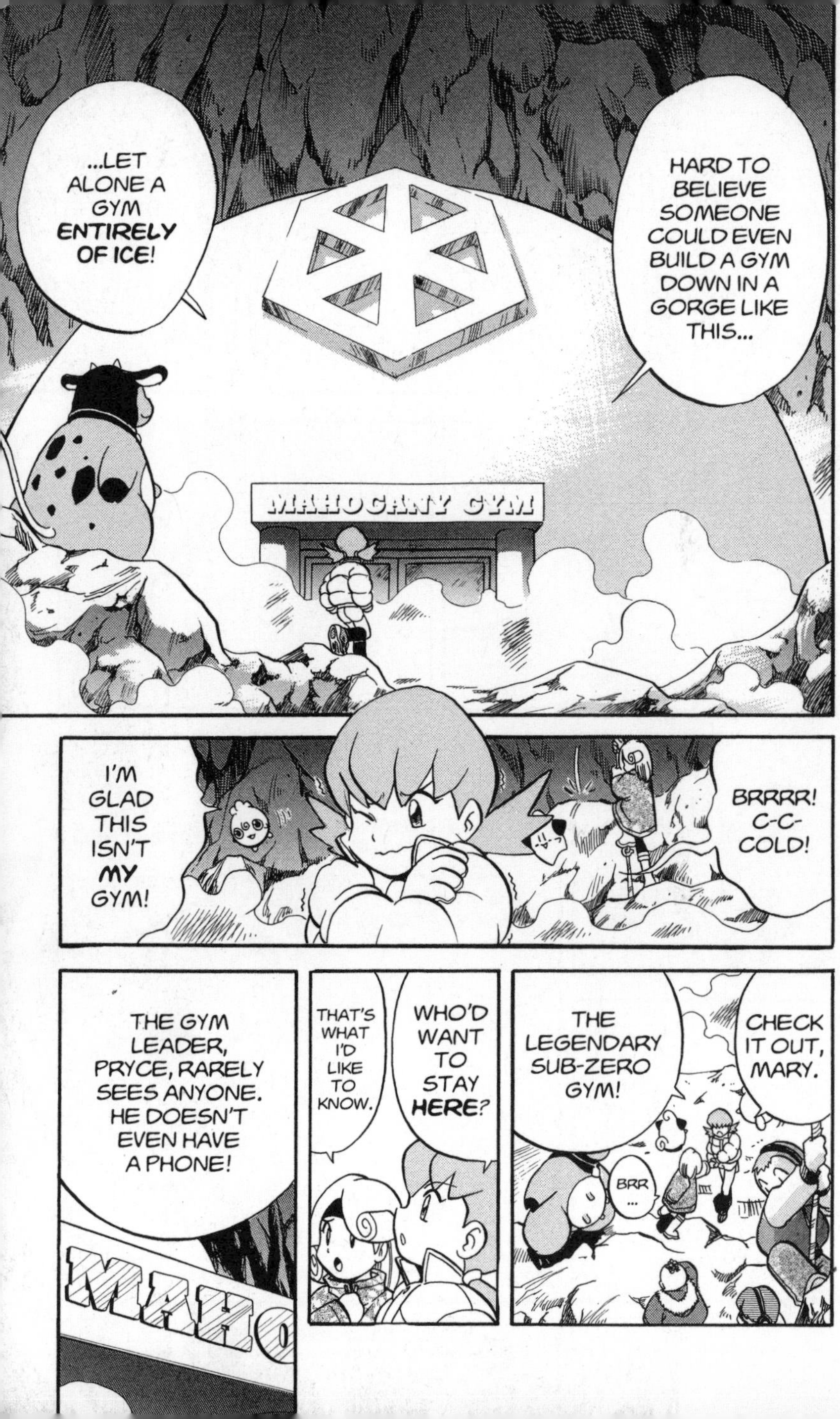
HARD TO BELIEVE SOMEONE COULD EVEN BUILD A GYM DOWN IN A GORGE LIKE THIS...
...LET ALONE A GYM ENTIRELY OF ICE!
MAHOGANY GYM
BRRRR! C-C-COLD!
I'M GLAD THIS ISN'T MY GYM!
CHECK IT OUT, MARY.
THE LEGENDARY SUB-ZERO GYM!
BRR...
WHO'D WANT TO STAY HERE?
THAT'S WHAT I'D LIKE TO KNOW.
THE GYM LEADER, PRYCE, RARELY SEES ANYONE. HE DOESN'T EVEN HAVE A PHONE!
MAHO

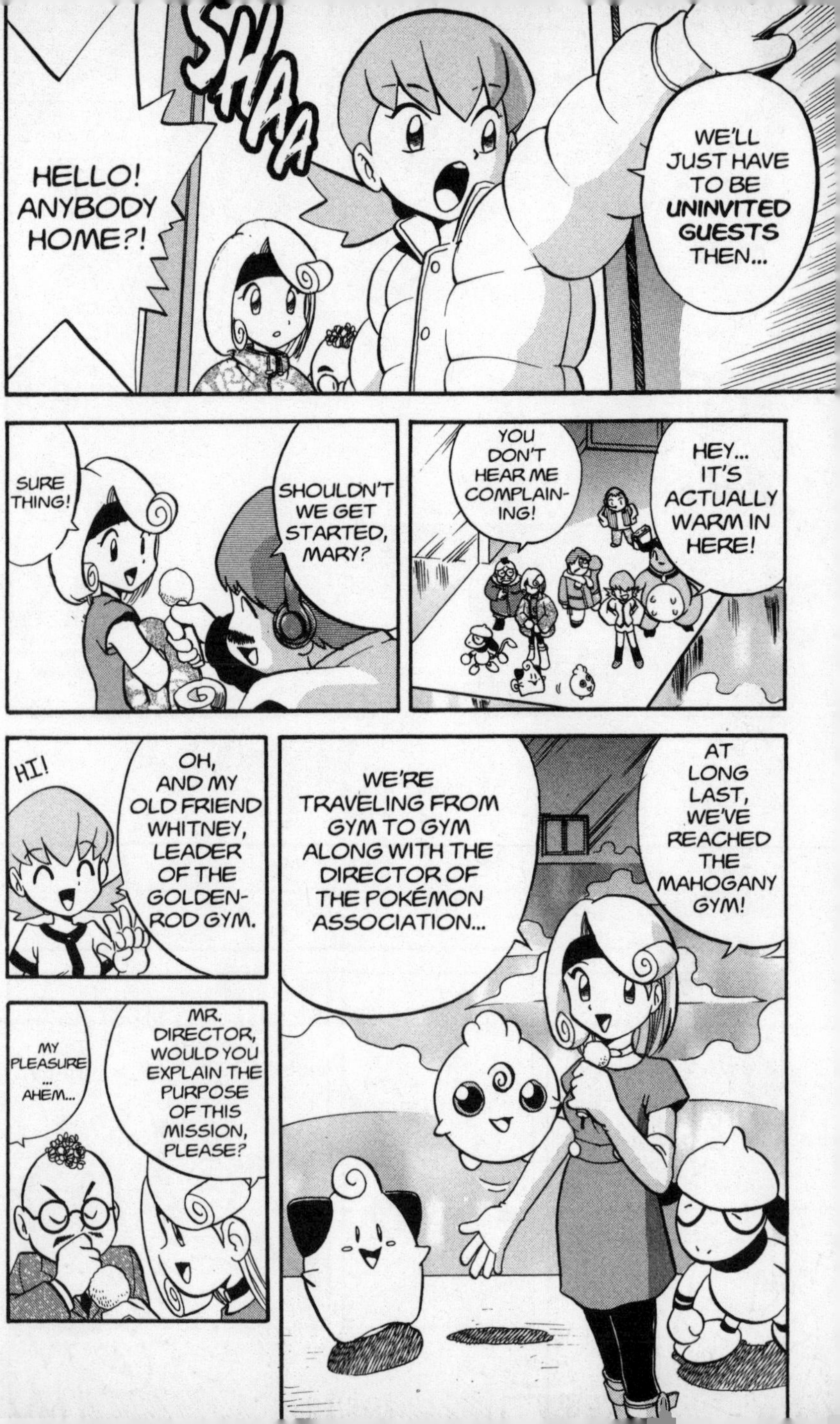
SHAA
WE'LL JUST HAVE TO BE UNINVITED GUESTS THEN...
HELLO! ANYBODY HOME?!
HEY... IT'S ACTUALLY WARM IN HERE!
YOU DON'T HEAR ME COMPLAIN-ING!
SHOULDN'T WE GET STARTED, MARY?
SURE THING!
AT LONG LAST, WE'VE REACHED THE MAHOGANY GYM!
WE'RE TRAVELING FROM GYM TO GYM ALONG WITH THE DIRECTOR OF THE POKÉMON ASSOCIATION...
OH, AND MY OLD FRIEND WHITNEY, LEADER OF THE GOLDEN-ROD GYM.
HI!
MR. DIRECTOR, WOULD YOU EXPLAIN THE PURPOSE OF THIS MISSION, PLEASE?
MY PLEASURE ... AHEM...

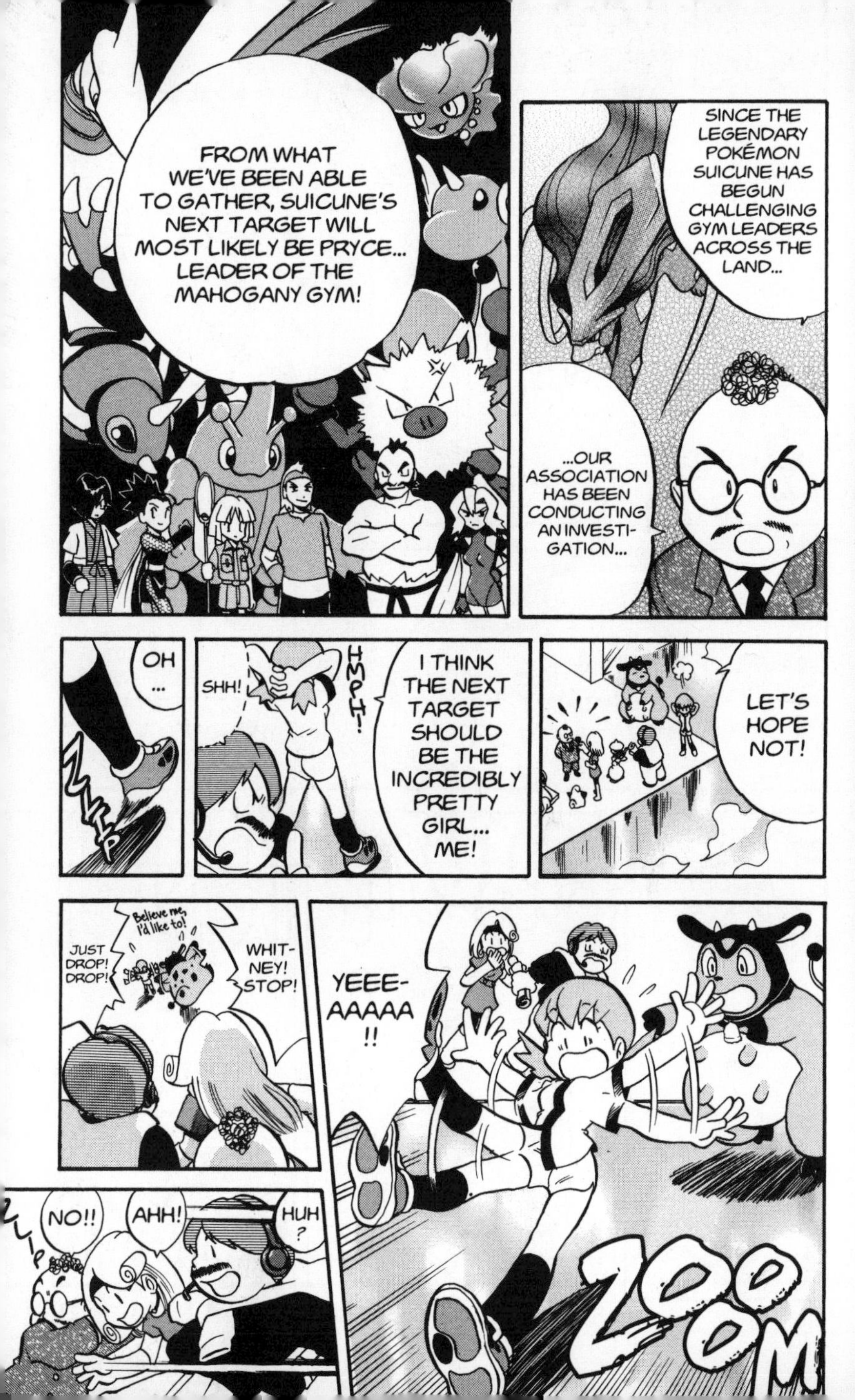
SINCE THE LEGENDARY POKÉMON SUICUNE HAS BEGUN CHALLENGING GYM LEADERS ACROSS THE LAND...
...OUR ASSOCIATION HAS BEEN CONDUCTING AN INVESTI-GATION...
FROM WHAT WE'VE BEEN ABLE TO GATHER, SUICUNE'S NEXT TARGET WILL MOST LIKELY BE PRYCE... LEADER OF THE MAHOGANY GYM!
LET'S HOPE NOT!
I THINK THE NEXT TARGET SHOULD BE THE INCREDIBLY PRETTY GIRL... ME!
HMPH!
SHH!
OH ...
YEEE-AAAAA !!
ZOOOM
WHIT-NEY! STOP!
Believe me, I'd like to!
JUST DROP! DROP!
HUH ?
AHH!
NO!!

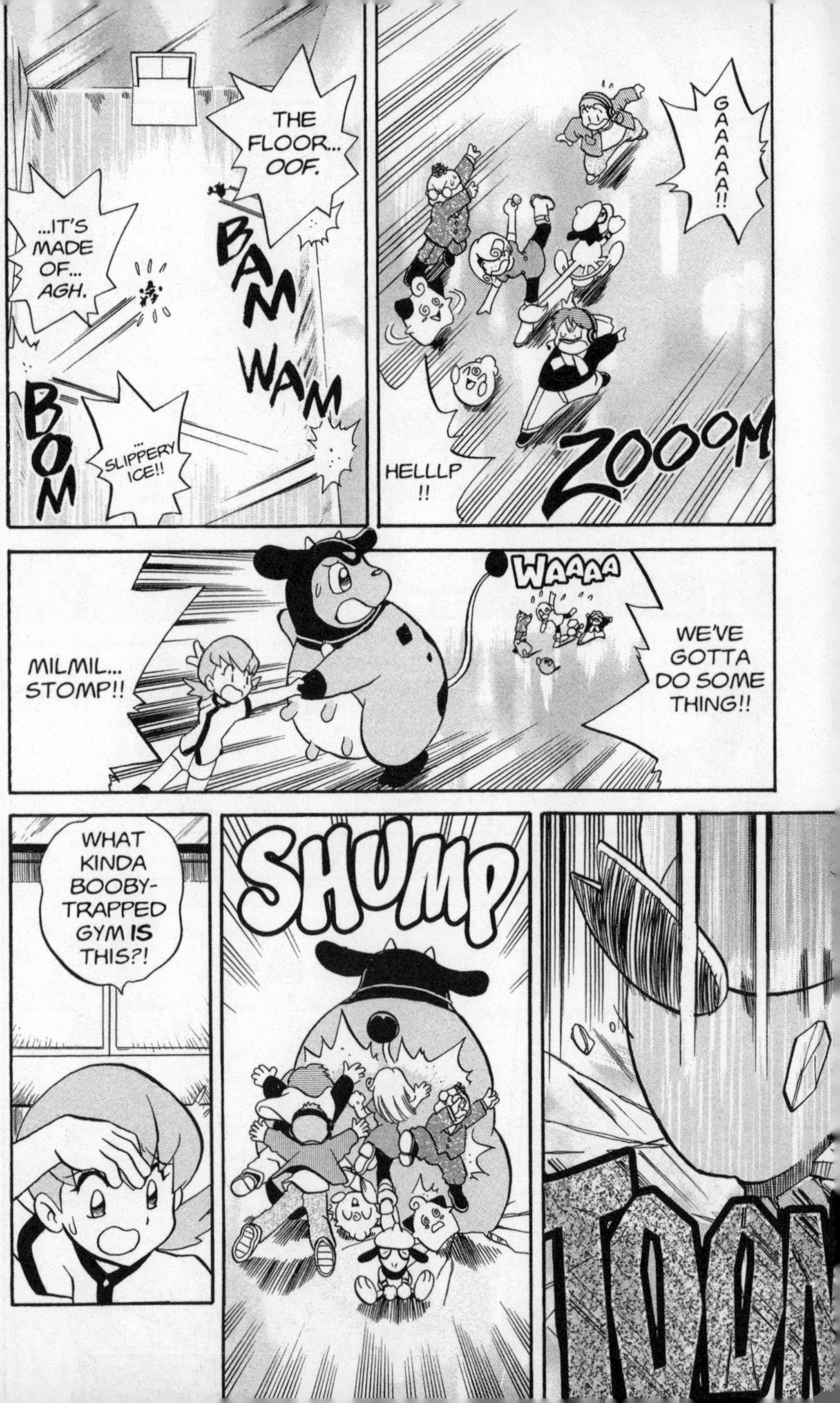
GAAAAAA!!
ZOOOOM
HELLLP!!
THE FLOOR... OOF.
BAM
WAM
...IT'S MADE OF... AGH.
...SLIPPERY ICE!!
BOM
WAAAA
WE'VE GOTTA DO SOME THING!!
MILMIL... STOMP!!
TOOM
SHUMP
WHAT KINDA BOOBY-TRAPPED GYM **IS** THIS?!

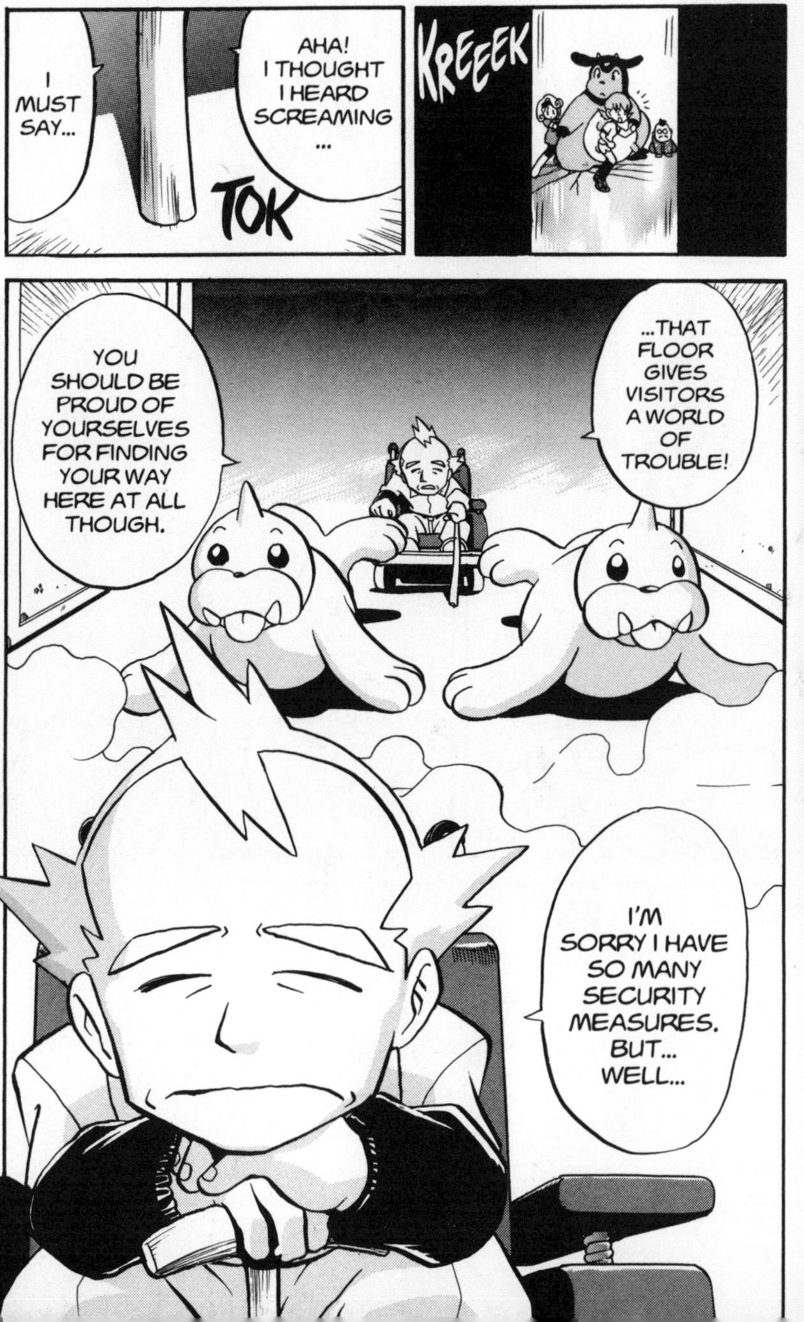
KREEEK
AHA! I THOUGHT I HEARD SCREAMING...
I MUST SAY...
TOK
...THAT FLOOR GIVES VISITORS A WORLD OF TROUBLE!
YOU SHOULD BE PROUD OF YOURSELVES FOR FINDING YOUR WAY HERE AT ALL THOUGH.
I'M SORRY I HAVE SO MANY SECURITY MEASURES. BUT... WELL...

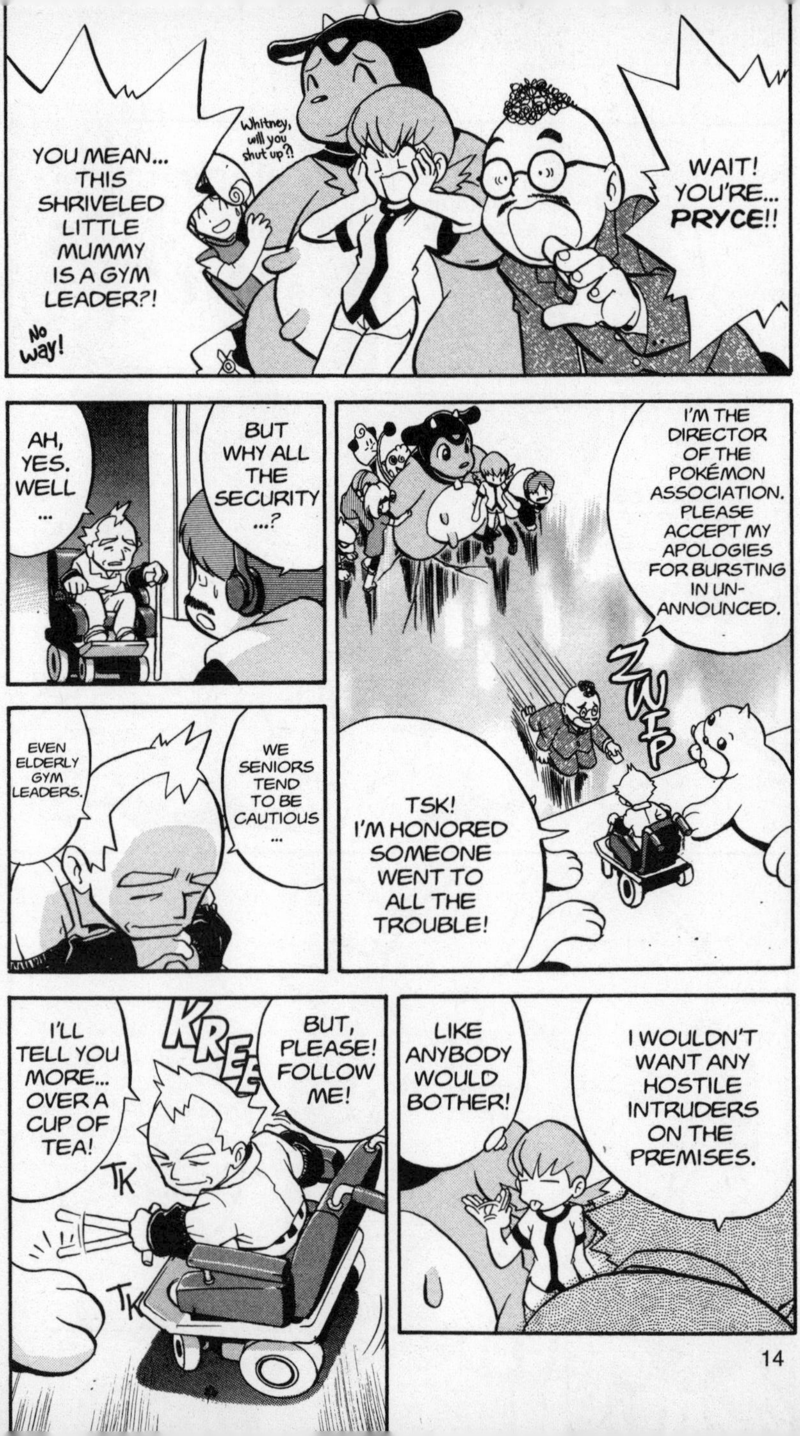
WAIT! YOU'RE... PRYCE!!
Whitney, will you shut up?!
YOU MEAN... THIS SHRIVELED LITTLE MUMMY IS A GYM LEADER?!
No way!
I'M THE DIRECTOR OF THE POKÉMON ASSOCIATION. PLEASE ACCEPT MY APOLOGIES FOR BURSTING IN UN-ANNOUNCED.
ZWIP
TSK! I'M HONORED SOMEONE WENT TO ALL THE TROUBLE!
BUT WHY ALL THE SECURITY ...?
AH, YES. WELL ...
WE SENIORS TEND TO BE CAUTIOUS ...
EVEN ELDERLY GYM LEADERS.
I WOULDN'T WANT ANY HOSTILE INTRUDERS ON THE PREMISES.
LIKE ANYBODY WOULD BOTHER!
BUT, PLEASE! FOLLOW ME!
KREE
I'LL TELL YOU MORE... OVER A CUP OF TEA!
TK
TK

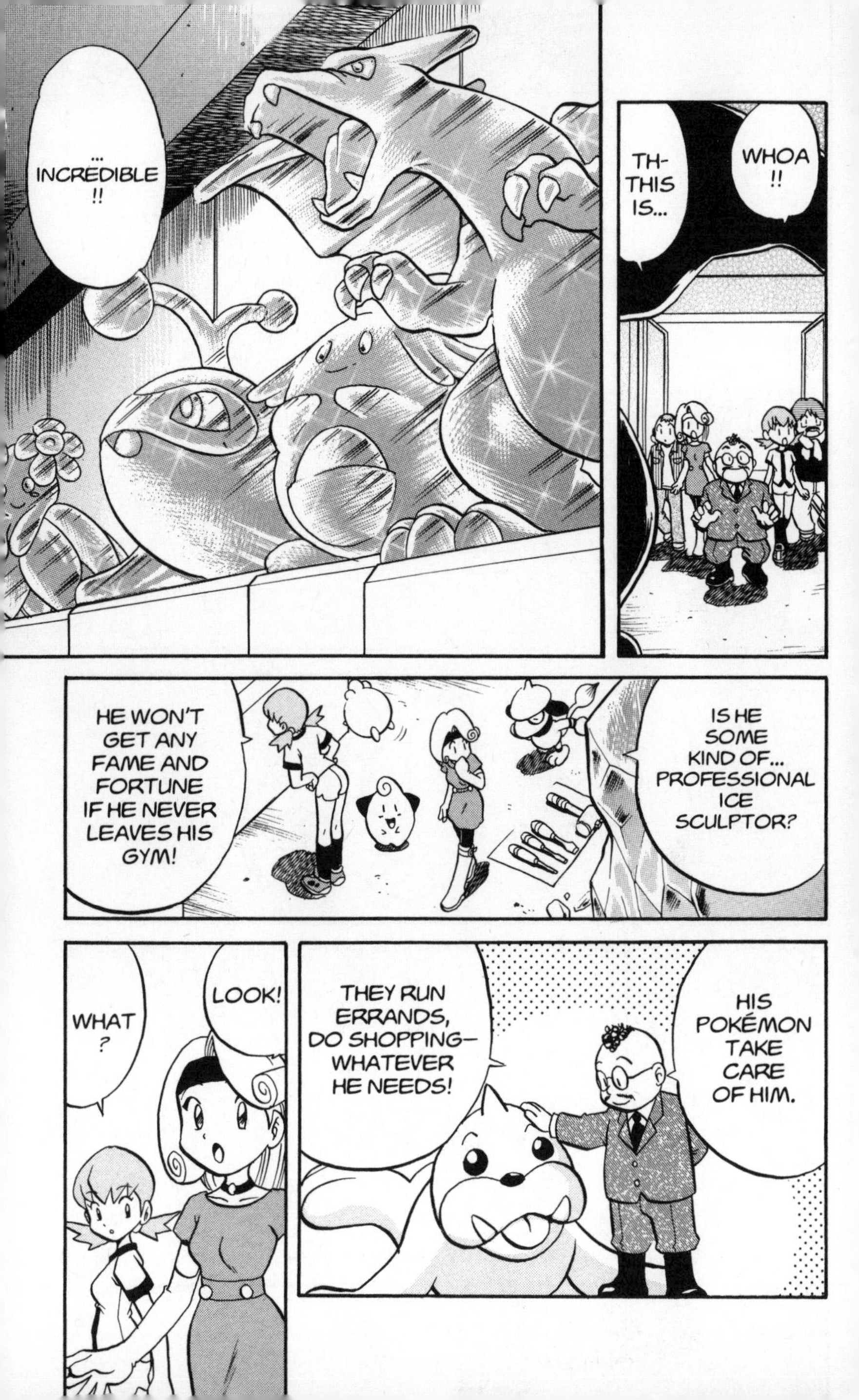
WHOA !!
TH- THIS IS...
... INCREDIBLE !!
IS HE SOME KIND OF... PROFESSIONAL ICE SCULPTOR?
HE WON'T GET ANY FAME AND FORTUNE IF HE NEVER LEAVES HIS GYM!
HIS POKÉMON TAKE CARE OF HIM.
THEY RUN ERRANDS, DO SHOPPING— WHATEVER HE NEEDS!
LOOK!
WHAT ?

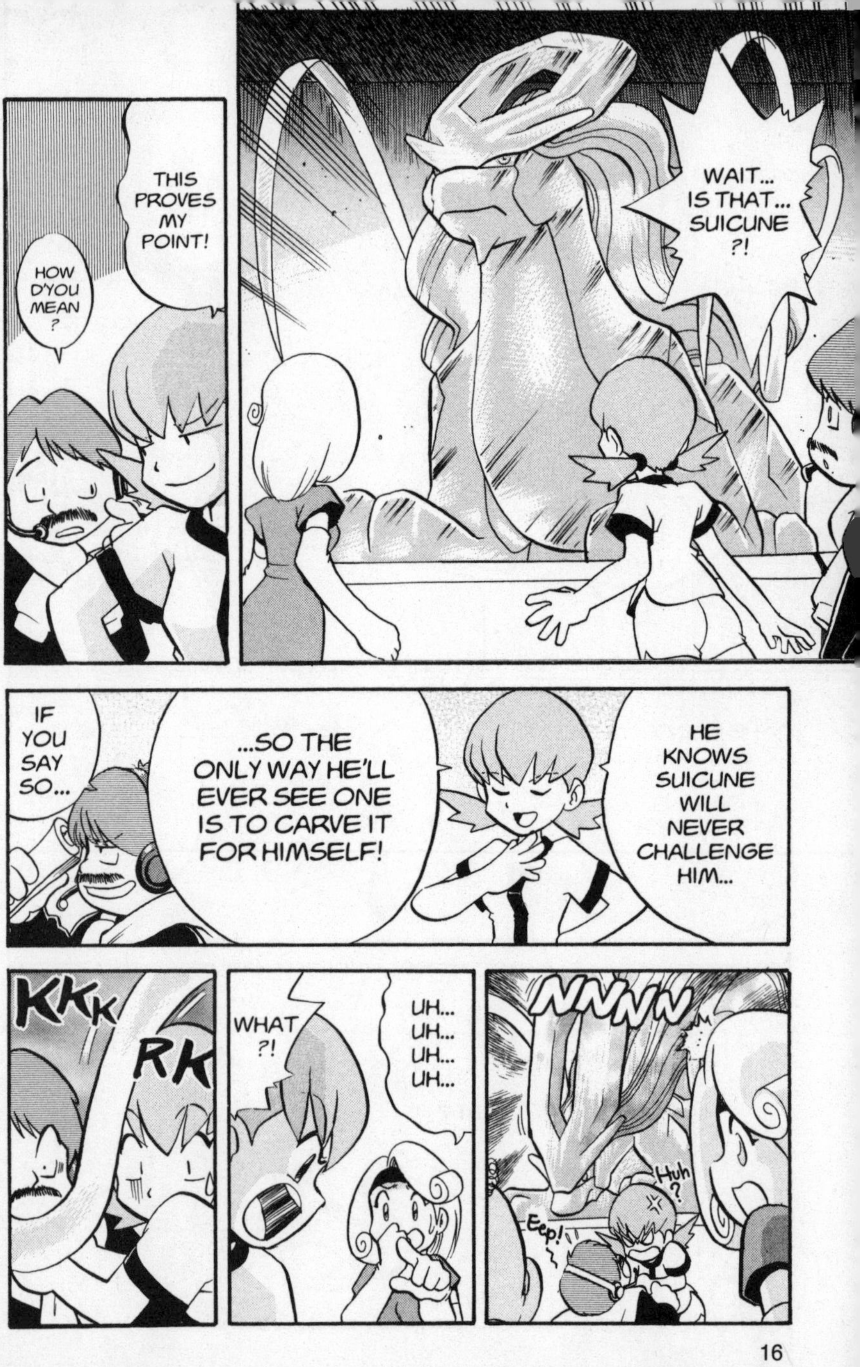
WAIT... IS THAT... SUICUNE?!
THIS PROVES MY POINT!
HOW D'YOU MEAN?
HE KNOWS SUICUNE WILL NEVER CHALLENGE HIM...
...SO THE ONLY WAY HE'LL EVER SEE ONE IS TO CARVE IT FOR HIMSELF!
IF YOU SAY SO...
NNNNM
Huh?
Eep!
UH... UH... UH... UH...
WHAT?!
KKK
RK

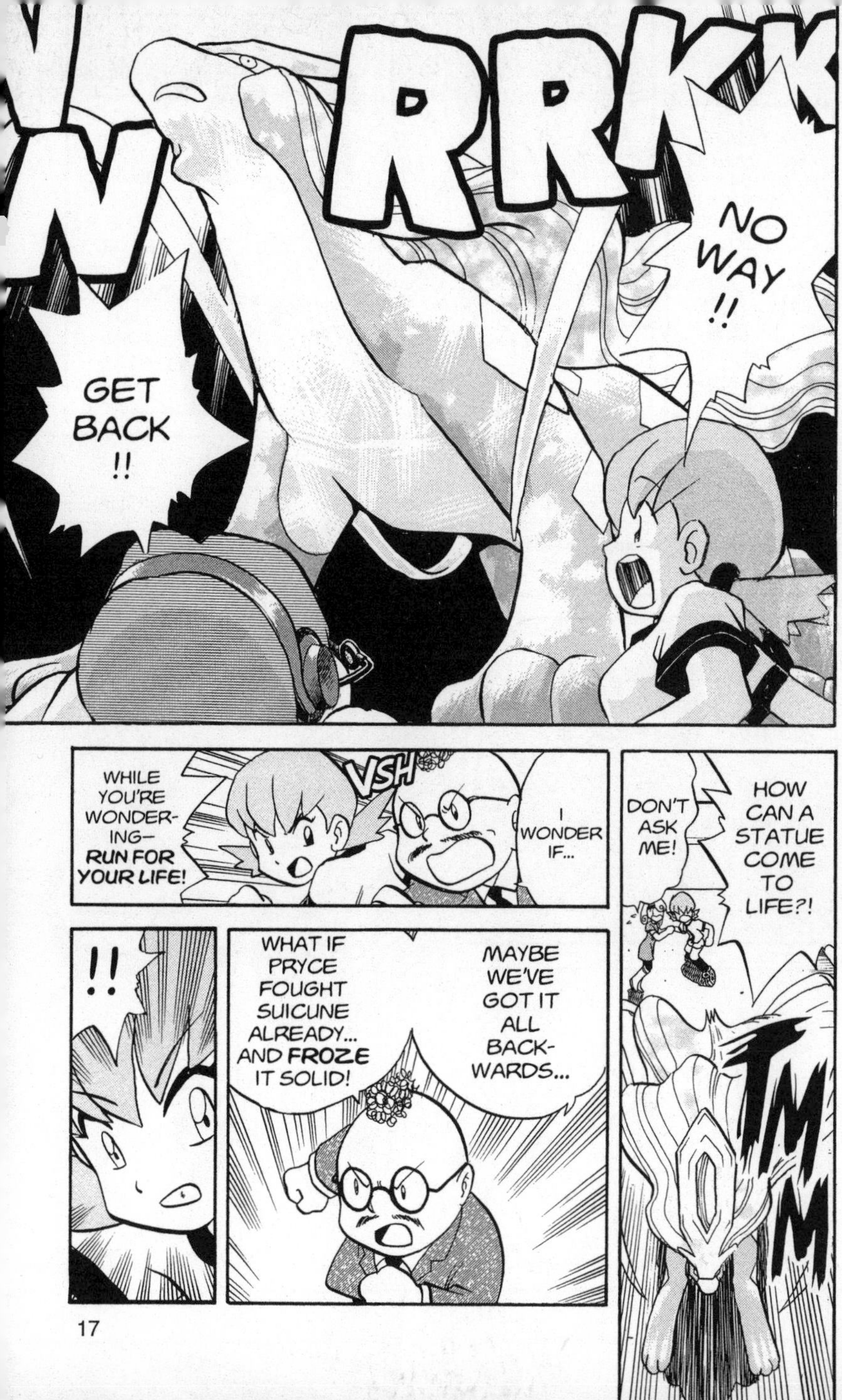
RRK
NO WAY!!
GET BACK!!
HOW CAN A STATUE COME TO LIFE?!
DON'T ASK ME!
I WONDER IF...
VSH
WHILE YOU'RE WONDERING— **RUN FOR YOUR LIFE!**
MAYBE WE'VE GOT IT ALL BACKWARDS...
WHAT IF PRYCE FOUGHT SUICUNE ALREADY... AND **FROZE** IT SOLID!
!!

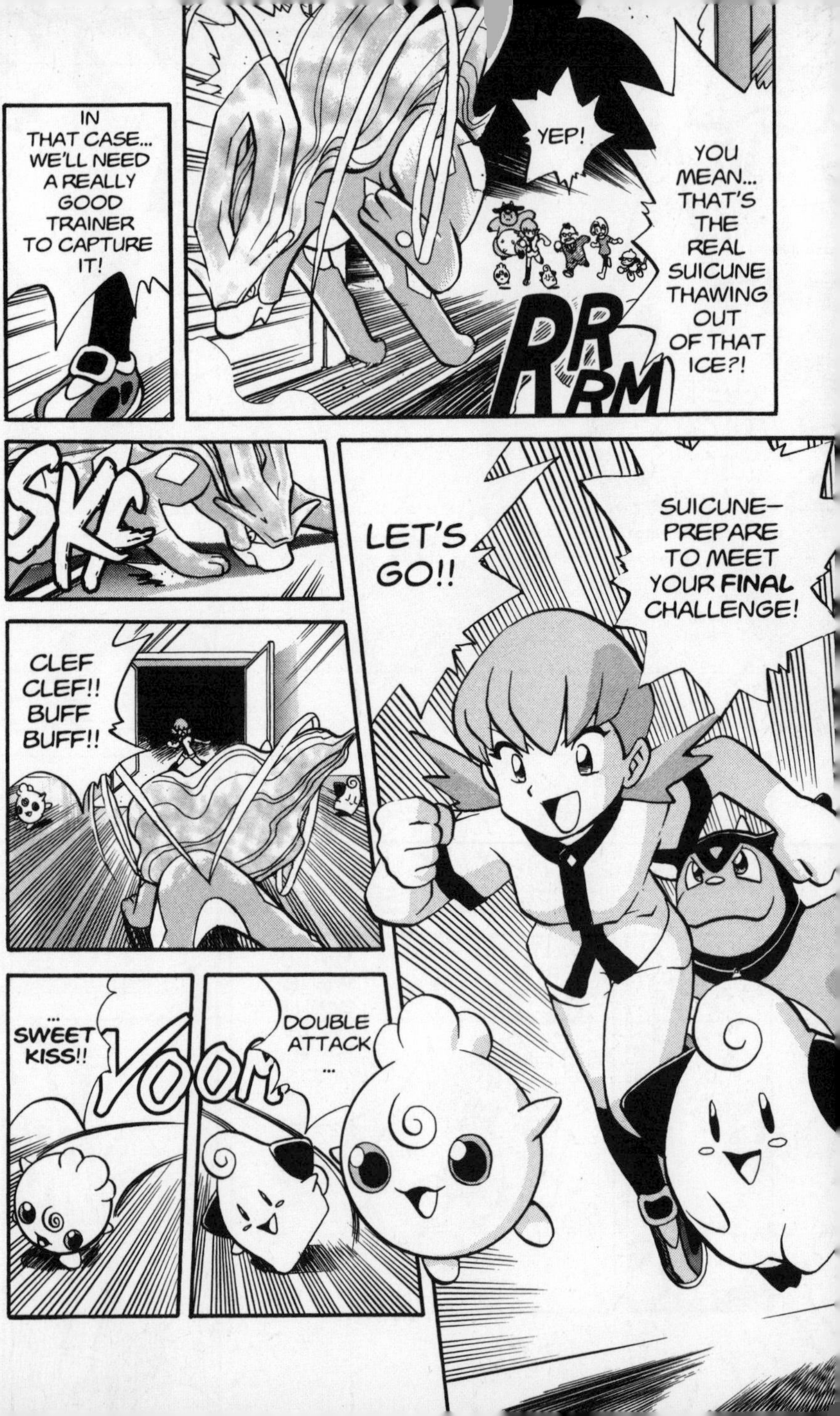
YOU MEAN... THAT'S THE REAL SUICUNE THAWING OUT OF THAT ICE?!
YEP!
RRRM
IN THAT CASE... WE'LL NEED A REALLY GOOD TRAINER TO CAPTURE IT!
SUICUNE—PREPARE TO MEET YOUR **FINAL** CHALLENGE!
LET'S GO!!
SKK
CLEF CLEF!! BUFF BUFF!!
DOUBLE ATTACK...
VOOM
...SWEET KISS!!

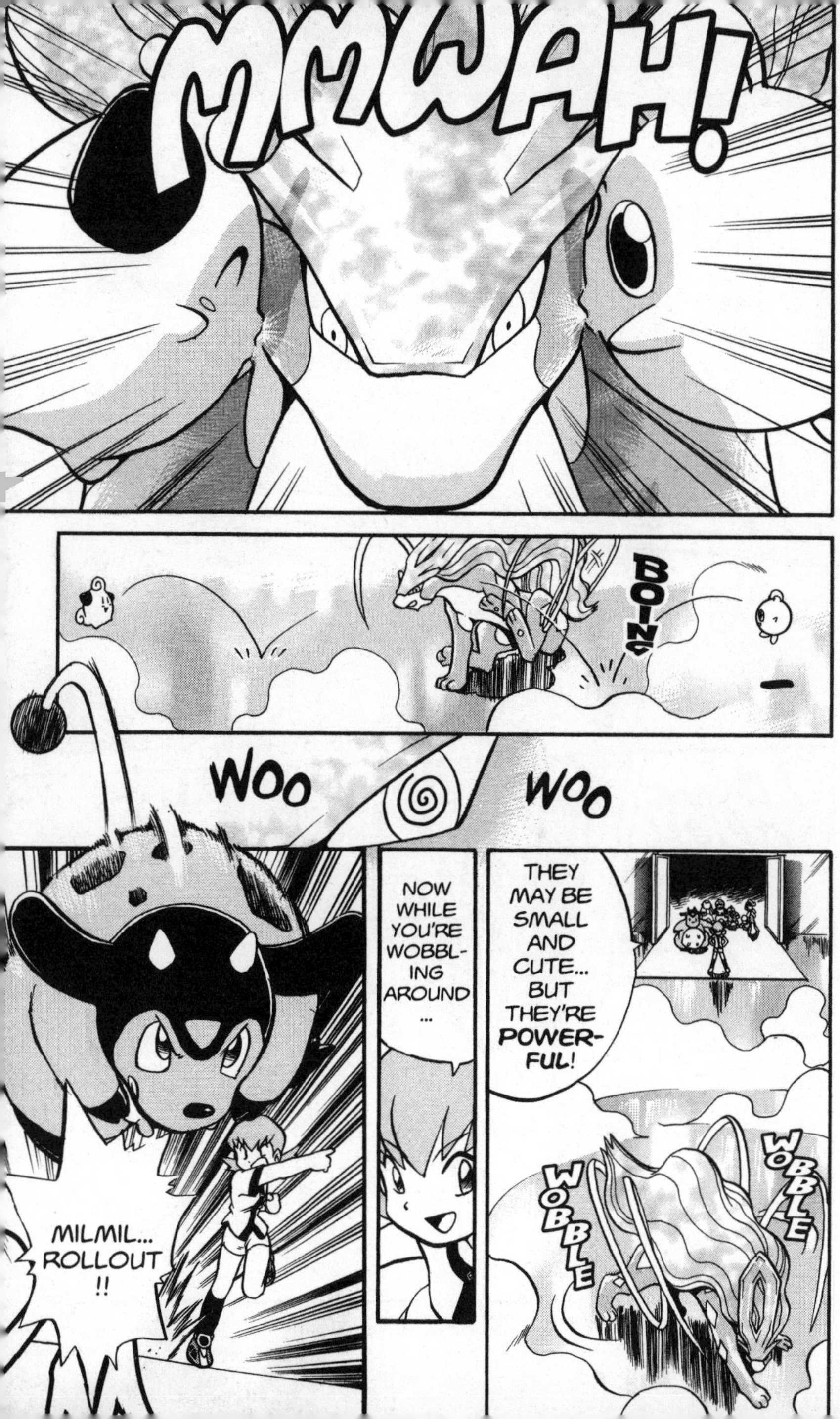
MMWAH!
BOING
WOO
WOO
THEY MAY BE SMALL AND CUTE... BUT THEY'RE **POWERFUL!**
WOBBLE
WOBBLE
NOW WHILE YOU'RE WOBBLING AROUND...
MILMIL... ROLLOUT!!

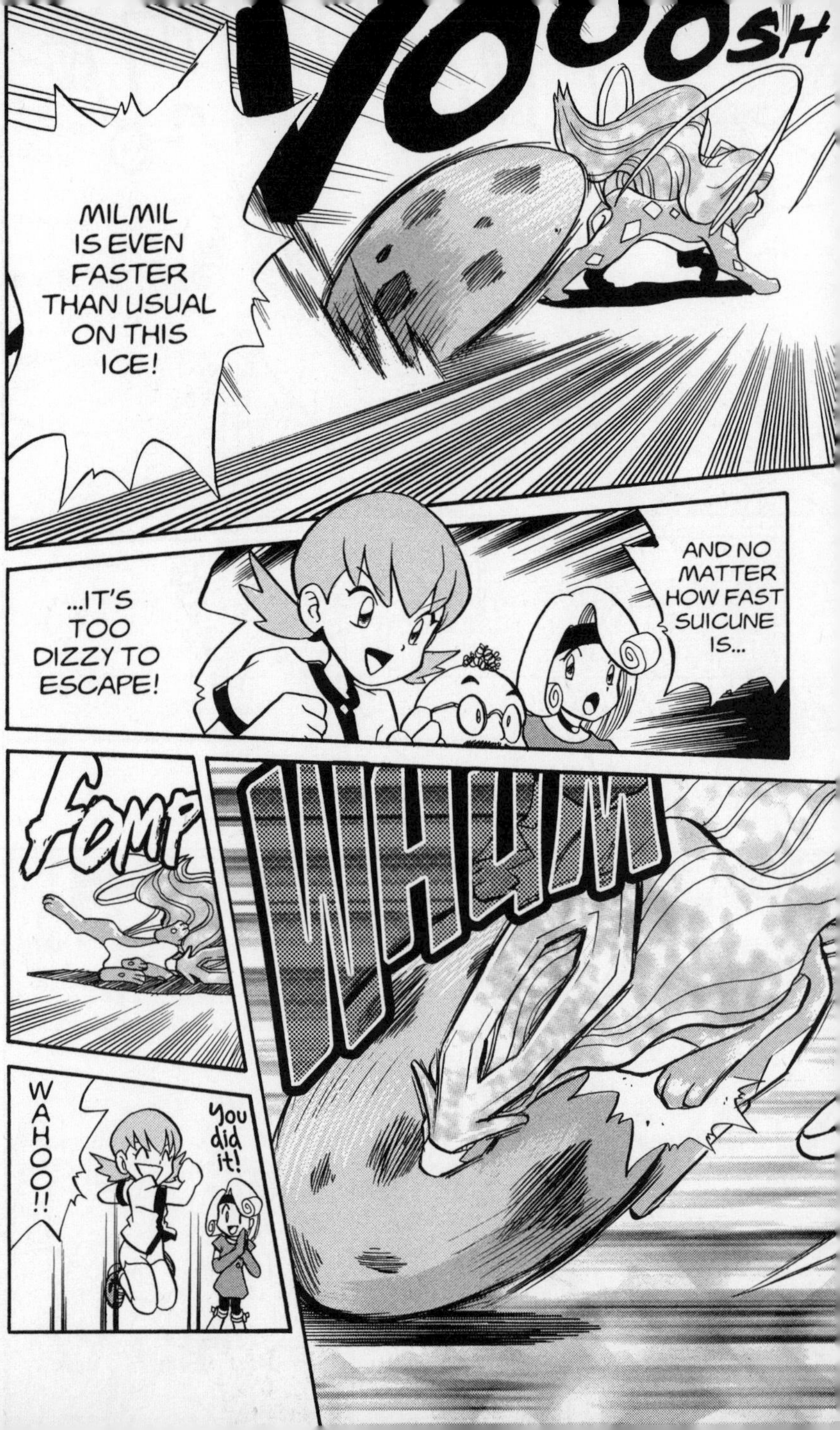
WOOOOSH
MILMIL IS EVEN FASTER THAN USUAL ON THIS ICE!
AND NO MATTER HOW FAST SUICUNE IS...
...IT'S TOO DIZZY TO ESCAPE!
WHAM
FOMP
You did it!
WAHOO!!

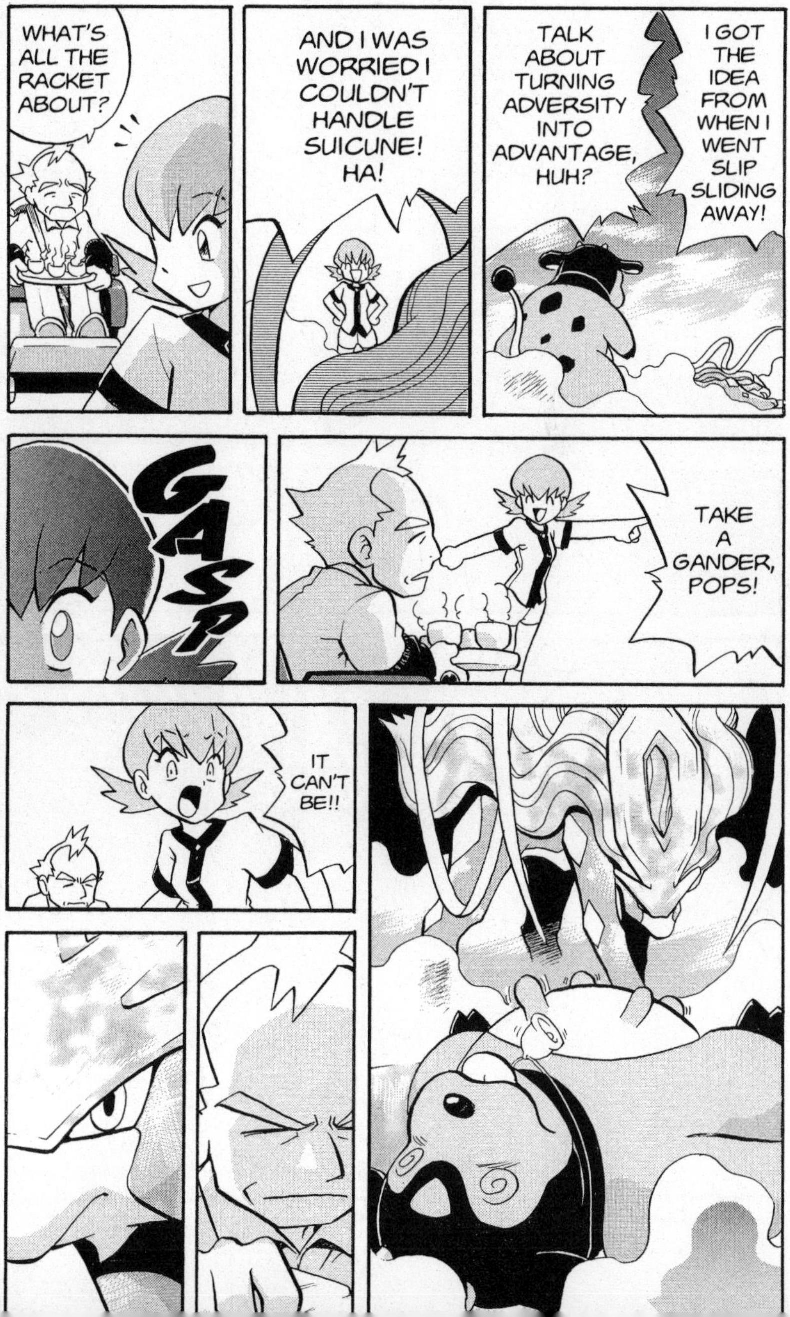
I GOT THE IDEA FROM WHEN I WENT SLIP SLIDING AWAY!
TALK ABOUT TURNING ADVERSITY INTO ADVANTAGE, HUH?
AND I WAS WORRIED I COULDN'T HANDLE SUICUNE! HA!
WHAT'S ALL THE RACKET ABOUT?
TAKE A GANDER, POPS!
GASP
IT CAN'T BE!!

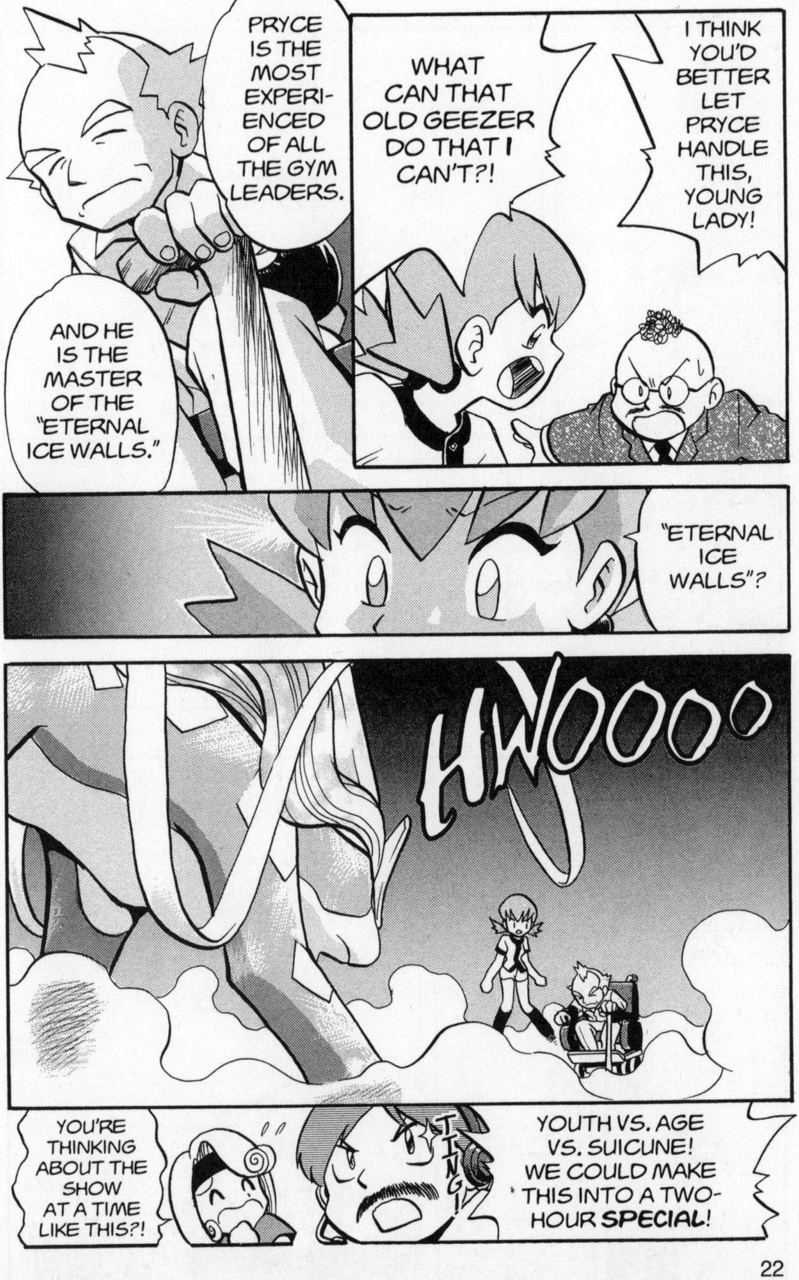
I THINK YOU'D BETTER LET PRYCE HANDLE THIS, YOUNG LADY!
WHAT CAN THAT OLD GEEZER DO THAT I CAN'T?!
PRYCE IS THE MOST EXPERI-ENCED OF ALL THE GYM LEADERS.
AND HE IS THE MASTER OF THE "ETERNAL ICE WALLS."
"ETERNAL ICE WALLS"?
HWOOOO
YOUTH VS. AGE VS. SUICUNE! WE COULD MAKE THIS INTO A TWO-HOUR **SPECIAL**!
TING!
YOU'RE THINKING ABOUT THE SHOW AT A TIME LIKE THIS?!

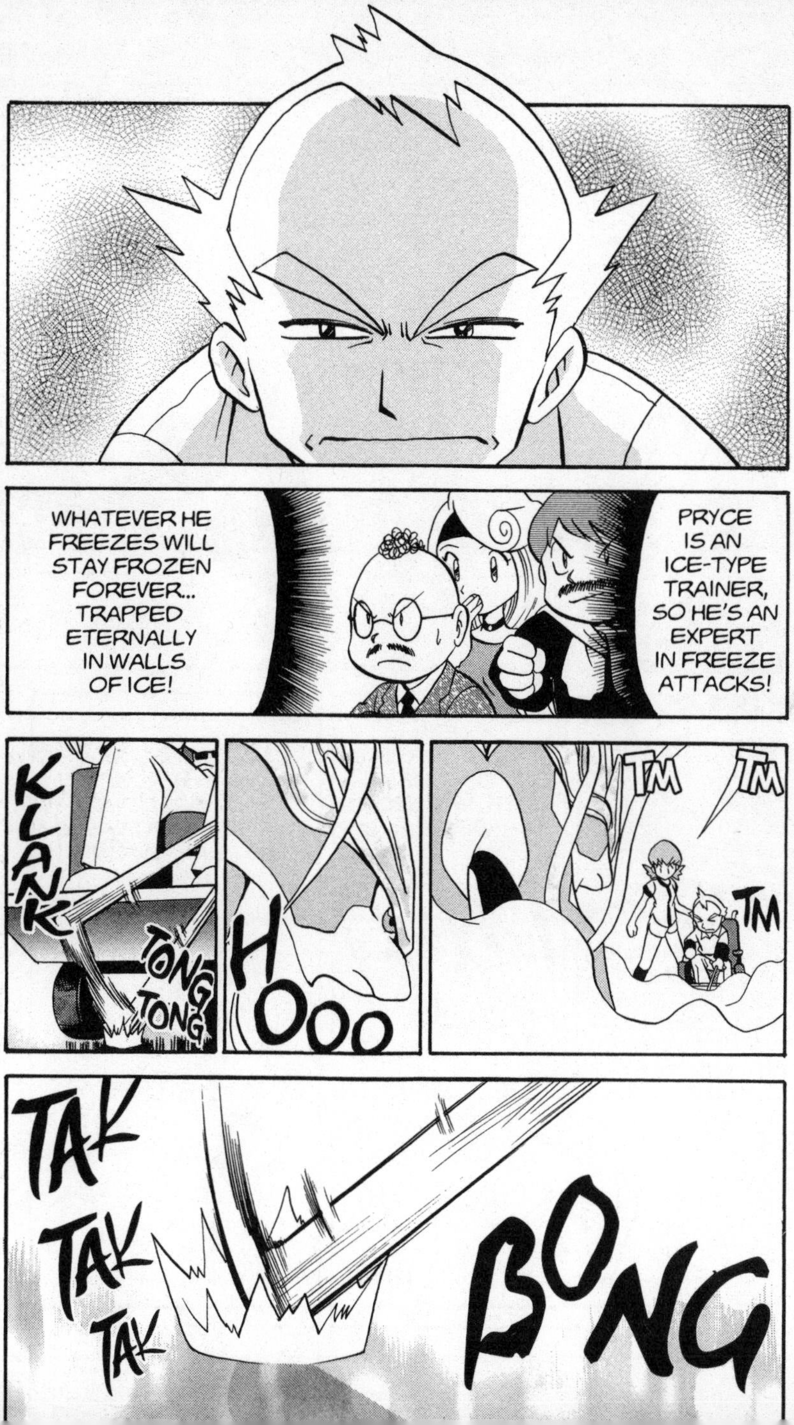
PRYCE IS AN ICE-TYPE TRAINER, SO HE'S AN EXPERT IN FREEZE ATTACKS!
WHATEVER HE FREEZES WILL STAY FROZEN FOREVER... TRAPPED ETERNALLY IN WALLS OF ICE!
TM TM
TM
HOOO
KLANK
TONG TONG
BONG
TAK TAK TAK

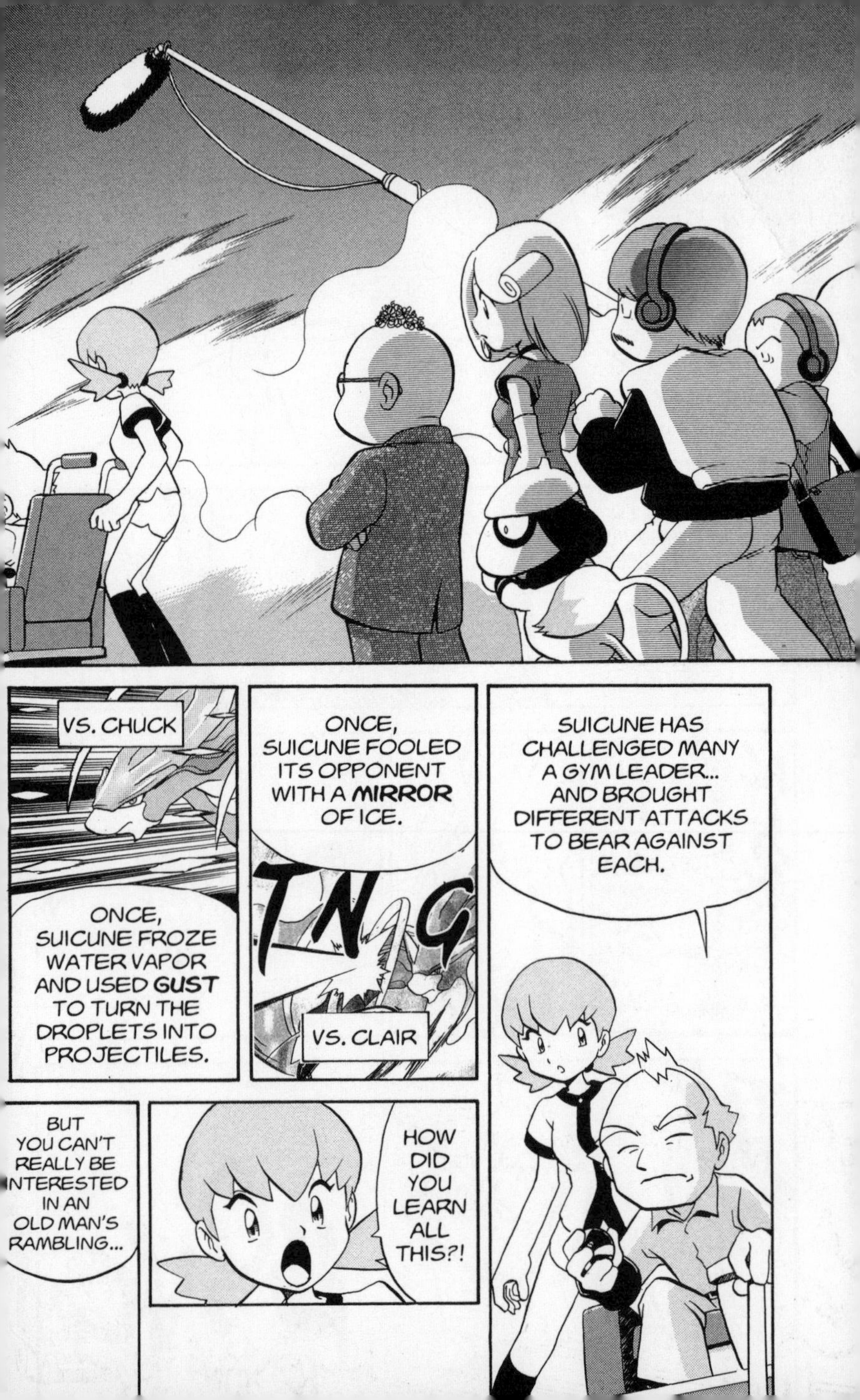
SUICUNE HAS CHALLENGED MANY A GYM LEADER... AND BROUGHT DIFFERENT ATTACKS TO BEAR AGAINST EACH.
ONCE, SUICUNE FOOLED ITS OPPONENT WITH A MIRROR OF ICE.
VS. CLAIR
VS. CHUCK
ONCE, SUICUNE FROZE WATER VAPOR AND USED GUST TO TURN THE DROPLETS INTO PROJECTILES.
HOW DID YOU LEARN ALL THIS?!
BUT YOU CAN'T REALLY BE INTERESTED IN AN OLD MAN'S RAMBLING...

144 Savvy Swinub

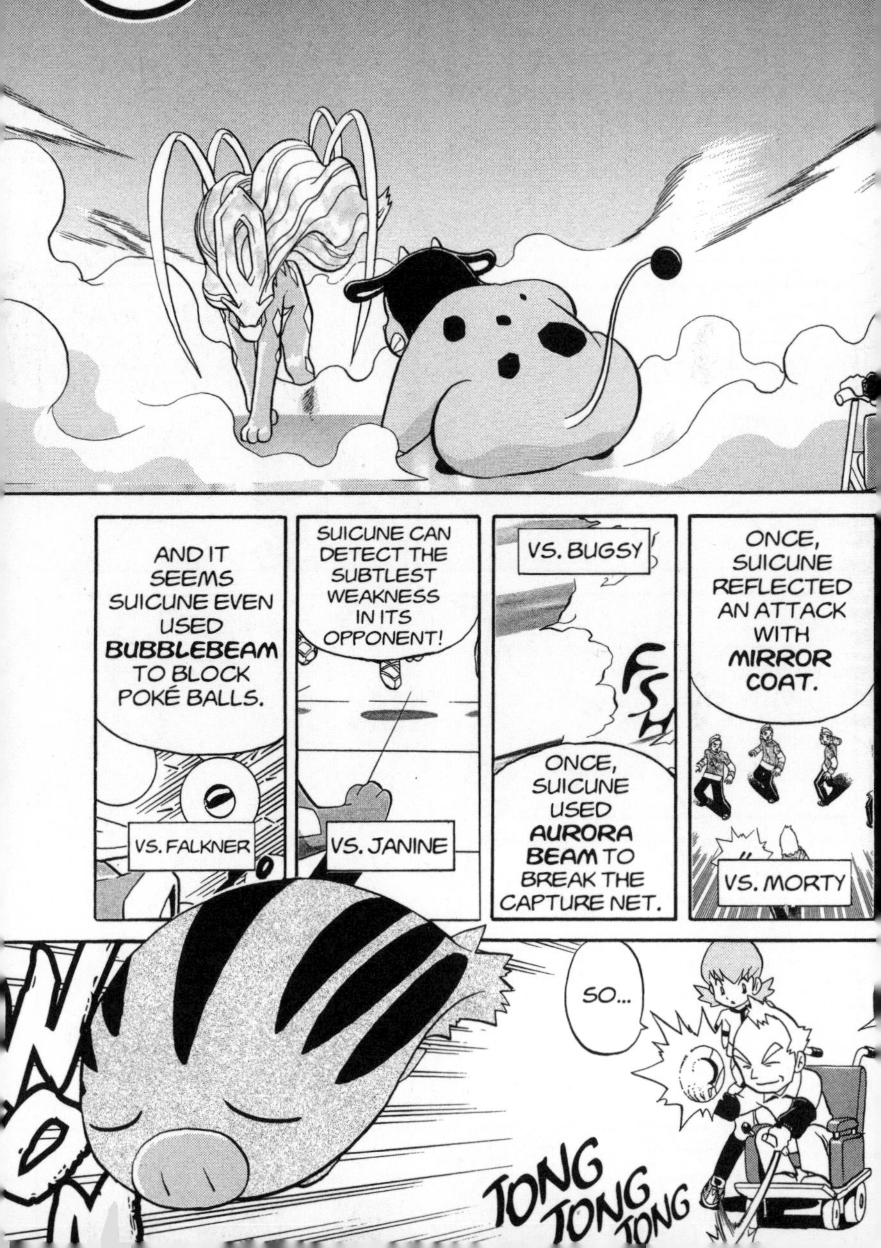

ONCE, SUICUNE REFLECTED AN ATTACK WITH **MIRROR COAT.**
VS. MORTY
VS. BUGSY
FSH
ONCE, SUICUNE USED **AURORA BEAM** TO BREAK THE CAPTURE NET.
SUICUNE CAN DETECT THE SUBTLEST WEAKNESS IN ITS OPPONENT!
VS. JANINE
AND IT SEEMS SUICUNE EVEN USED **BUBBLEBEAM** TO BLOCK POKÉ BALLS.
VS. FALKNER
SO...
TONG TONG TONG

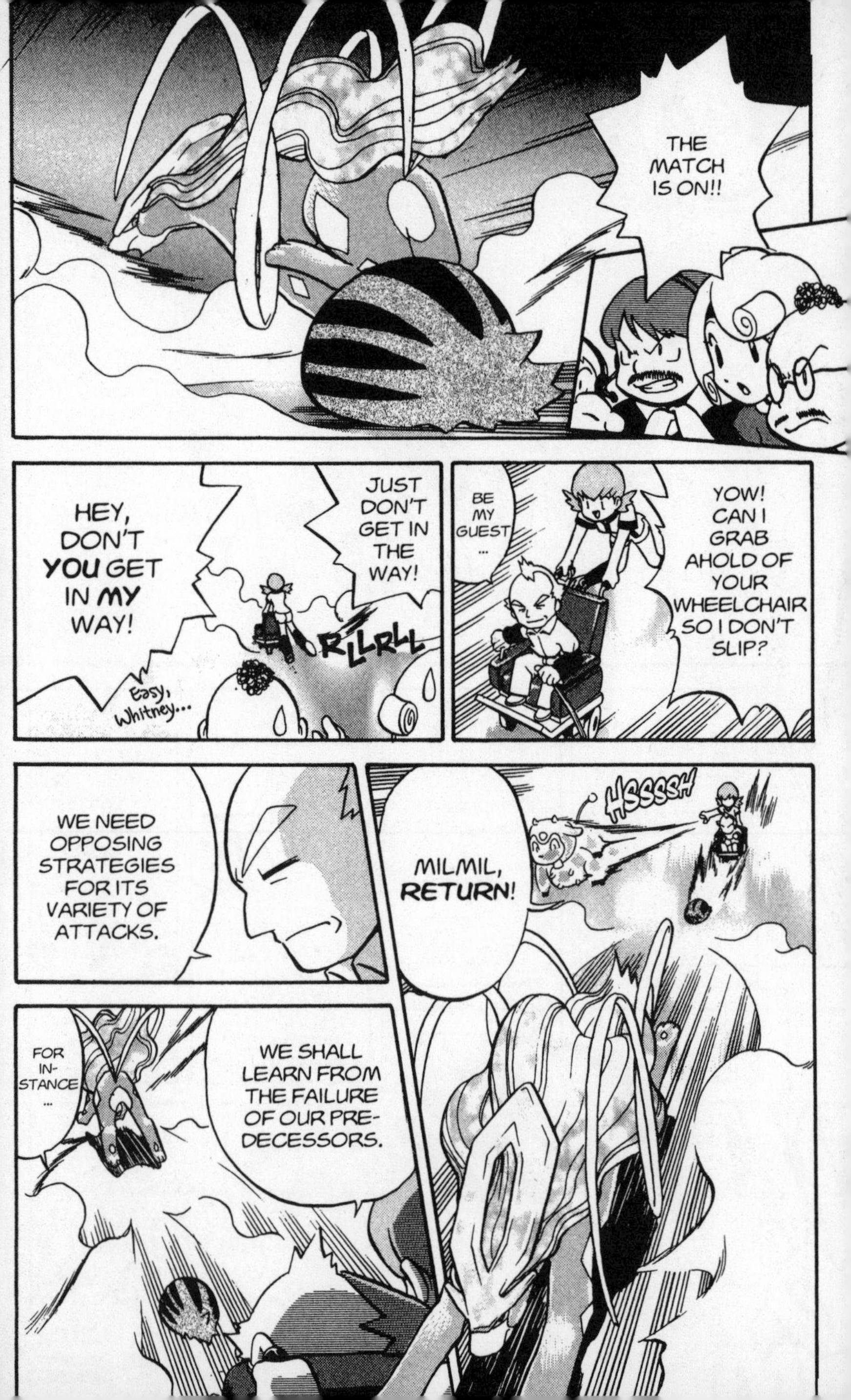
THE MATCH IS ON!!
YOW! CAN I GRAB AHOLD OF YOUR WHEELCHAIR SO I DON'T SLIP?
BE MY GUEST...
JUST DON'T GET IN THE WAY!
HEY, DON'T **YOU** GET IN **MY** WAY!
RLLRLL
Easy, Whitney...
HSSSSH
MILMIL, **RETURN**!
WE NEED OPPOSING STRATEGIES FOR ITS VARIETY OF ATTACKS.
WE SHALL LEARN FROM THE FAILURE OF OUR PRE-DECESSORS.
FOR IN-STANCE...

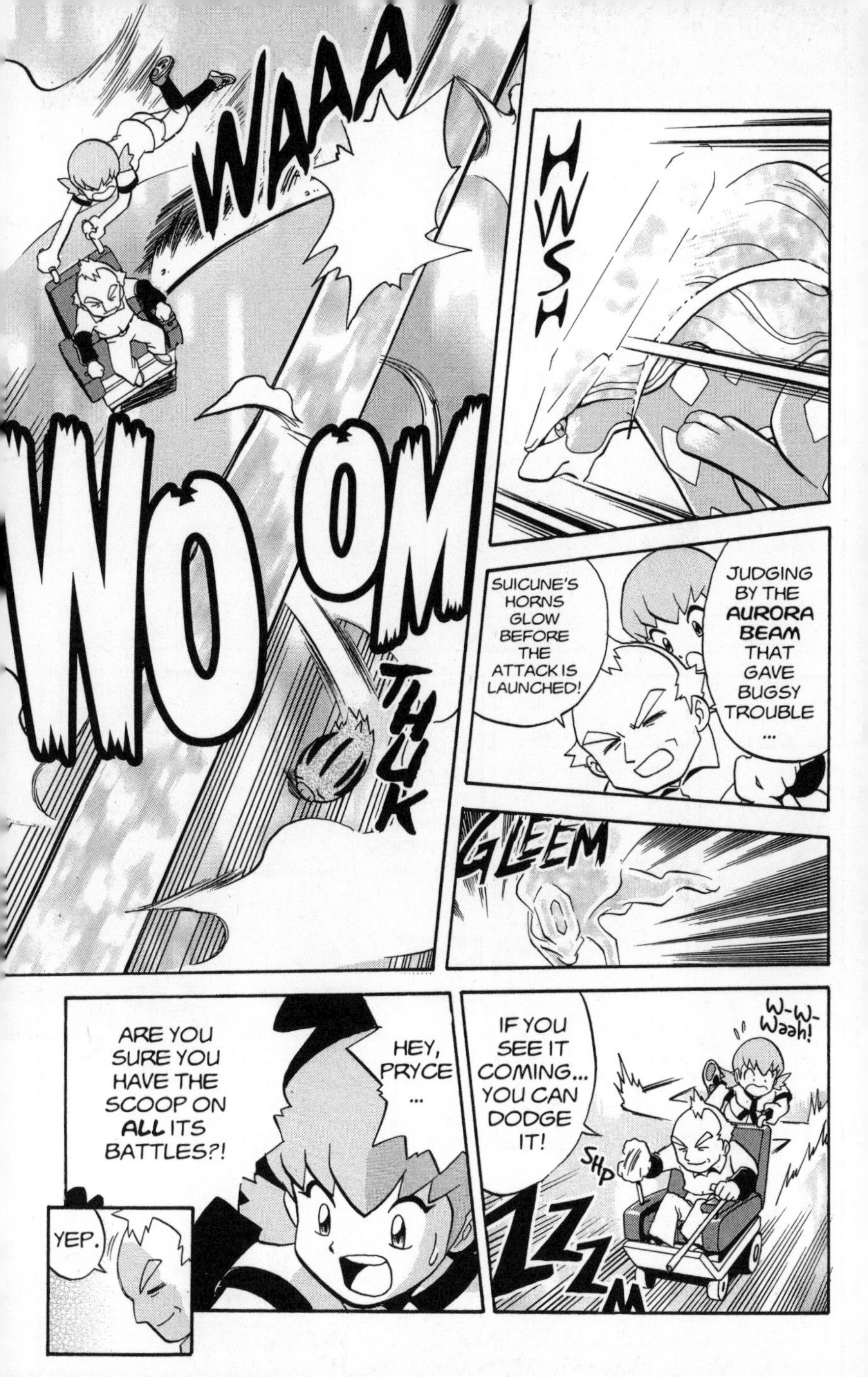
HWSH
JUDGING BY THE AURORA BEAM THAT GAVE BUGSY TROUBLE ...
SUICUNE'S HORNS GLOW BEFORE THE ATTACK IS LAUNCHED!
GLEEM
WAAA
WOOM
THUK
W-W-Waah!
IF YOU SEE IT COMING... YOU CAN DODGE IT!
SHP
ZZZM
HEY, PRYCE ...
ARE YOU SURE YOU HAVE THE SCOOP ON ALL ITS BATTLES?!
YEP.

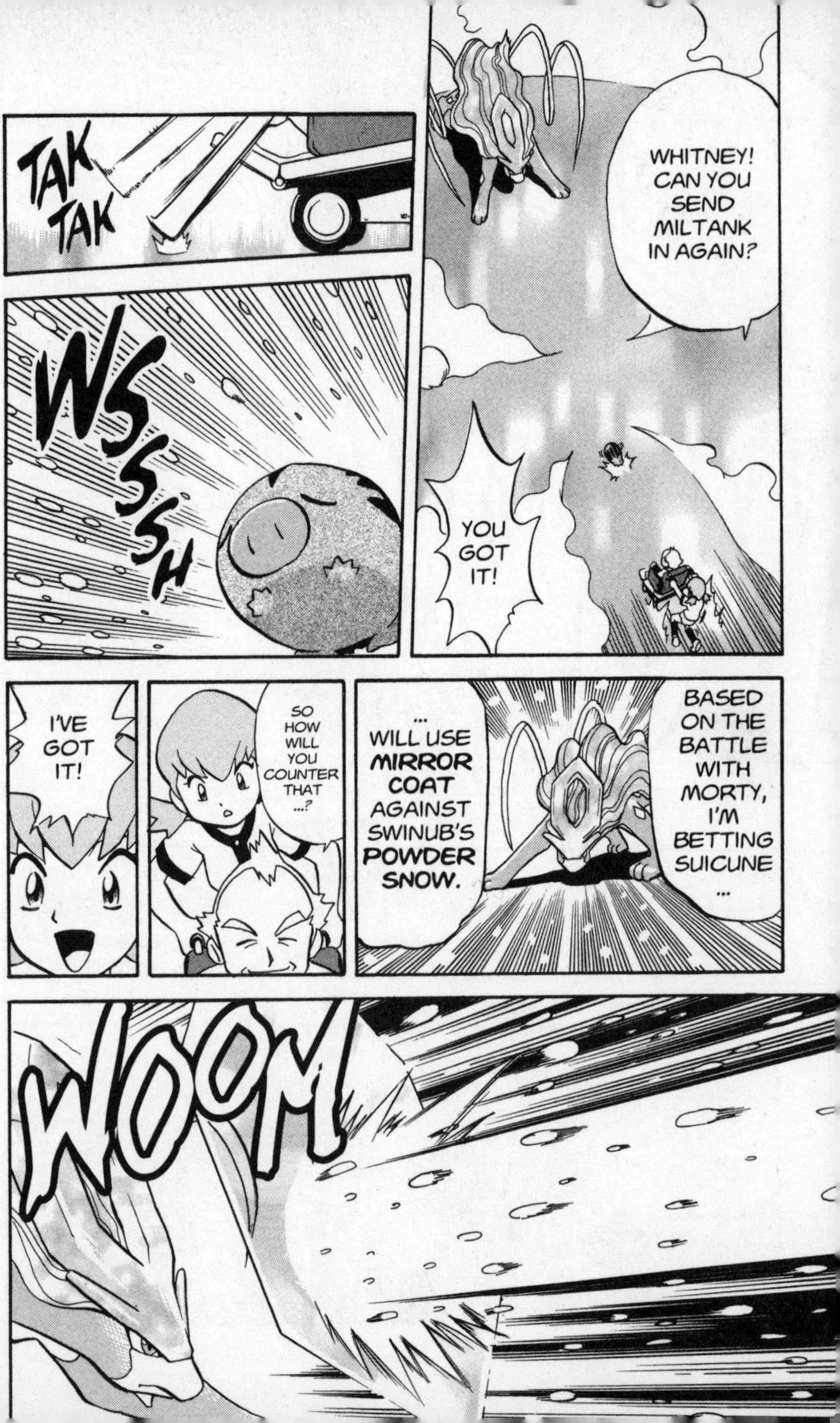
WHITNEY! CAN YOU SEND MILTANK IN AGAIN?
YOU GOT IT!
TAK TAK
WSSSH
BASED ON THE BATTLE WITH MORTY, I'M BETTING SUICUNE ...
... WILL USE **MIRROR COAT** AGAINST SWINUB'S **POWDER SNOW.**
SO HOW WILL YOU COUNTER THAT ...?
I'VE GOT IT!
WOOM

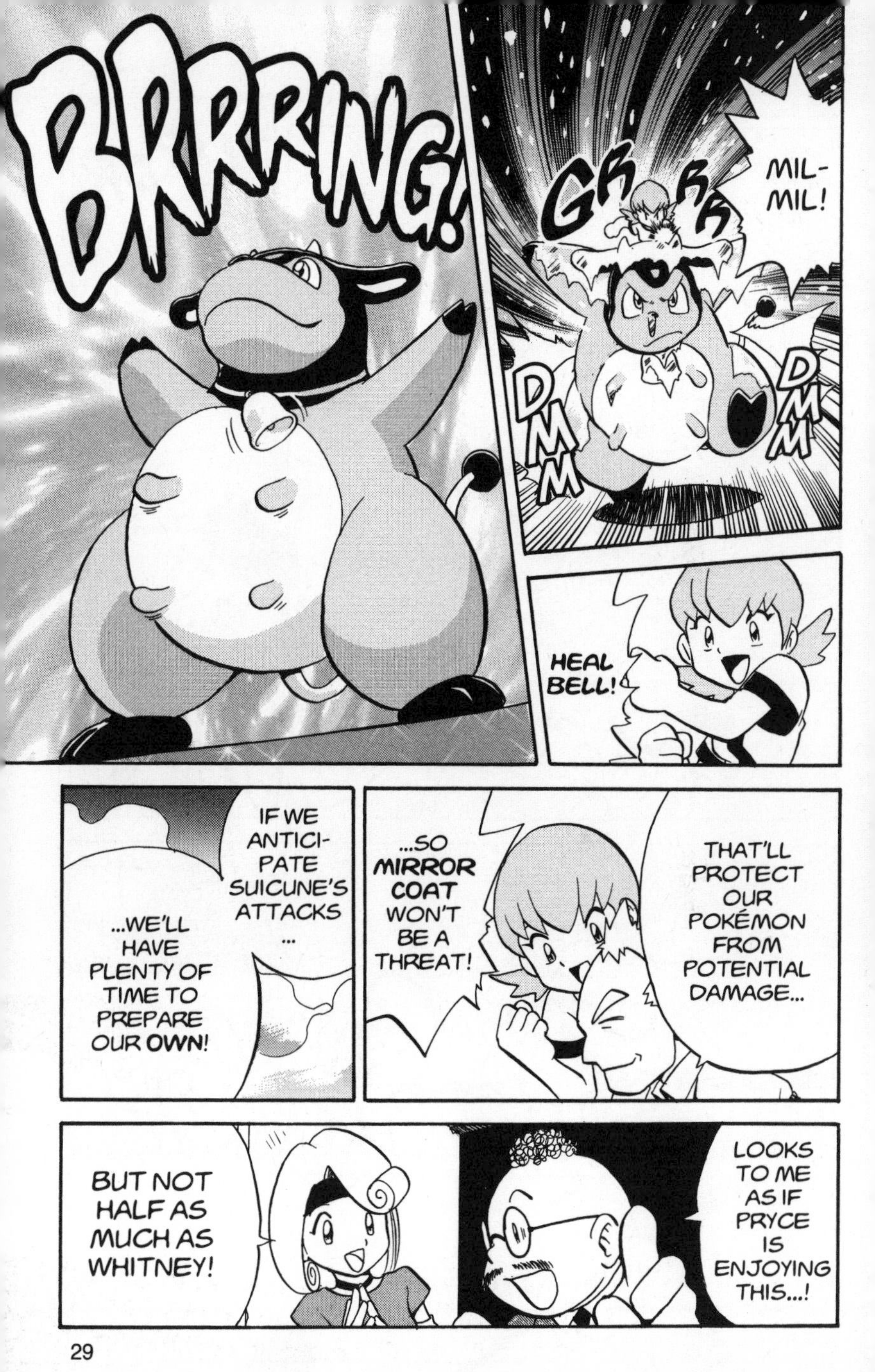
MIL-MIL!
GRRR
DMM
DMM
HEAL BELL!
BRRRING!
THAT'LL PROTECT OUR POKÉMON FROM POTENTIAL DAMAGE...
...SO **MIRROR COAT** WON'T BE A THREAT!
IF WE ANTICIPATE SUICUNE'S ATTACKS...
...WE'LL HAVE PLENTY OF TIME TO PREPARE OUR **OWN**!
LOOKS TO ME AS IF PRYCE IS ENJOYING THIS...!
BUT NOT HALF AS MUCH AS WHITNEY!

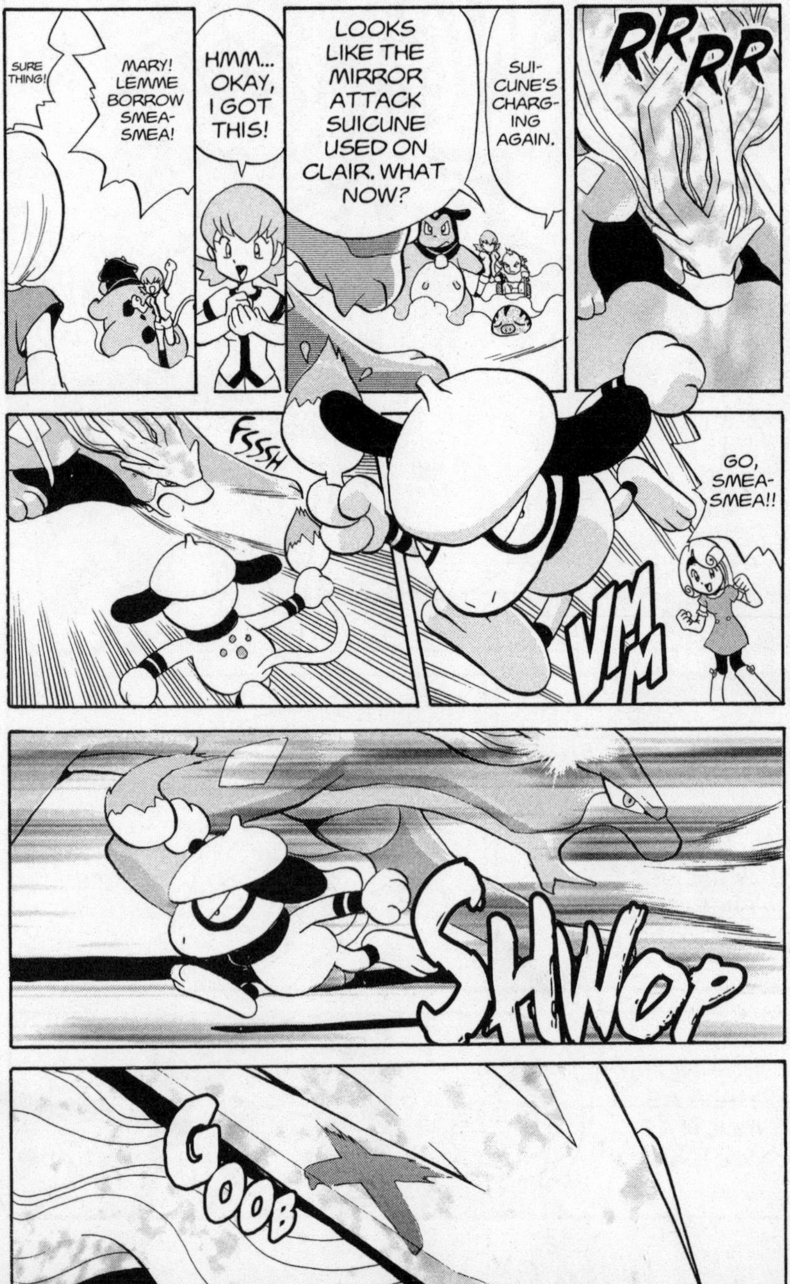
RRRR
SUICUNE'S CHARGING AGAIN.
LOOKS LIKE THE MIRROR ATTACK SUICUNE USED ON CLAIR. WHAT NOW?
HMM... OKAY, I GOT THIS!
MARY! LEMME BORROW SMEA-SMEA!
SURE THING!
GO, SMEA-SMEA!!
VMM
FSSSH
SHWOP
GOOB

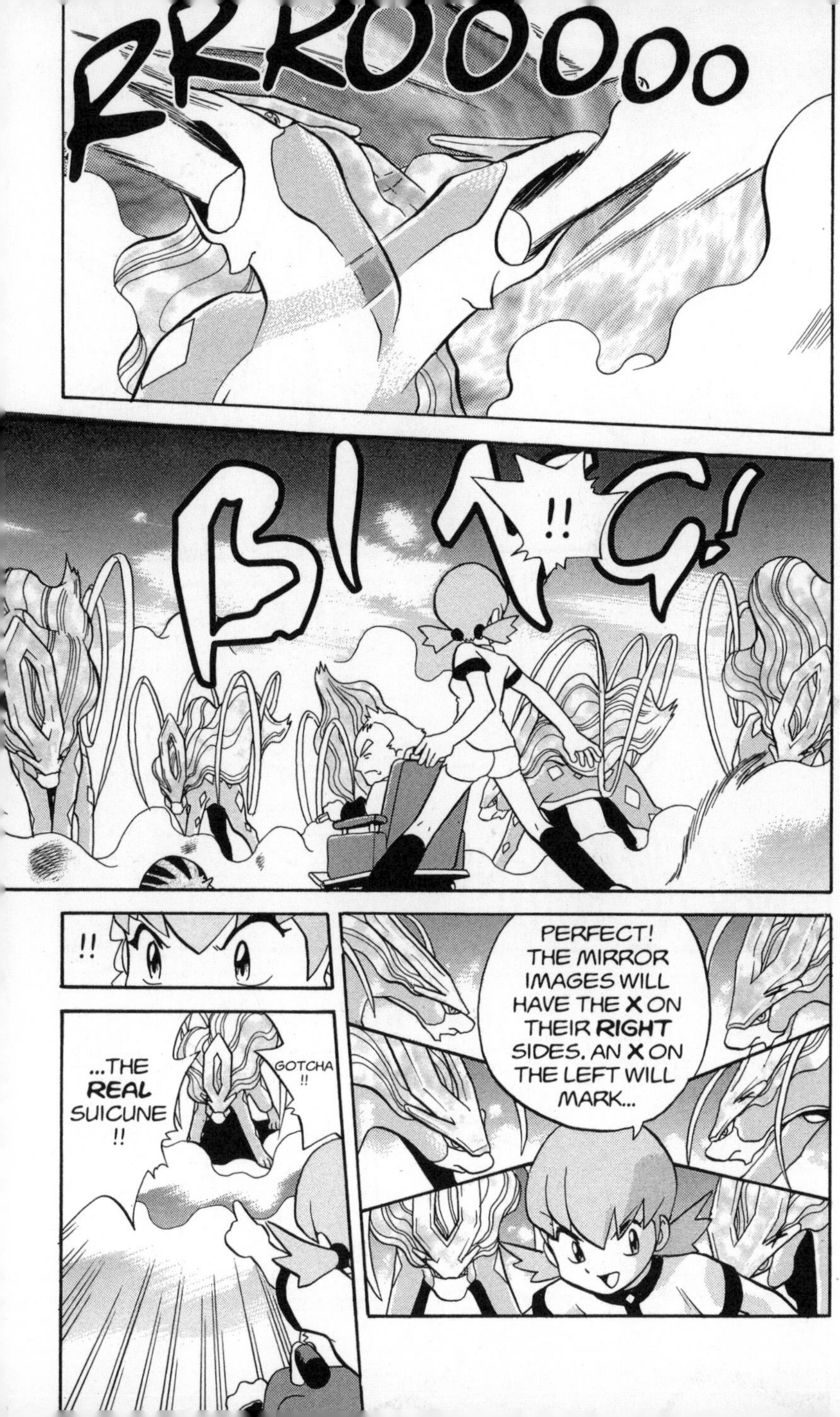
RRROOOOOO
!!
PERFECT! THE MIRROR IMAGES WILL HAVE THE **X** ON THEIR **RIGHT** SIDES. AN **X** ON THE LEFT WILL MARK...
!!
GOTCHA !!
...THE **REAL** SUICUNE !!

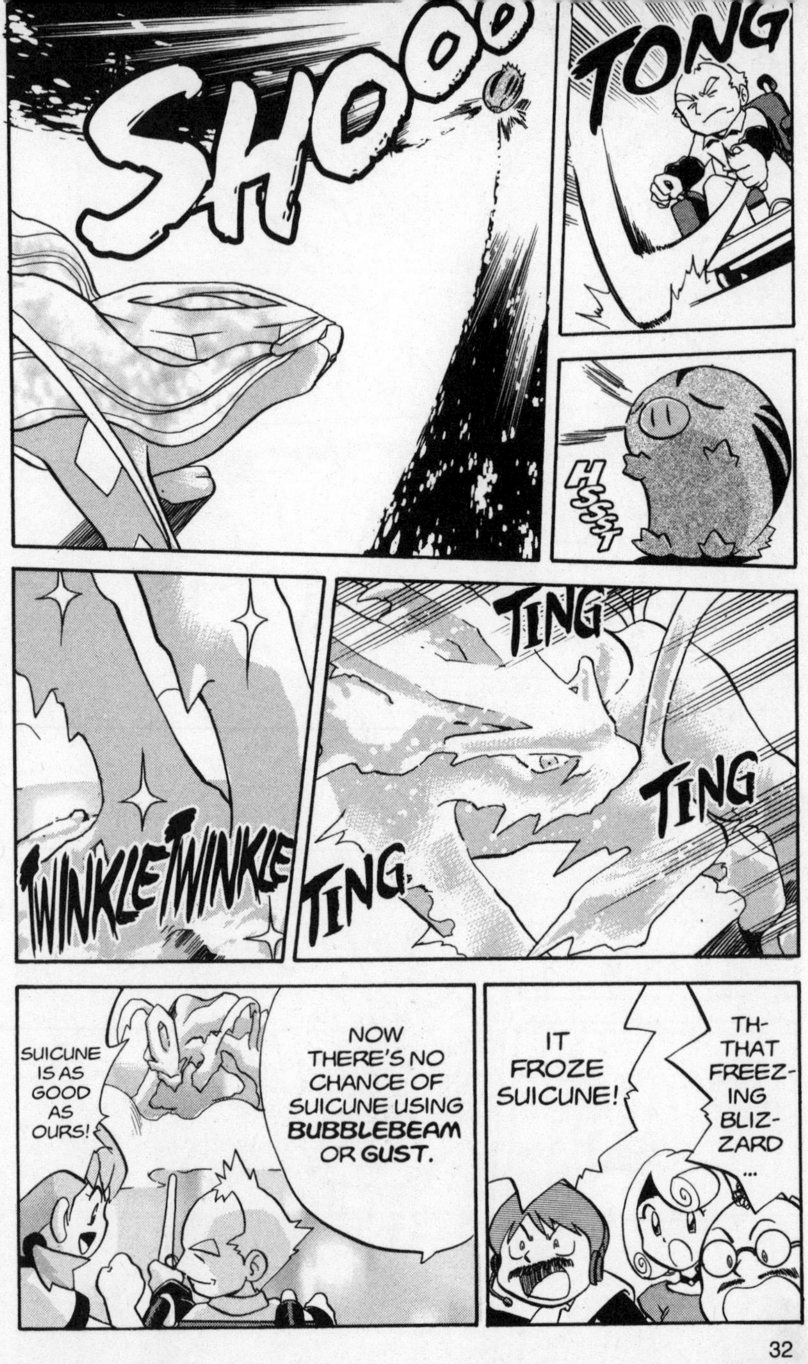
TONG
HSSST
SHOOO
TING
TING
TING
TWINKLE TWINKLE
TH-THAT FREEZING BLIZZARD...
IT FROZE SUICUNE!
NOW THERE'S NO CHANCE OF SUICUNE USING **BUBBLEBEAM** OR **GUST**.
SUICUNE IS AS GOOD AS OURS!

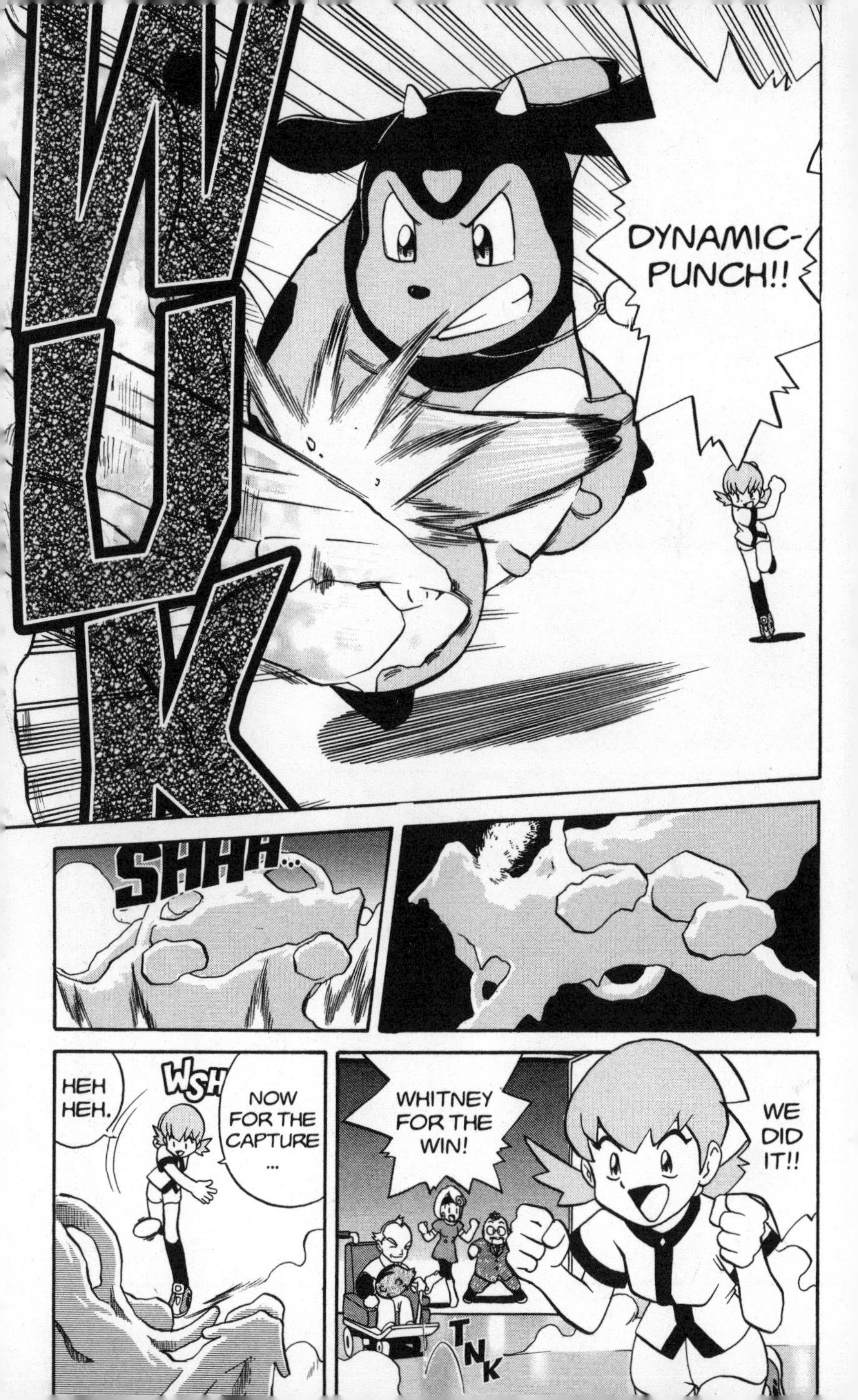
DYNAMIC-PUNCH!!
SHHH...
WE DID IT!!
WHITNEY FOR THE WIN!
TNK
WSH
NOW FOR THE CAPTURE ...
HEH HEH.

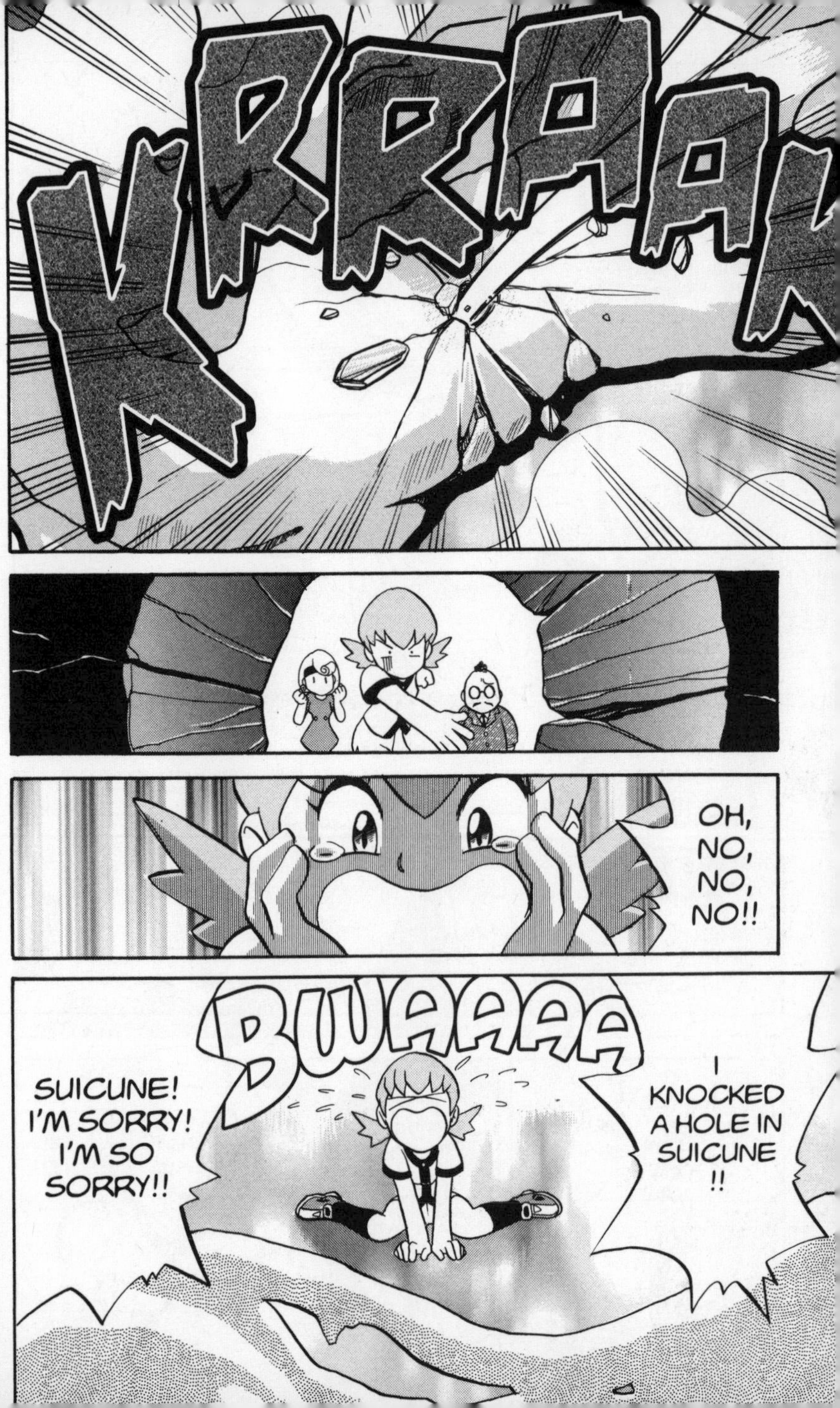
KRRAA
OH, NO, NO, NO!!
BWAAAAA
I KNOCKED A HOLE IN SUICUNE!!
SUICUNE! I'M SORRY! I'M SO SORRY!!

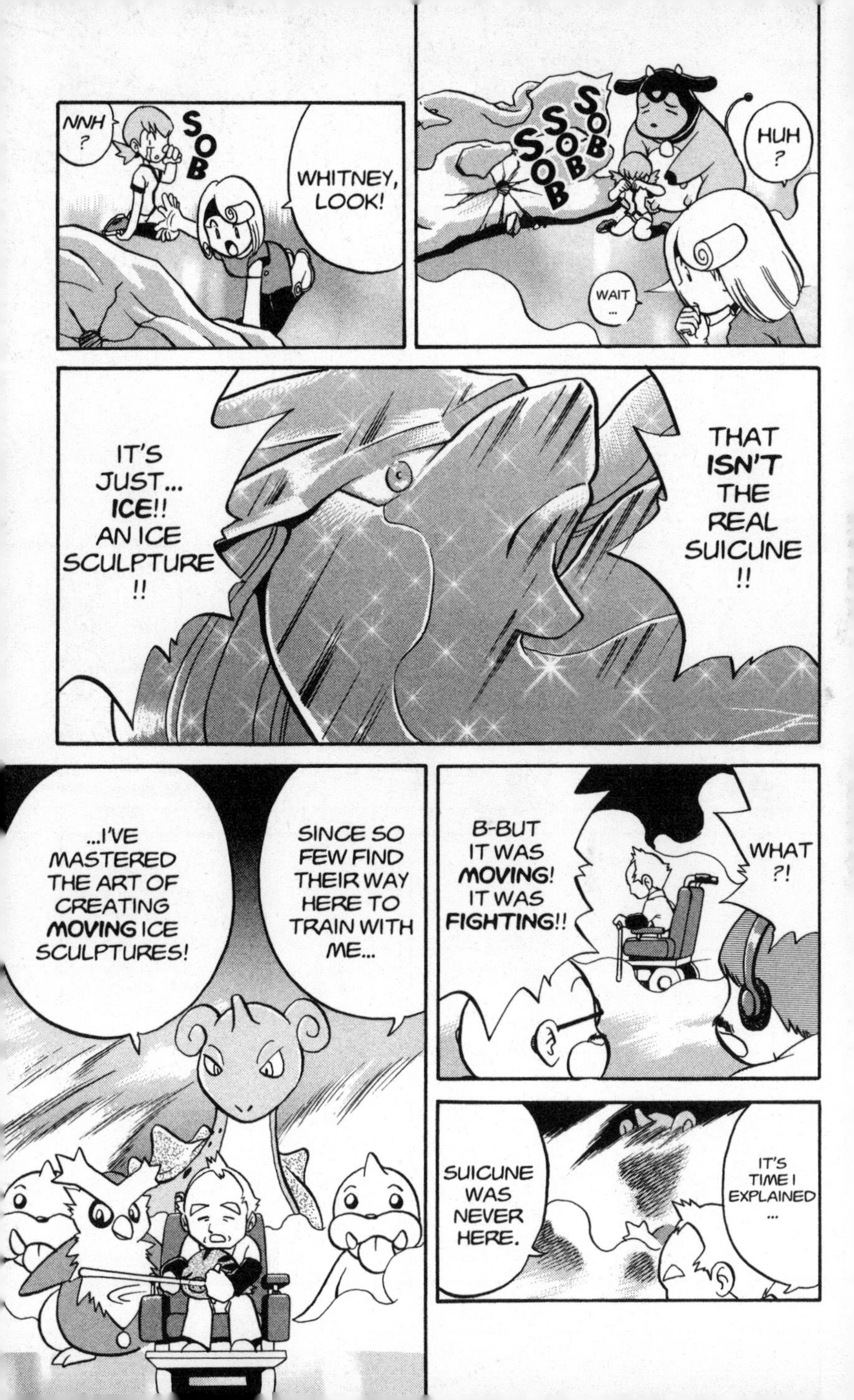

SOB SOB SOB SOB
HUH ?
WAIT ...
WHITNEY, LOOK!
NNH ?
SOB
THAT ISN'T THE REAL SUICUNE !!
IT'S JUST... ICE!! AN ICE SCULPTURE !!
WHAT ?!
B-BUT IT WAS MOVING! IT WAS FIGHTING!!
IT'S TIME I EXPLAINED ...
SUICUNE WAS NEVER HERE.
SINCE SO FEW FIND THEIR WAY HERE TO TRAIN WITH ME...
...I'VE MASTERED THE ART OF CREATING MOVING ICE SCULPTURES!

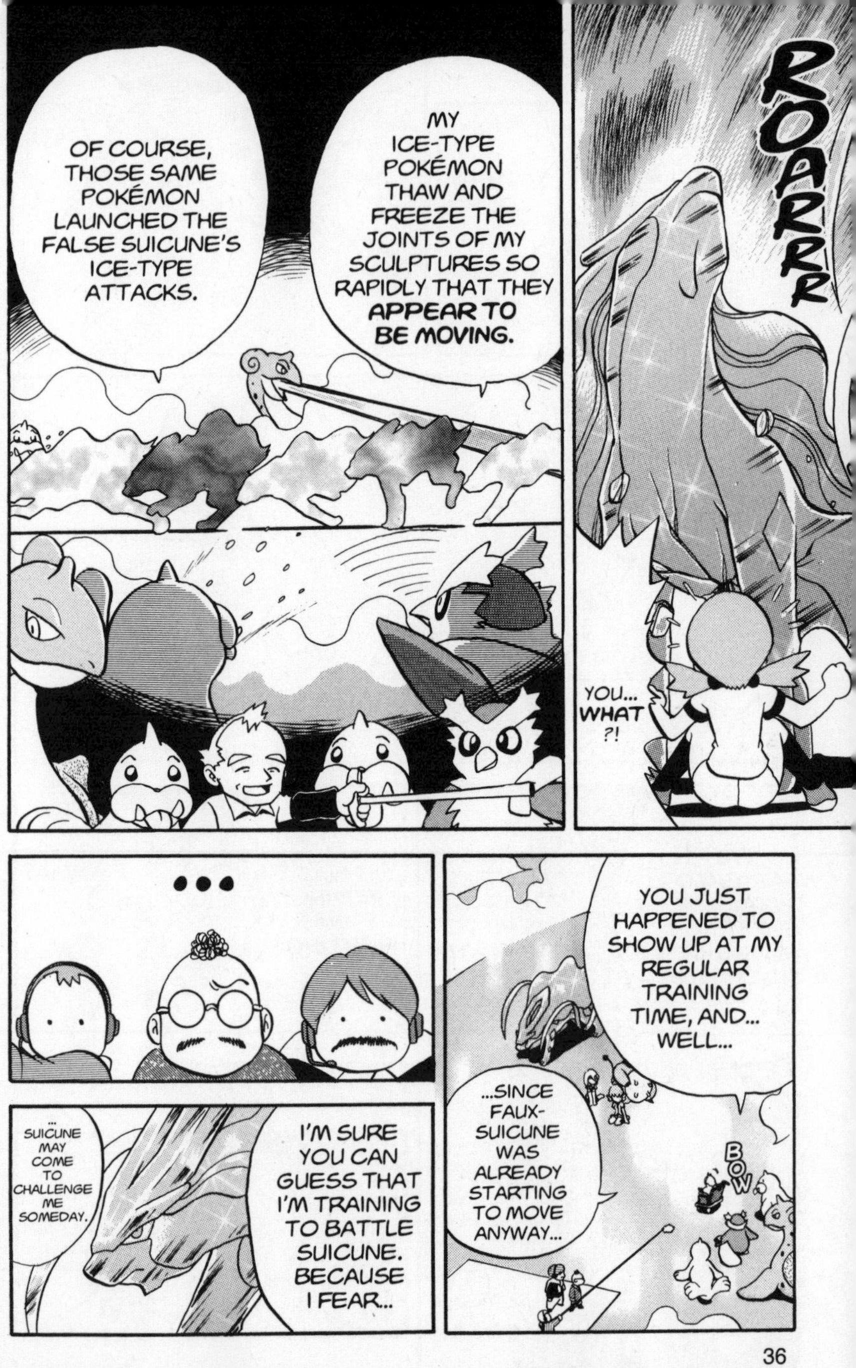
ROARRR
YOU... WHAT?!
MY ICE-TYPE POKÉMON THAW AND FREEZE THE JOINTS OF MY SCULPTURES SO RAPIDLY THAT THEY **APPEAR TO BE MOVING.**
OF COURSE, THOSE SAME POKÉMON LAUNCHED THE FALSE SUICUNE'S ICE-TYPE ATTACKS.
YOU JUST HAPPENED TO SHOW UP AT MY REGULAR TRAINING TIME, AND... WELL...
...SINCE FAUX-SUICUNE WAS ALREADY STARTING TO MOVE ANYWAY...
BOW
•••
I'M SURE YOU CAN GUESS THAT I'M TRAINING TO BATTLE SUICUNE. BECAUSE I FEAR...
...SUICUNE MAY COME TO CHALLENGE ME SOMEDAY.

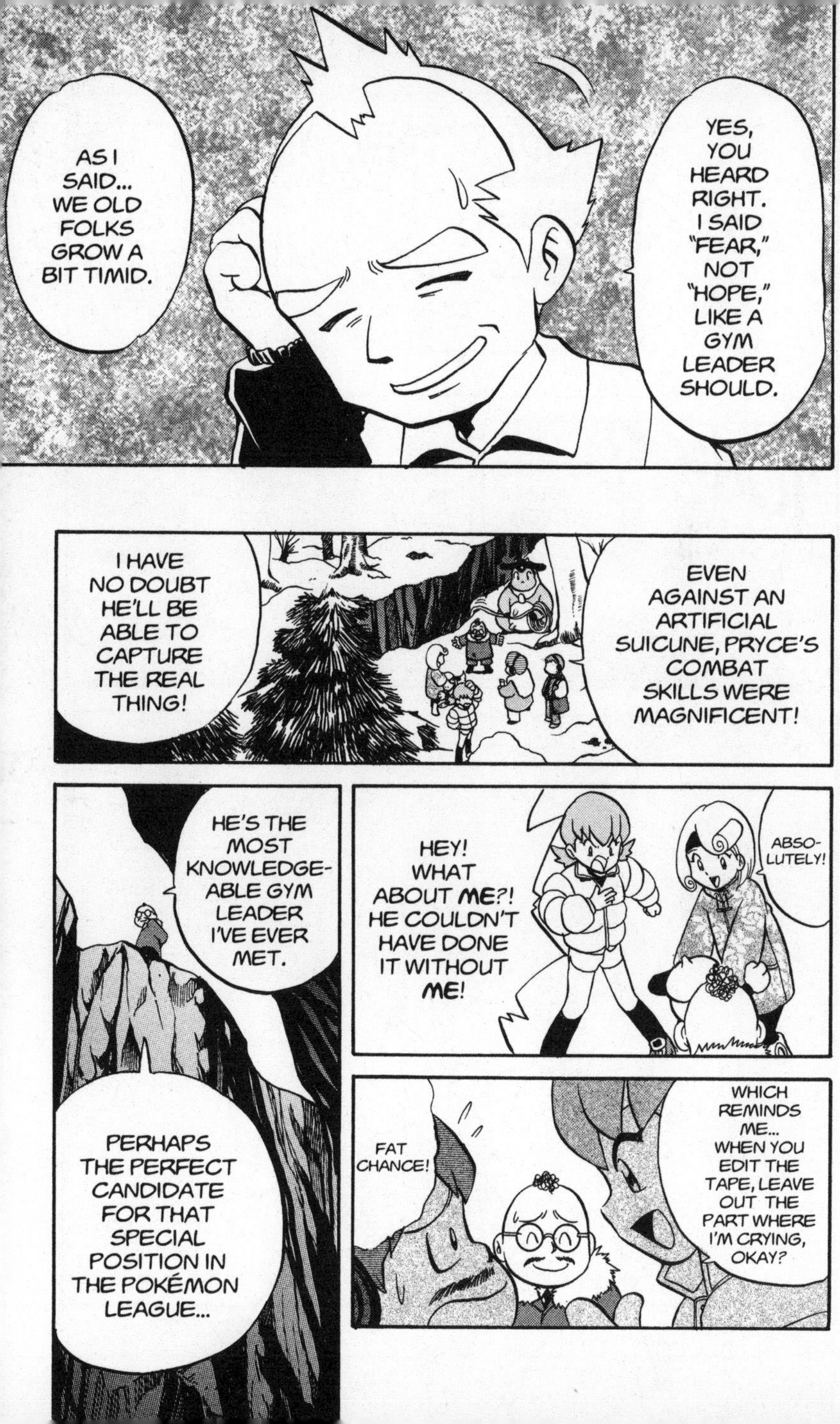
YES, YOU HEARD RIGHT. I SAID "FEAR," NOT "HOPE," LIKE A GYM LEADER SHOULD.
AS I SAID... WE OLD FOLKS GROW A BIT TIMID.
EVEN AGAINST AN ARTIFICIAL SUICUNE, PRYCE'S COMBAT SKILLS WERE MAGNIFICENT!
I HAVE NO DOUBT HE'LL BE ABLE TO CAPTURE THE REAL THING!
ABSO-LUTELY!
HEY! WHAT ABOUT ME?! HE COULDN'T HAVE DONE IT WITHOUT ME!
WHICH REMINDS ME... WHEN YOU EDIT THE TAPE, LEAVE OUT THE PART WHERE I'M CRYING, OKAY?
FAT CHANCE!
HE'S THE MOST KNOWLEDGE-ABLE GYM LEADER I'VE EVER MET.
PERHAPS THE PERFECT CANDIDATE FOR THAT SPECIAL POSITION IN THE POKÉMON LEAGUE...

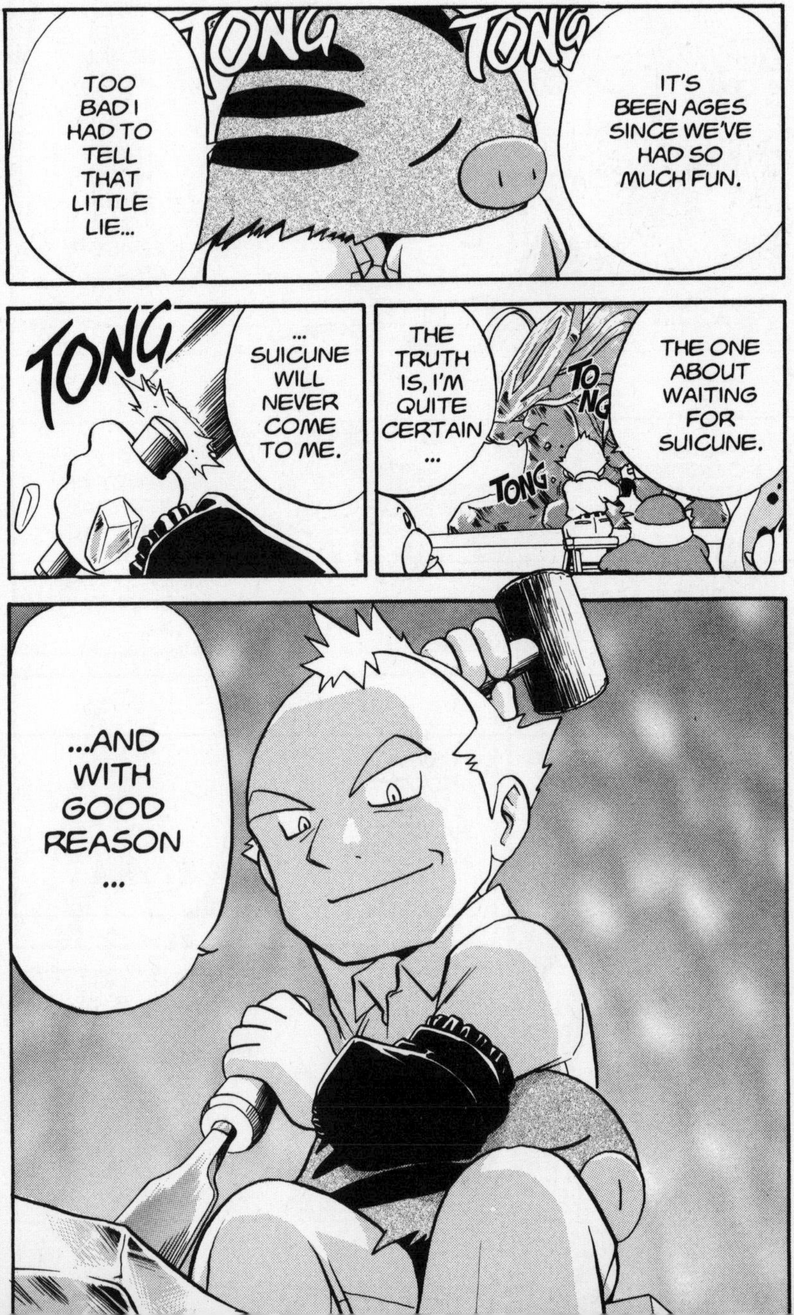
IT'S BEEN AGES SINCE WE'VE HAD SO MUCH FUN.
TONG
TONG
TOO BAD I HAD TO TELL THAT LITTLE LIE...
THE ONE ABOUT WAITING FOR SUICUNE.
TONG
TONG
THE TRUTH IS, I'M QUITE CERTAIN ...
... SUICUNE WILL NEVER COME TO ME.
TONG
...AND WITH GOOD REASON ...

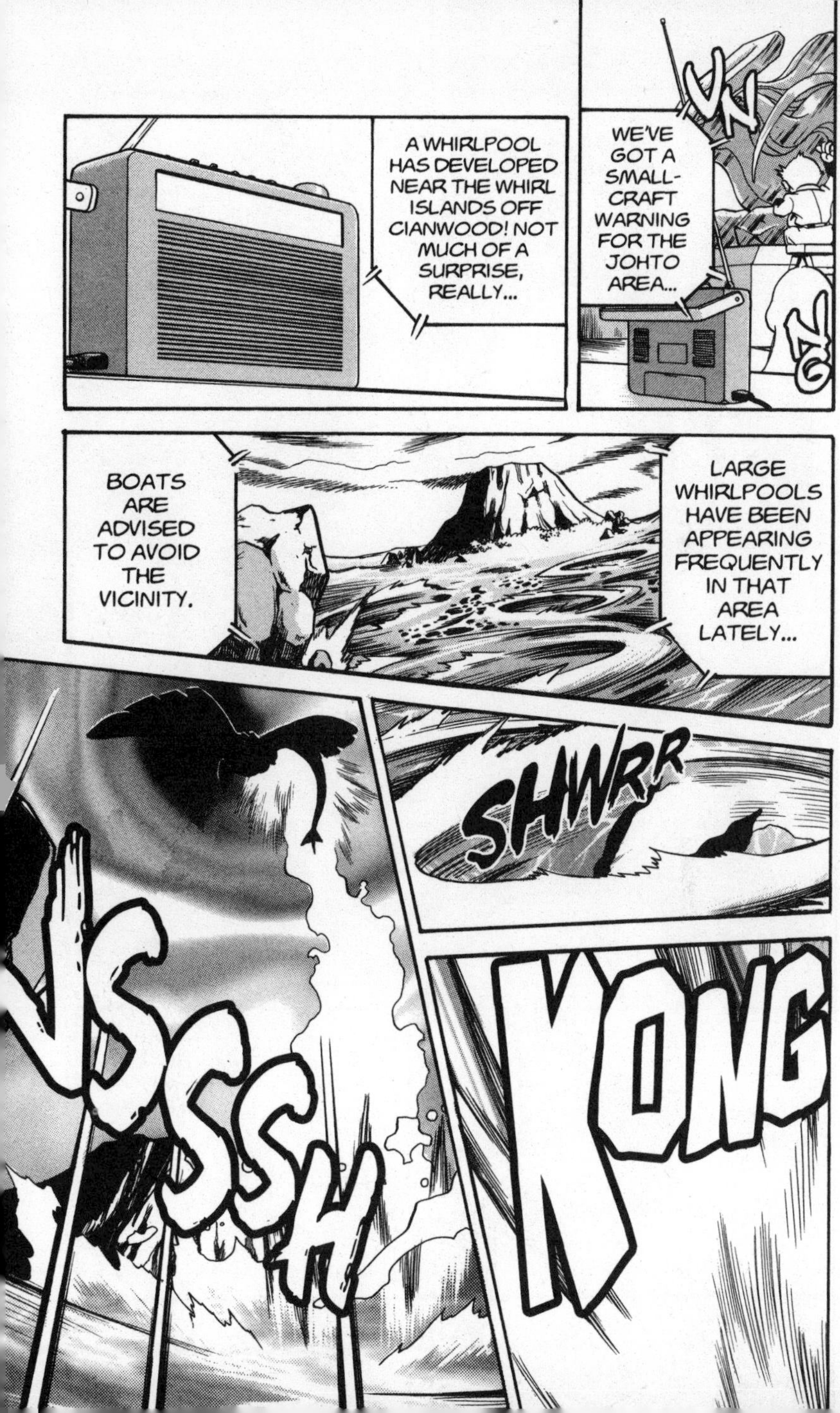
WE'VE GOT A SMALL-CRAFT WARNING FOR THE JOHTO AREA...
A WHIRLPOOL HAS DEVELOPED NEAR THE WHIRL ISLANDS OFF CIANWOOD! NOT MUCH OF A SURPRISE, REALLY...
LARGE WHIRLPOOLS HAVE BEEN APPEARING FREQUENTLY IN THAT AREA LATELY...
BOATS ARE ADVISED TO AVOID THE VICINITY.
SHWRR
KONG
SSSH

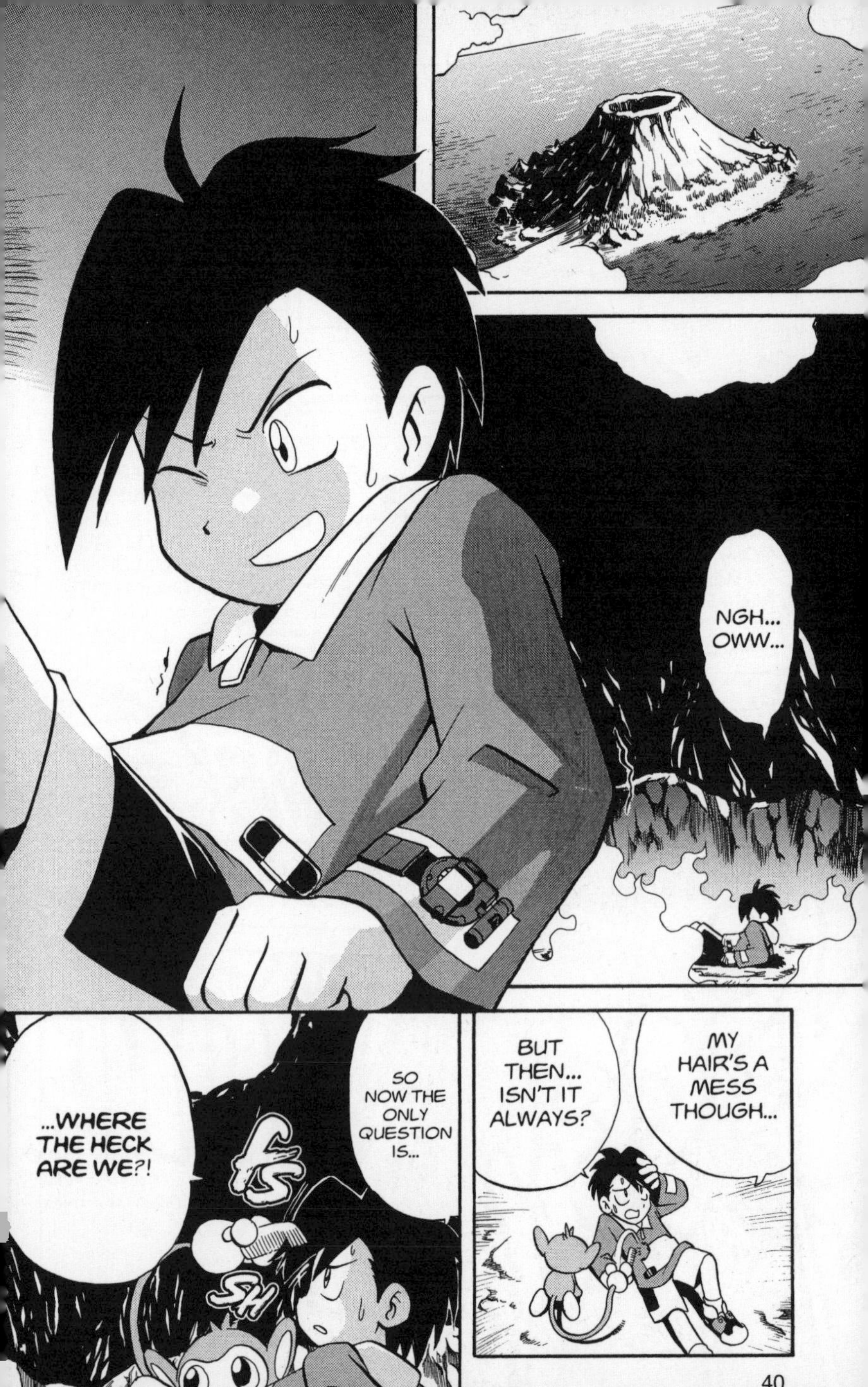
NGH... OWW...
MY HAIR'S A MESS THOUGH...
BUT THEN... ISN'T IT ALWAYS?
SO NOW THE ONLY QUESTION IS...
FS
SH
...WHERE THE HECK ARE WE?!

145 Sandslash Surprise

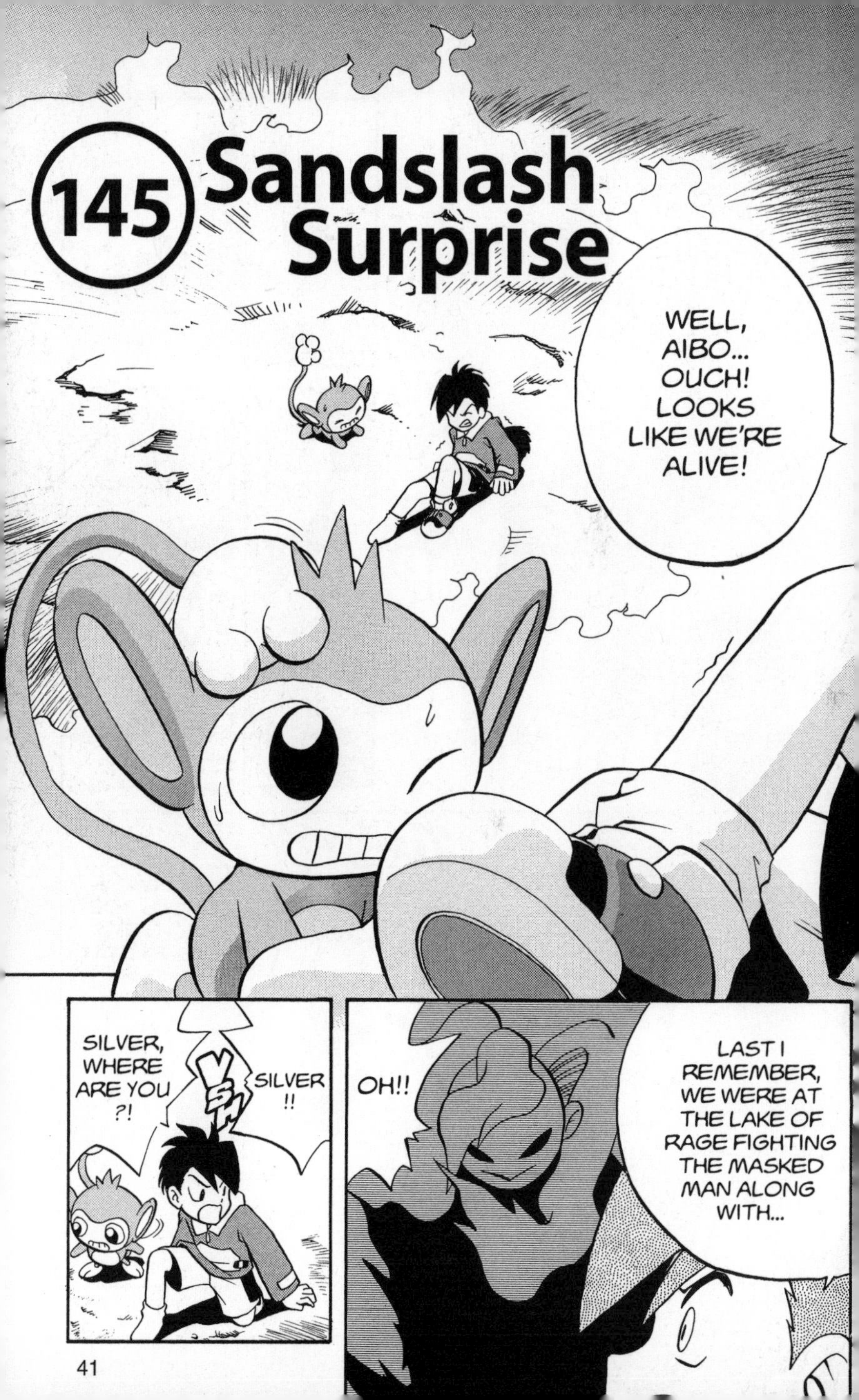
WELL, AIBO... OUCH! LOOKS LIKE WE'RE ALIVE!
LAST I REMEMBER, WE WERE AT THE LAKE OF RAGE FIGHTING THE MASKED MAN ALONG WITH...
OH!!
SILVER !!
SILVER, WHERE ARE YOU ?!

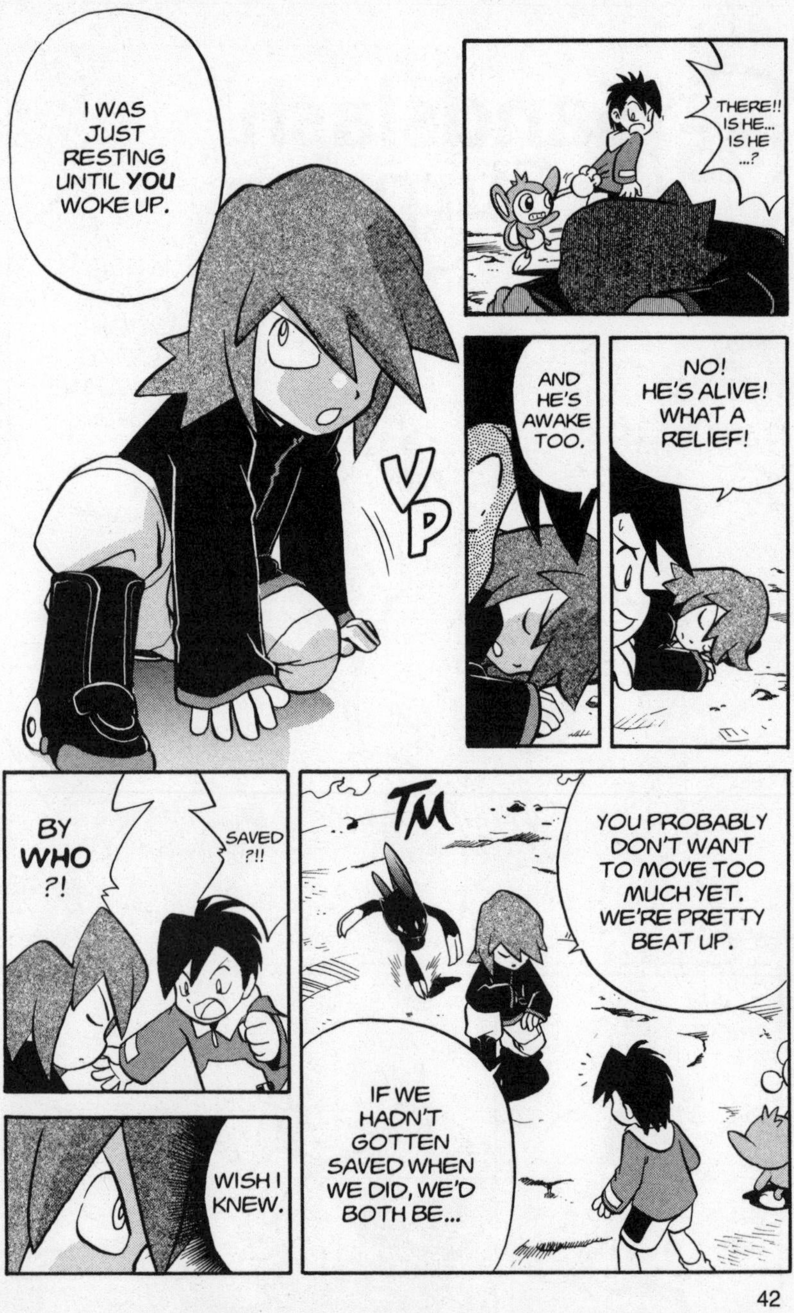
THERE!! IS HE... IS HE ...?
NO! HE'S ALIVE! WHAT A RELIEF!
AND HE'S AWAKE TOO.
I WAS JUST RESTING UNTIL **YOU** WOKE UP.
VP
TM
YOU PROBABLY DON'T WANT TO MOVE TOO MUCH YET. WE'RE PRETTY BEAT UP.
IF WE HADN'T GOTTEN SAVED WHEN WE DID, WE'D BOTH BE...
SAVED ?!!
BY **WHO** ?!
WISH I KNEW.

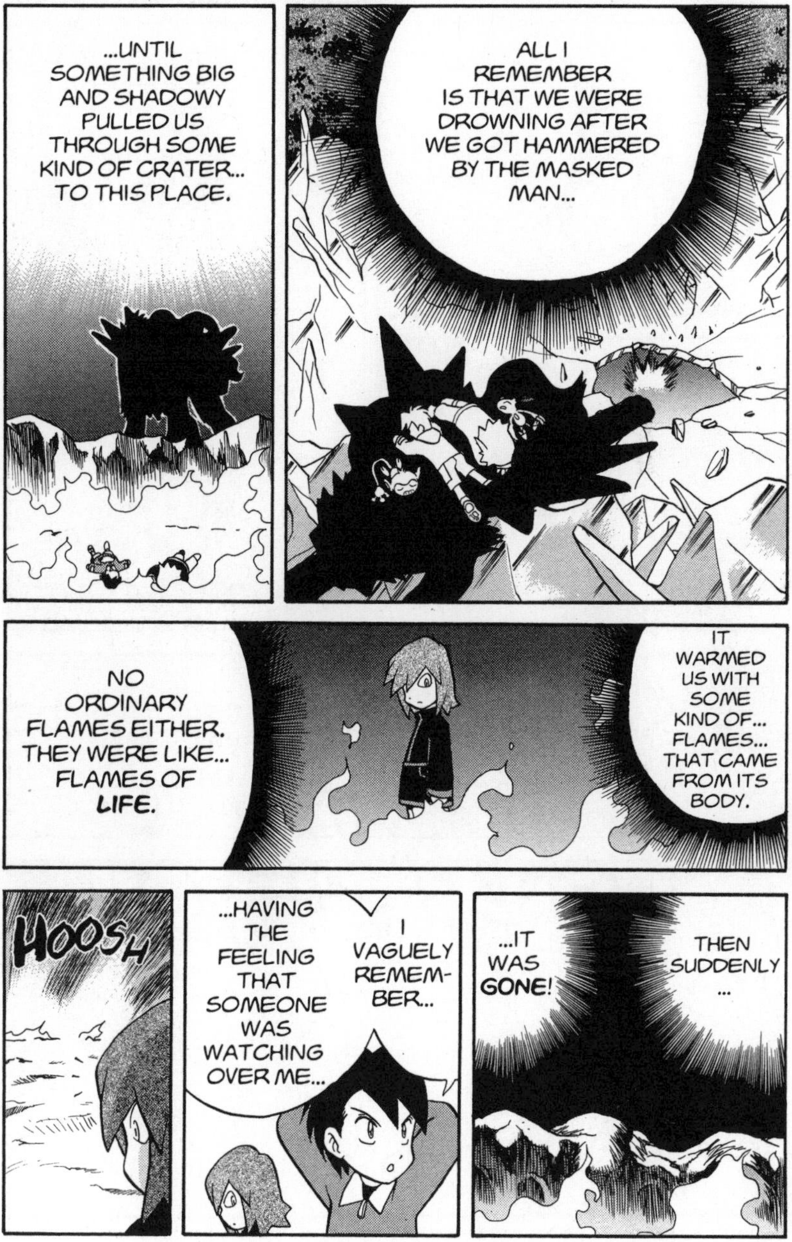
ALL I REMEMBER IS THAT WE WERE DROWNING AFTER WE GOT HAMMERED BY THE MASKED MAN...
...UNTIL SOMETHING BIG AND SHADOWY PULLED US THROUGH SOME KIND OF CRATER... TO THIS PLACE.
IT WARMED US WITH SOME KIND OF... FLAMES... THAT CAME FROM ITS BODY.
NO ORDINARY FLAMES EITHER. THEY WERE LIKE... FLAMES OF **LIFE**.
THEN SUDDENLY ...
...IT WAS **GONE**!
I VAGUELY REMEMBER...
...HAVING THE FEELING THAT SOMEONE WAS WATCHING OVER ME...
HOOSH

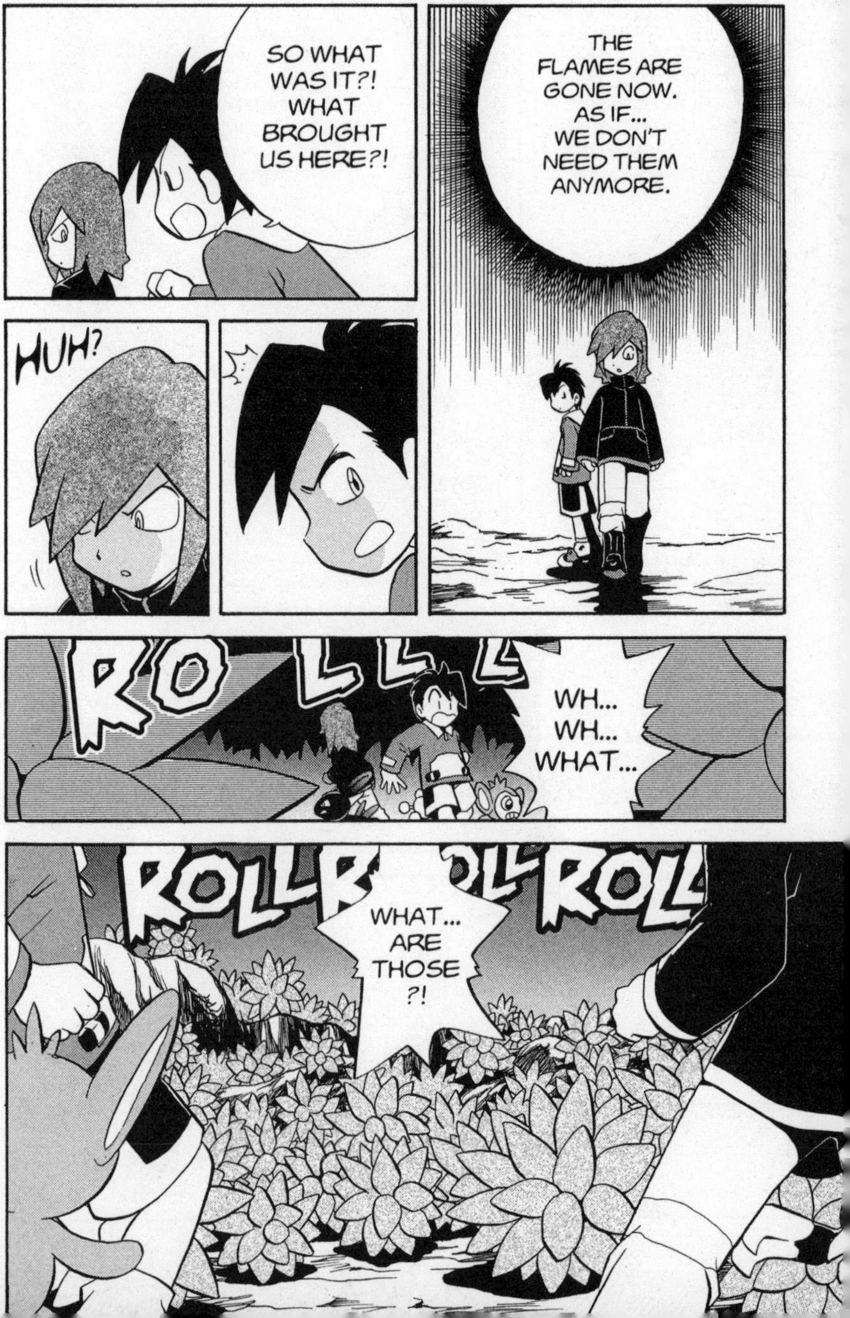
THE FLAMES ARE GONE NOW. AS IF... WE DON'T NEED THEM ANYMORE.
SO WHAT WAS IT?! WHAT BROUGHT US HERE?!
HUH?
WH... WH... WHAT...
ROLL
ROLL
WHAT... ARE THOSE?!

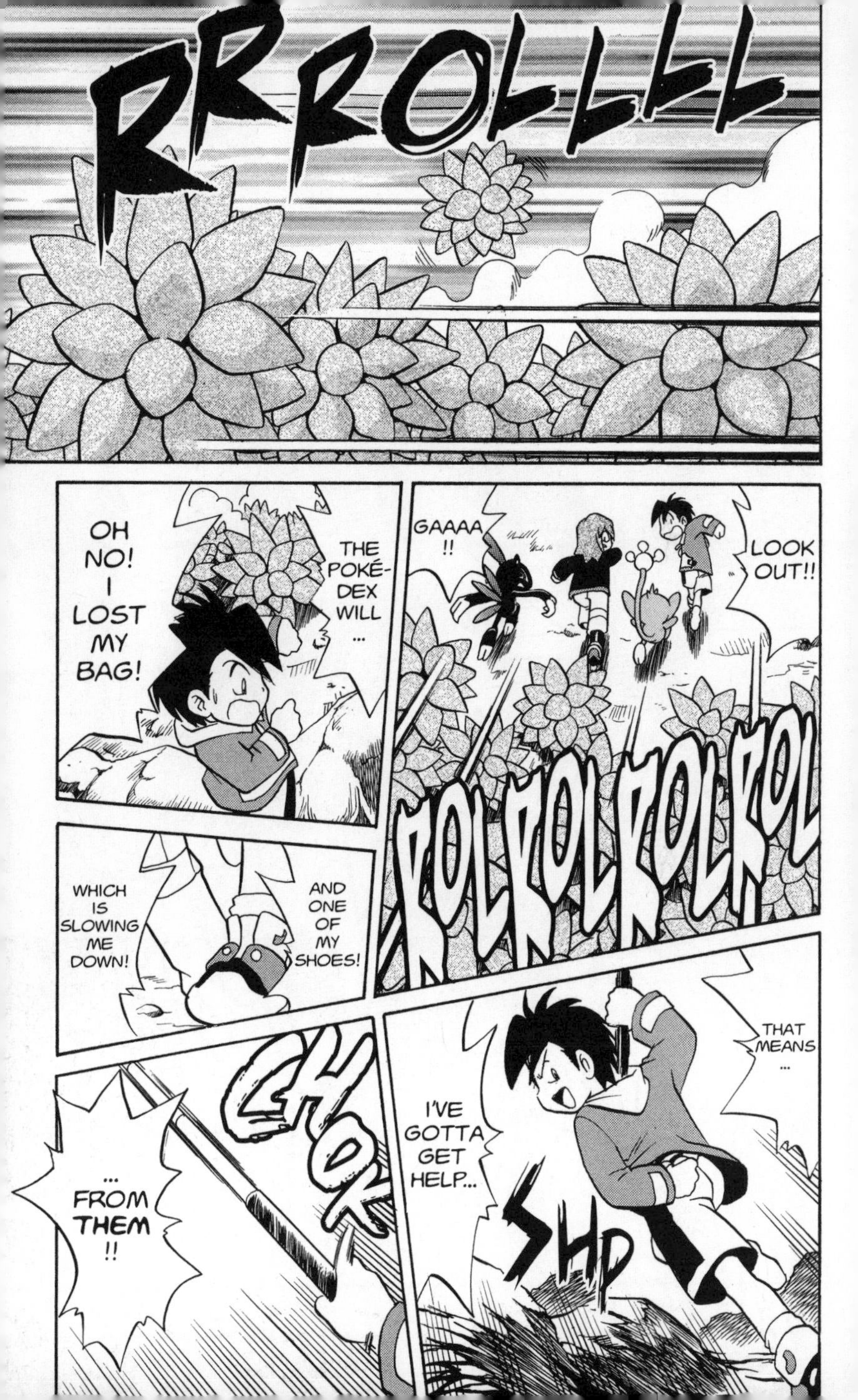
RRROLLLL
LOOK OUT!!
GAAAA !!
ROLROLROLROL
THE POKÉ-DEX WILL ...
OH NO! I LOST MY BAG!
AND ONE OF MY SHOES!
WHICH IS SLOWING ME DOWN!
THAT MEANS ...
I'VE GOTTA GET HELP...
SHP
CHOK
... FROM THEM !!

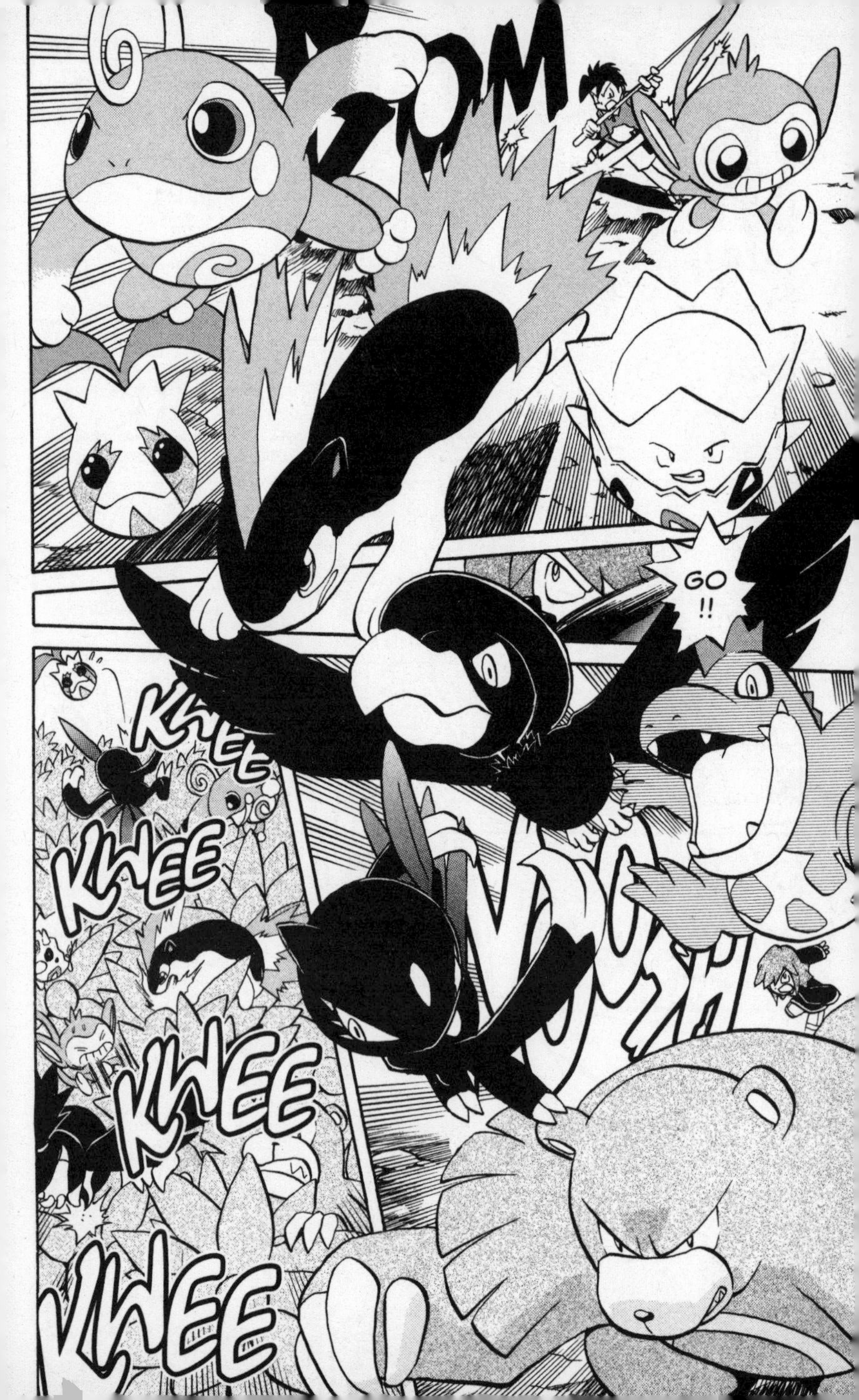
GO !!
VOOSH
KWEE
KWEE
KWEE
KWEE

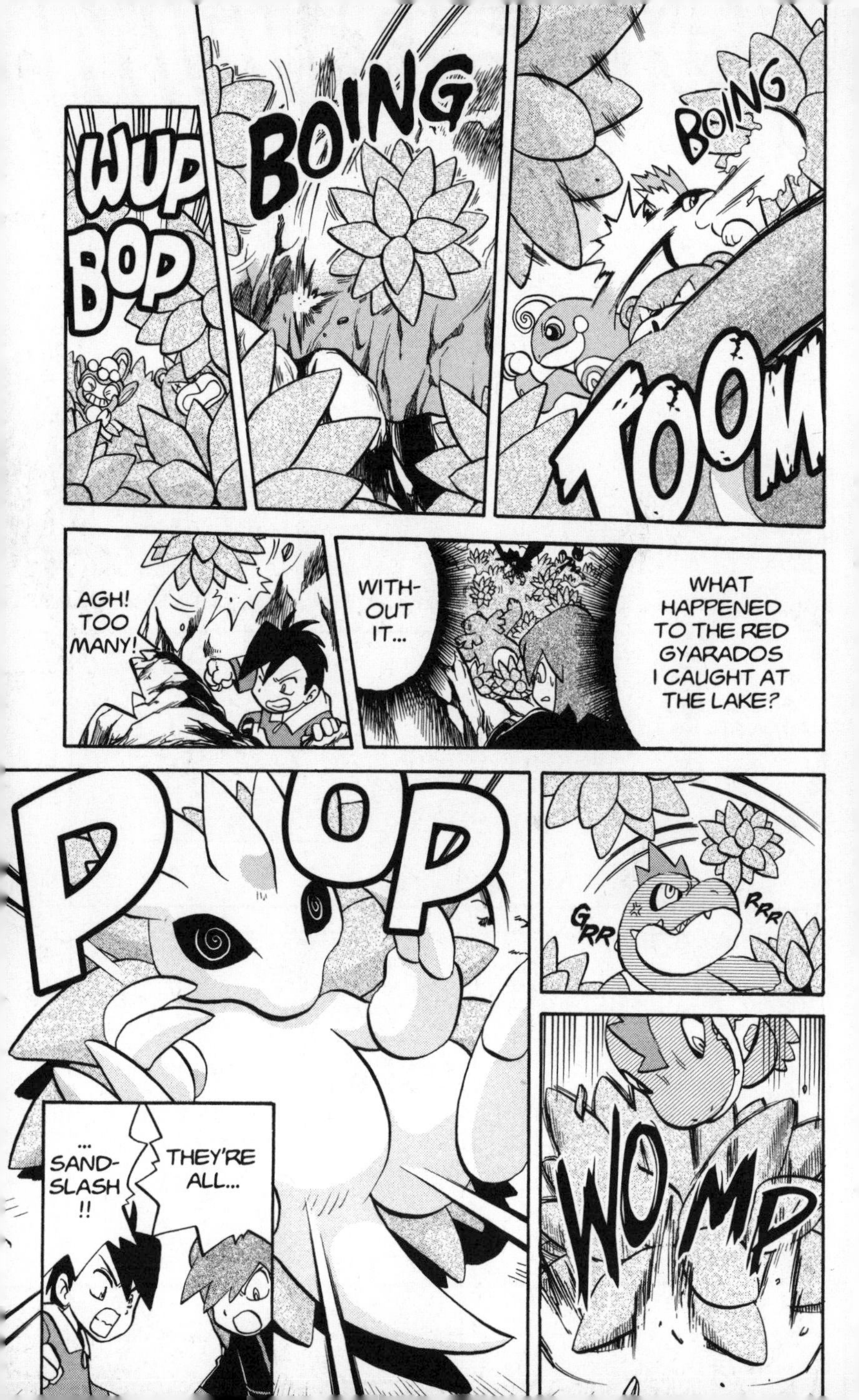
BOING
TOOM
BOING
WUP BOP
WHAT HAPPENED TO THE RED GYARADOS I CAUGHT AT THE LAKE?
WITH-OUT IT...
AGH! TOO MANY!
GRR RRR
WOMP
POP
THEY'RE ALL...
... SAND-SLASH !!

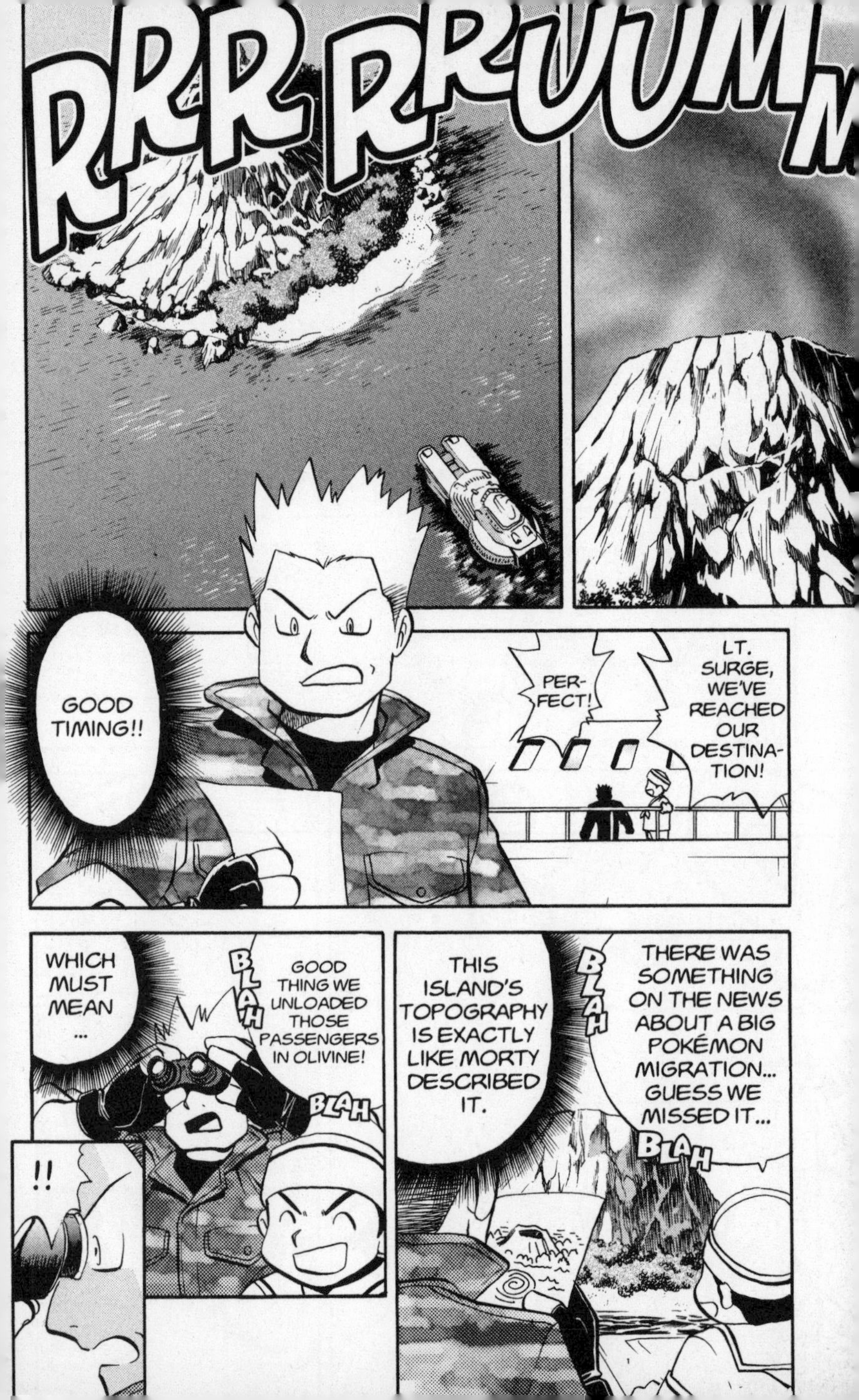
RRRRRUUMM
LT. SURGE, WE'VE REACHED OUR DESTINATION!
PER-FECT!
GOOD TIMING!!
THERE WAS SOMETHING ON THE NEWS ABOUT A BIG POKÉMON MIGRATION... GUESS WE MISSED IT...
BLAH
BLAH
THIS ISLAND'S TOPOGRAPHY IS EXACTLY LIKE MORTY DESCRIBED IT.
GOOD THING WE UNLOADED THOSE PASSENGERS IN OLIVINE!
BLAH
BLAH
WHICH MUST MEAN ...
!!

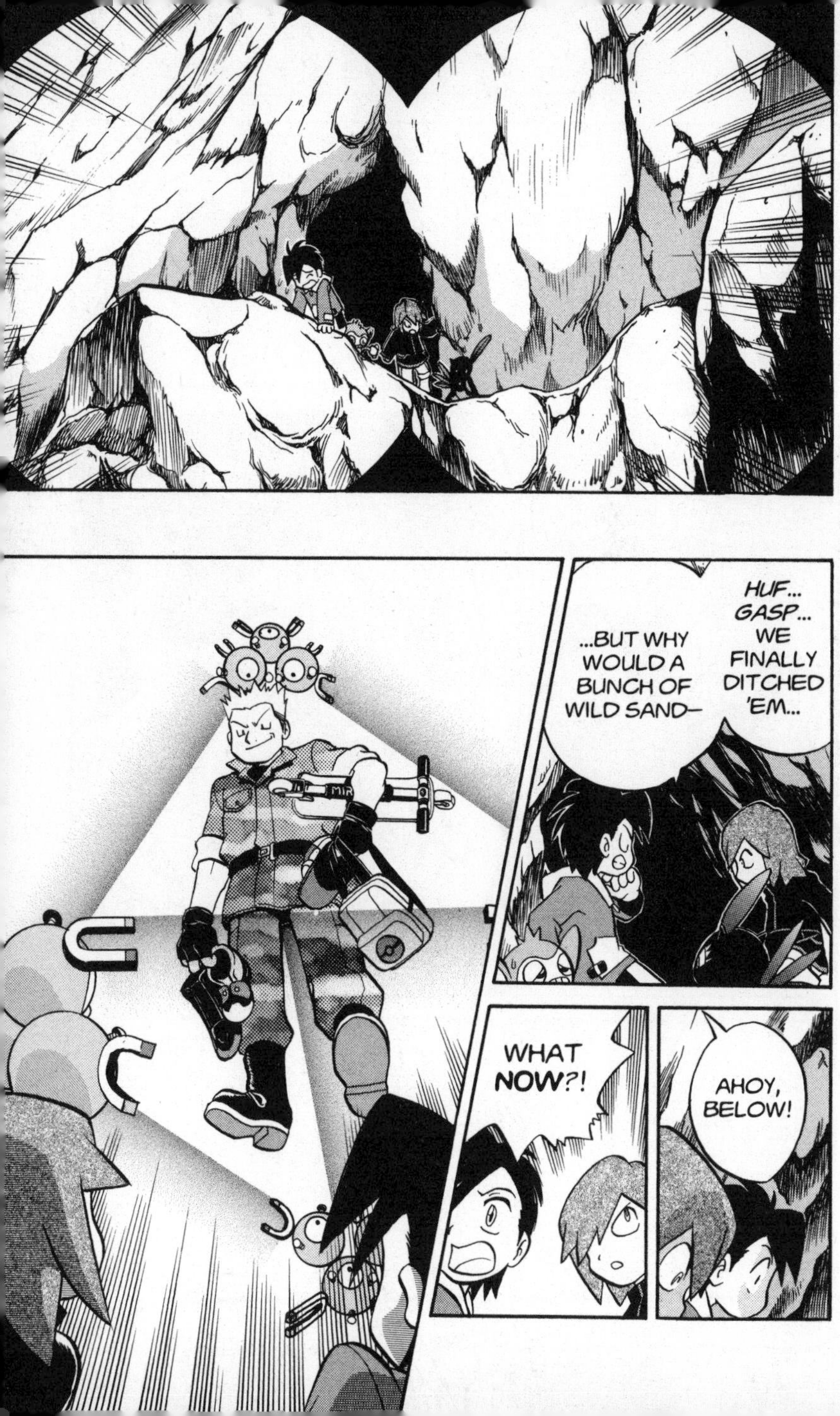
HUF... GASP... WE FINALLY DITCHED 'EM...
...BUT WHY WOULD A BUNCH OF WILD SAND—
AHOY, BELOW!
WHAT **NOW**?!

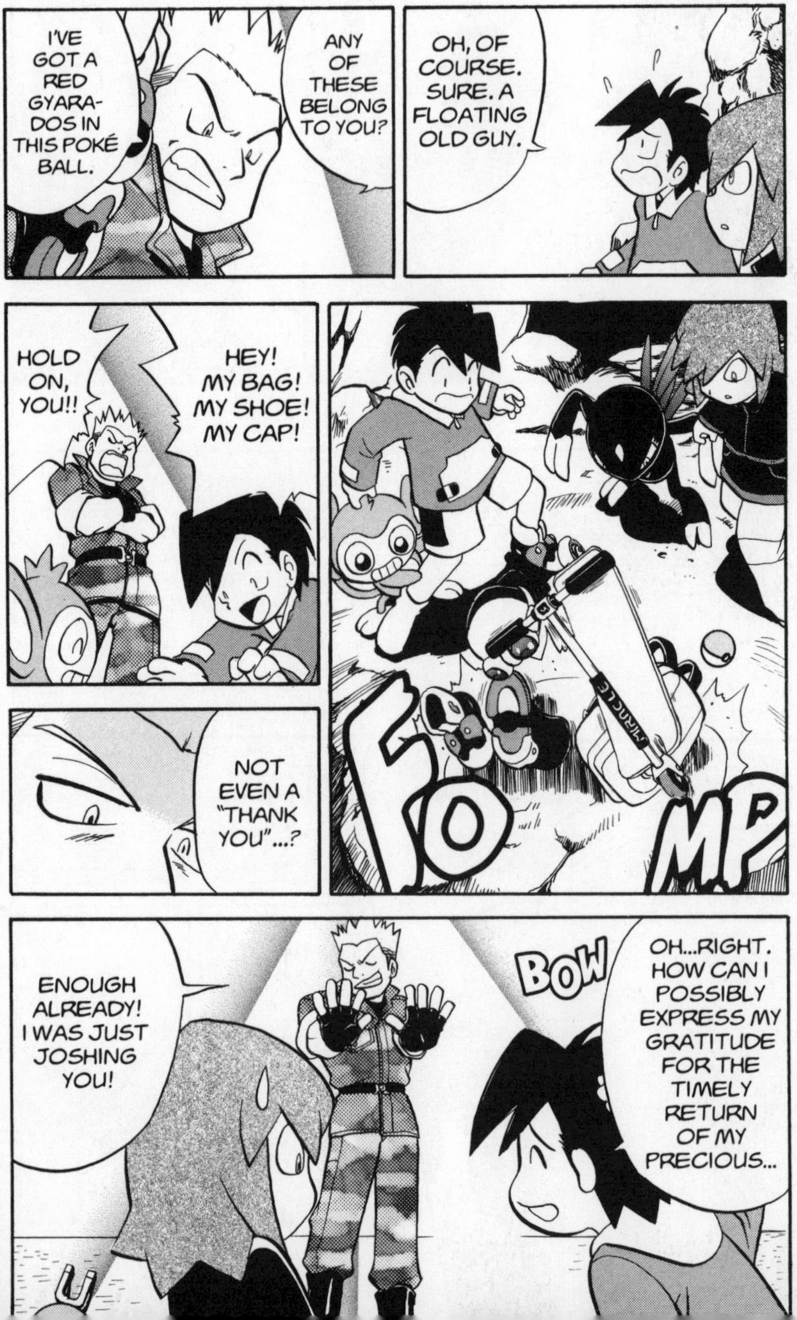
OH, OF COURSE. SURE. A FLOATING OLD GUY.
ANY OF THESE BELONG TO YOU?
I'VE GOT A RED GYARA-DOS IN THIS POKÉ BALL.
TOMP
HEY! MY BAG! MY SHOE! MY CAP!
HOLD ON, YOU!!
NOT EVEN A "THANK YOU"...?
OH...RIGHT. HOW CAN I POSSIBLY EXPRESS MY GRATITUDE FOR THE TIMELY RETURN OF MY PRECIOUS...
BOW
ENOUGH ALREADY! I WAS JUST JOSHING YOU!

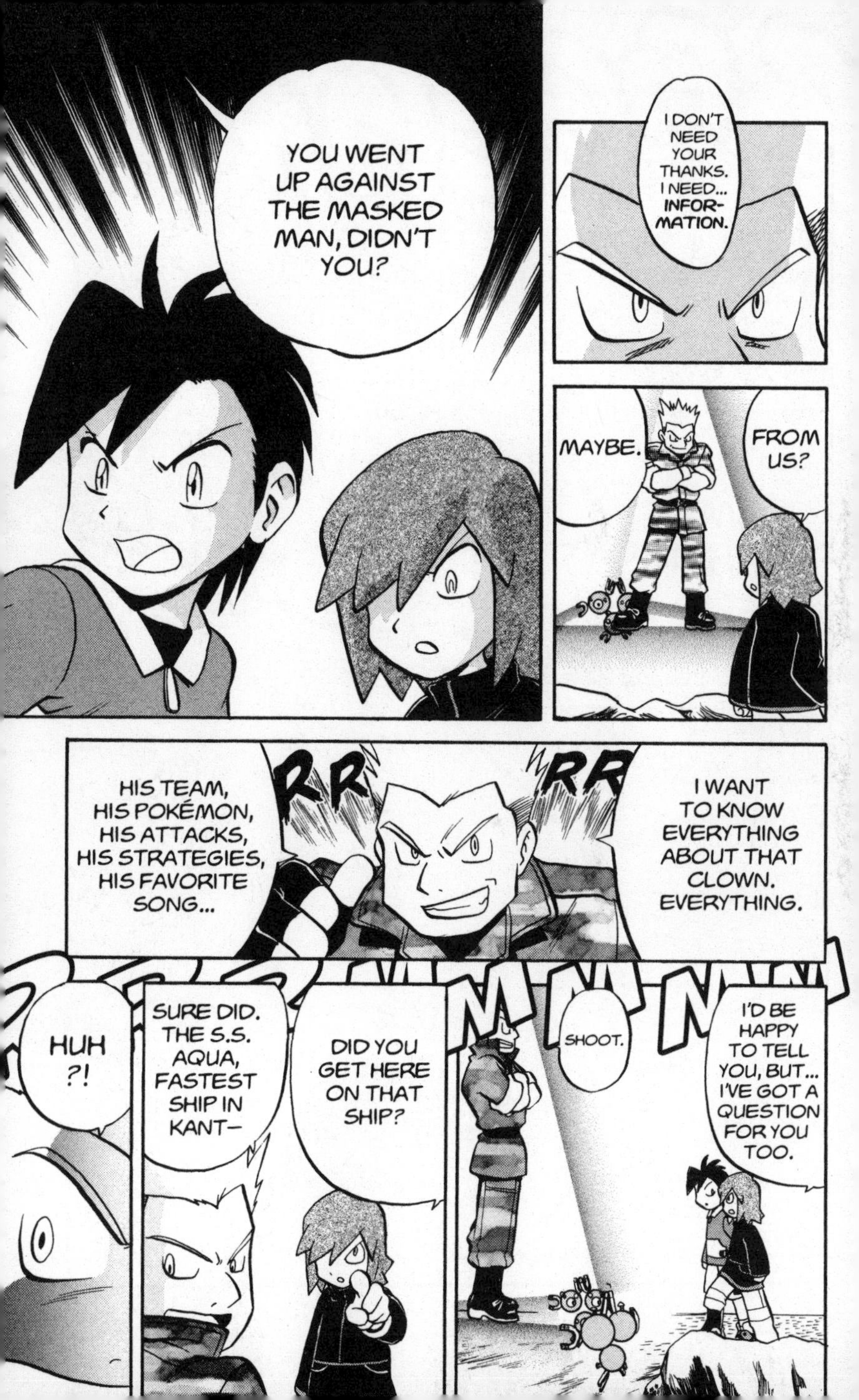

I DON'T NEED YOUR THANKS. I NEED... **INFORMATION.**
FROM US?
MAYBE.
YOU WENT UP AGAINST THE MASKED MAN, DIDN'T YOU?
RR
RR
I WANT TO KNOW EVERYTHING ABOUT THAT CLOWN. EVERYTHING.
HIS TEAM, HIS POKÉMON, HIS ATTACKS, HIS STRATEGIES, HIS FAVORITE SONG...
I'D BE HAPPY TO TELL YOU, BUT... I'VE GOT A QUESTION FOR YOU TOO.
SHOOT.
DID YOU GET HERE ON THAT SHIP?
SURE DID. THE S.S. AQUA, FASTEST SHIP IN KANT—
HUH ?!

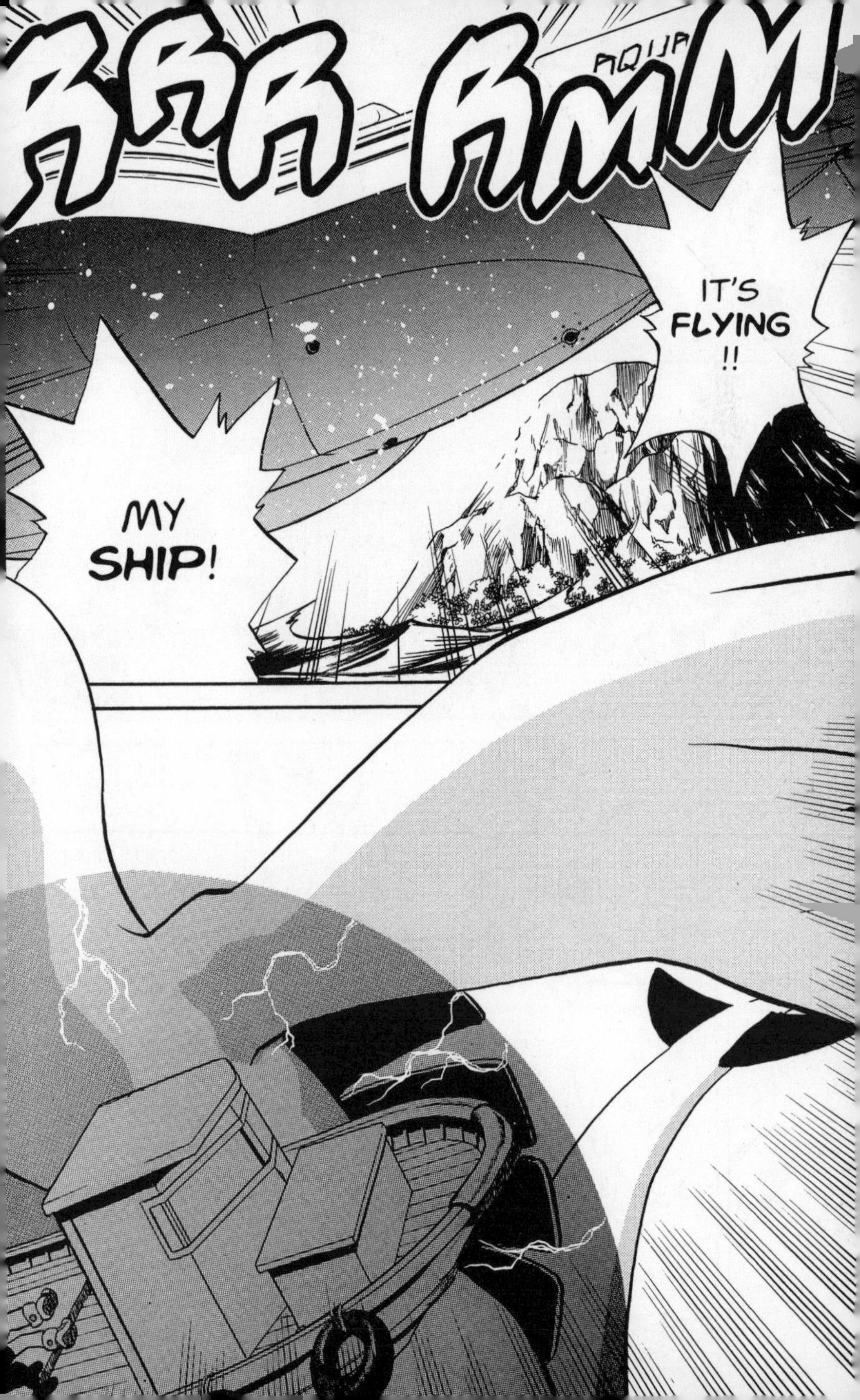
BRR RMM
AQUA
IT'S FLYING !!
MY SHIP!

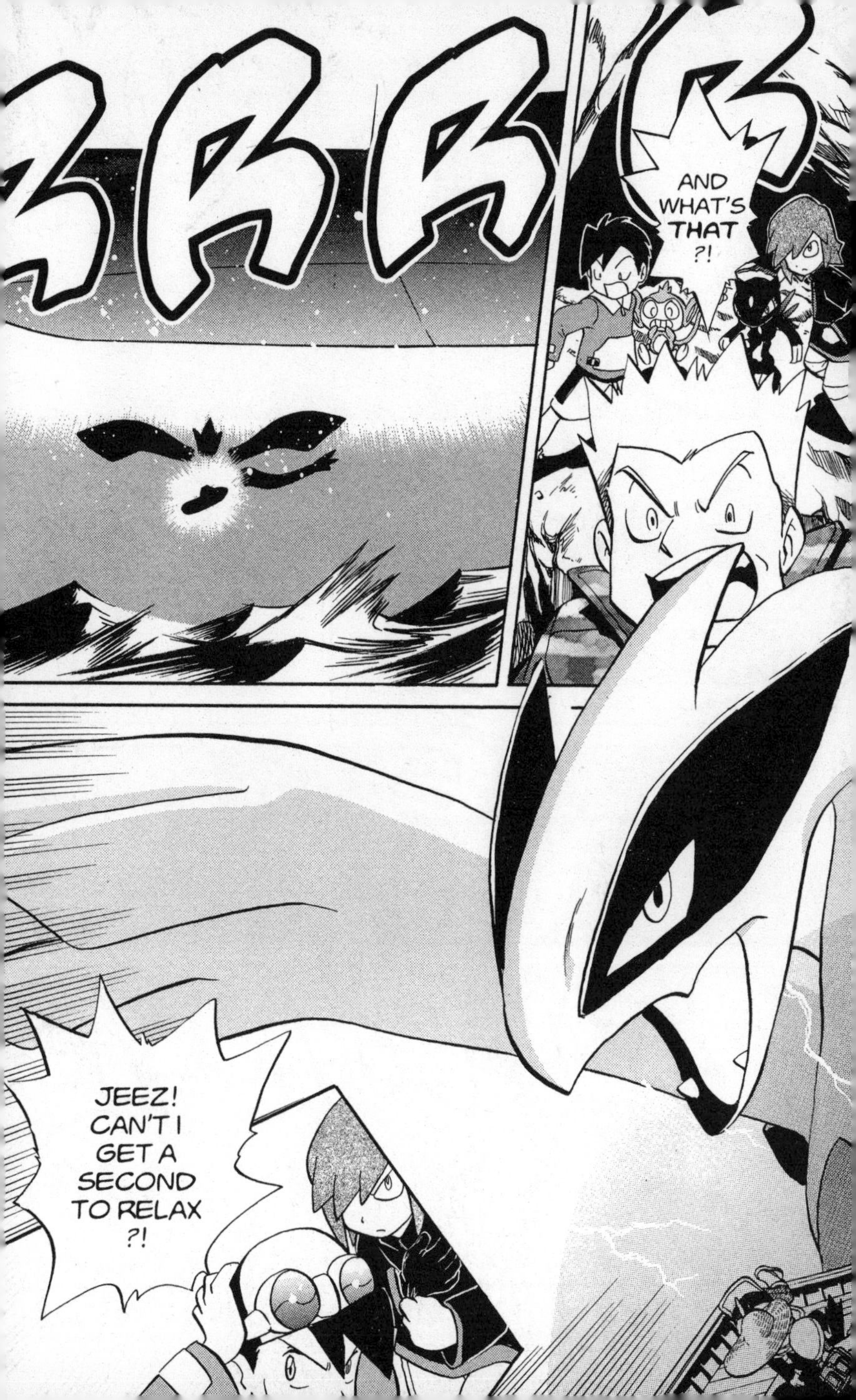
AND WHAT'S THAT ?!
JEEZ! CAN'T I GET A SECOND TO RELAX ?!

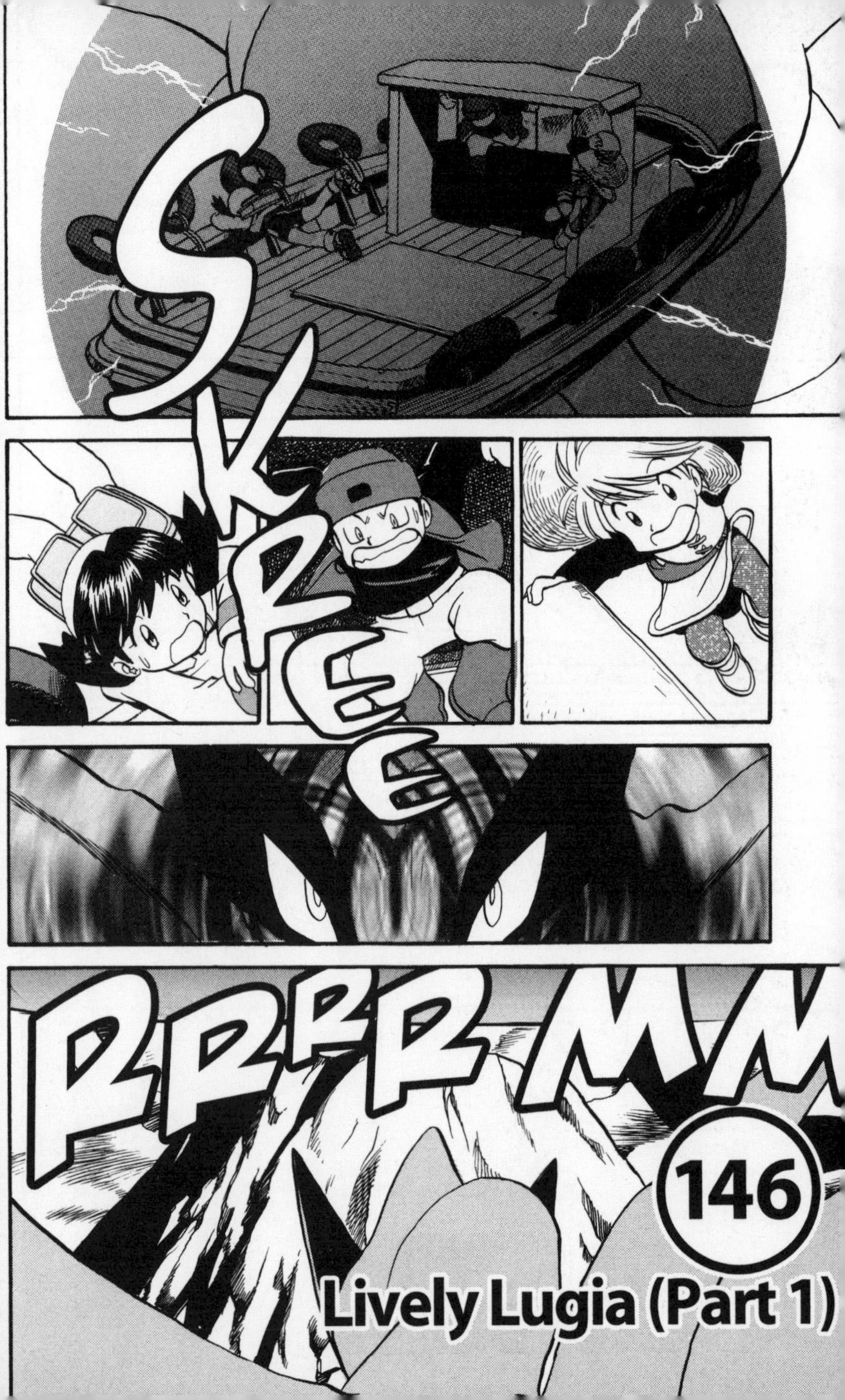
SKREEE
RRRRMMM
146
Lively Lugia (Part 1)

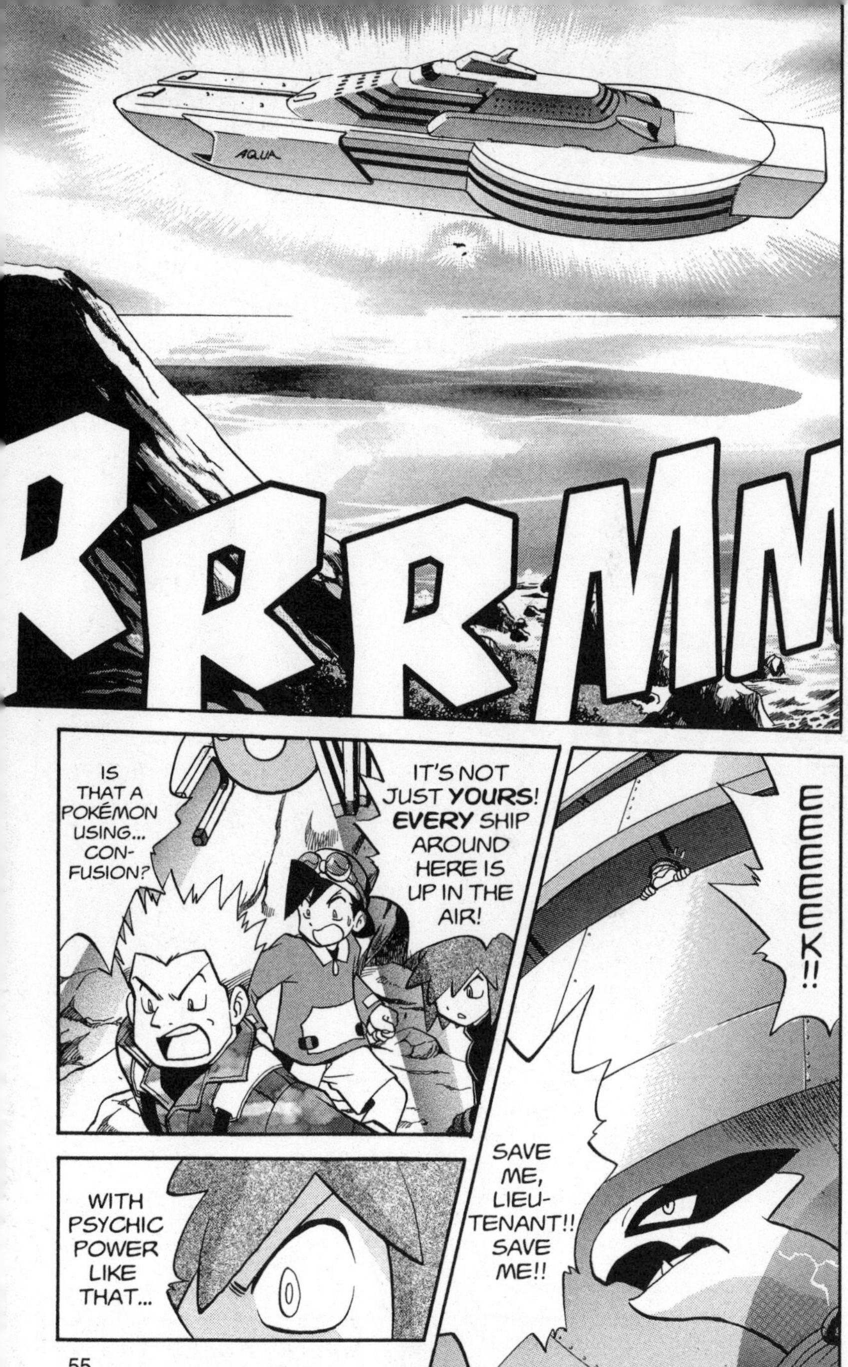
RRRMM
EEEEEK!!
SAVE ME, LIEUTENANT!! SAVE ME!!
IT'S NOT JUST **YOURS**! **EVERY** SHIP AROUND HERE IS UP IN THE AIR!
IS THAT A POKÉMON USING... CONFUSION?
WITH PSYCHIC POWER LIKE THAT...

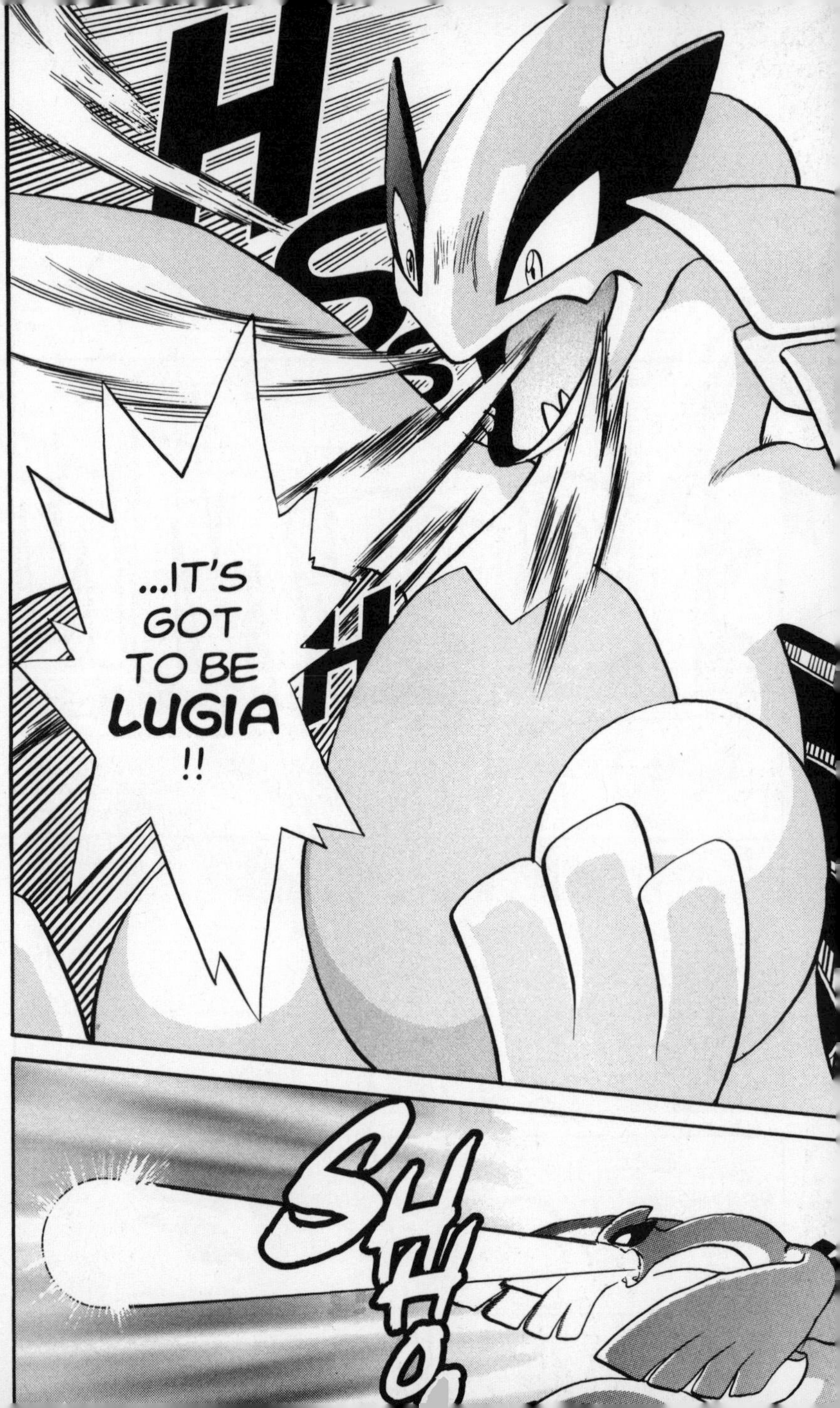
...IT'S GOT TO BE **LUGIA** !!

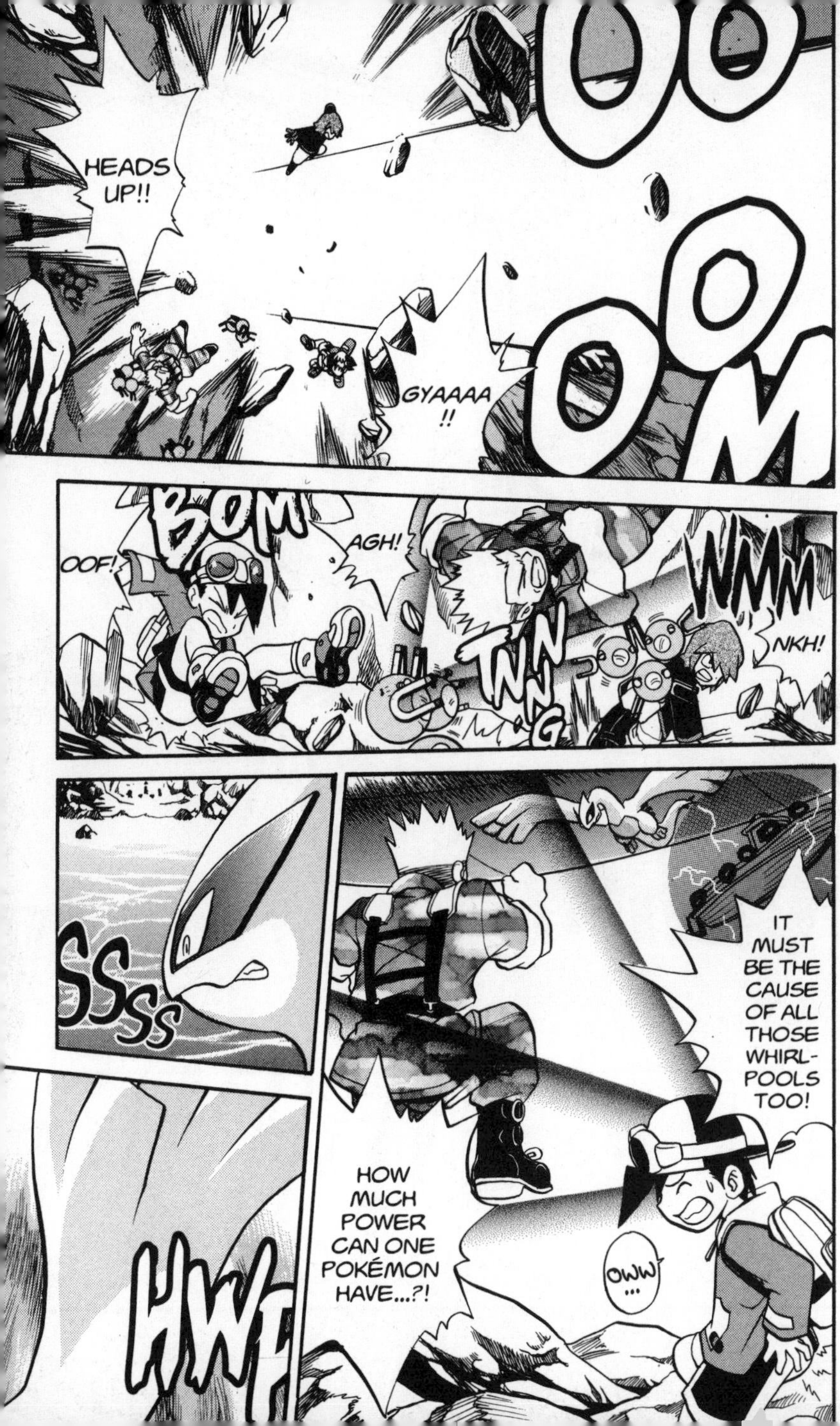
OOOOOM
HEADS UP!!
GYAAAA!!
WMM
NKH!
TNNNG
AGH!
BOM
OOF!
IT MUST BE THE CAUSE OF ALL THOSE WHIRL-POOLS TOO!
HOW MUCH POWER CAN ONE POKÉMON HAVE...?!
OWW...
SSSS
HWF

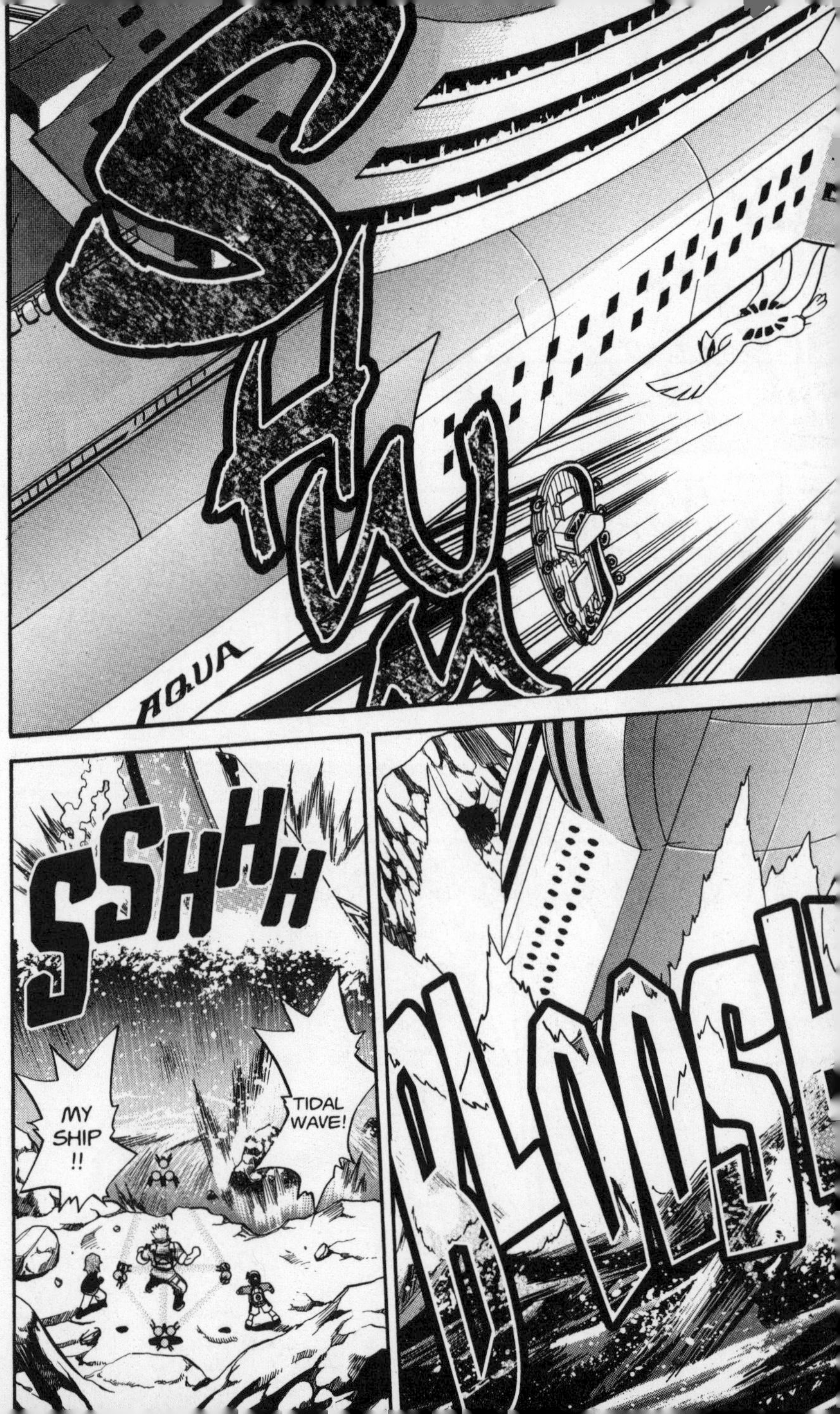
AQUA
SSHHH
TIDAL WAVE!
MY SHIP !!

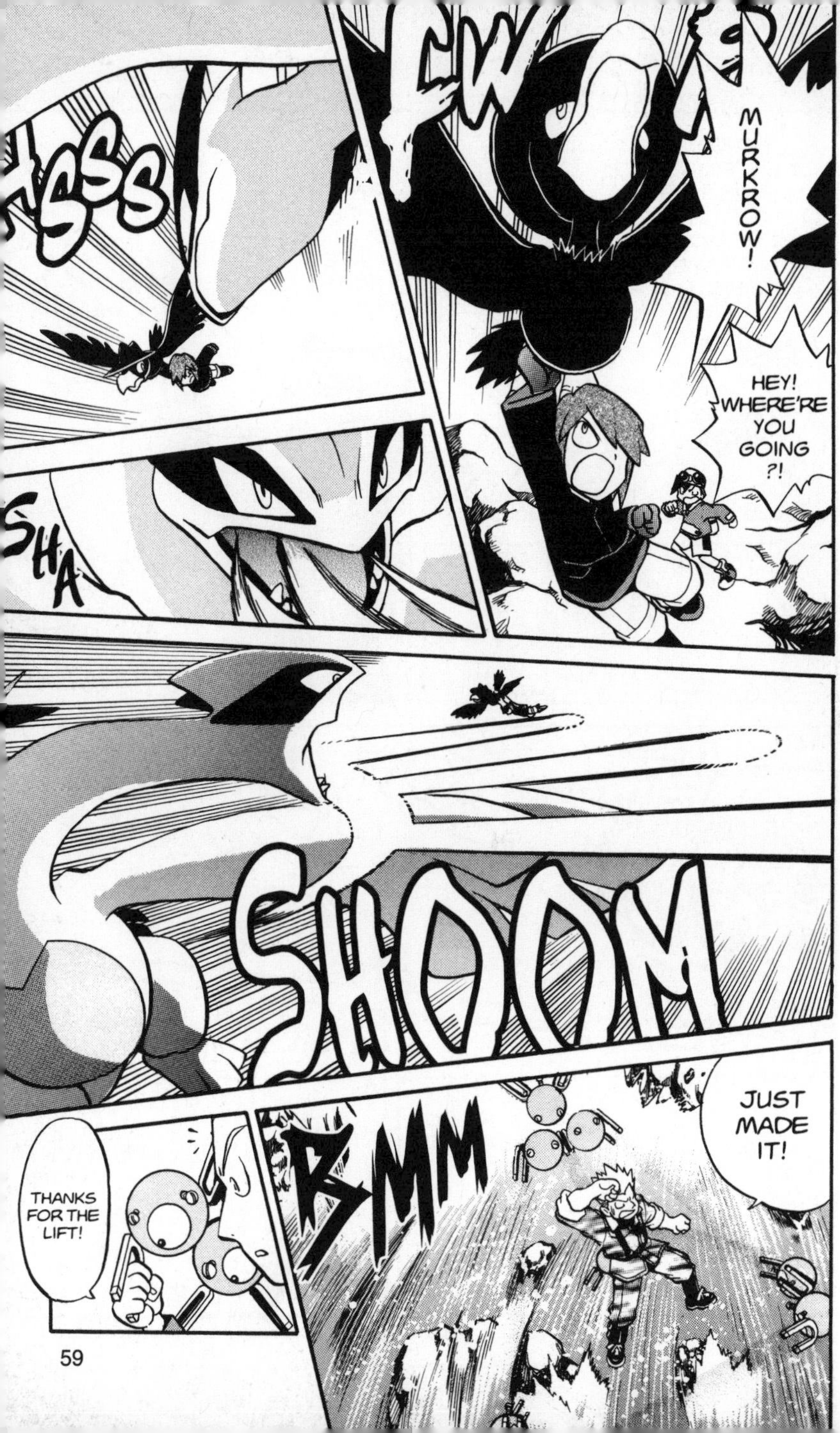
MURKROW!
HEY! WHERE'RE YOU GOING ?!
HSSS
SHA
SHOOM
JUST MADE IT!
BMM
THANKS FOR THE LIFT!

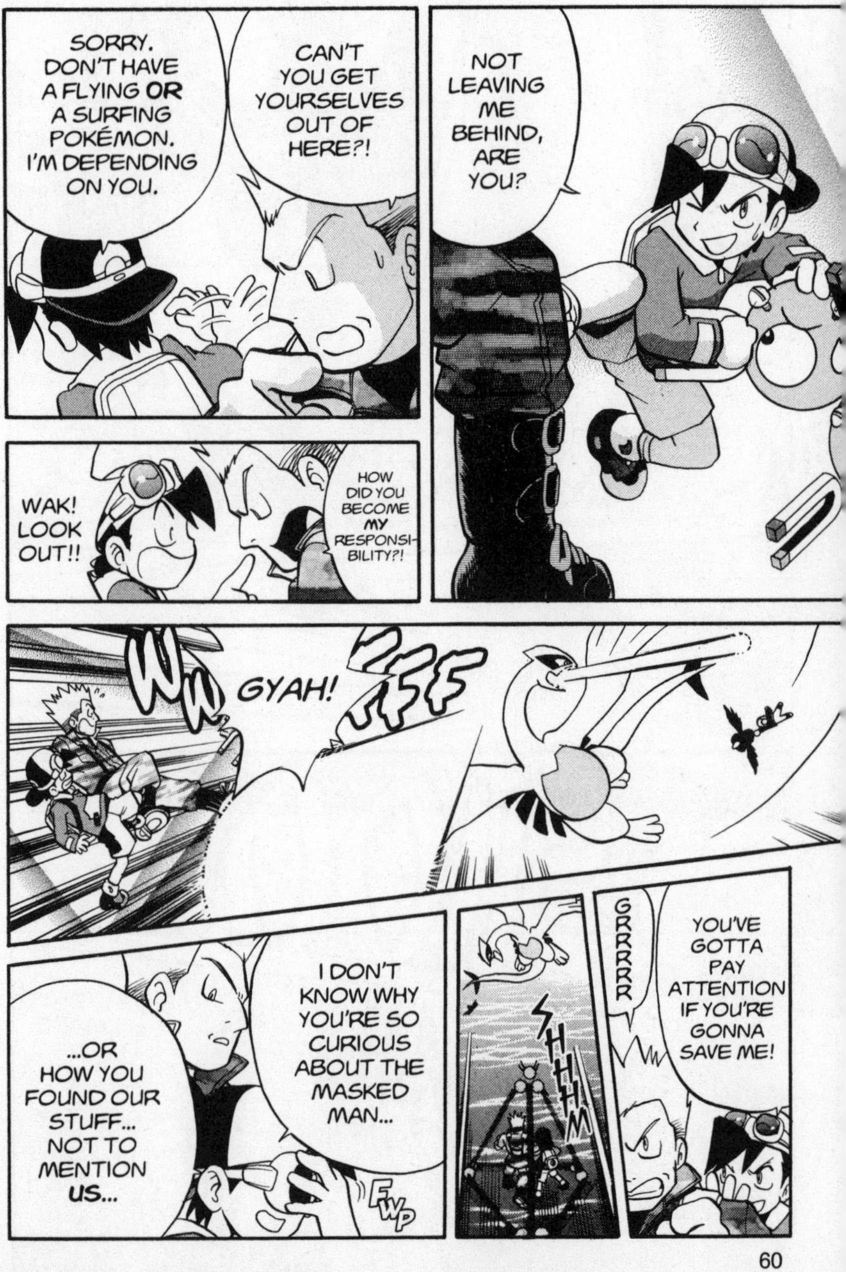
NOT LEAVING ME BEHIND, ARE YOU?
CAN'T YOU GET YOURSELVES OUT OF HERE?!
SORRY. DON'T HAVE A FLYING **OR** A SURFING POKÉMON. I'M DEPENDING ON YOU.
HOW DID YOU BECOME **MY** RESPONSIBILITY?!
WAK! LOOK OUT!!
GYAH!
GRRRRR
YOU'VE GOTTA PAY ATTENTION IF YOU'RE GONNA SAVE ME!
I DON'T KNOW WHY YOU'RE SO CURIOUS ABOUT THE MASKED MAN...
...OR HOW YOU FOUND OUR STUFF... NOT TO MENTION **US**...
FWP

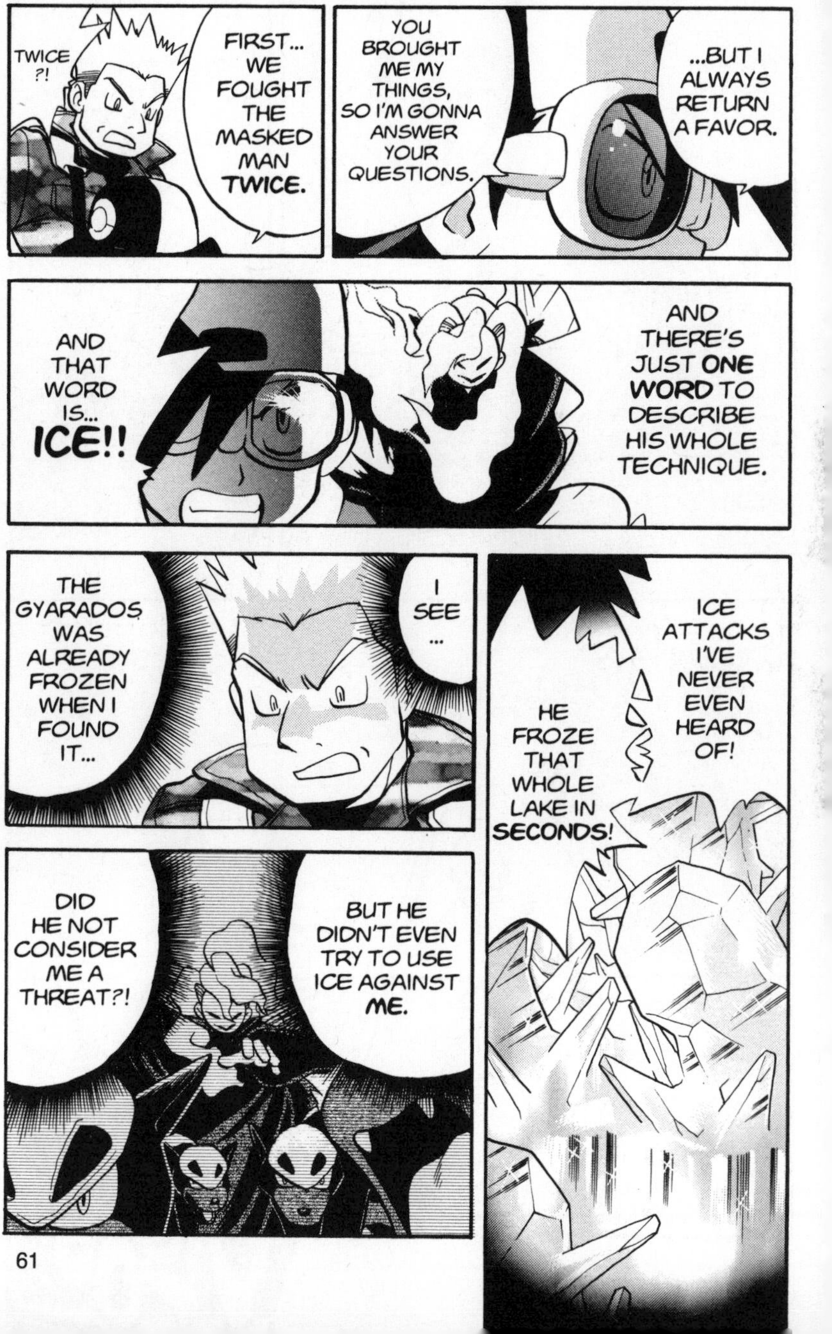
YOU BROUGHT ME MY THINGS, SO I'M GONNA ANSWER YOUR QUESTIONS.
...BUT I ALWAYS RETURN A FAVOR.
FIRST... WE FOUGHT THE MASKED MAN **TWICE.**
TWICE?!
AND THERE'S JUST **ONE WORD** TO DESCRIBE HIS WHOLE TECHNIQUE.
AND THAT WORD IS... **ICE!!**
ICE ATTACKS I'VE NEVER EVEN HEARD OF!
HE FROZE THAT WHOLE LAKE IN **SECONDS!**
I SEE...
THE GYARADOS WAS ALREADY FROZEN WHEN I FOUND IT...
BUT HE DIDN'T EVEN TRY TO USE ICE AGAINST **ME.**
DID HE NOT CONSIDER ME A THREAT?!

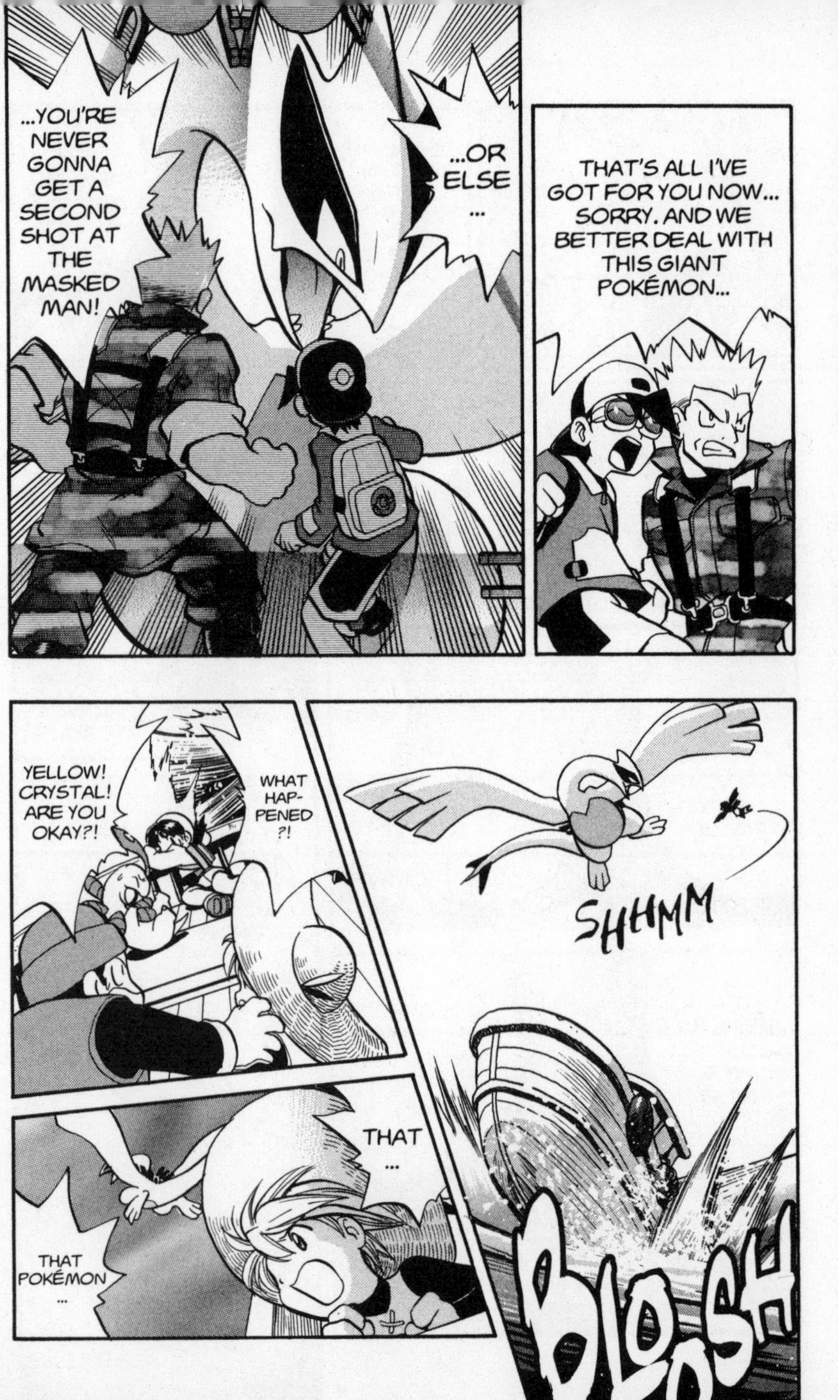
THAT'S ALL I'VE GOT FOR YOU NOW... SORRY. AND WE BETTER DEAL WITH THIS GIANT POKÉMON...
...OR ELSE ...
...YOU'RE NEVER GONNA GET A SECOND SHOT AT THE MASKED MAN!
SHHMM
BLOOSH
WHAT HAP-PENED ?!
YELLOW! CRYSTAL! ARE YOU OKAY?!
THAT ...
THAT POKÉMON ...

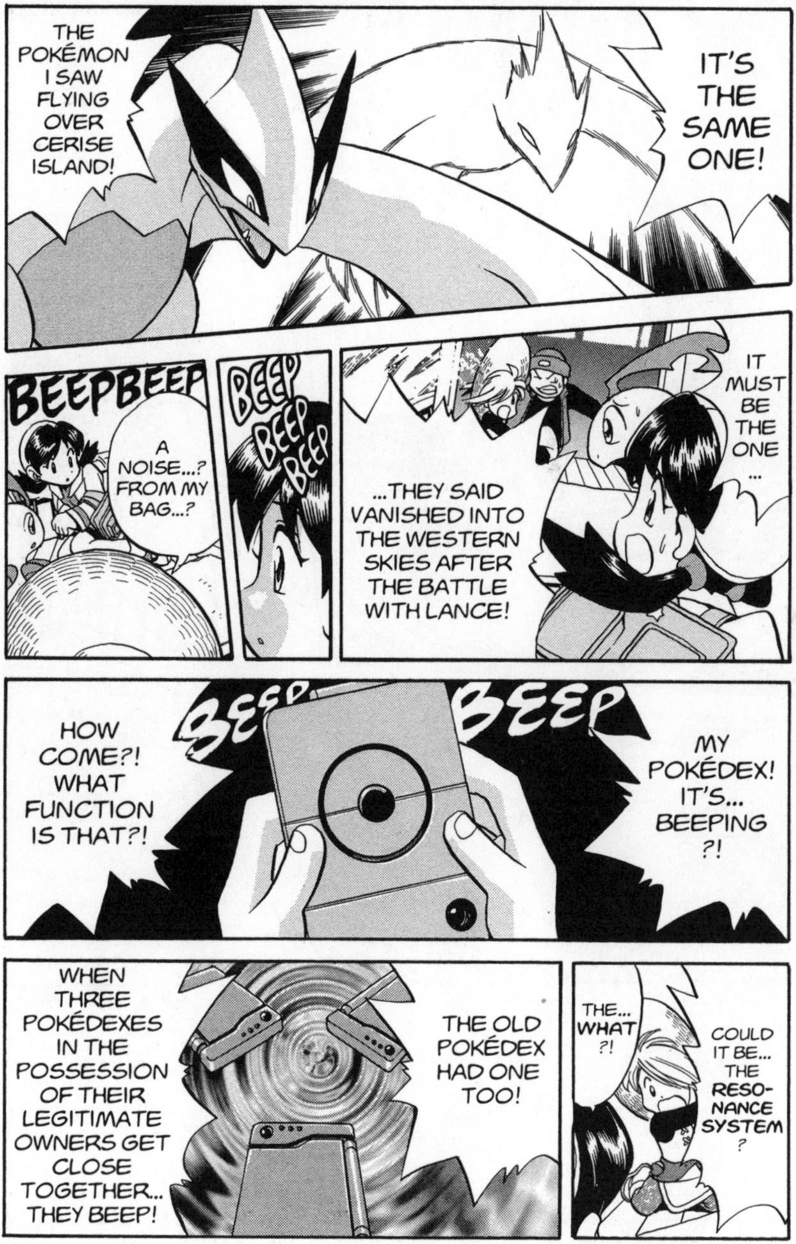
IT'S THE SAME ONE!
THE POKÉMON I SAW FLYING OVER CERISE ISLAND!
IT MUST BE THE ONE...
...THEY SAID VANISHED INTO THE WESTERN SKIES AFTER THE BATTLE WITH LANCE!
BEEP BEEP BEEP
BEEPBEEP
A NOISE...? FROM MY BAG...?
BEEP
MY POKÉDEX! IT'S... BEEPING?!
HOW COME?! WHAT FUNCTION IS THAT?!
COULD IT BE... THE RESONANCE SYSTEM?
THE... WHAT?!
THE OLD POKÉDEX HAD ONE TOO!
WHEN THREE POKÉDEXES IN THE POSSESSION OF THEIR LEGITIMATE OWNERS GET CLOSE TOGETHER... THEY BEEP!

SEE VOL. 11.

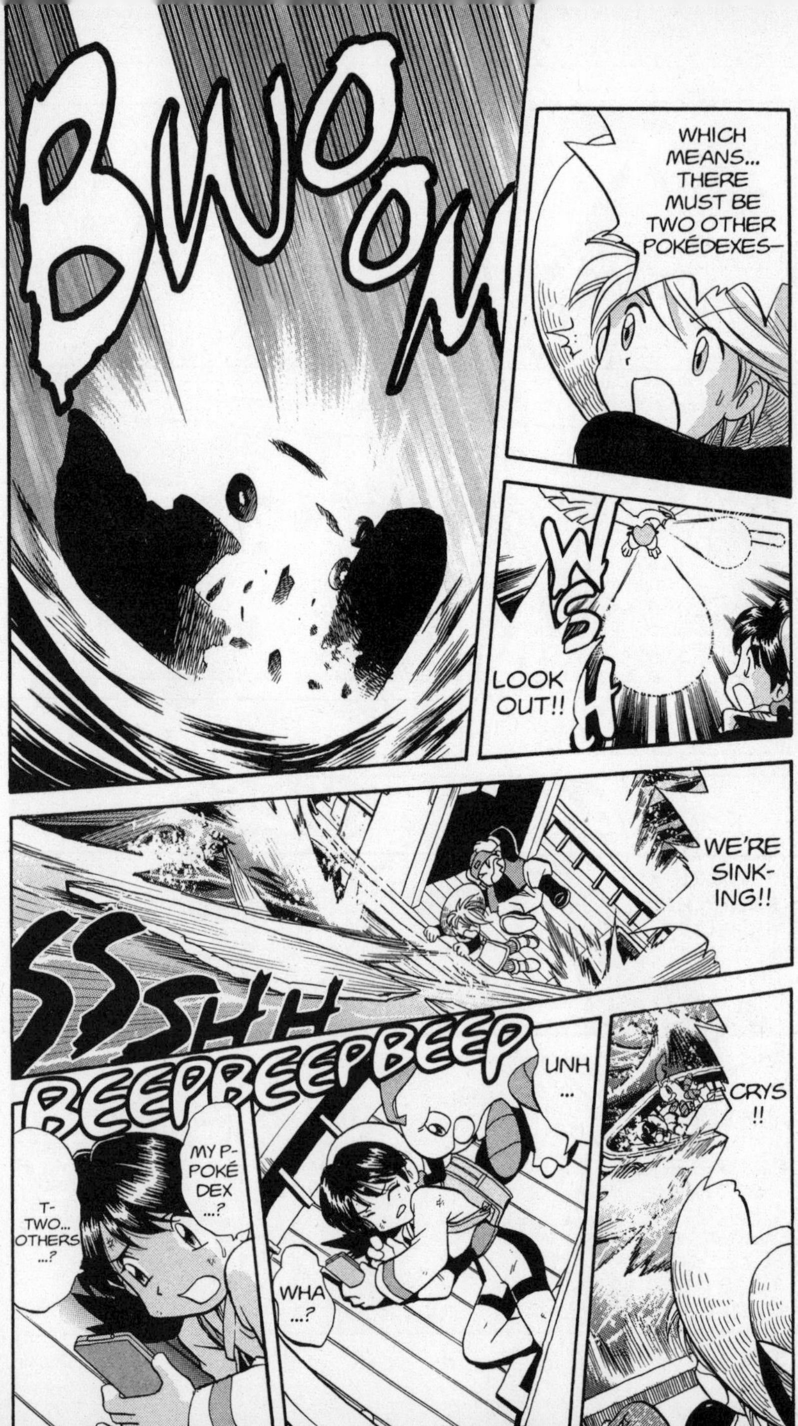
WHICH MEANS... THERE MUST BE TWO OTHER POKÉDEXES—
WSH
LOOK OUT!!
BWOOM
WE'RE SINK-ING!!
SSHH
CRYS!!
UNH...
WHA...?
BEEPBEEPBEEP
MY P-POKÉDEX...?
T-TWO... OTHERS...?

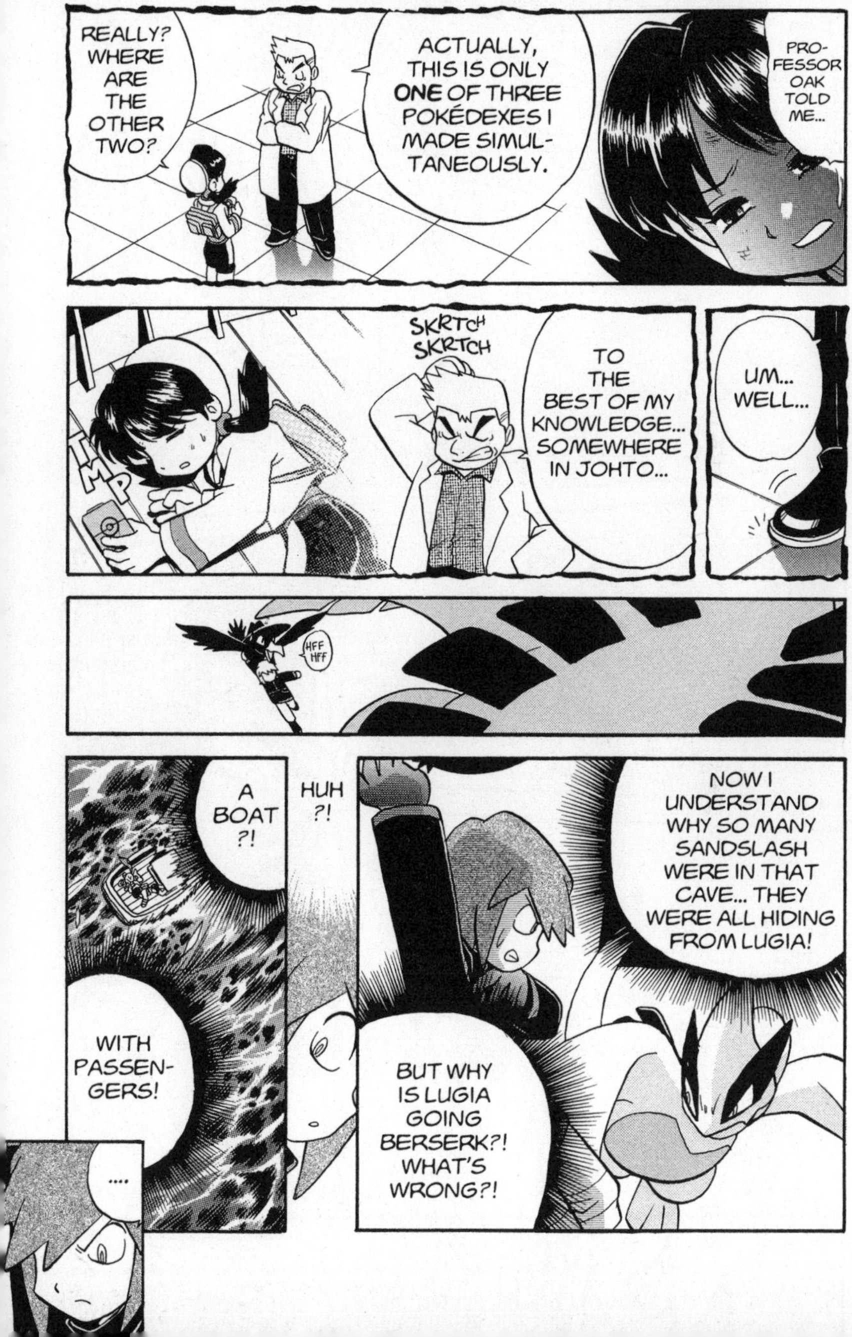
PRO-FESSOR OAK TOLD ME...
ACTUALLY, THIS IS ONLY **ONE** OF THREE POKÉDEXES I MADE SIMUL-TANEOUSLY.
REALLY? WHERE ARE THE OTHER TWO?
UM... WELL...
SKRTCH SKRTCH
TO THE BEST OF MY KNOWLEDGE... SOMEWHERE IN JOHTO...
TMP
HFF HFF
NOW I UNDERSTAND WHY SO MANY SANDSLASH WERE IN THAT CAVE... THEY WERE ALL HIDING FROM LUGIA!
BUT WHY IS LUGIA GOING BERSERK?! WHAT'S WRONG?!
HUH ?!
A BOAT ?!
WITH PASSEN-GERS!
....

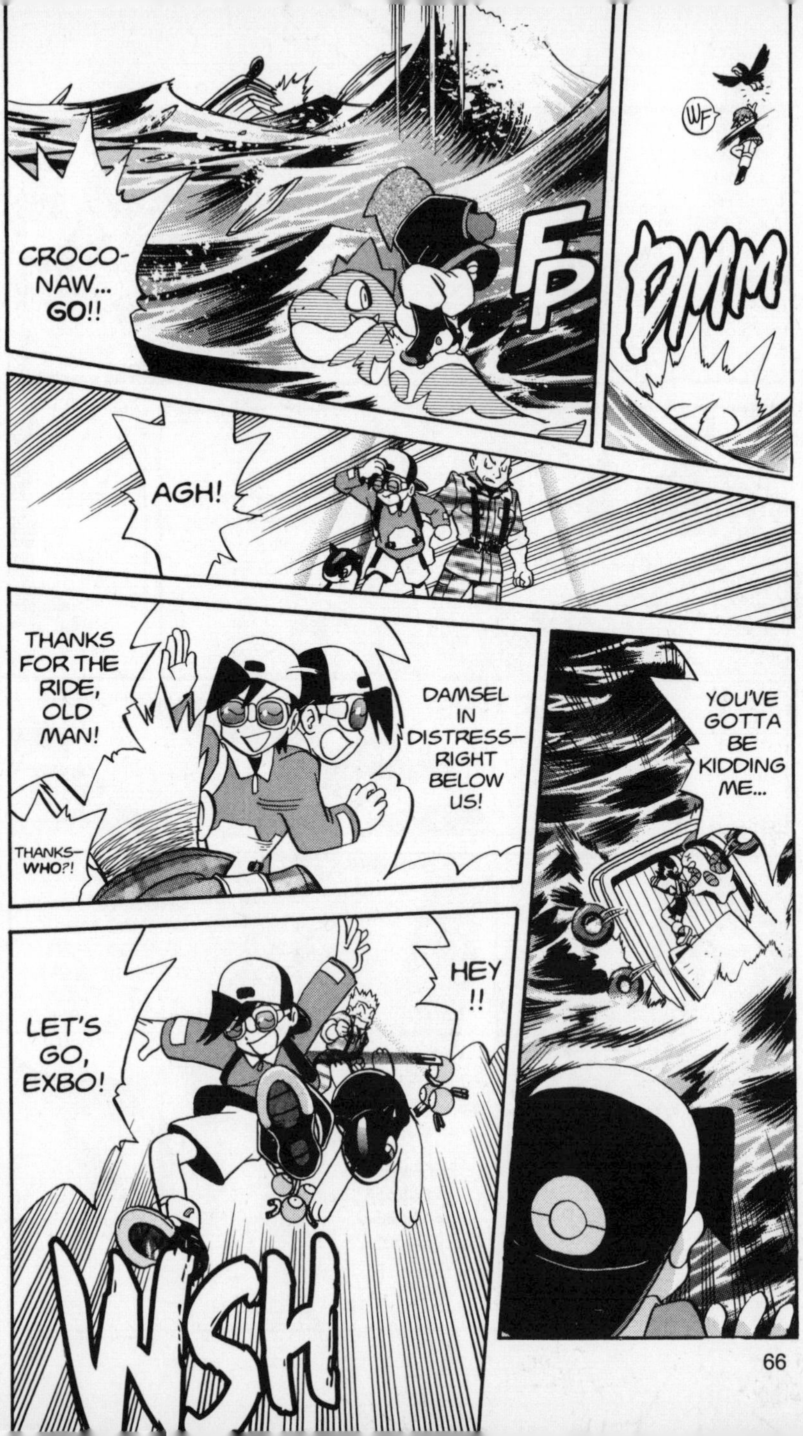
WF
DMM
FP
CROCO-NAW... GO!!
AGH!
YOU'VE GOTTA BE KIDDING ME...
DAMSEL IN DISTRESS—RIGHT BELOW US!
THANKS FOR THE RIDE, OLD MAN!
THANKS—WHO?!
HEY !!
LET'S GO, EXBO!
WSH

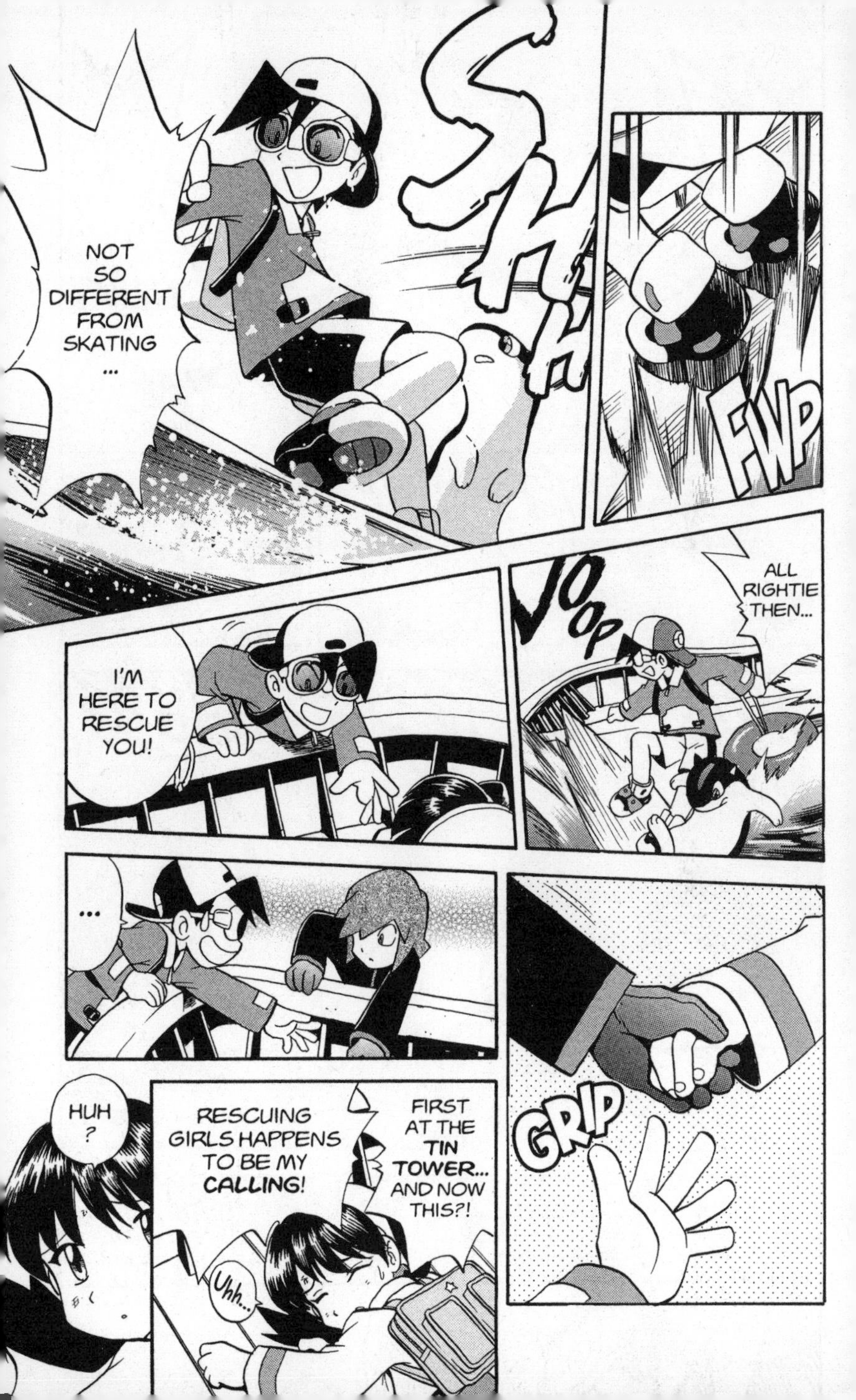
FWP
NOT SO DIFFERENT FROM SKATING ...
SH
ALL RIGHTIE THEN...
VOOP
I'M HERE TO RESCUE YOU!
GRIP
...
FIRST AT THE TIN TOWER... AND NOW THIS?!
RESCUING GIRLS HAPPENS TO BE MY CALLING!
Uhh...
HUH ?

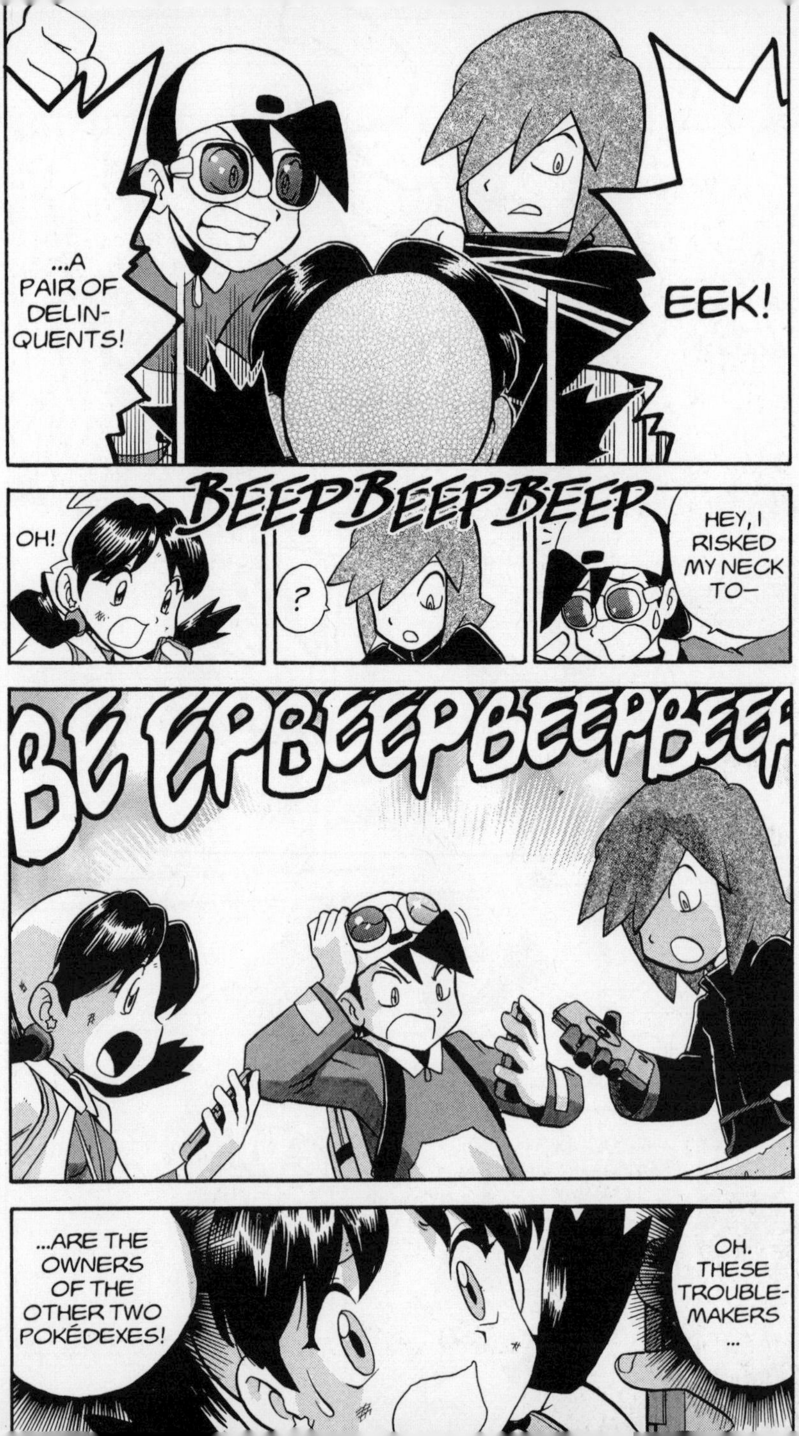
EEK!
...A PAIR OF DELIN-QUENTS!
BEEPBEEPBEEP
HEY, I RISKED MY NECK TO–
?
OH!
BEEPBEEPBEEPBEEP
OH. THESE TROUBLE-MAKERS ...
...ARE THE OWNERS OF THE OTHER TWO POKÉDEXES!

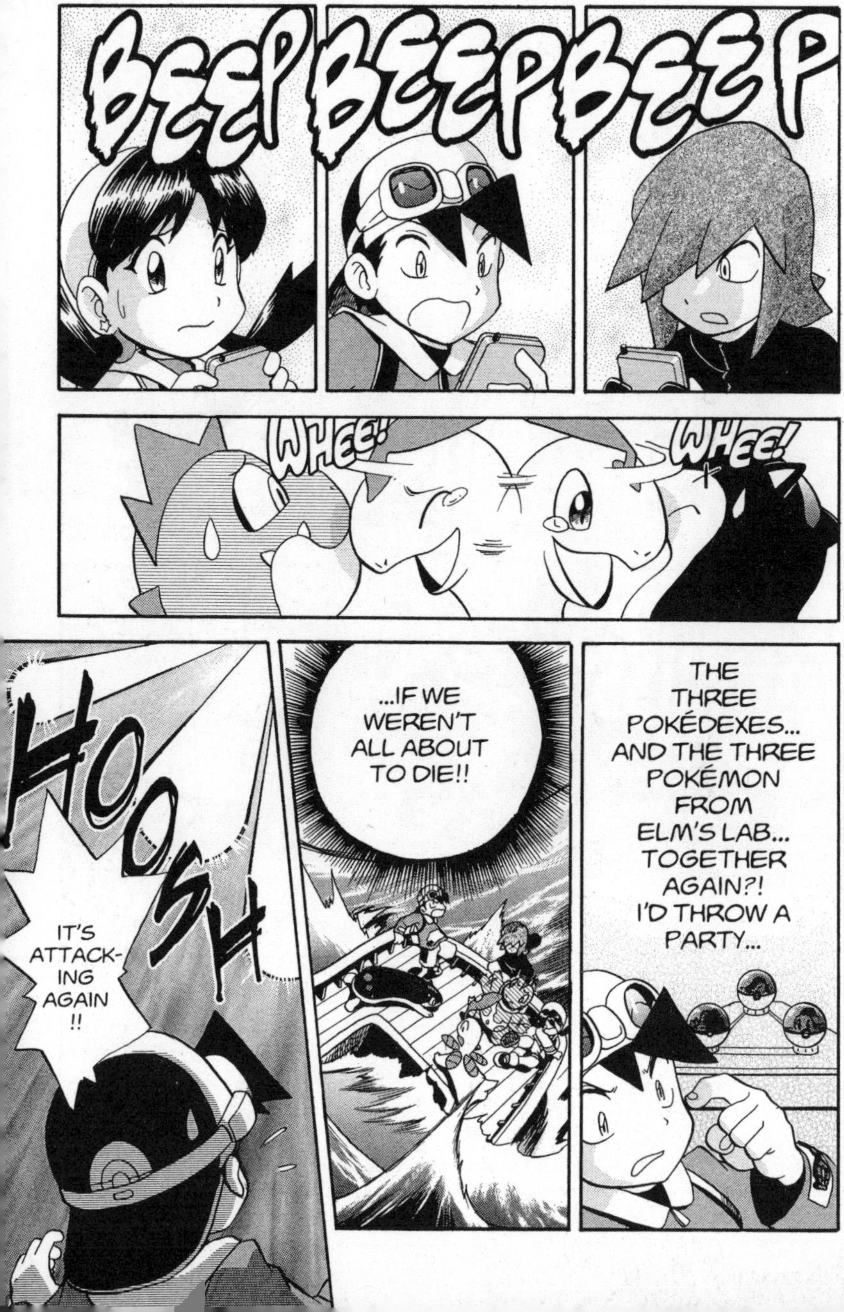
BEEP
BEEP
BEEP
WHEE!
WHEE!
THE THREE POKÉDEXES... AND THE THREE POKÉMON FROM ELM'S LAB... TOGETHER AGAIN?! I'D THROW A PARTY...
...IF WE WEREN'T ALL ABOUT TO DIE!!
HOOSH
IT'S ATTACK-ING AGAIN!!

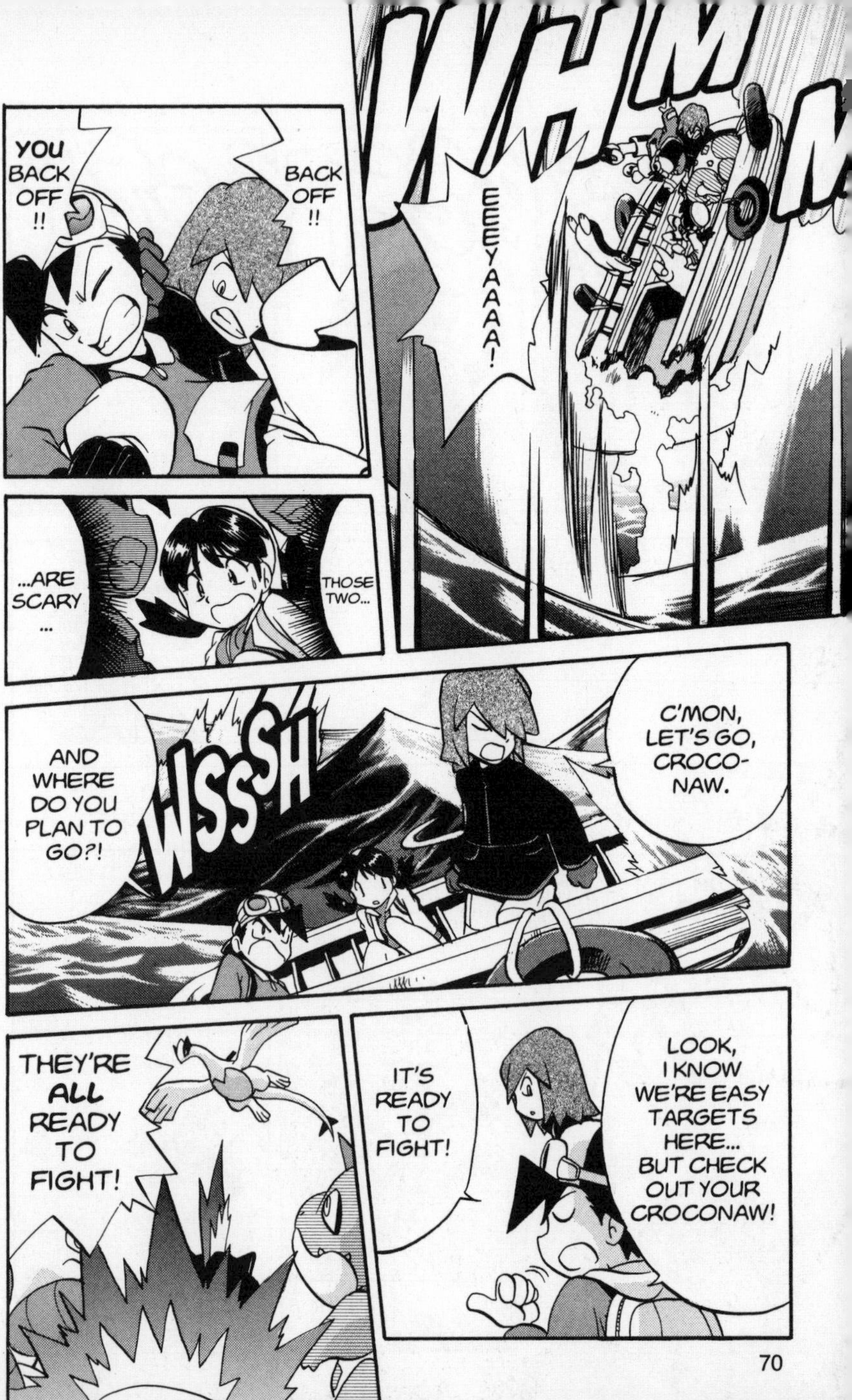
WHMM
EEEYAAAA!
BACK OFF!!
YOU BACK OFF!!
THOSE TWO...
...ARE SCARY...
C'MON, LET'S GO, CROCO-NAW.
WSSSH
AND WHERE DO YOU PLAN TO GO?!
LOOK, I KNOW WE'RE EASY TARGETS HERE... BUT CHECK OUT YOUR CROCONAW!
IT'S READY TO FIGHT!
THEY'RE ALL READY TO FIGHT!

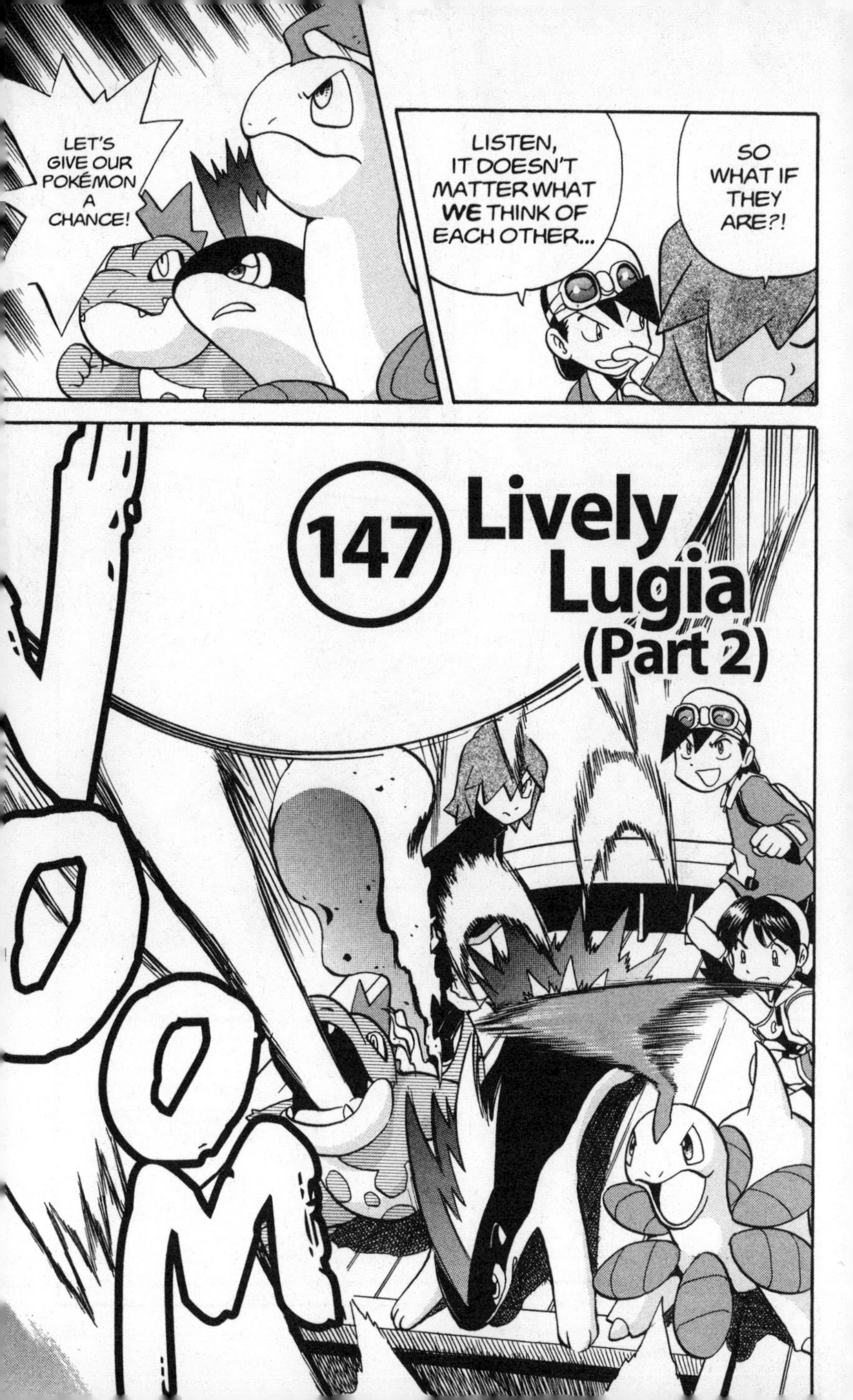
SO WHAT IF THEY ARE?!
LISTEN, IT DOESN'T MATTER WHAT WE THINK OF EACH OTHER...
LET'S GIVE OUR POKÉMON A CHANCE!
147 Lively Lugia (Part 2)

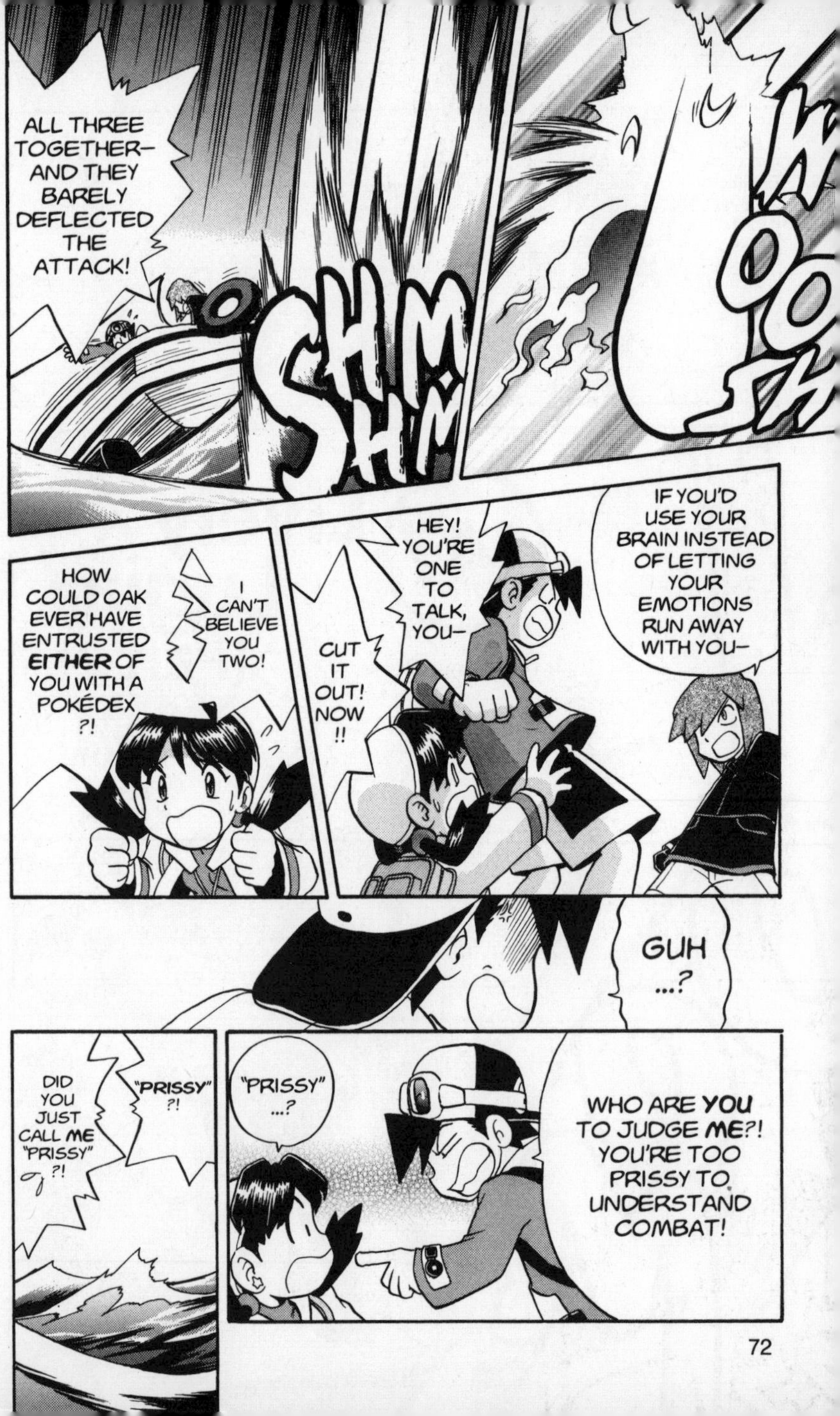
SHM SHM
ALL THREE TOGETHER—AND THEY BARELY DEFLECTED THE ATTACK!
IF YOU'D USE YOUR BRAIN INSTEAD OF LETTING YOUR EMOTIONS RUN AWAY WITH YOU—
HEY! YOU'RE ONE TO TALK, YOU—
CUT IT OUT! NOW!!
I CAN'T BELIEVE YOU TWO!
HOW COULD OAK EVER HAVE ENTRUSTED **EITHER** OF YOU WITH A POKÉDEX?!
GUH...?
WHO ARE **YOU** TO JUDGE **ME**?! YOU'RE TOO PRISSY TO UNDERSTAND COMBAT!
"PRISSY"...?
"**PRISSY**"?!
DID YOU JUST CALL **ME** "PRISSY"?!

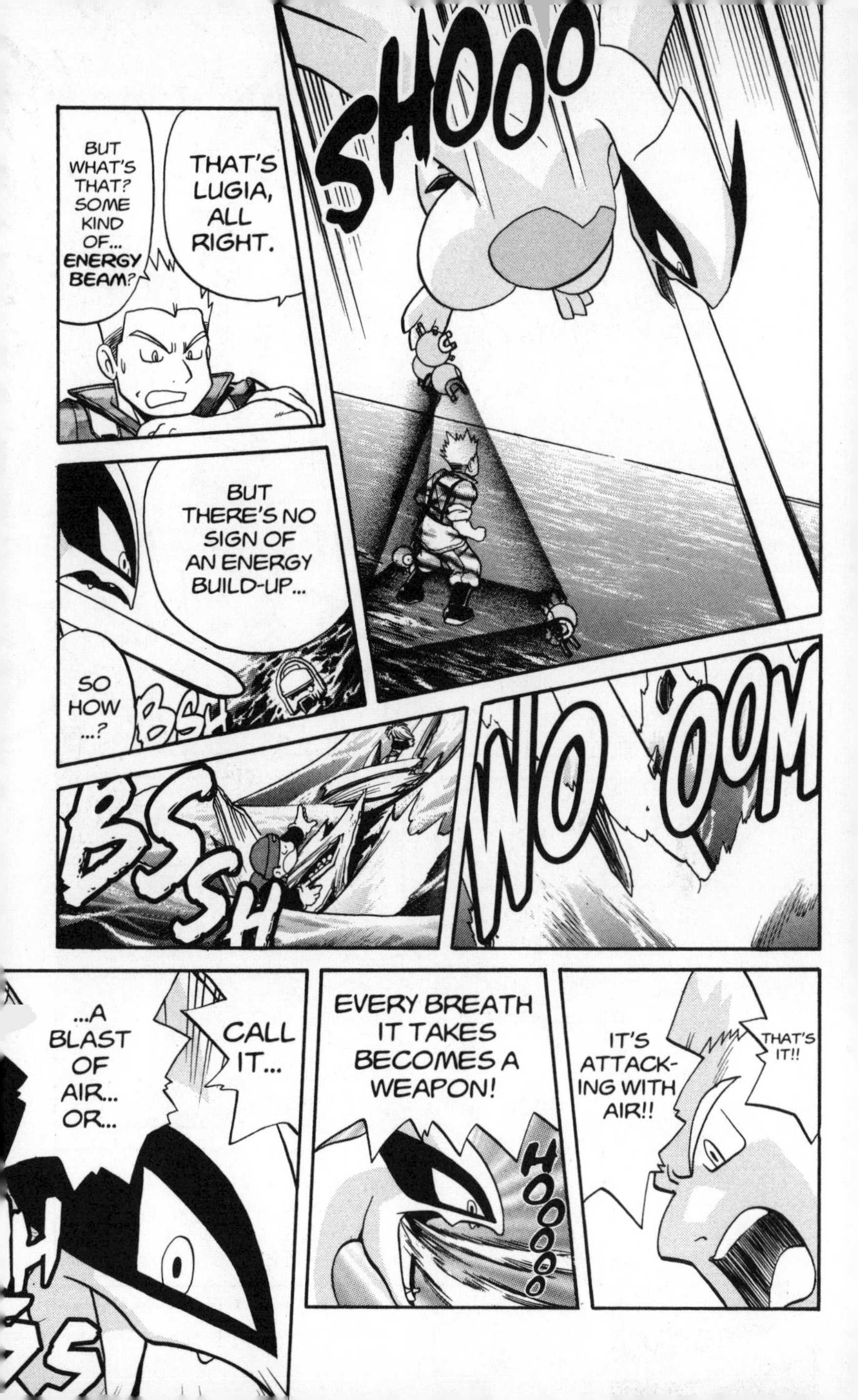
SHOOO
THAT'S LUGIA, ALL RIGHT.
BUT WHAT'S THAT? SOME KIND OF... ENERGY BEAM?
BUT THERE'S NO SIGN OF AN ENERGY BUILD-UP...
SO HOW ...?
BSH
WOOOM
BSSH
IT'S ATTACKING WITH AIR!!
THAT'S IT!!
EVERY BREATH IT TAKES BECOMES A WEAPON!
HOOOOOO
CALL IT...
...A BLAST OF AIR... OR...

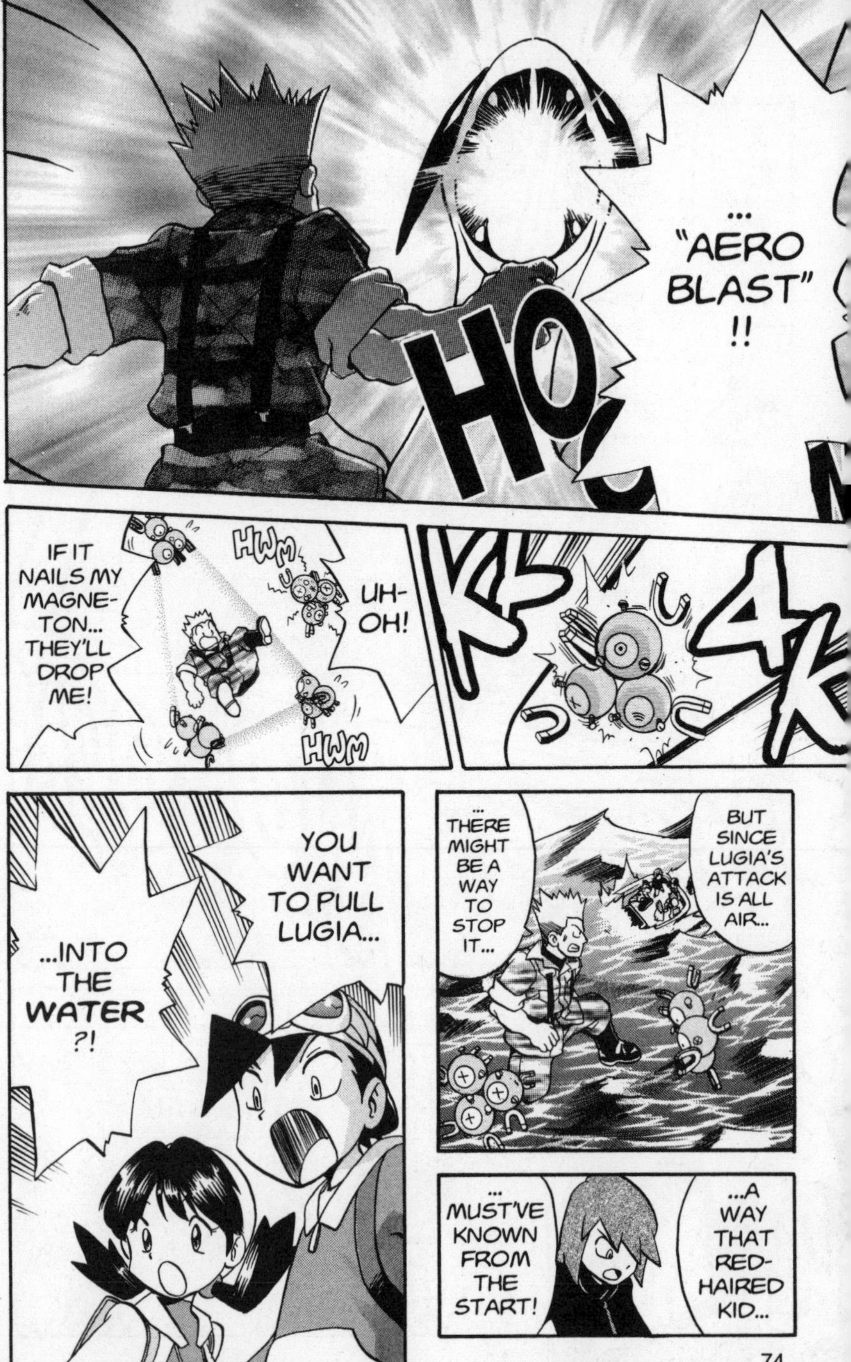
... "AERO BLAST" !!
HO
HWM
UH-OH!
IF IT NAILS MY MAGNETON... THEY'LL DROP ME!
HWM
BUT SINCE LUGIA'S ATTACK IS ALL AIR...
... THERE MIGHT BE A WAY TO STOP IT...
...A WAY THAT RED-HAIRED KID...
... MUST'VE KNOWN FROM THE START!
YOU WANT TO PULL LUGIA...
...INTO THE **WATER** ?!

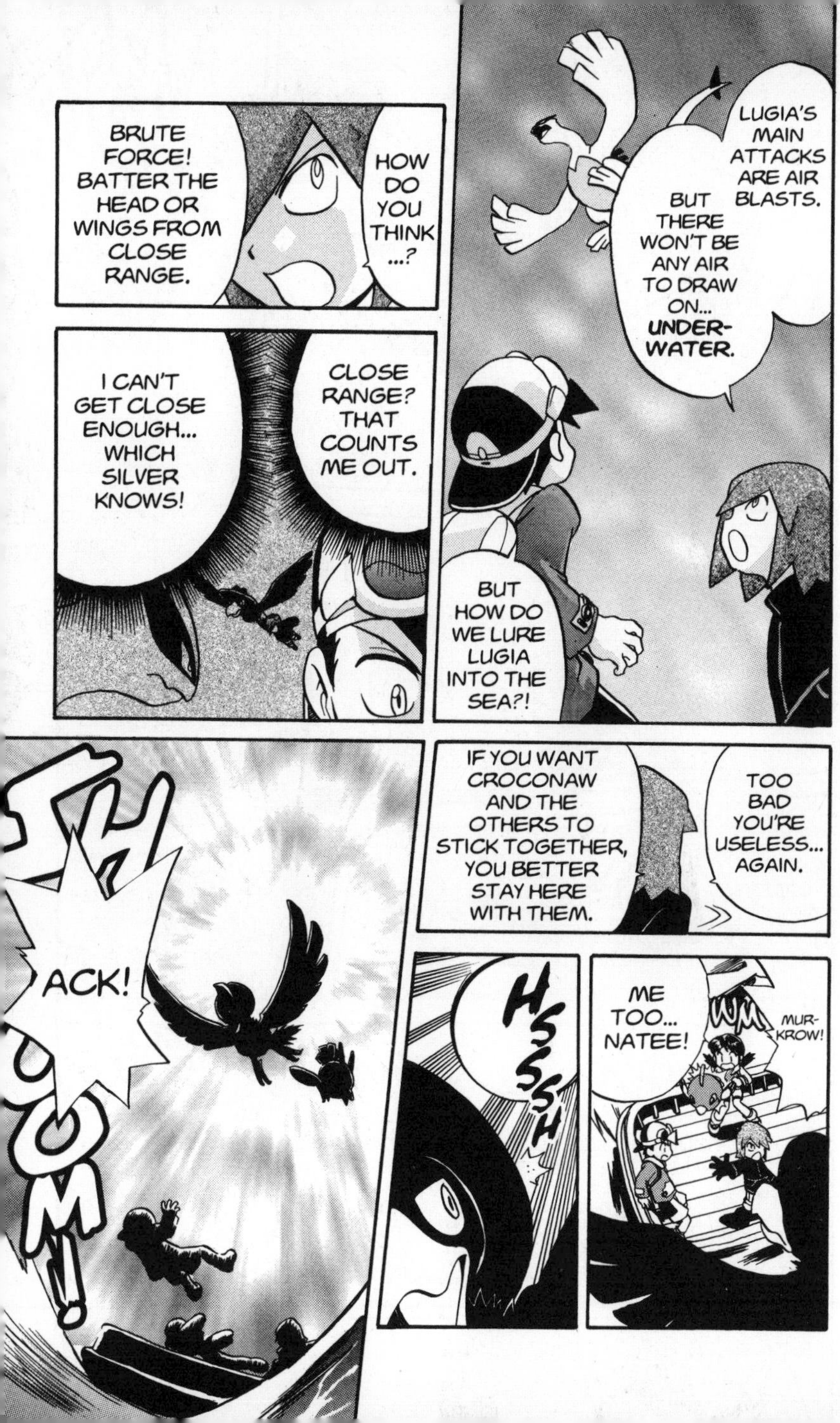
LUGIA'S MAIN ATTACKS ARE AIR BLASTS.
BUT THERE WON'T BE ANY AIR TO DRAW ON... **UNDER-WATER.**
BUT HOW DO WE LURE LUGIA INTO THE SEA?!
HOW DO YOU THINK ...?
BRUTE FORCE! BATTER THE HEAD OR WINGS FROM CLOSE RANGE.
CLOSE RANGE? THAT COUNTS ME OUT.
I CAN'T GET CLOSE ENOUGH... WHICH SILVER KNOWS!
TOO BAD YOU'RE USELESS... AGAIN.
IF YOU WANT CROCONAW AND THE OTHERS TO STICK TOGETHER, YOU BETTER STAY HERE WITH THEM.
MUR-KROW!
ME TOO... NATEE!
HSSSH
ACK!

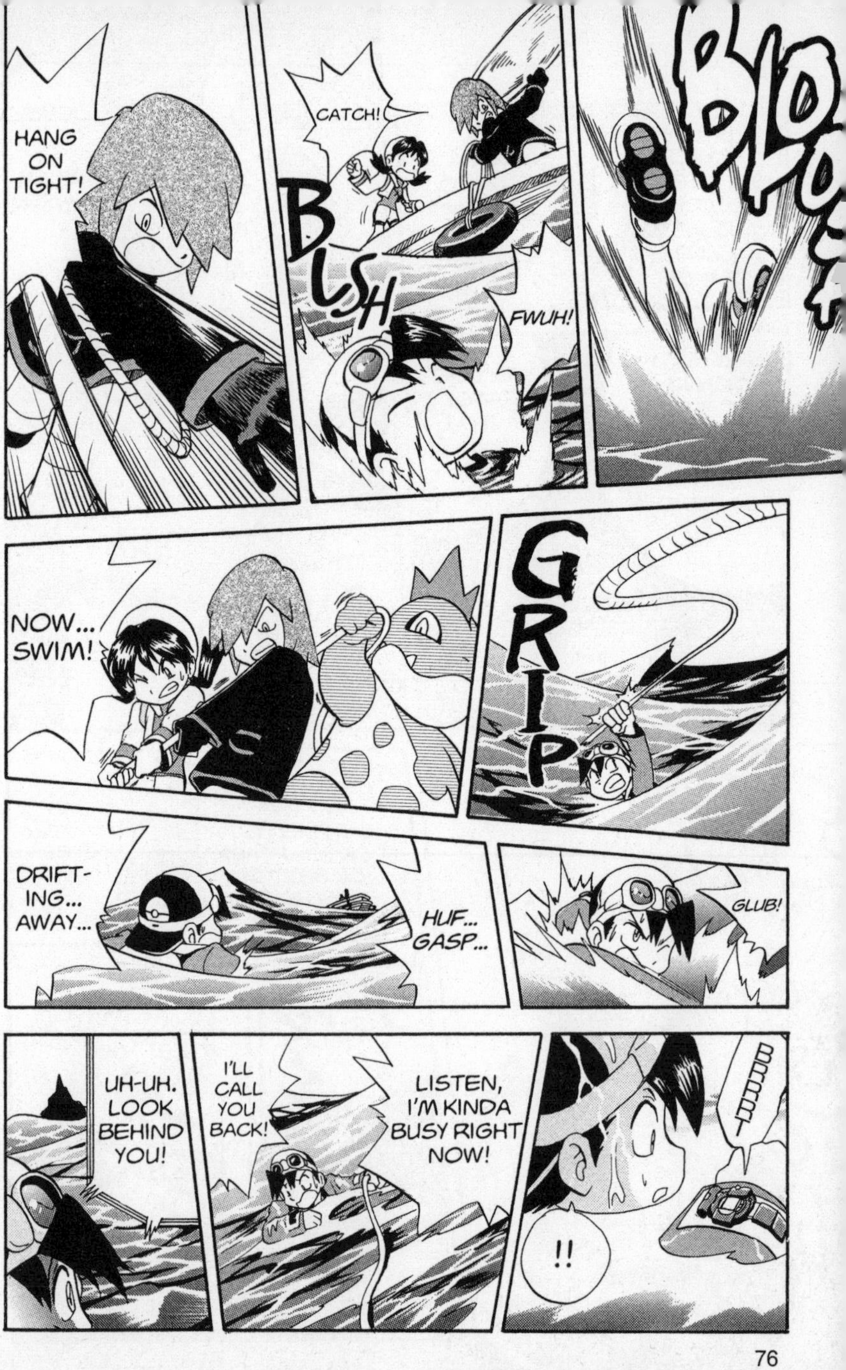
CATCH!
BLSH
FWUH!
HANG ON TIGHT!
GRIP
NOW... SWIM!
GLUB!
HUF... GASP...
DRIFTING... AWAY...
BRRRRT
!!
LISTEN, I'M KINDA BUSY RIGHT NOW!
I'LL CALL YOU BACK!
UH-UH. LOOK BEHIND YOU!

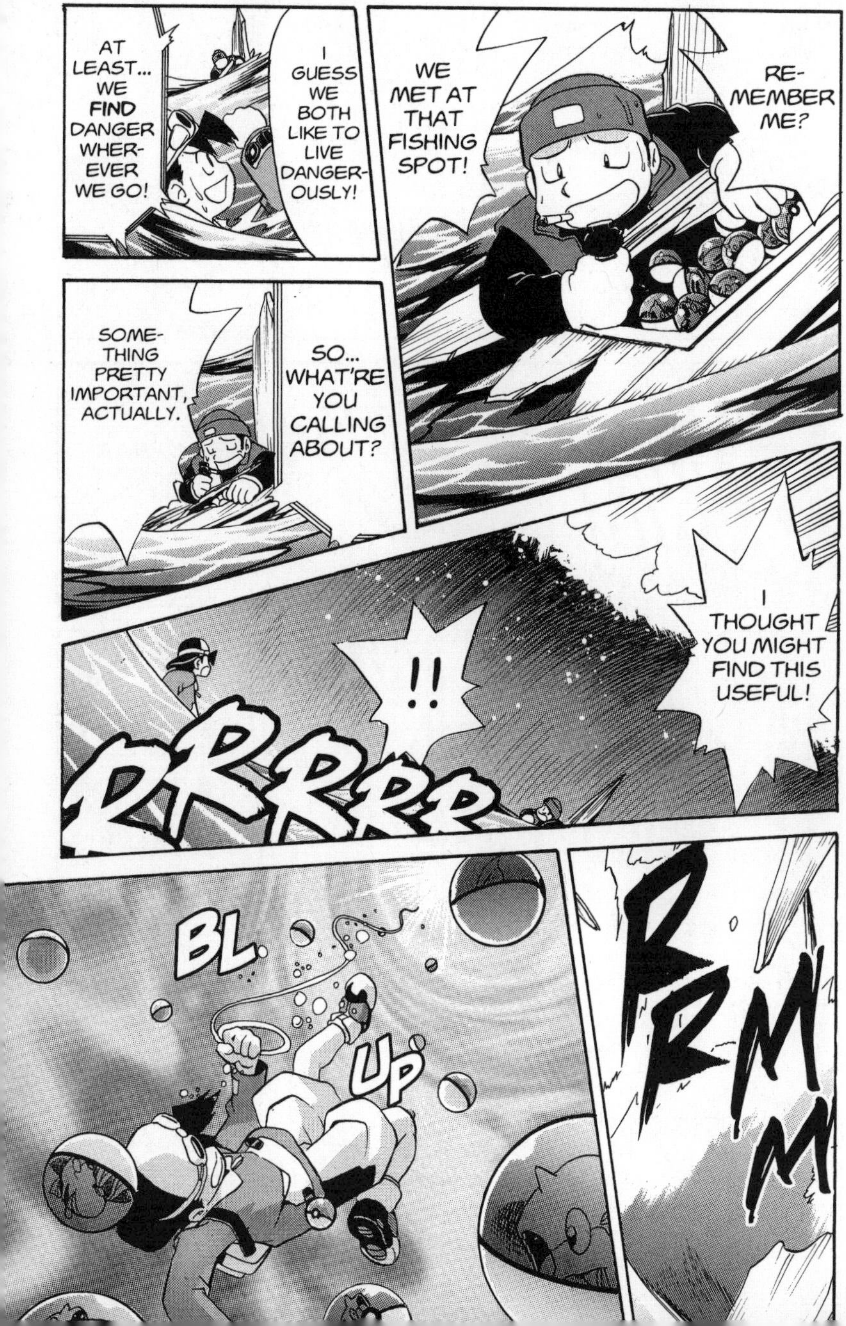
RE-MEMBER ME?
WE MET AT THAT FISHING SPOT!
I GUESS WE BOTH LIKE TO LIVE DANGER-OUSLY!
AT LEAST... WE **FIND** DANGER WHER-EVER WE GO!
SO... WHAT'RE YOU CALLING ABOUT?
SOME-THING PRETTY IMPORTANT, ACTUALLY.
I THOUGHT YOU MIGHT FIND THIS USEFUL!
!!
DRRRRR
RRMMM
BL
UP

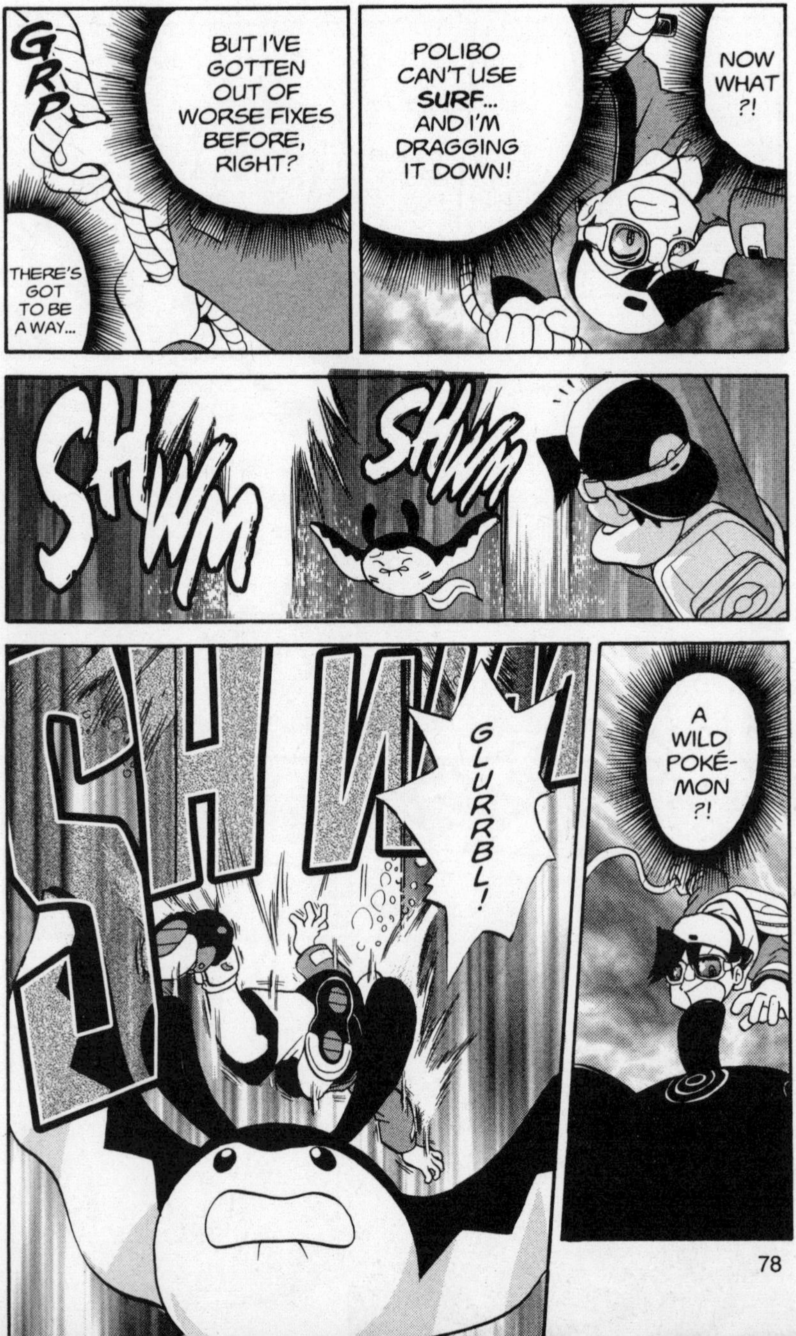
NOW WHAT ?!
POLIBO CAN'T USE **SURF**... AND I'M DRAGGING IT DOWN!
GRP
BUT I'VE GOTTEN OUT OF WORSE FIXES BEFORE, RIGHT?
THERE'S GOT TO BE A WAY...
SHWM
SHWM
A WILD POKÉ-MON ?!
GLURRBL!

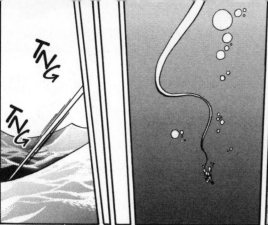

TNG

TNG

TOO WEAK... I CAN'T...

NO...

SNAP

OH!!

WAGH!

WHAT A DRAG...

RRRMM

WHAT'S THAT SOUND?!

OH NO!!

!!

RRRMMM

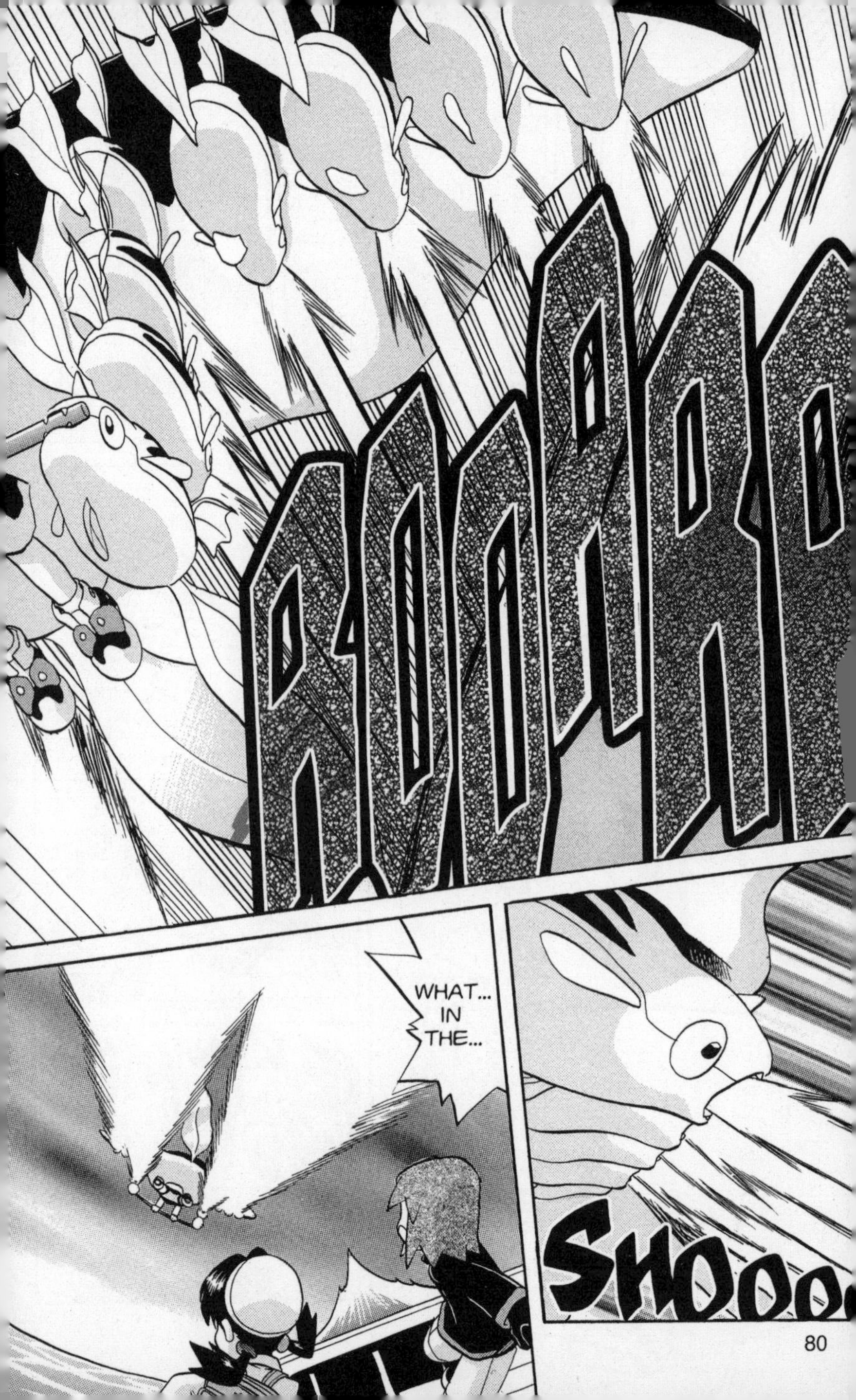
SHOOO...
WHAT... IN THE...

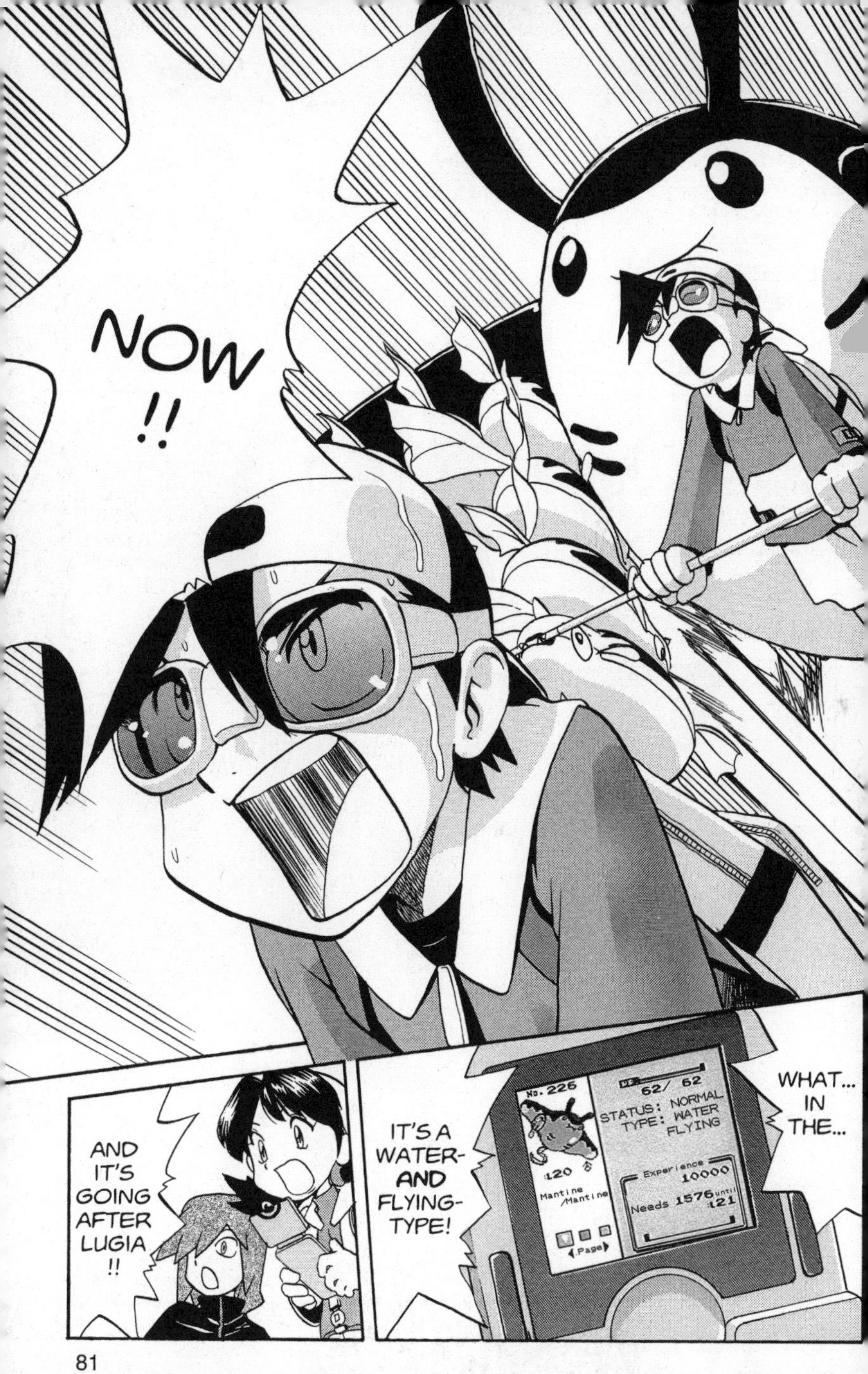
NOW!!
WHAT... IN THE...
No. 226
HP 62/ 62
STATUS: NORMAL
TYPE: WATER FLYING
Experience 10000
Needs 1576 until :21
Mantine /Mantine
Page
IT'S A WATER- AND FLYING-TYPE!
AND IT'S GOING AFTER LUGIA!!

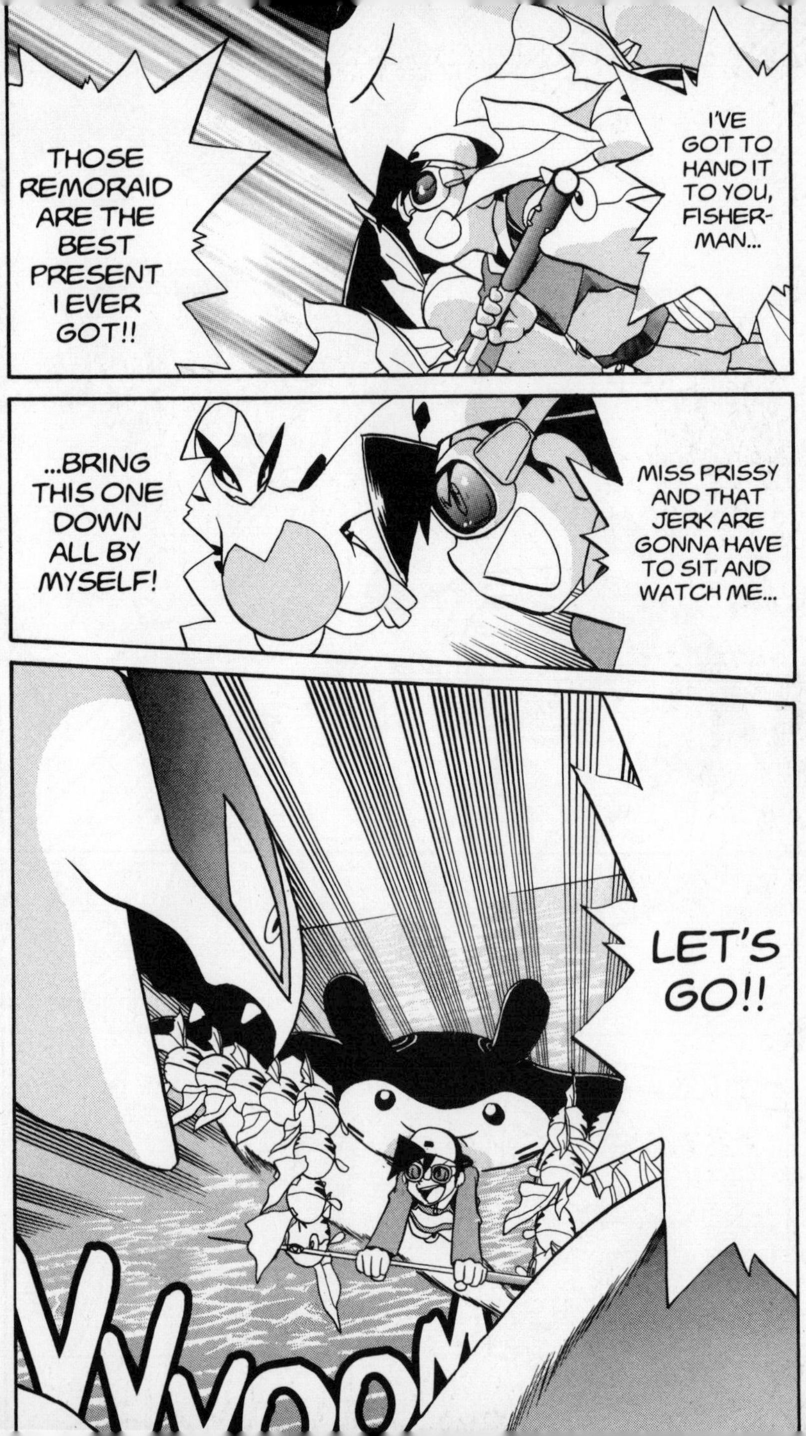
I'VE GOT TO HAND IT TO YOU, FISHERMAN...
THOSE REMORAID ARE THE BEST PRESENT I EVER GOT!!
MISS PRISSY AND THAT JERK ARE GONNA HAVE TO SIT AND WATCH ME...
...BRING THIS ONE DOWN ALL BY MYSELF!
LET'S GO!!
VVVOOM

148 Lively Lugia (Part 3)

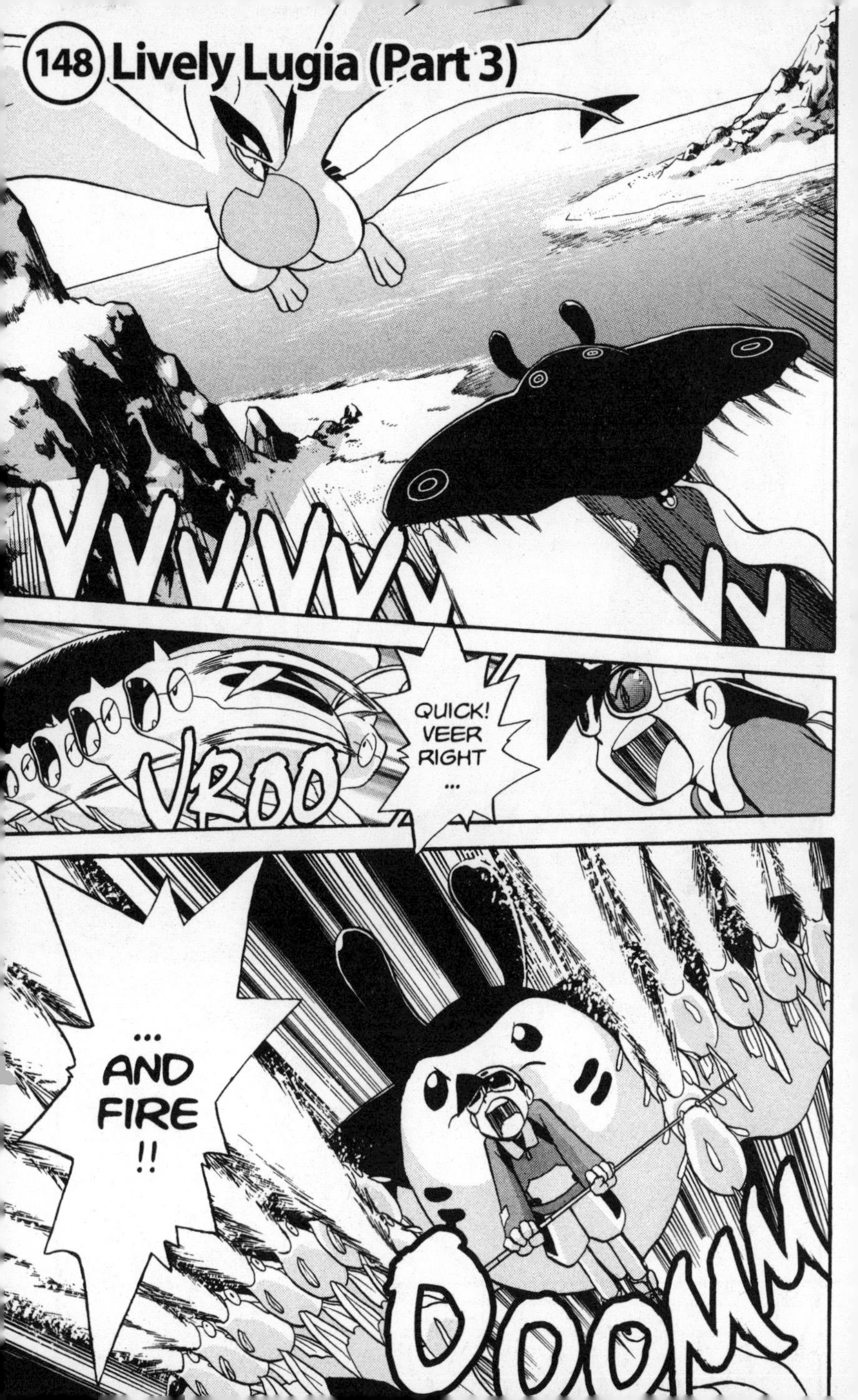
VVVVVV
VV
QUICK! VEER RIGHT ...
VROO
... AND FIRE !!
DOOM

148 Lively Lugia (Part 3)

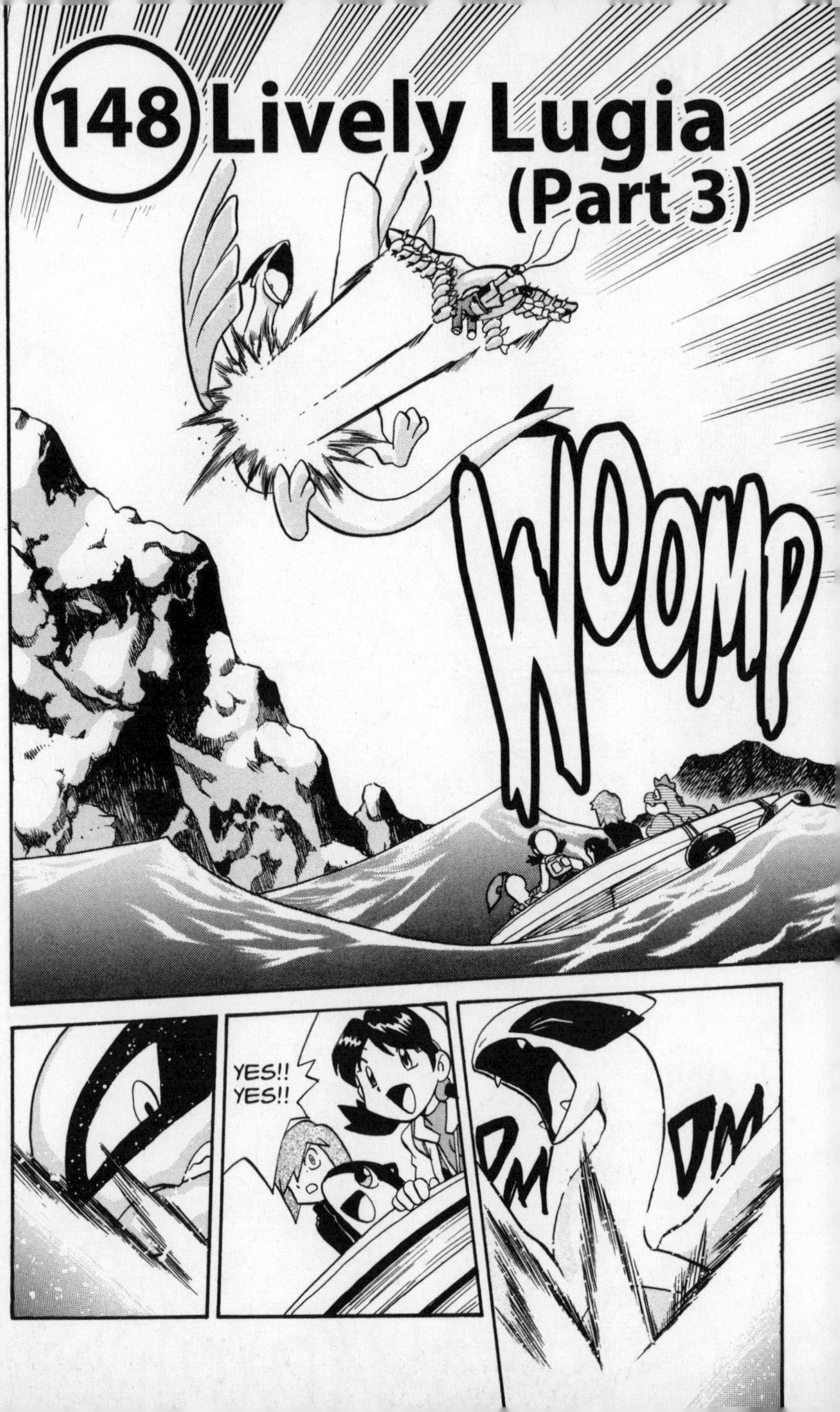
WOOMP
DM
DM
YES!!
YES!!

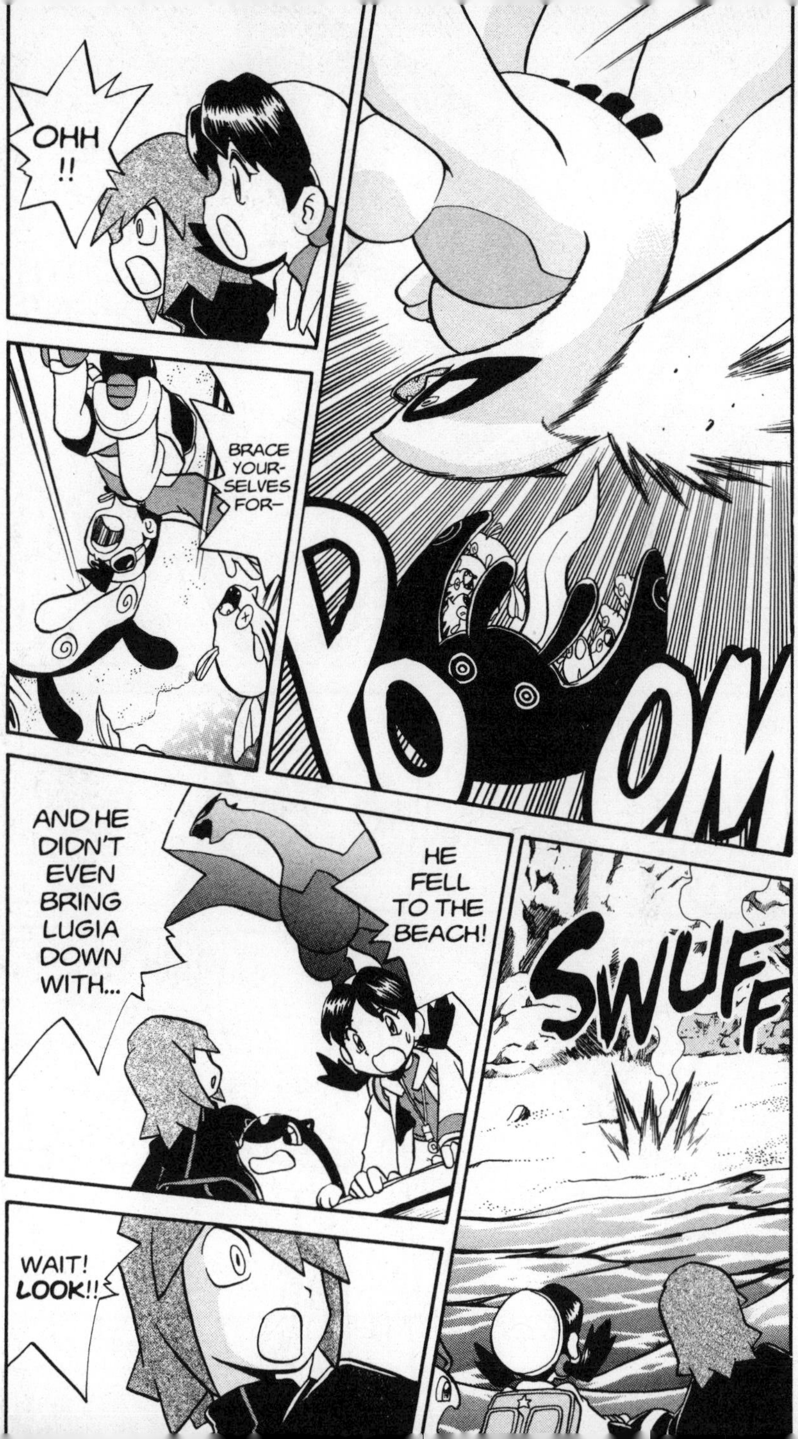

BOOM
OHH !!
BRACE YOUR-SELVES FOR–
SWUFF
HE FELL TO THE BEACH!
AND HE DIDN'T EVEN BRING LUGIA DOWN WITH...
WAIT! **LOOK!!**

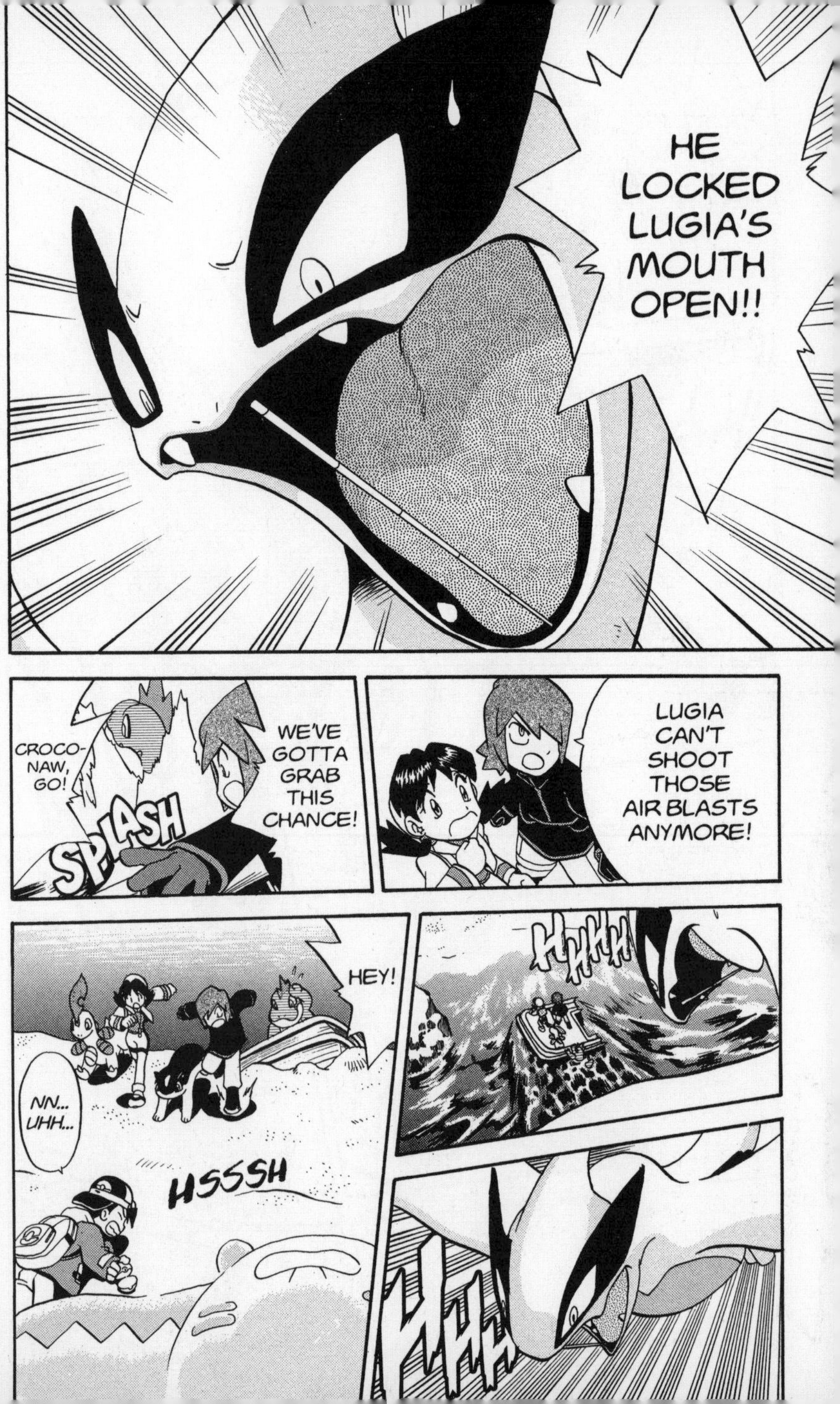
HE LOCKED LUGIA'S MOUTH OPEN!!
LUGIA CAN'T SHOOT THOSE AIR BLASTS ANYMORE!
WE'VE GOTTA GRAB THIS CHANCE!
CROCO-NAW, GO!
SPLASH
HHHH
HHHH
HEY!
NN... UHH...
HSSSH

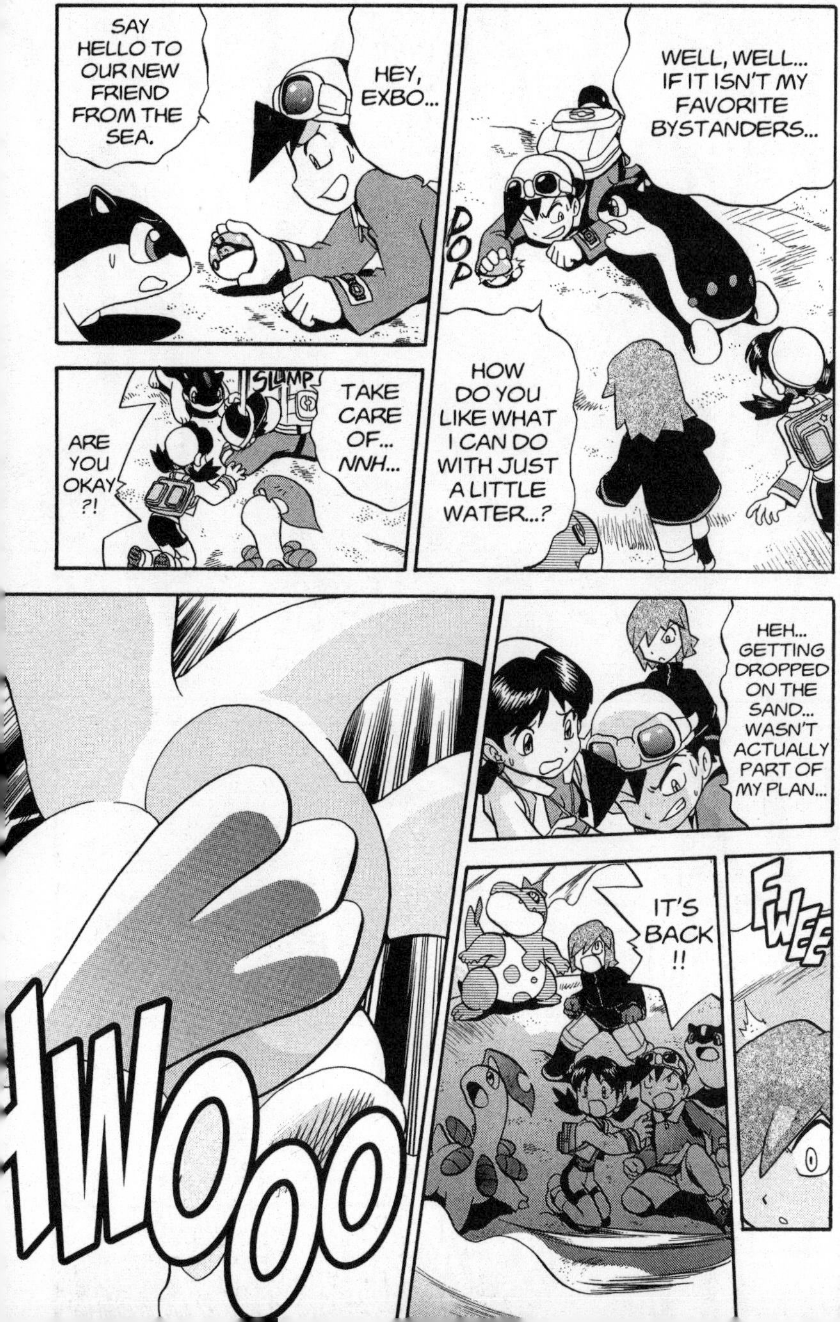
WELL, WELL... IF IT ISN'T MY FAVORITE BYSTANDERS...
POP
HEY, EXBO...
SAY HELLO TO OUR NEW FRIEND FROM THE SEA.
HOW DO YOU LIKE WHAT I CAN DO WITH JUST A LITTLE WATER...?
TAKE CARE OF... NNH...
SLUMP
ARE YOU OKAY?!
HEH... GETTING DROPPED ON THE SAND... WASN'T ACTUALLY PART OF MY PLAN...
FWEE
IT'S BACK!!
HWOOOO

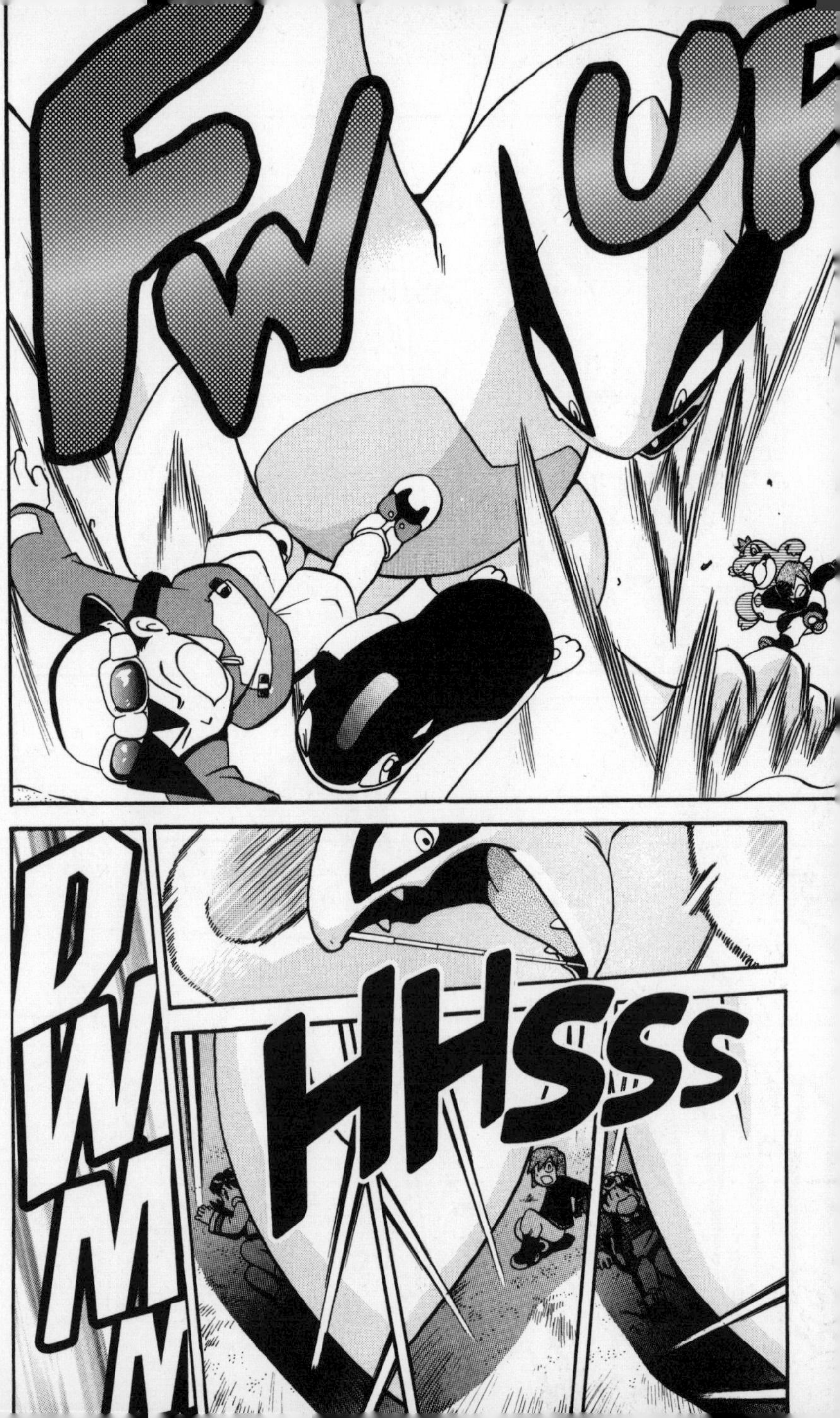
FWUP
HHSSS
DWMM

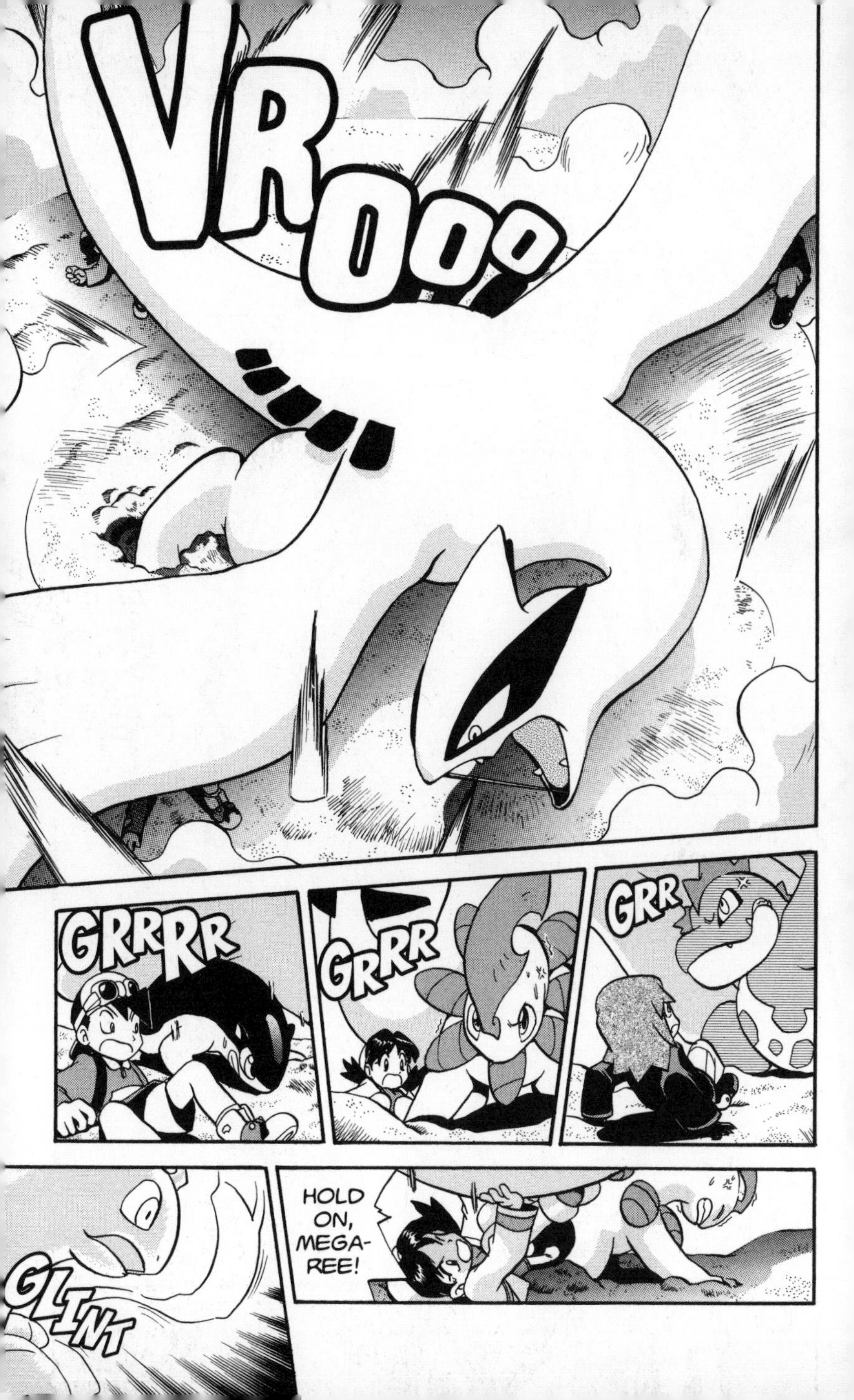
VROOO
GRR
GRRR
GRRRR
HOLD ON, MEGA-REE!
GLINT

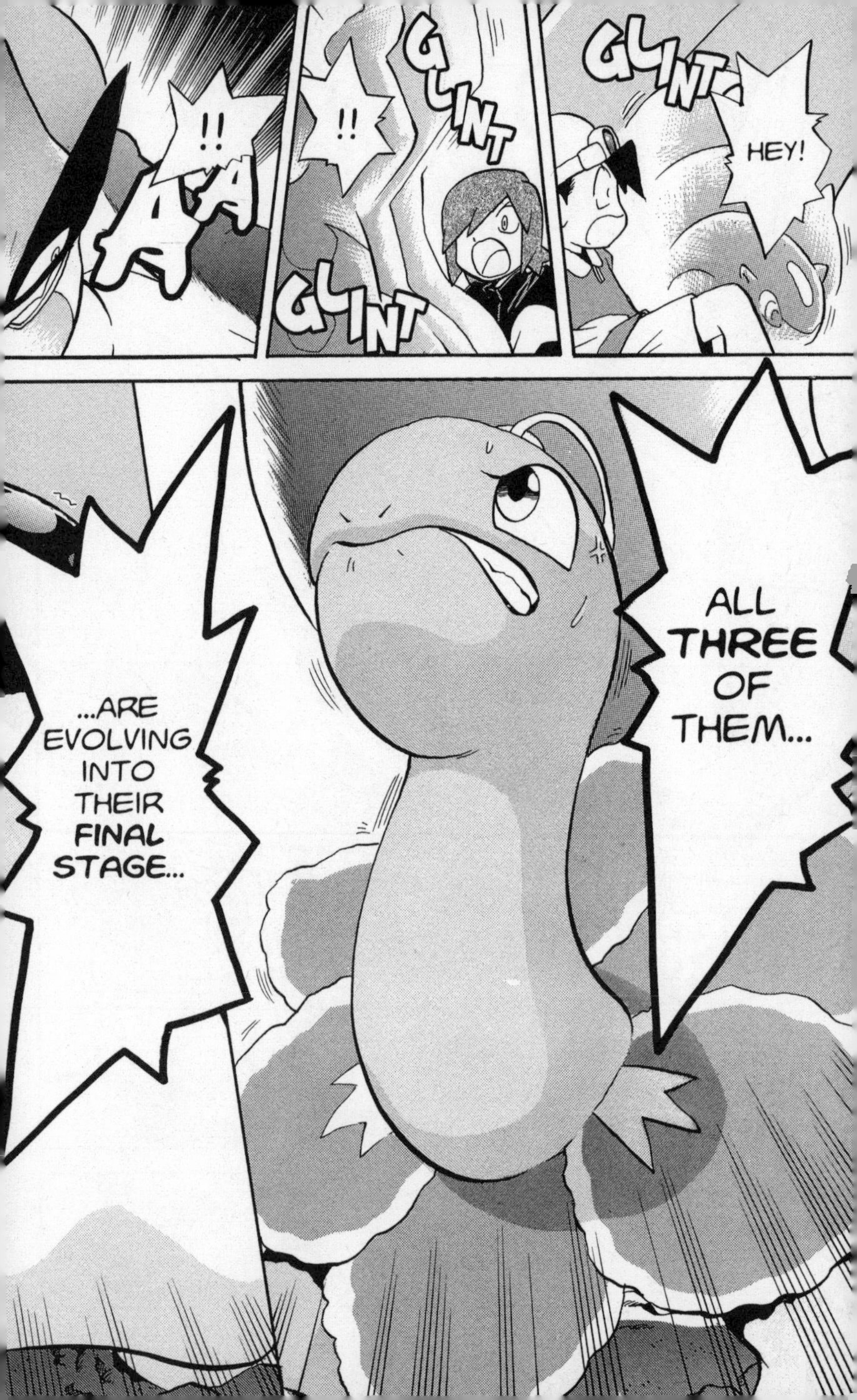
GLINT
HEY!
GLINT
!!
GLINT
!!
ALL THREE OF THEM...
...ARE EVOLVING INTO THEIR FINAL STAGE...

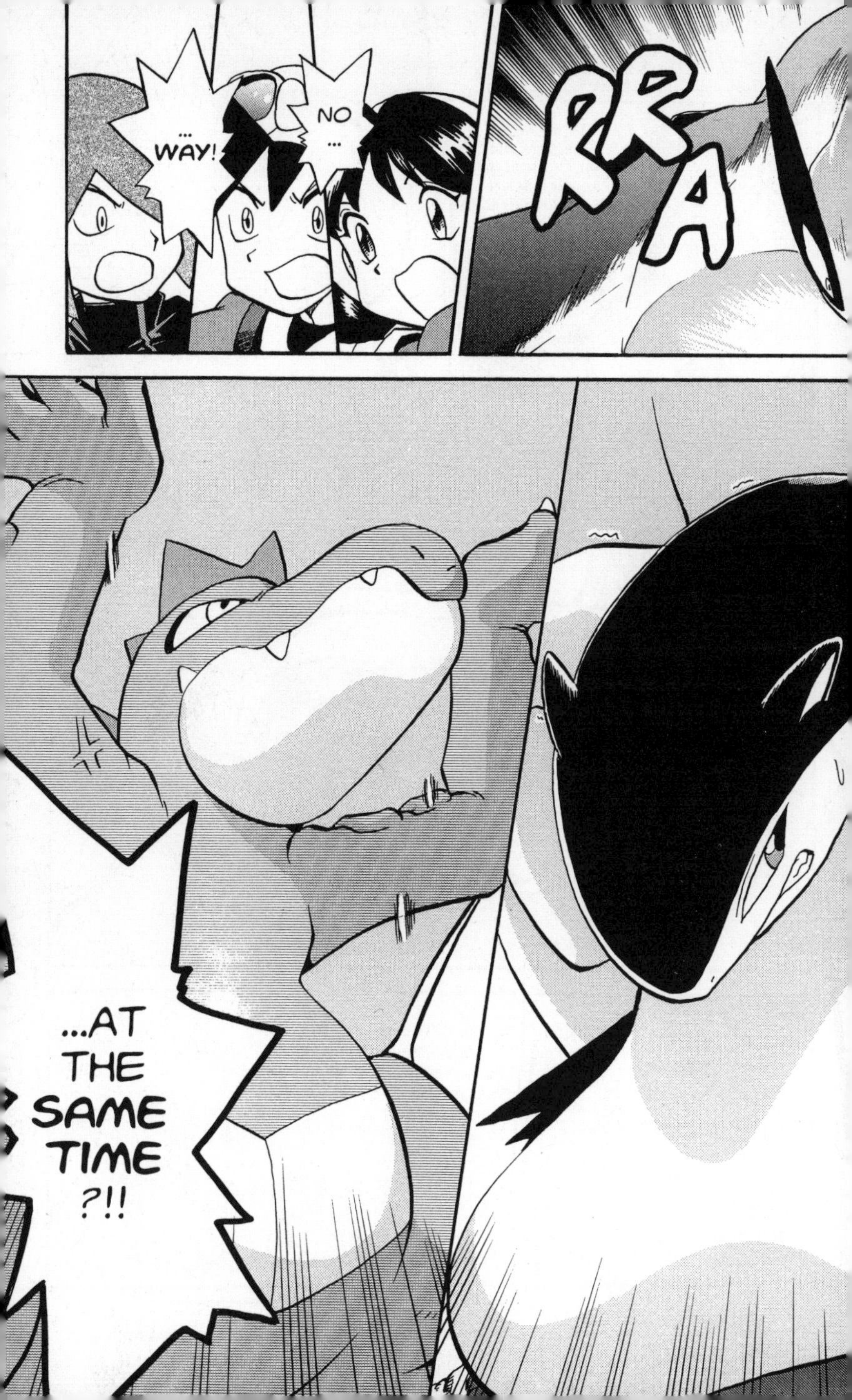
RRA
NO ...
... WAY!
...AT THE SAME TIME ?!!

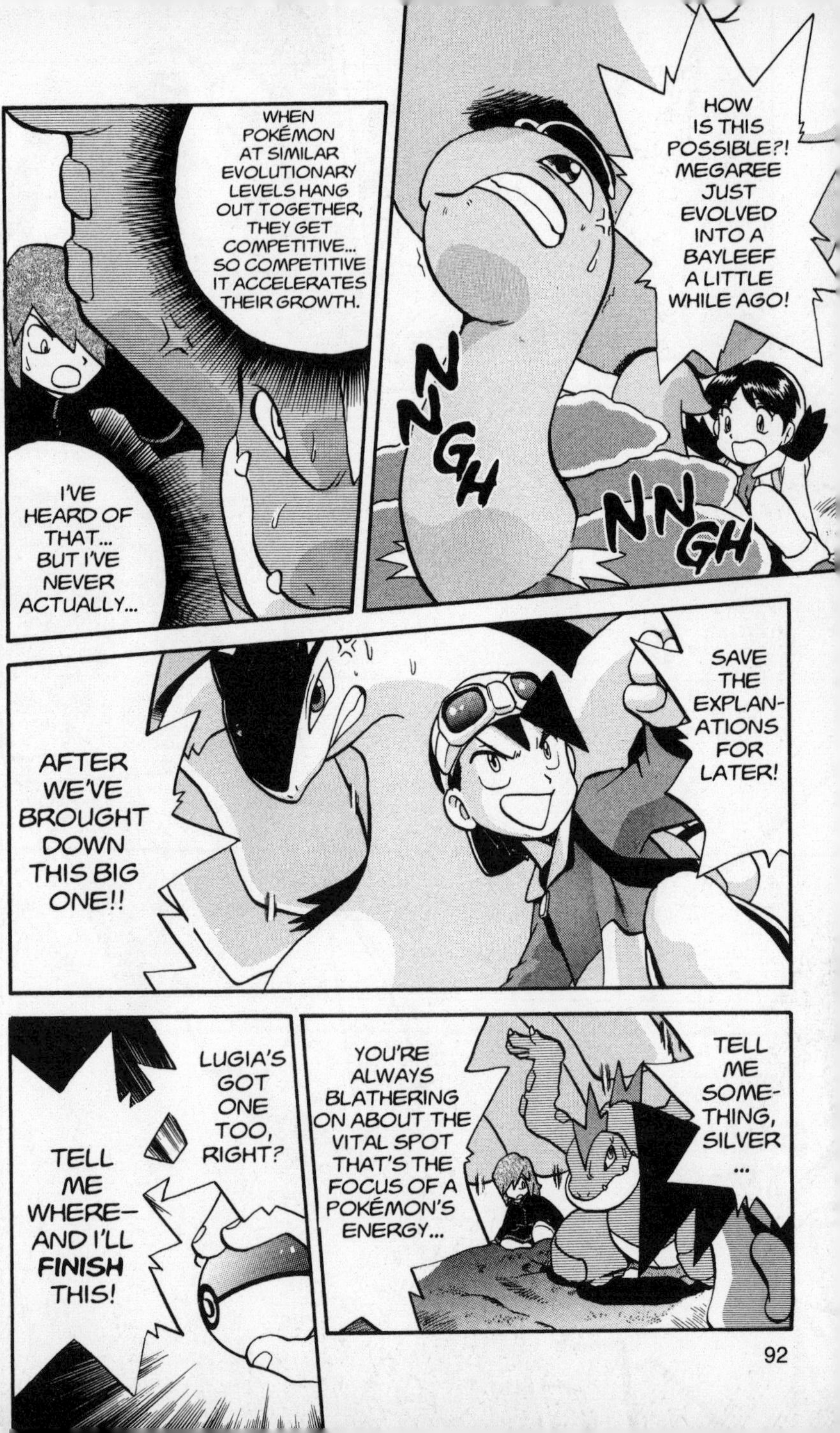

HOW IS THIS POSSIBLE?! MEGAREE JUST EVOLVED INTO A BAYLEEF A LITTLE WHILE AGO!
NNGH
NNGH
WHEN POKÉMON AT SIMILAR EVOLUTIONARY LEVELS HANG OUT TOGETHER, THEY GET COMPETITIVE... SO COMPETITIVE IT ACCELERATES THEIR GROWTH.
I'VE HEARD OF THAT... BUT I'VE NEVER ACTUALLY...
SAVE THE EXPLAN-ATIONS FOR LATER!
AFTER WE'VE BROUGHT DOWN THIS BIG ONE!!
TELL ME SOME-THING, SILVER ...
YOU'RE ALWAYS BLATHERING ON ABOUT THE VITAL SPOT THAT'S THE FOCUS OF A POKÉMON'S ENERGY...
LUGIA'S GOT ONE TOO, RIGHT?
TELL ME WHERE— AND I'LL **FINISH** THIS!

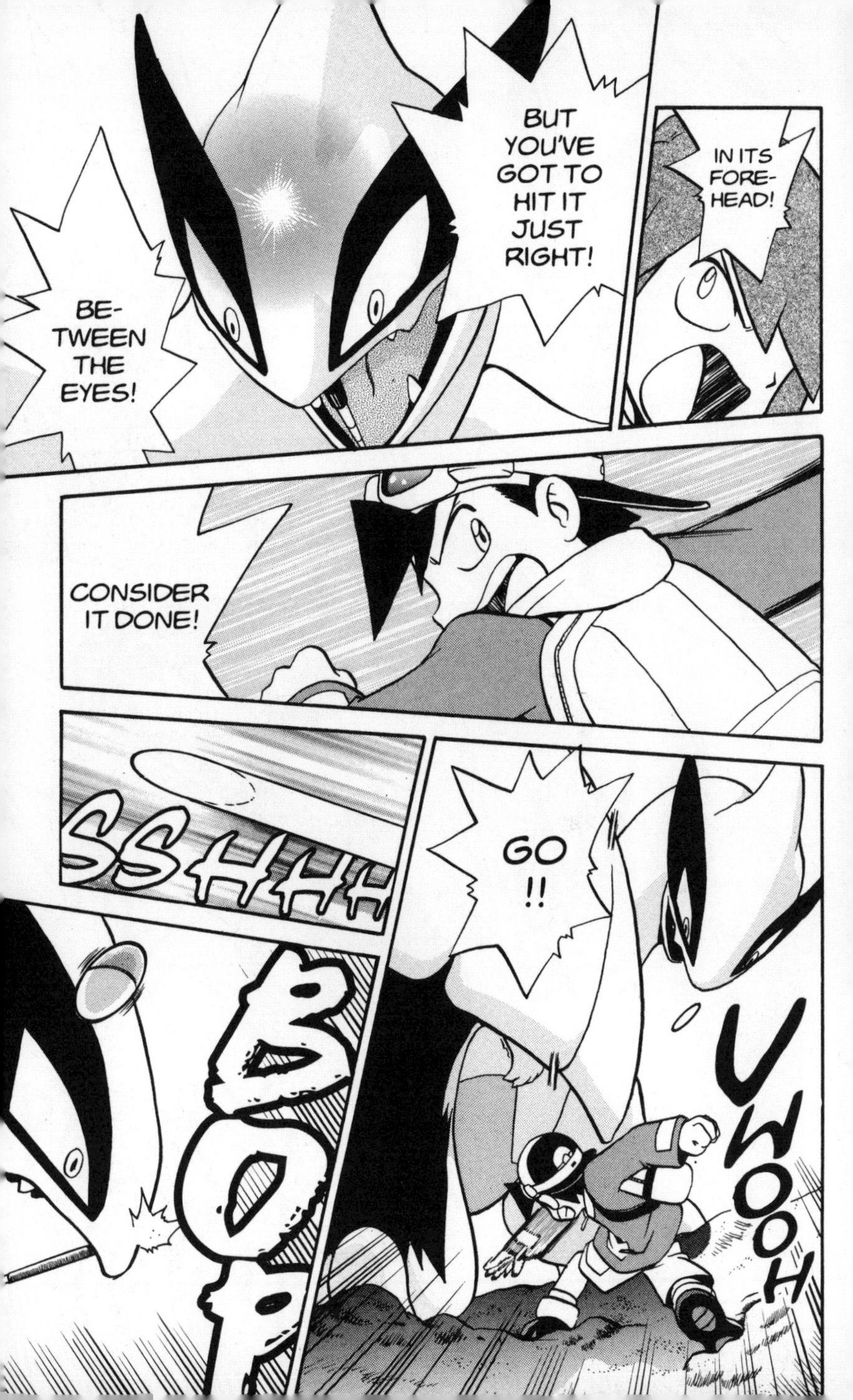
IN ITS FORE-HEAD!
BUT YOU'VE GOT TO HIT IT JUST RIGHT!
BE-TWEEN THE EYES!
CONSIDER IT DONE!
GO !!
VWOOOH
SSHHH
BOO

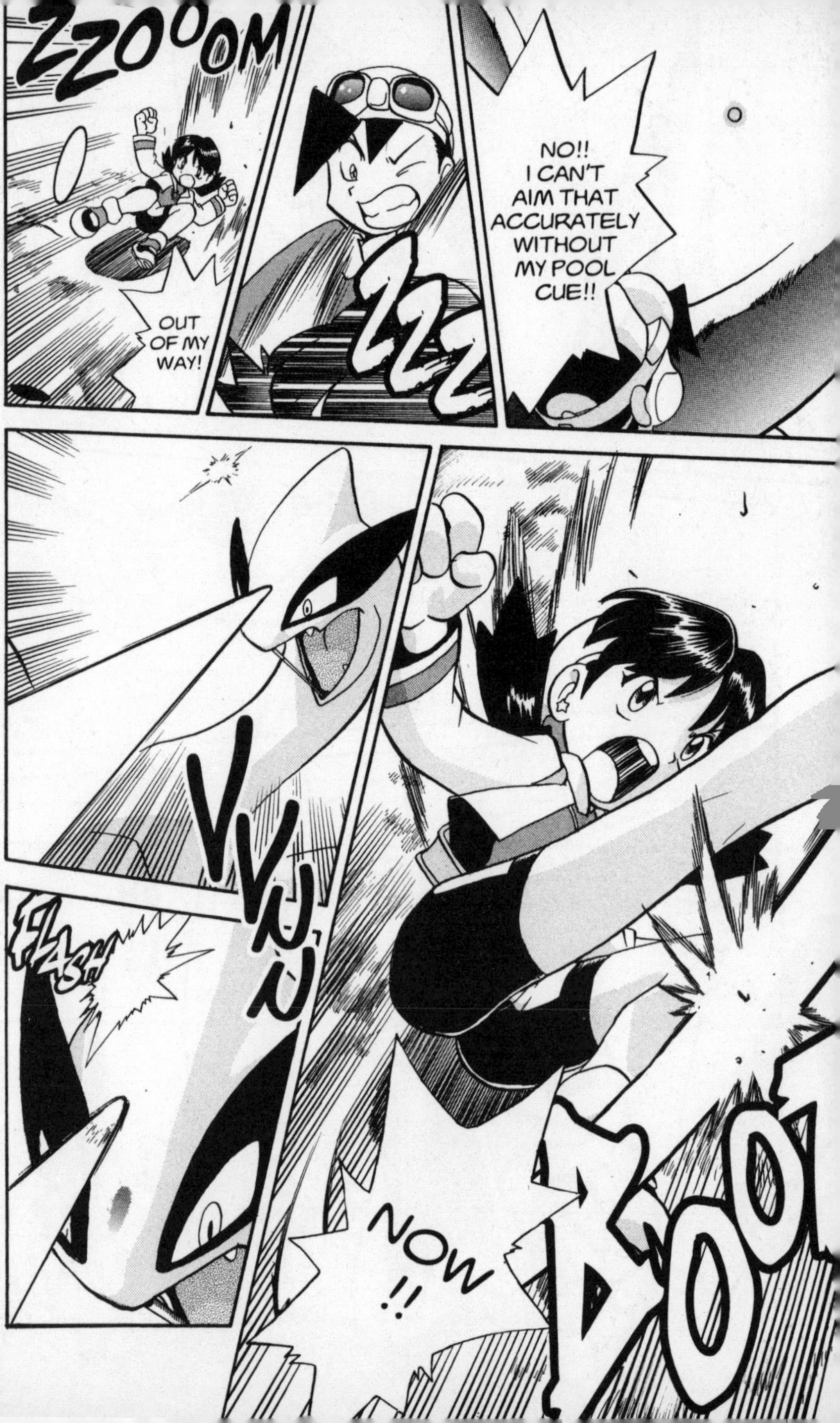
NO!! I CAN'T AIM THAT ACCURATELY WITHOUT MY POOL CUE!!
ZZOOOM
OUT OF MY WAY!
NOW!!
FLASH

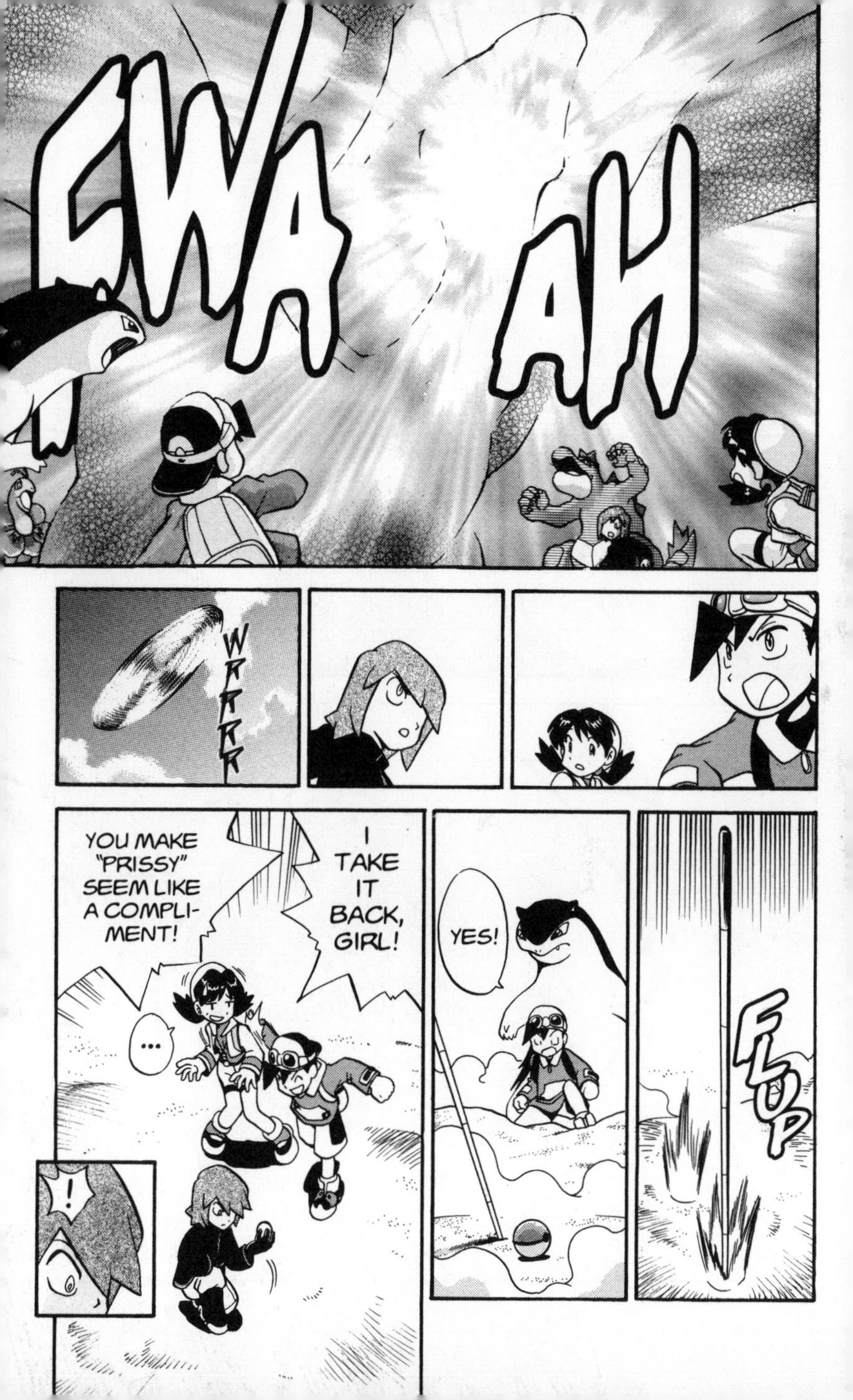
GWA AH
WRRRRR
FLOP
YES!
I TAKE IT BACK, GIRL!
YOU MAKE "PRISSY" SEEM LIKE A COMPLI-MENT!
...
!

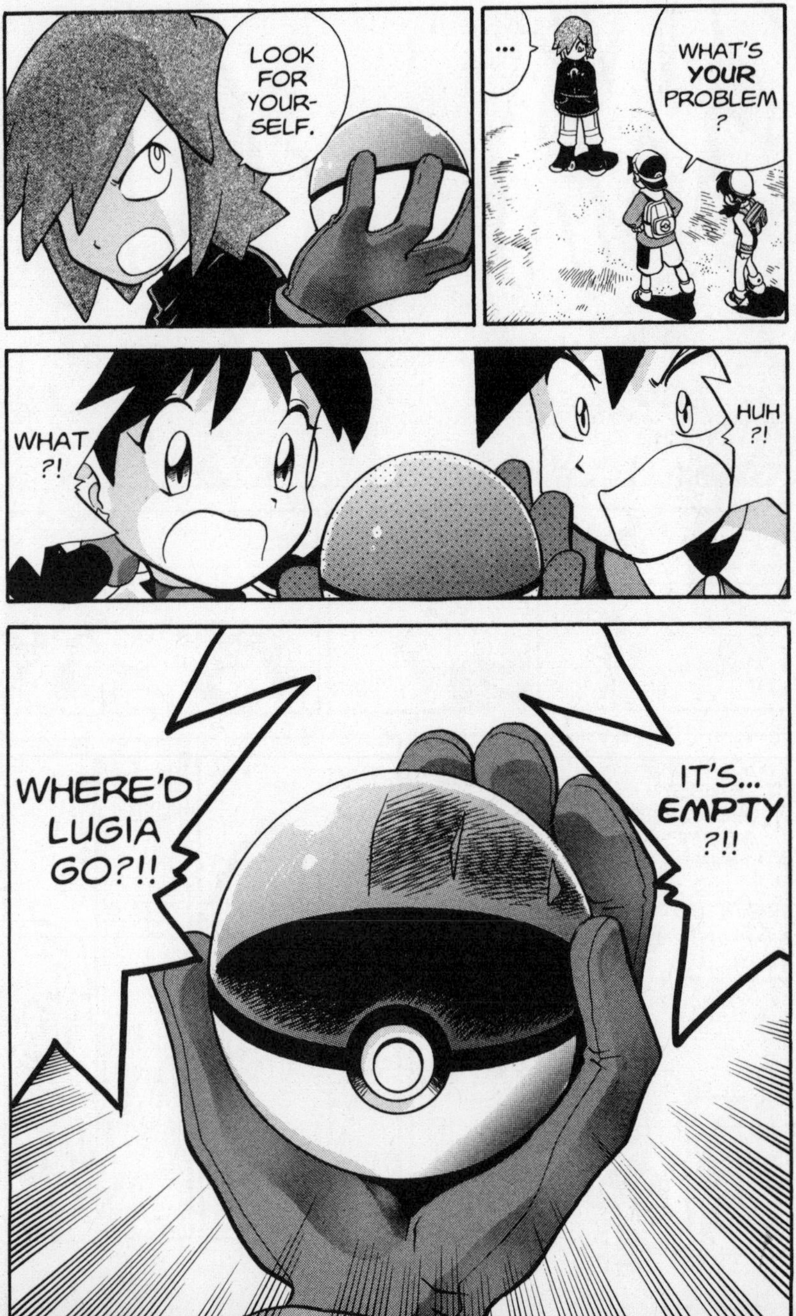

WHAT'S YOUR PROBLEM?
...
LOOK FOR YOURSELF.
HUH?!
WHAT?!
IT'S... EMPTY?!!
WHERE'D LUGIA GO?!!

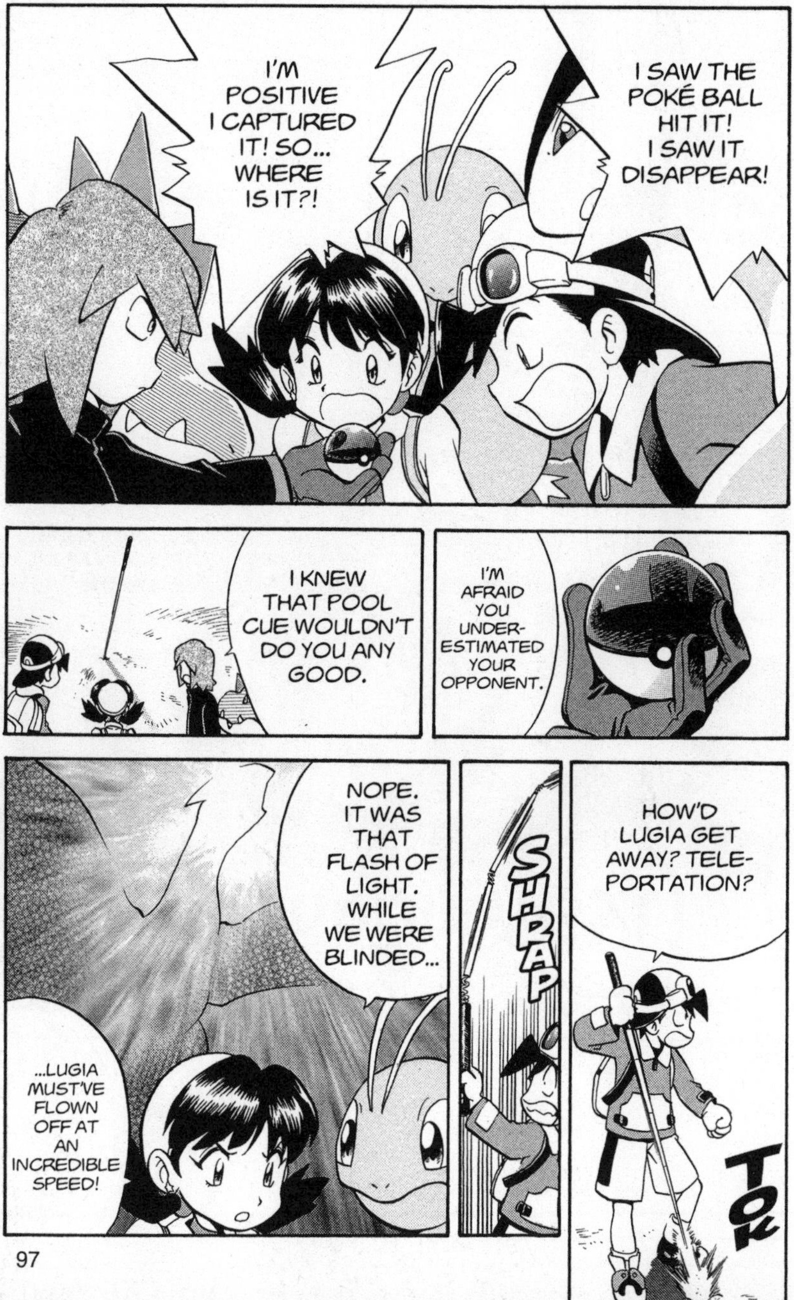
I SAW THE POKÉ BALL HIT IT! I SAW IT DISAPPEAR!
I'M POSITIVE I CAPTURED IT! SO... WHERE IS IT?!
I'M AFRAID YOU UNDER-ESTIMATED YOUR OPPONENT.
I KNEW THAT POOL CUE WOULDN'T DO YOU ANY GOOD.
HOW'D LUGIA GET AWAY? TELE-PORTATION?
TOK
SHRAP
NOPE. IT WAS THAT FLASH OF LIGHT. WHILE WE WERE BLINDED...
...LUGIA MUST'VE FLOWN OFF AT AN INCREDIBLE SPEED!

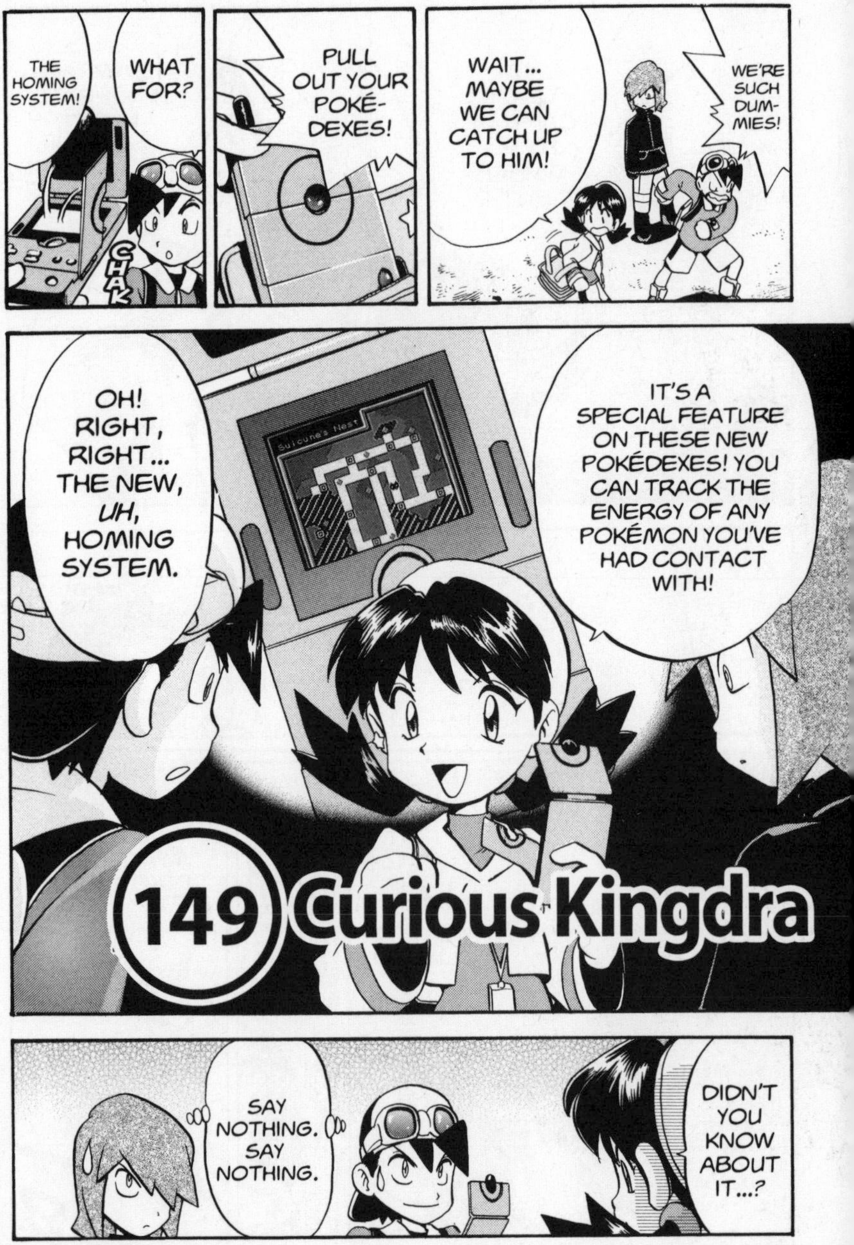
WE'RE SUCH DUM-MIES!
WAIT... MAYBE WE CAN CATCH UP TO HIM!
PULL OUT YOUR POKÉ-DEXES!
WHAT FOR?
THE HOMING SYSTEM!
CHAK
IT'S A SPECIAL FEATURE ON THESE NEW POKÉDEXES! YOU CAN TRACK THE ENERGY OF ANY POKÉMON YOU'VE HAD CONTACT WITH!
Suicune's Nest
OH! RIGHT, RIGHT... THE NEW, *UH*, HOMING SYSTEM.
149 Curious Kingdra
DIDN'T YOU KNOW ABOUT IT...?
SAY NOTHING. SAY NOTHING.

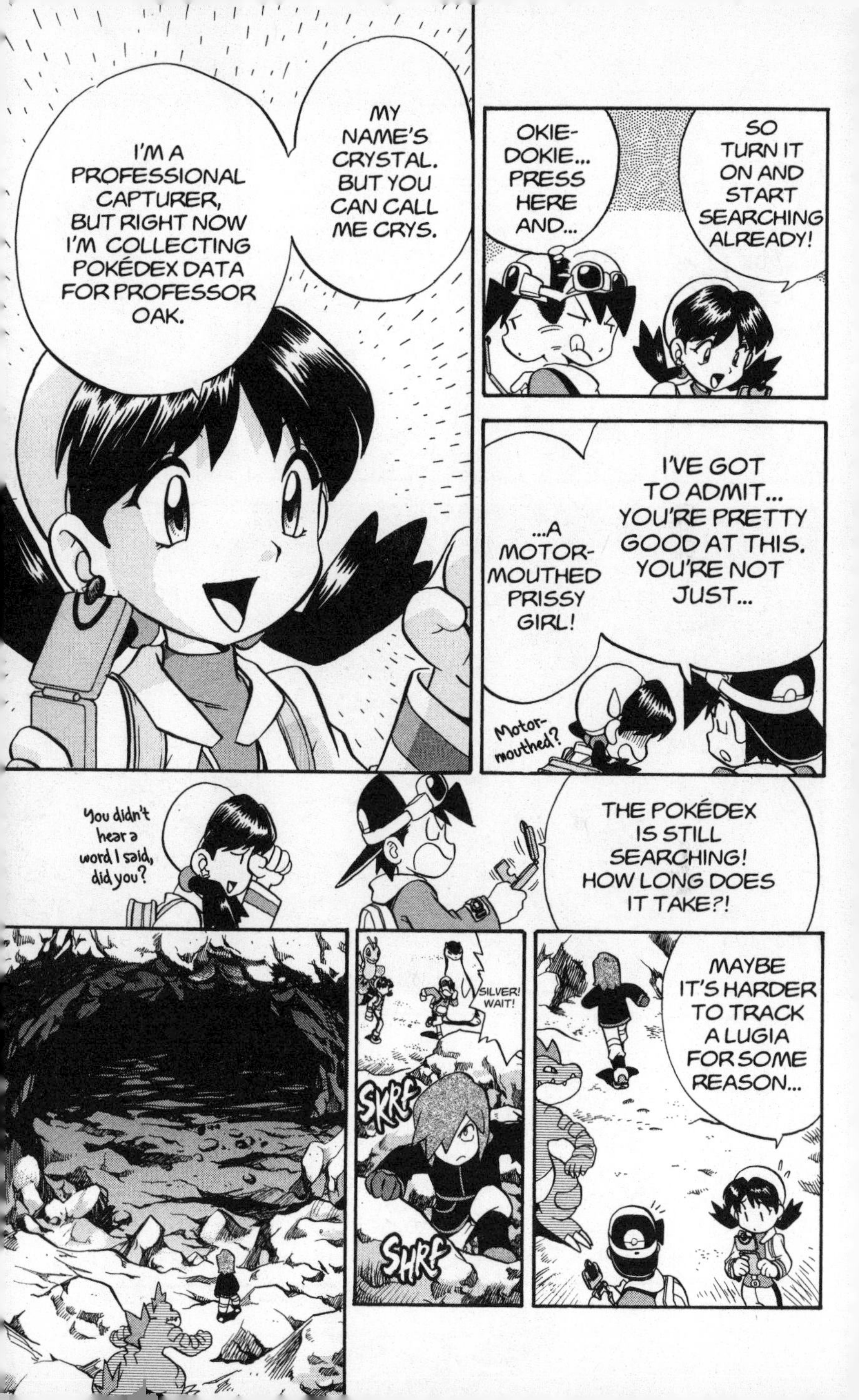
MY NAME'S CRYSTAL. BUT YOU CAN CALL ME CRYS.
I'M A PROFESSIONAL CAPTURER, BUT RIGHT NOW I'M COLLECTING POKÉDEX DATA FOR PROFESSOR OAK.
SO TURN IT ON AND START SEARCHING ALREADY!
OKIE-DOKIE... PRESS HERE AND...
I'VE GOT TO ADMIT... YOU'RE PRETTY GOOD AT THIS. YOU'RE NOT JUST...
...A MOTOR-MOUTHED PRISSY GIRL!
Motor-mouthed?
THE POKÉDEX IS STILL SEARCHING! HOW LONG DOES IT TAKE?!
You didn't hear a word I said, did you?
MAYBE IT'S HARDER TO TRACK A LUGIA FOR SOME REASON...
SILVER! WAIT!
SKRF
SHRF

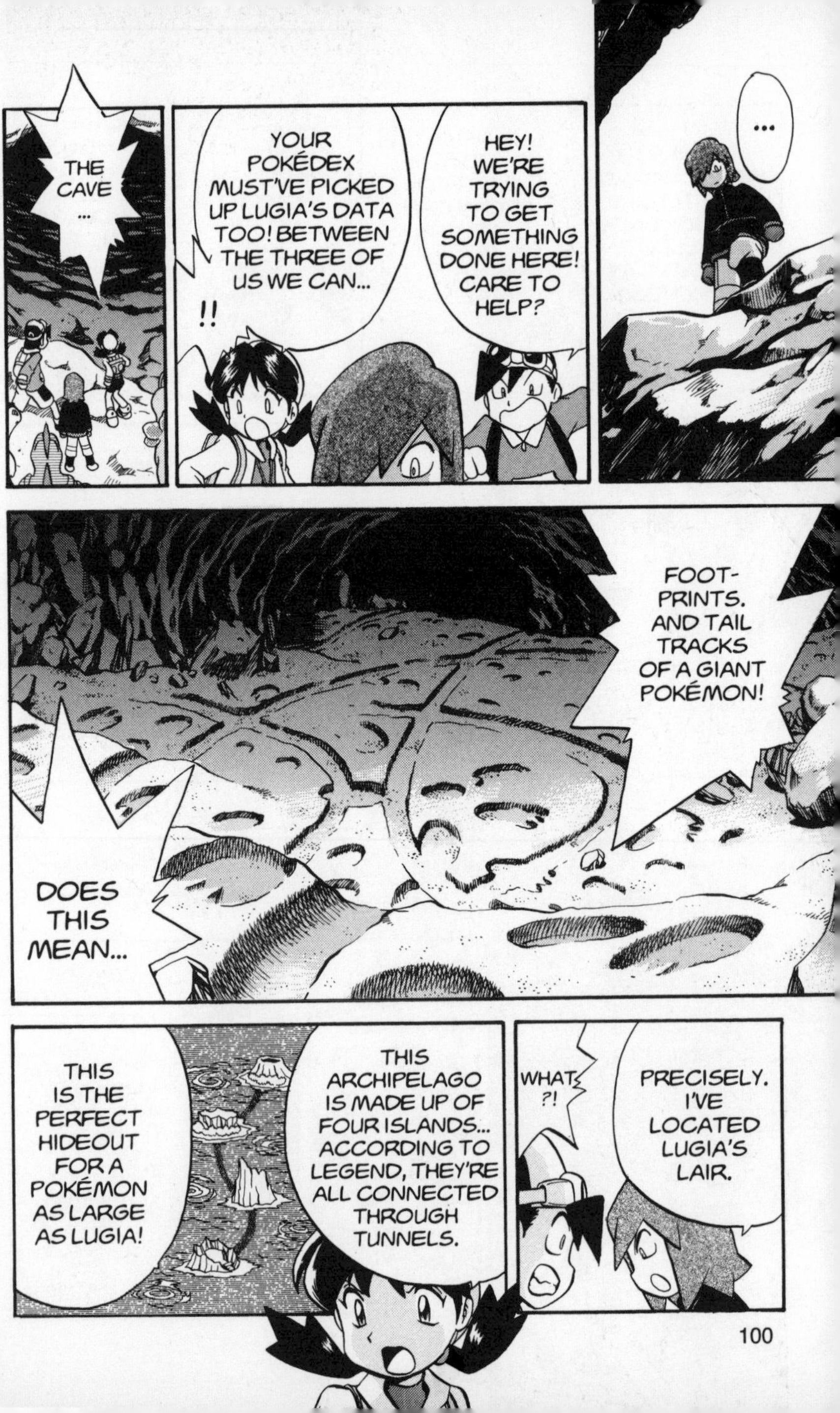
...
HEY! WE'RE TRYING TO GET SOMETHING DONE HERE! CARE TO HELP?
YOUR POKÉDEX MUST'VE PICKED UP LUGIA'S DATA TOO! BETWEEN THE THREE OF US WE CAN...
!!
THE CAVE ...
FOOT-PRINTS. AND TAIL TRACKS OF A GIANT POKÉMON!
DOES THIS MEAN...
PRECISELY. I'VE LOCATED LUGIA'S LAIR.
WHAT?!
THIS ARCHIPELAGO IS MADE UP OF FOUR ISLANDS... ACCORDING TO LEGEND, THEY'RE ALL CONNECTED THROUGH TUNNELS.
THIS IS THE PERFECT HIDEOUT FOR A POKÉMON AS LARGE AS LUGIA!

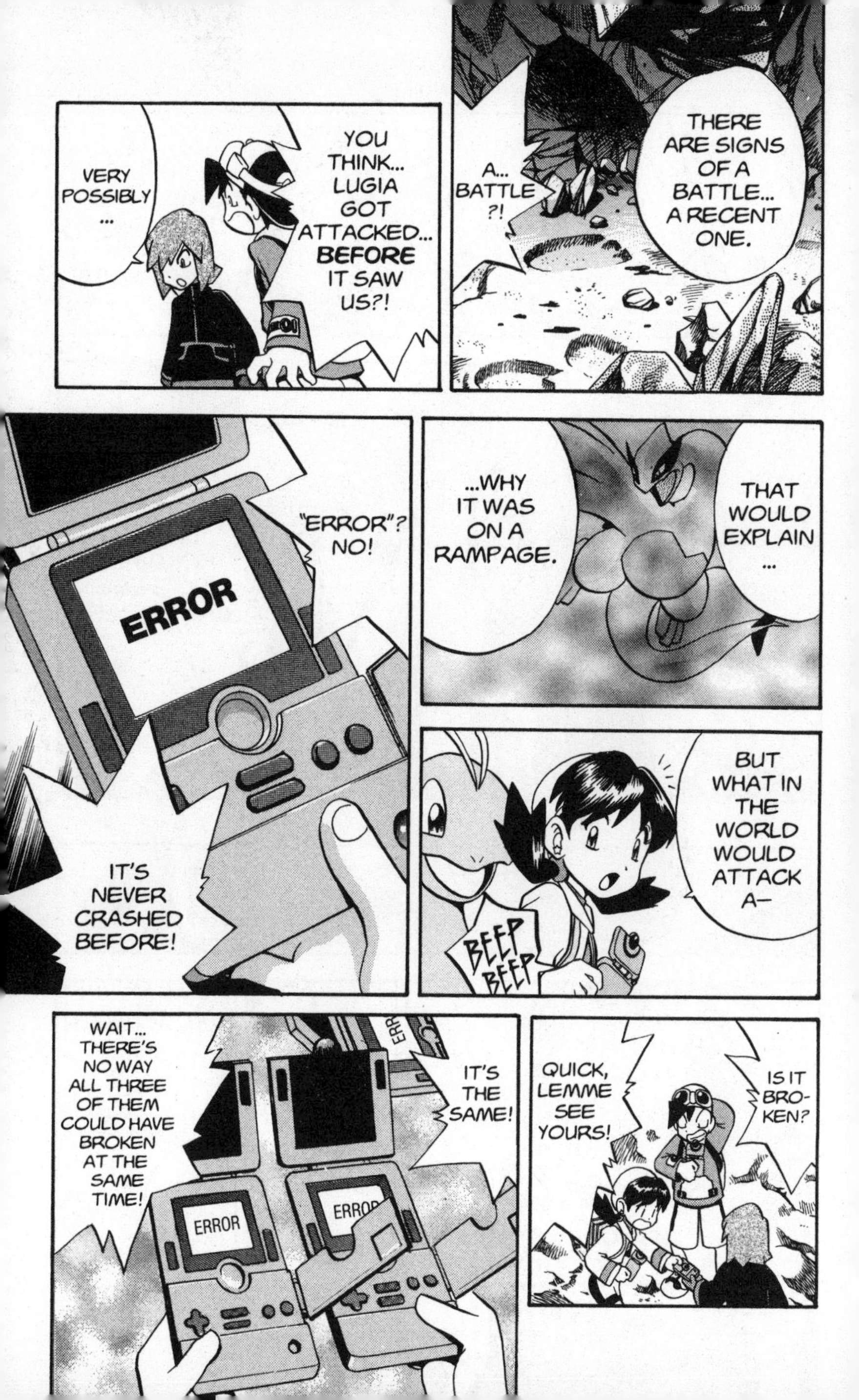
THERE ARE SIGNS OF A BATTLE... A RECENT ONE.
A... BATTLE?!
YOU THINK... LUGIA GOT ATTACKED... BEFORE IT SAW US?!
VERY POSSIBLY...
THAT WOULD EXPLAIN...
...WHY IT WAS ON A RAMPAGE.
BUT WHAT IN THE WORLD WOULD ATTACK A—
BEEP BEEP
ERROR
"ERROR"? NO!
IT'S NEVER CRASHED BEFORE!
IS IT BROKEN?
QUICK, LEMME SEE YOURS!
IT'S THE SAME!
WAIT... THERE'S NO WAY ALL THREE OF THEM COULD HAVE BROKEN AT THE SAME TIME!
ERROR

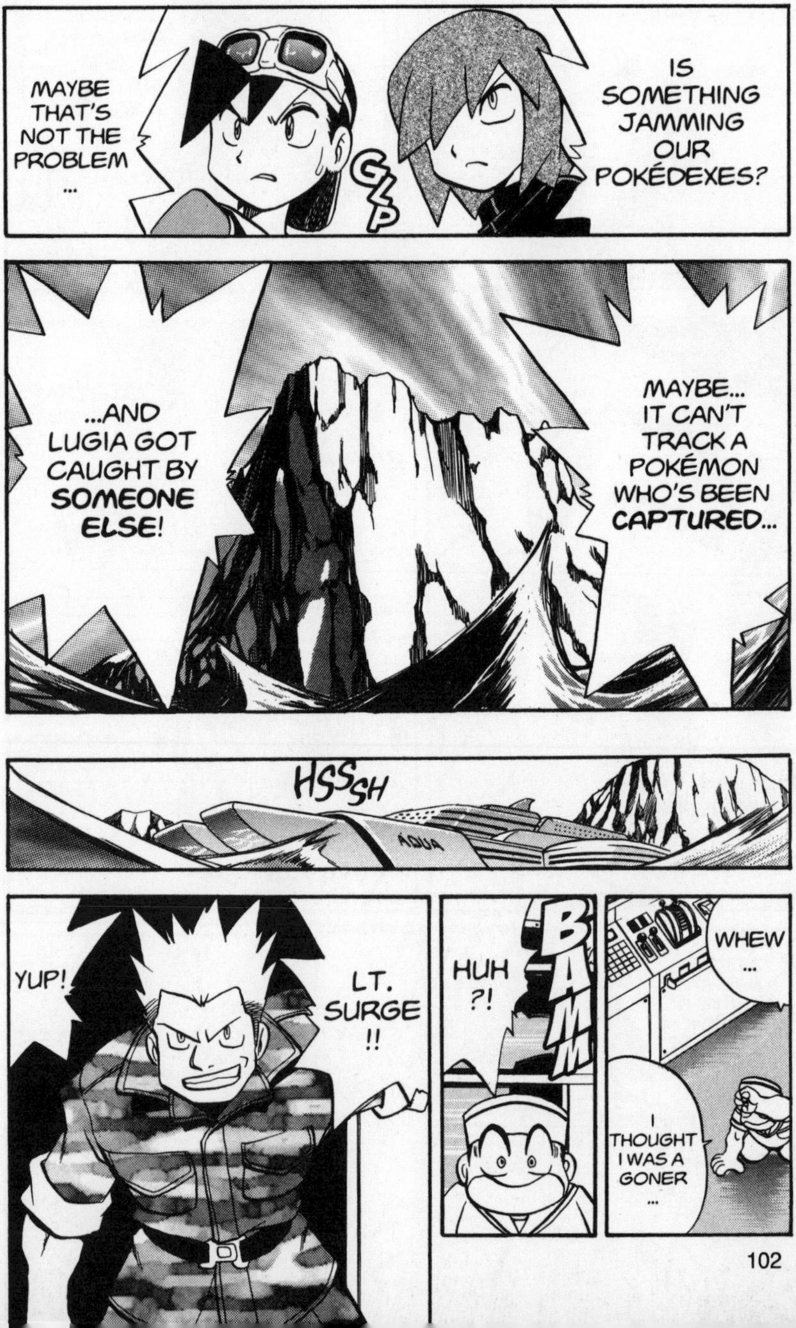
IS SOMETHING JAMMING OUR POKÉDEXES?
GLP
MAYBE THAT'S NOT THE PROBLEM ...
MAYBE... IT CAN'T TRACK A POKÉMON WHO'S BEEN CAPTURED...
...AND LUGIA GOT CAUGHT BY SOMEONE ELSE!
HSSSH
WHEW ...
I THOUGHT I WAS A GONER ...
BAMM
HUH ?!
LT. SURGE !!
YUP!

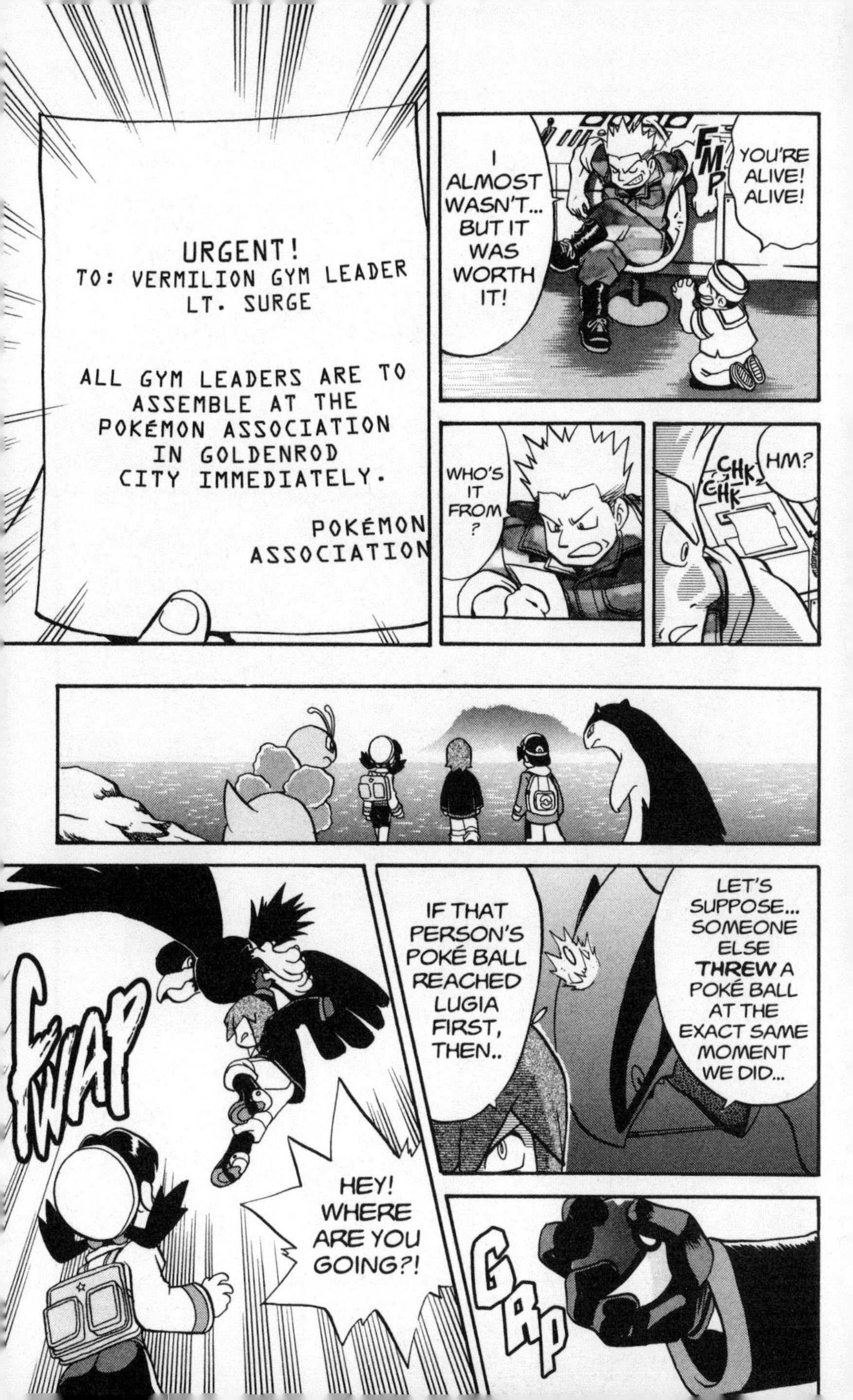
YOU'RE ALIVE! ALIVE!
FMP
I ALMOST WASN'T... BUT IT WAS WORTH IT!
HM?
CHK CHK
WHO'S IT FROM?
URGENT!
TO: VERMILION GYM LEADER LT. SURGE
ALL GYM LEADERS ARE TO ASSEMBLE AT THE POKÉMON ASSOCIATION IN GOLDENROD CITY IMMEDIATELY.
POKÉMON ASSOCIATION
LET'S SUPPOSE... SOMEONE ELSE THREW A POKÉ BALL AT THE EXACT SAME MOMENT WE DID...
IF THAT PERSON'S POKÉ BALL REACHED LUGIA FIRST, THEN..
GAP
FWAP
HEY! WHERE ARE YOU GOING?!

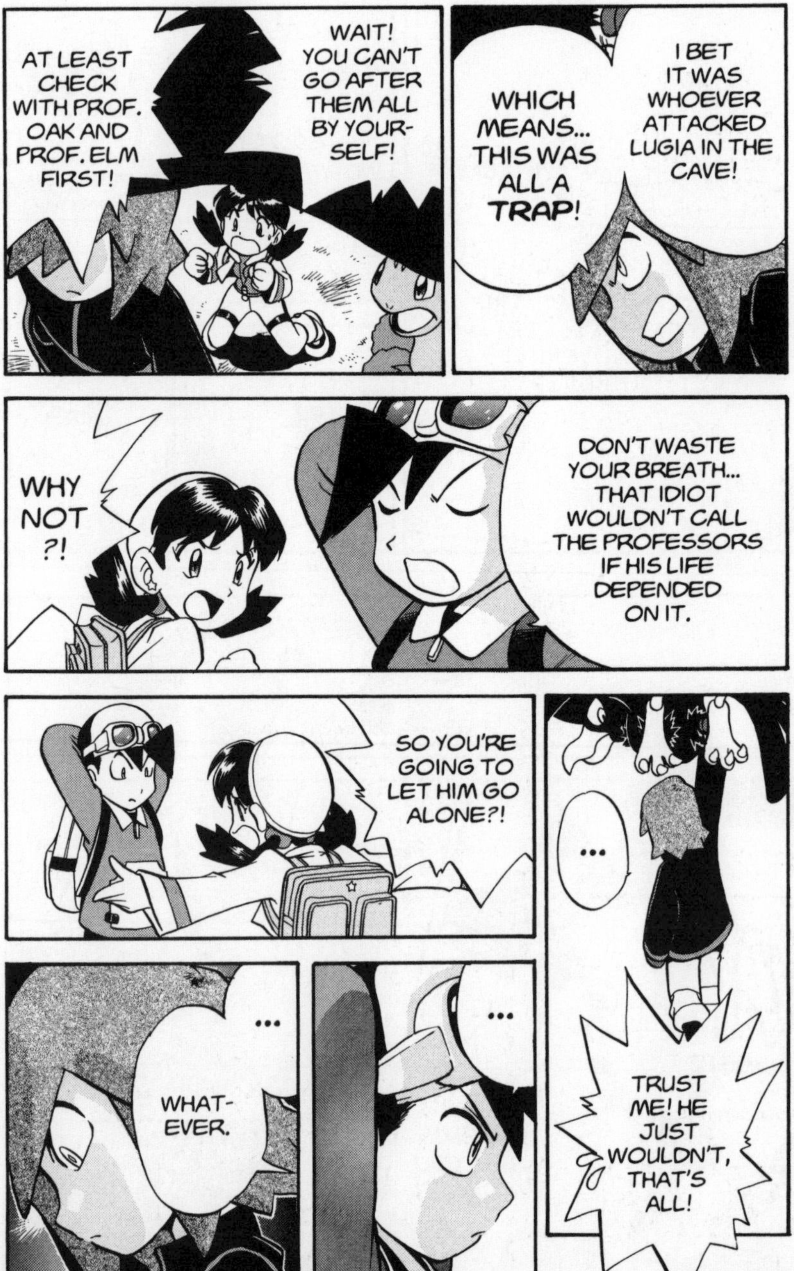
I BET IT WAS WHOEVER ATTACKED LUGIA IN THE CAVE!
WHICH MEANS... THIS WAS ALL A TRAP!
WAIT! YOU CAN'T GO AFTER THEM ALL BY YOURSELF!
AT LEAST CHECK WITH PROF. OAK AND PROF. ELM FIRST!
DON'T WASTE YOUR BREATH... THAT IDIOT WOULDN'T CALL THE PROFESSORS IF HIS LIFE DEPENDED ON IT.
WHY NOT?!
...
TRUST ME! HE JUST WOULDN'T, THAT'S ALL!
SO YOU'RE GOING TO LET HIM GO ALONE?!
...
...
WHATEVER.

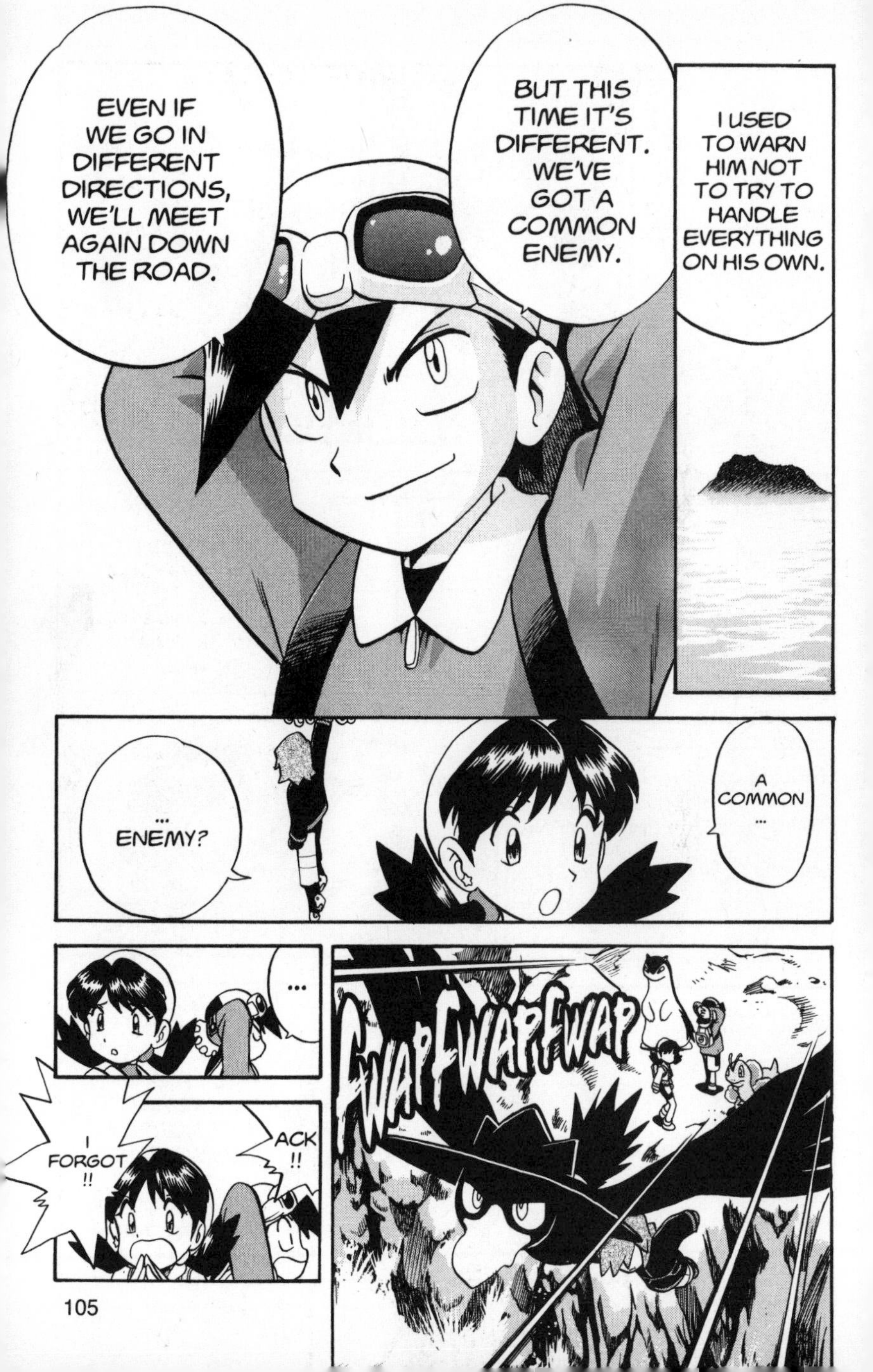
I USED TO WARN HIM NOT TO TRY TO HANDLE EVERYTHING ON HIS OWN.
BUT THIS TIME IT'S DIFFERENT. WE'VE GOT A COMMON ENEMY.
EVEN IF WE GO IN DIFFERENT DIRECTIONS, WE'LL MEET AGAIN DOWN THE ROAD.
A COMMON ...
... ENEMY?
FWAPFWAPFWAP
...
ACK !!
I FORGOT !!

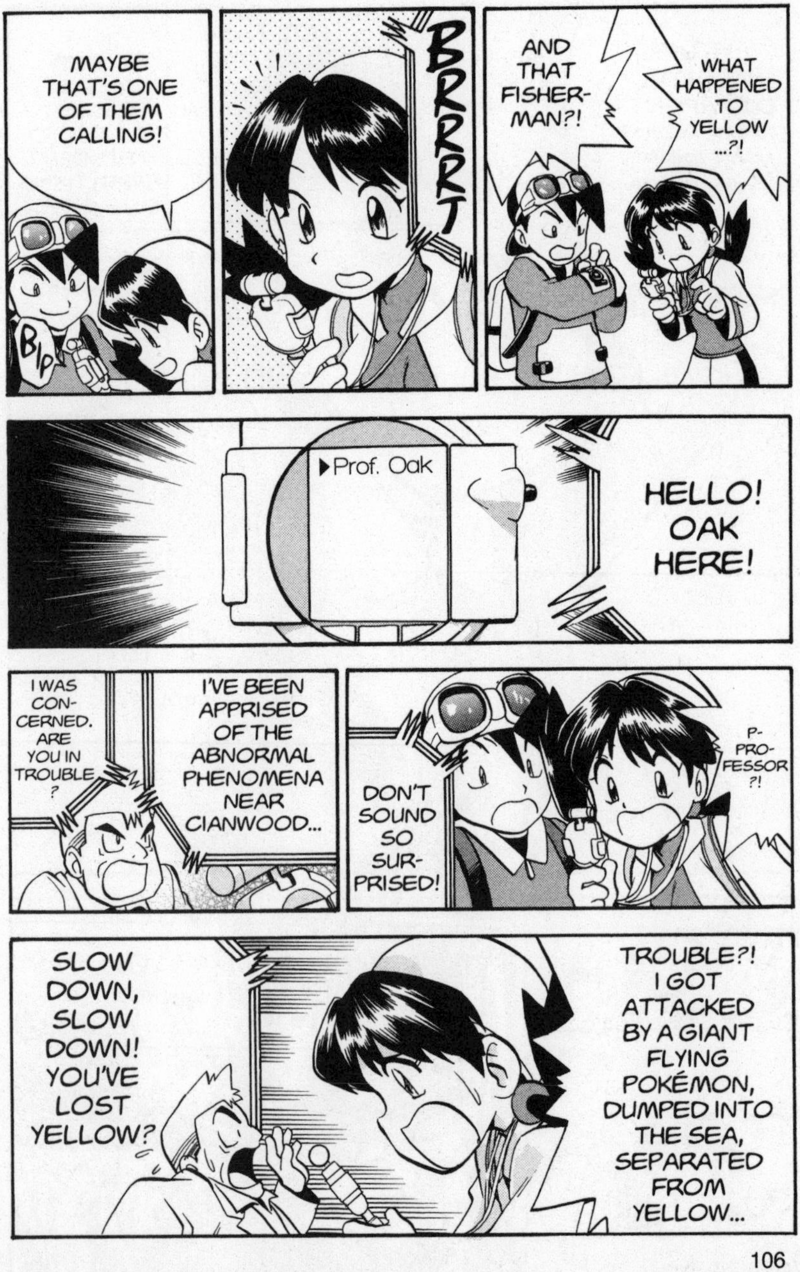
WHAT HAPPENED TO YELLOW ...?!
AND THAT FISHERMAN?!
BRRRRT
MAYBE THAT'S ONE OF THEM CALLING!
BLIP
▶Prof. Oak
HELLO! OAK HERE!
P-PROFESSOR?!
DON'T SOUND SO SURPRISED!
I'VE BEEN APPRISED OF THE ABNORMAL PHENOMENA NEAR CIANWOOD...
I WAS CONCERNED. ARE YOU IN TROUBLE?
TROUBLE?! I GOT ATTACKED BY A GIANT FLYING POKÉMON, DUMPED INTO THE SEA, SEPARATED FROM YELLOW...
SLOW DOWN, SLOW DOWN! YOU'VE LOST YELLOW?

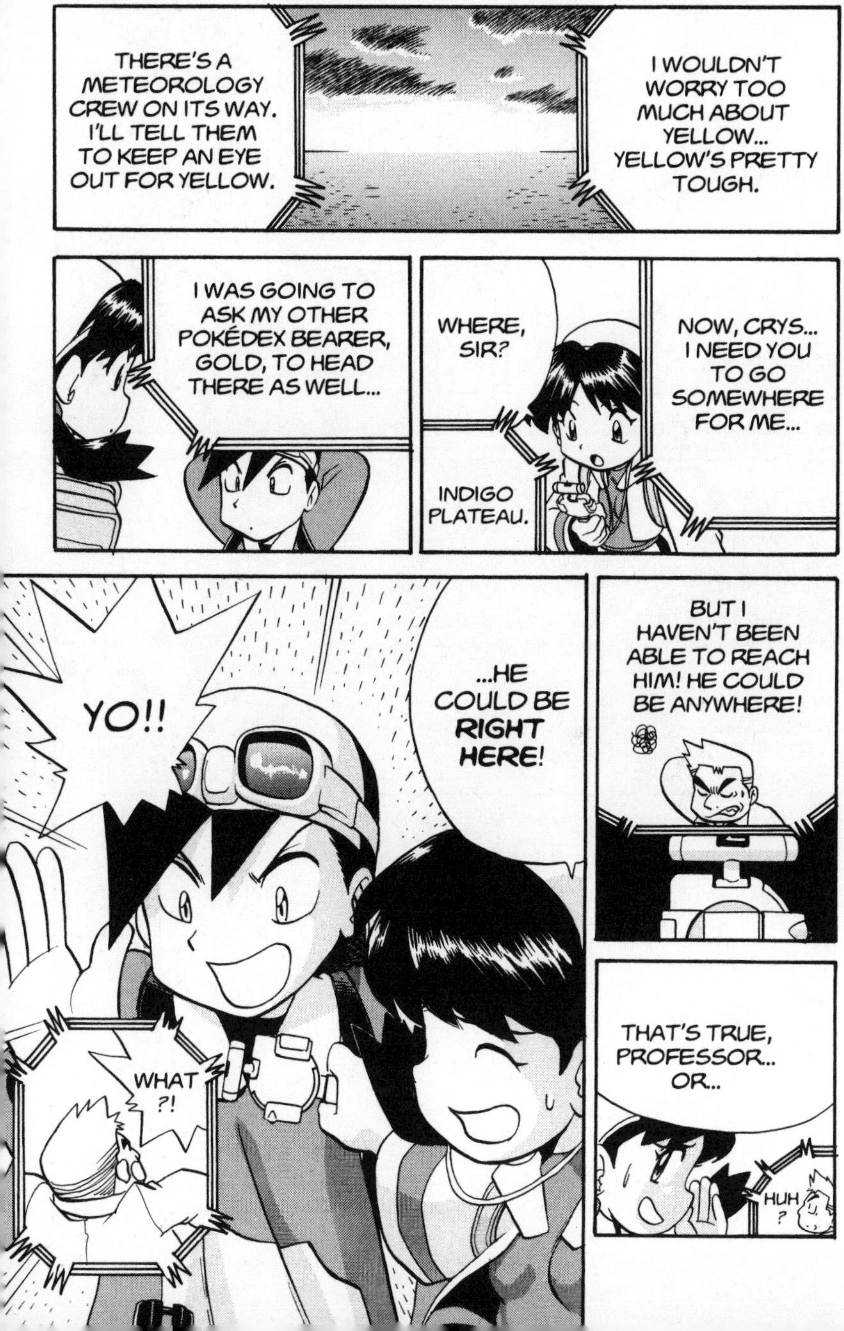
I WOULDN'T WORRY TOO MUCH ABOUT YELLOW... YELLOW'S PRETTY TOUGH.
THERE'S A METEOROLOGY CREW ON ITS WAY. I'LL TELL THEM TO KEEP AN EYE OUT FOR YELLOW.
NOW, CRYS... I NEED YOU TO GO SOMEWHERE FOR ME...
WHERE, SIR?
INDIGO PLATEAU.
I WAS GOING TO ASK MY OTHER POKÉDEX BEARER, GOLD, TO HEAD THERE AS WELL...
BUT I HAVEN'T BEEN ABLE TO REACH HIM! HE COULD BE ANYWHERE!
THAT'S TRUE, PROFESSOR... OR...
HUH ?
...HE COULD BE **RIGHT HERE**!
YO!!
WHAT ?!

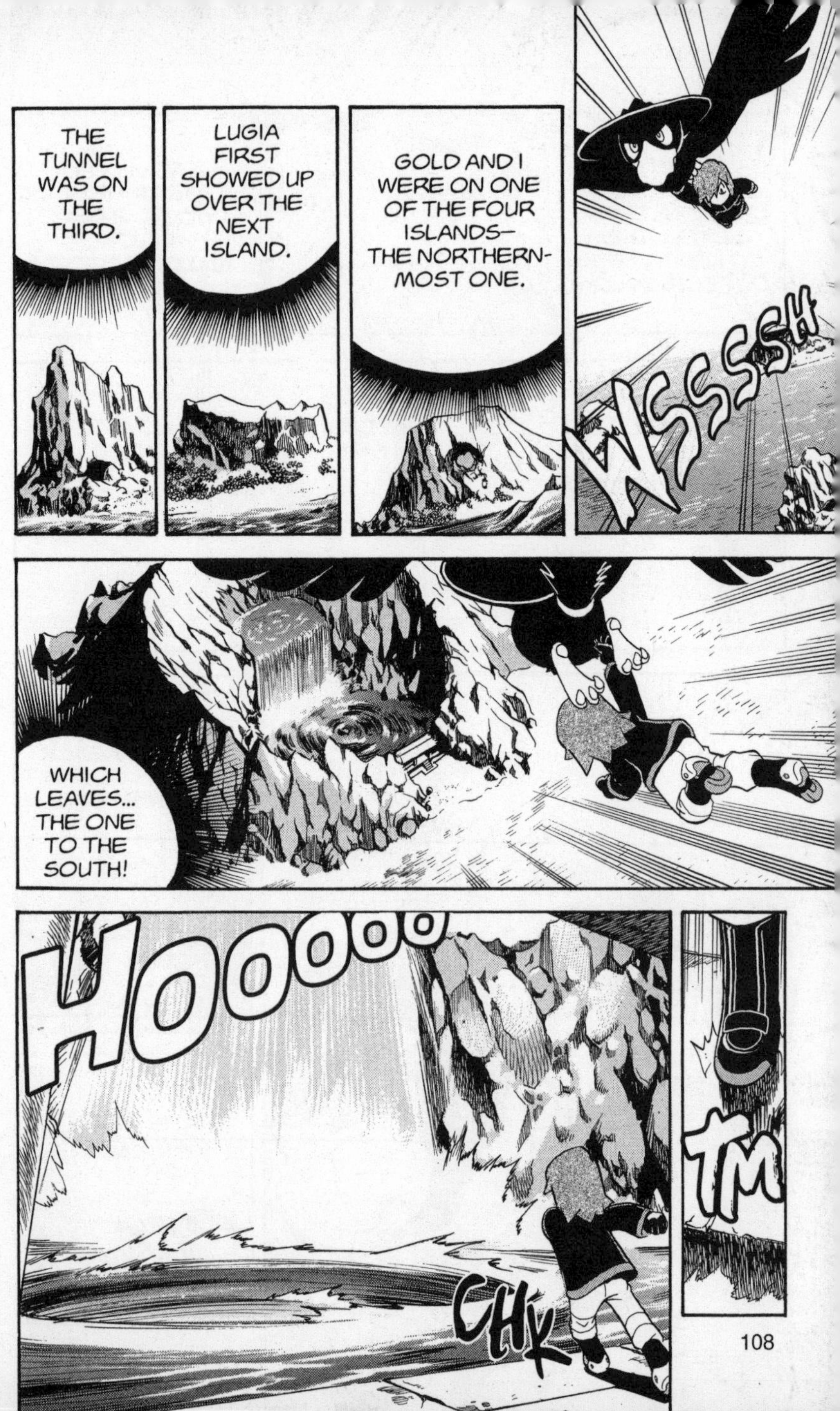
WSSSSH
GOLD AND I WERE ON ONE OF THE FOUR ISLANDS— THE NORTHERN-MOST ONE.
LUGIA FIRST SHOWED UP OVER THE NEXT ISLAND.
THE TUNNEL WAS ON THE THIRD.
WHICH LEAVES... THE ONE TO THE SOUTH!
TM
HOOOOOO
CHK

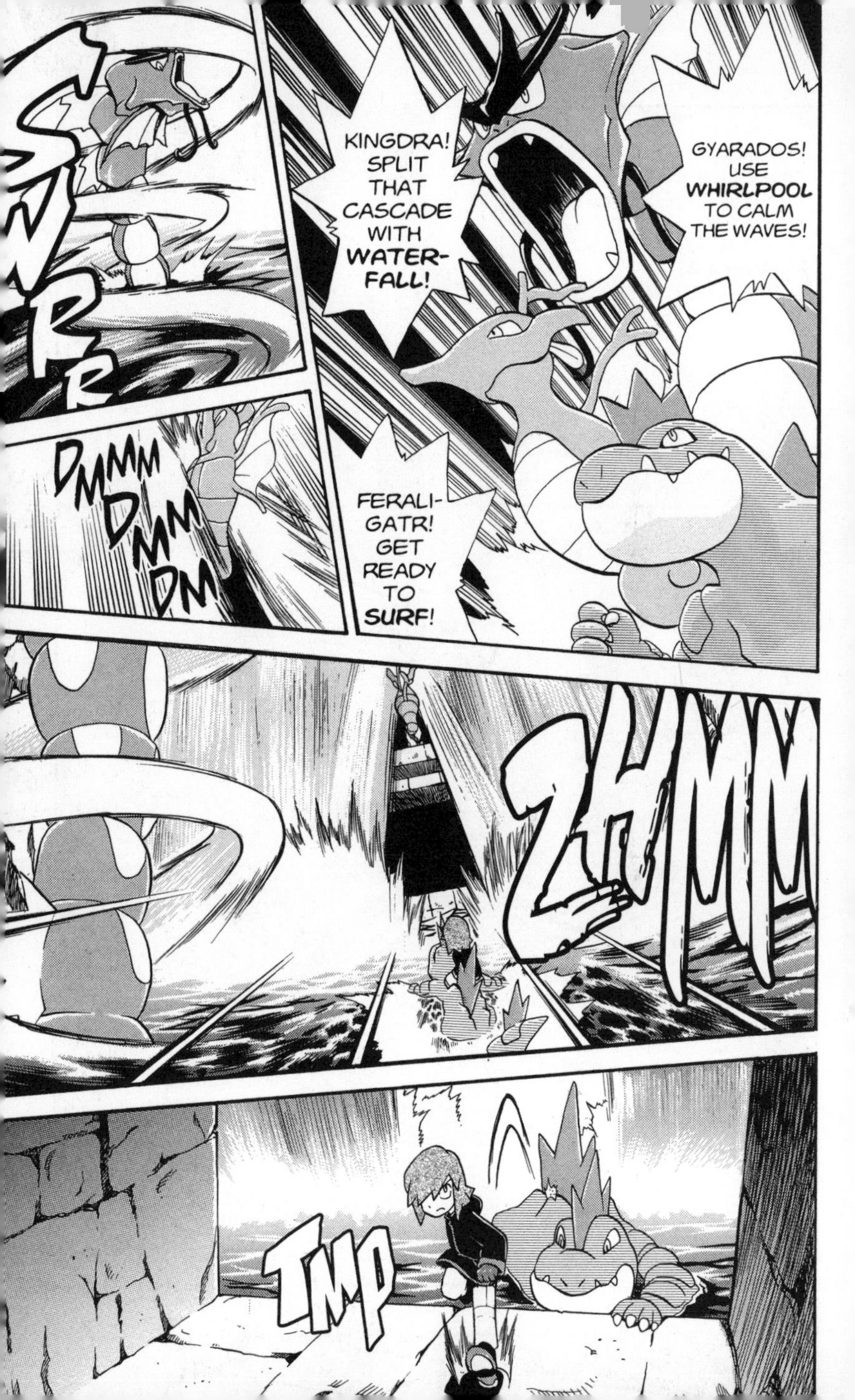
GYARADOS! USE **WHIRLPOOL** TO CALM THE WAVES!
KINGDRA! SPLIT THAT CASCADE WITH **WATER-FALL!**
FERALI-GATR! GET READY TO **SURF!**
SWRR
DMMM DMM DM
ZHMM
TMP

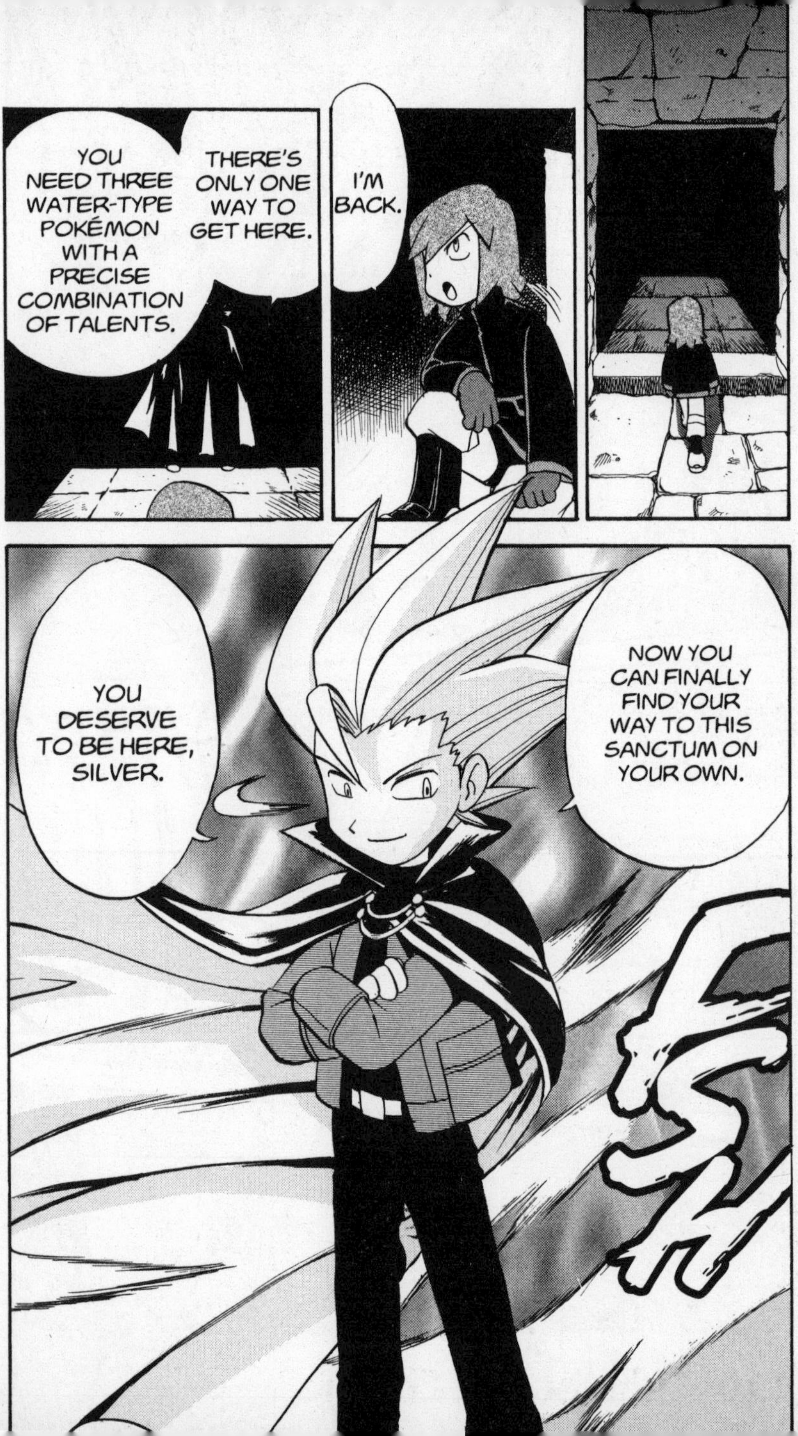
I'M BACK.
THERE'S ONLY ONE WAY TO GET HERE.
YOU NEED THREE WATER-TYPE POKÉMON WITH A PRECISE COMBINATION OF TALENTS.
NOW YOU CAN FINALLY FIND YOUR WAY TO THIS SANCTUM ON YOUR OWN.
YOU DESERVE TO BE HERE, SILVER.

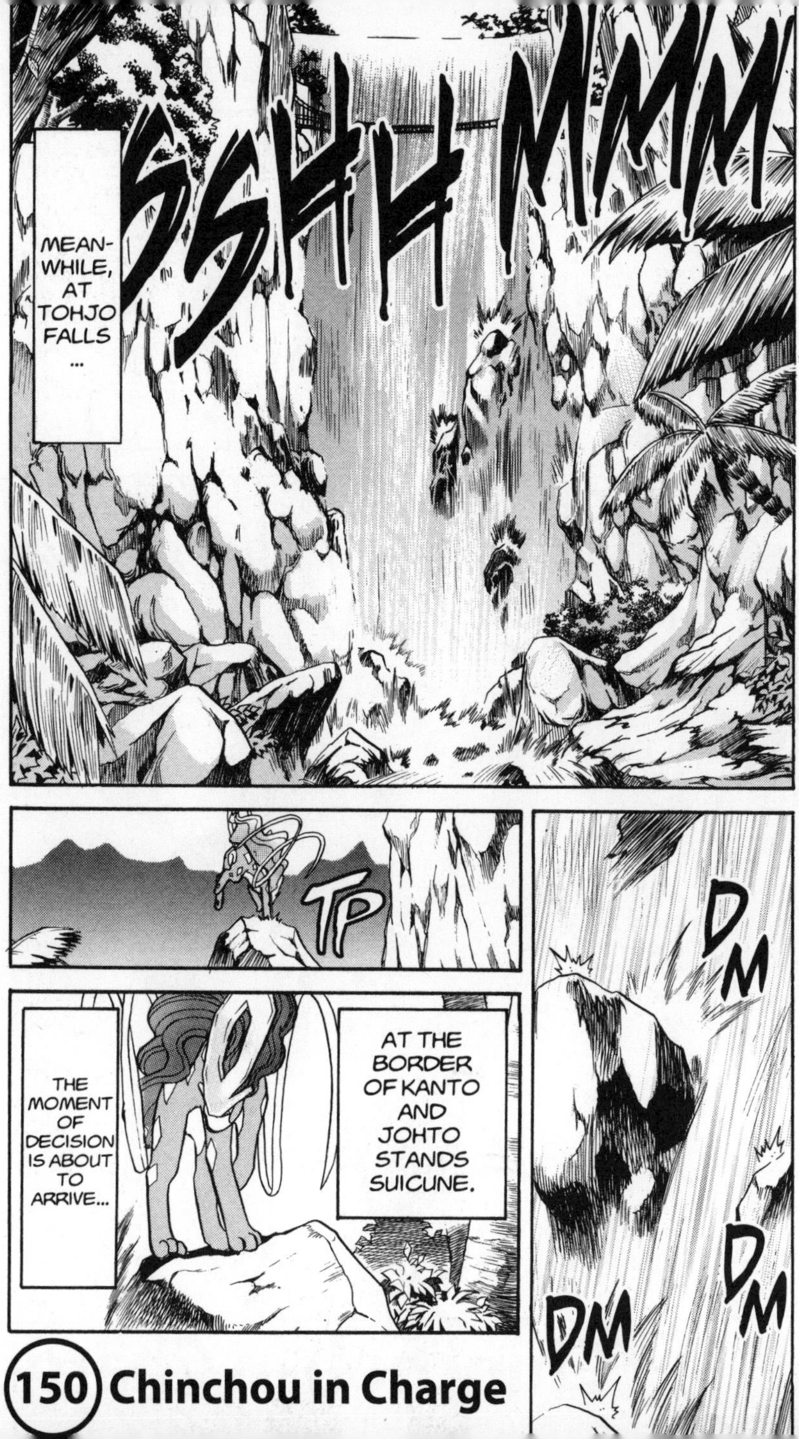
SSHHMMM
MEAN-WHILE, AT TOHJO FALLS ...
DM
DM
DM
DM
TP
AT THE BORDER OF KANTO AND JOHTO STANDS SUICUNE.
THE MOMENT OF DECISION IS ABOUT TO ARRIVE...

150 Chinchou in Charge

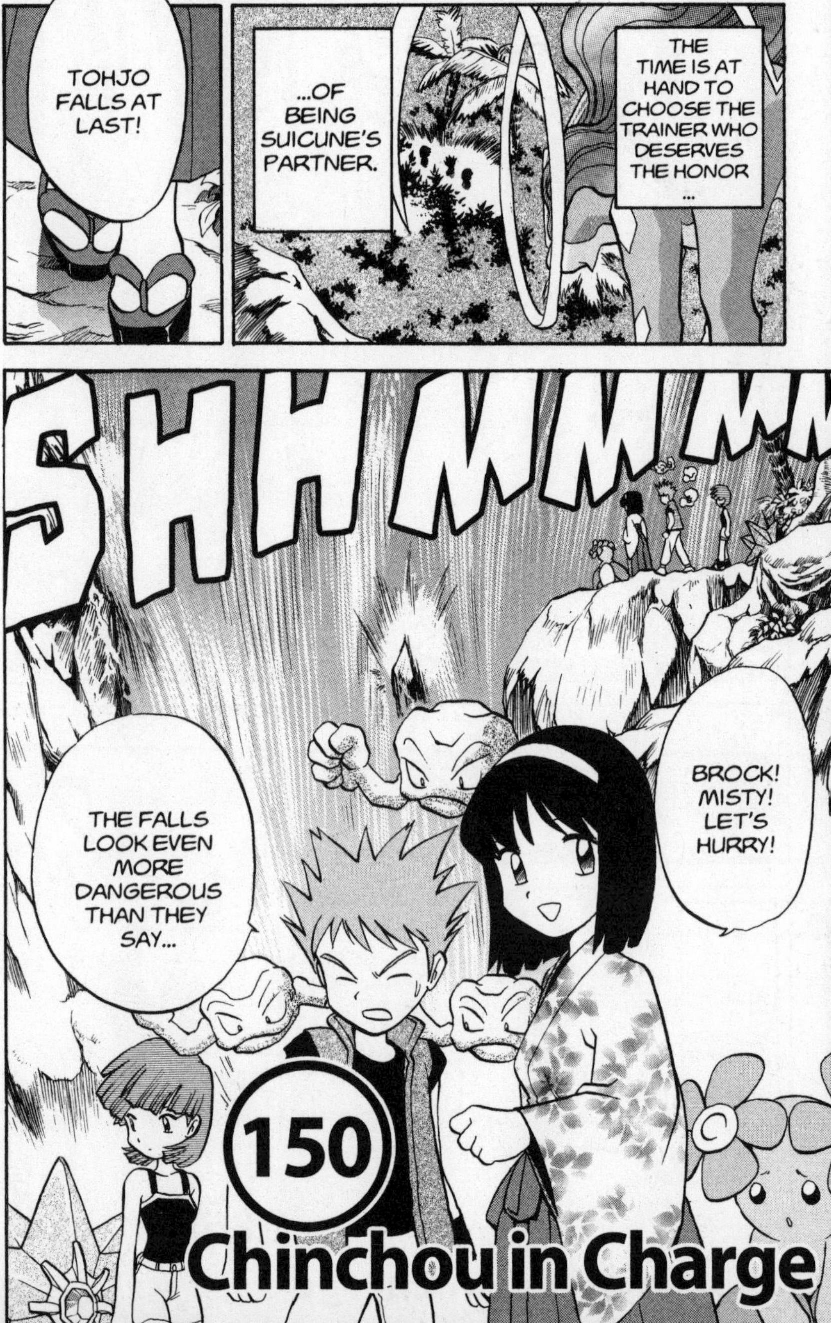
THE TIME IS AT HAND TO CHOOSE THE TRAINER WHO DESERVES THE HONOR ...
...OF BEING SUICUNE'S PARTNER.
TOHJO FALLS AT LAST!
SHMMMMM
BROCK! MISTY! LET'S HURRY!
THE FALLS LOOK EVEN MORE DANGEROUS THAN THEY SAY...
150
Chinchou in Charge

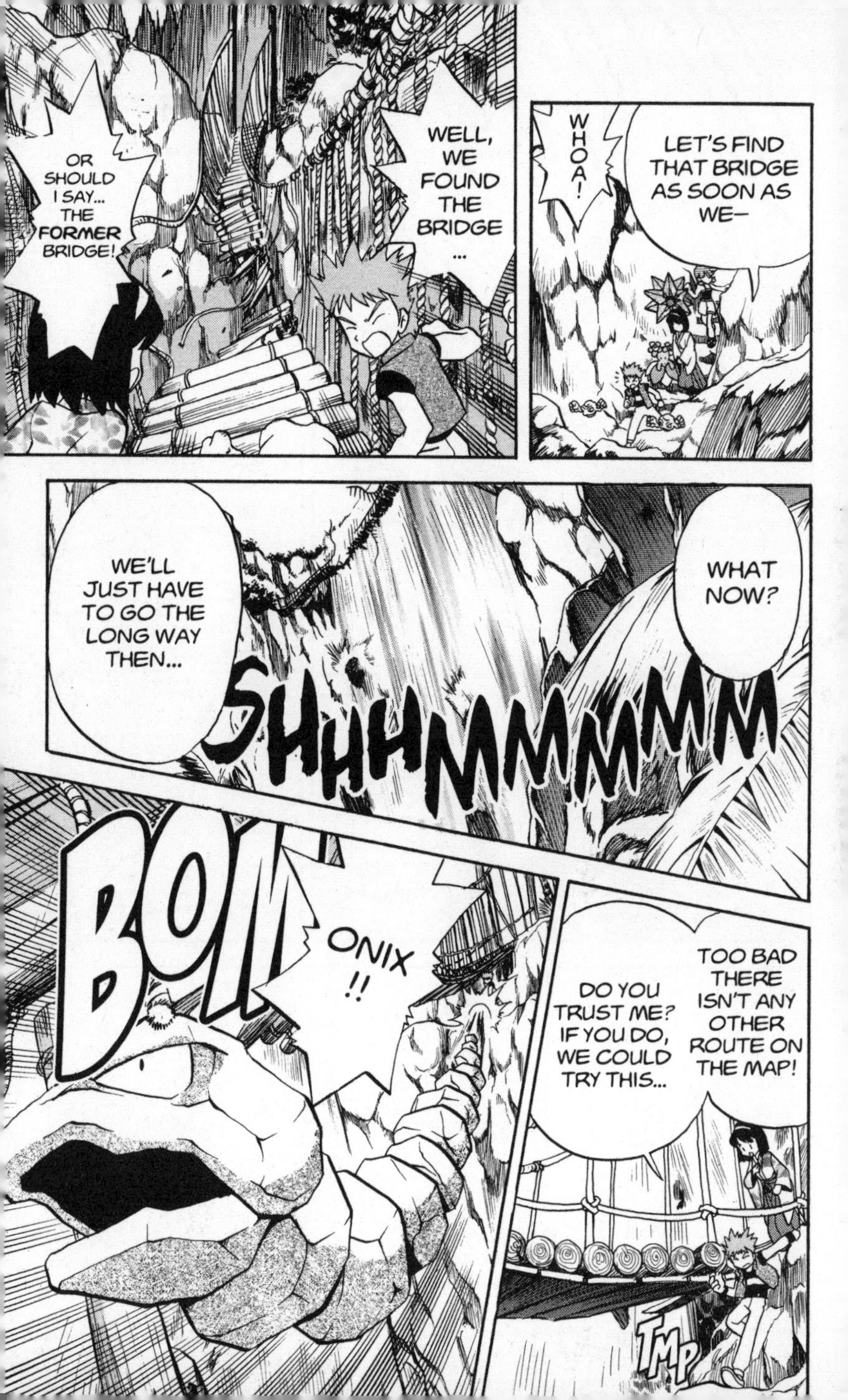
LET'S FIND THAT BRIDGE AS SOON AS WE—
WHOA!
WELL, WE FOUND THE BRIDGE ...
OR SHOULD I SAY... THE **FORMER** BRIDGE!
WHAT NOW?
WE'LL JUST HAVE TO GO THE LONG WAY THEN...
SHHHMMMMMM
TOO BAD THERE ISN'T ANY OTHER ROUTE ON THE MAP!
DO YOU TRUST ME? IF YOU DO, WE COULD TRY THIS...
TMP
BOM
ONIX !!

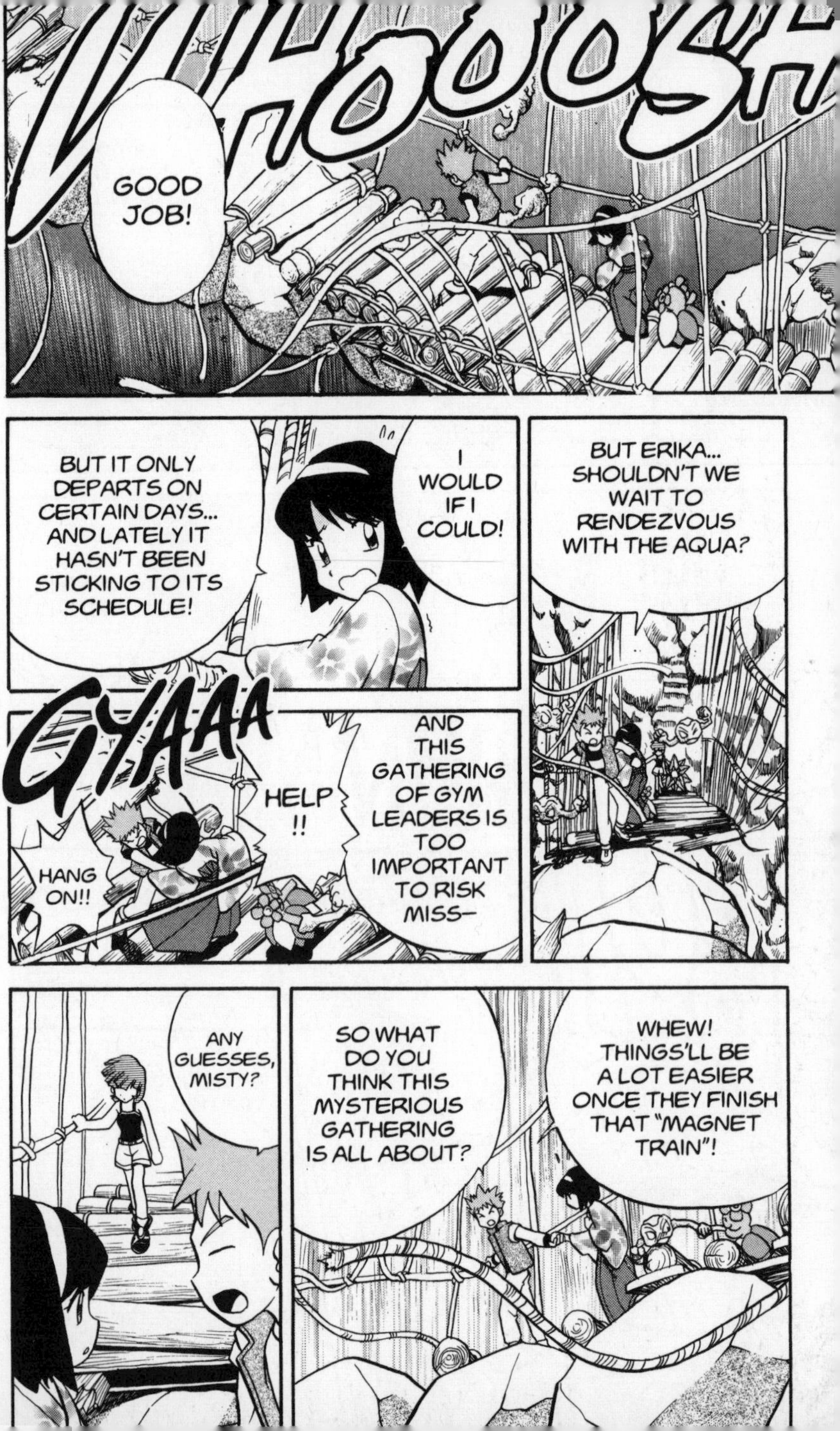
WHOOOSH
GOOD JOB!
BUT ERIKA... SHOULDN'T WE WAIT TO RENDEZVOUS WITH THE AQUA?
I WOULD IF I COULD!
BUT IT ONLY DEPARTS ON CERTAIN DAYS... AND LATELY IT HASN'T BEEN STICKING TO ITS SCHEDULE!
AND THIS GATHERING OF GYM LEADERS IS TOO IMPORTANT TO RISK MISS–
HELP !!
GYAAA
HANG ON!!
WHEW! THINGS'LL BE A LOT EASIER ONCE THEY FINISH THAT "MAGNET TRAIN"!
SO WHAT DO YOU THINK THIS MYSTERIOUS GATHERING IS ALL ABOUT?
ANY GUESSES, MISTY?

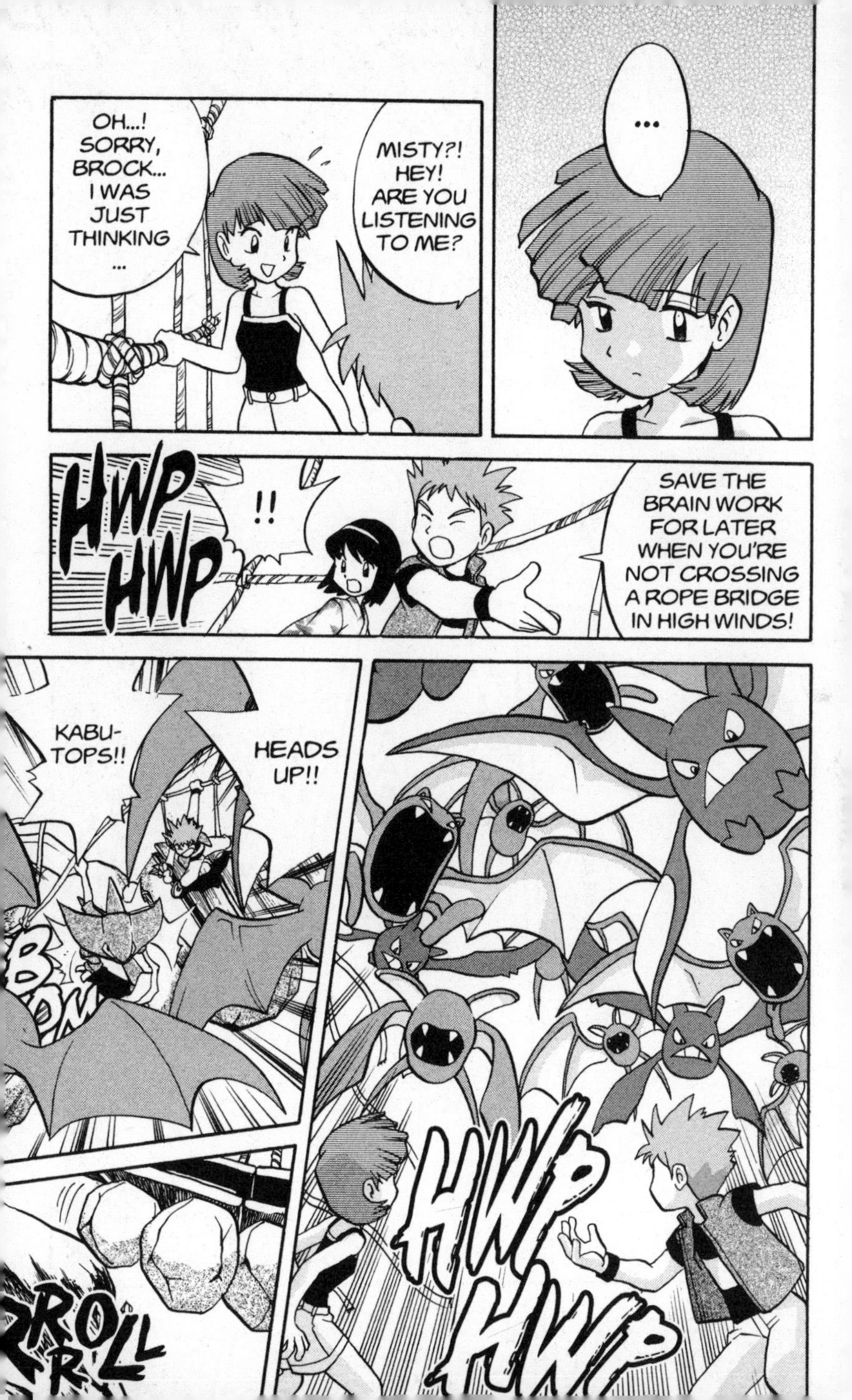
...
MISTY?! HEY! ARE YOU LISTENING TO ME?
OH...! SORRY, BROCK... I WAS JUST THINKING ...
SAVE THE BRAIN WORK FOR LATER WHEN YOU'RE NOT CROSSING A ROPE BRIDGE IN HIGH WINDS!
!!
HWP HWP
HWP HWP
HEADS UP!!
KABU-TOPS!!

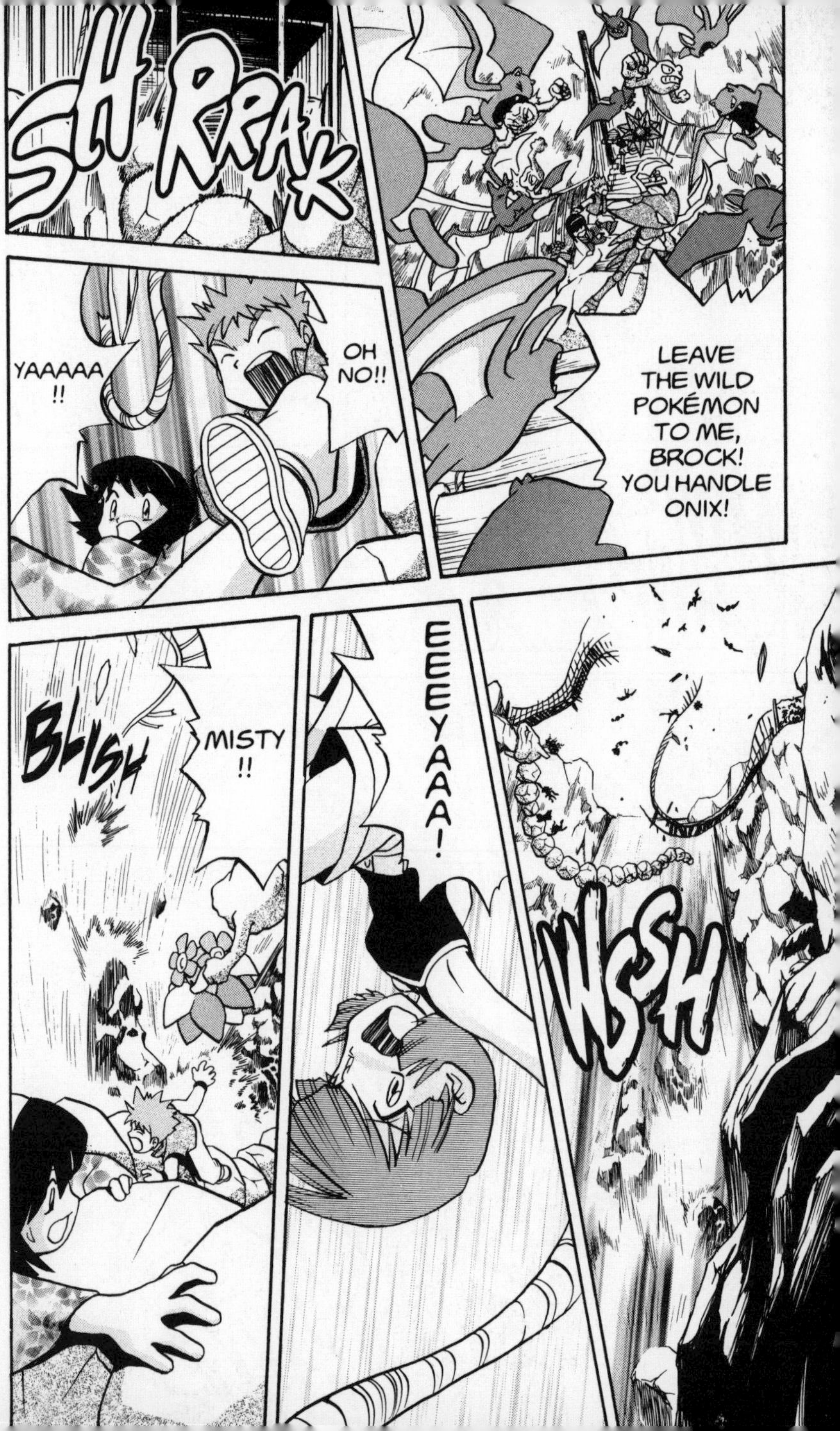

LEAVE THE WILD POKÉMON TO ME, BROCK! YOU HANDLE ONIX!
SHRRPAK
OH NO!!
YAAAAA!!
WSH
EEEYAAA!
MISTY!!
BLISH

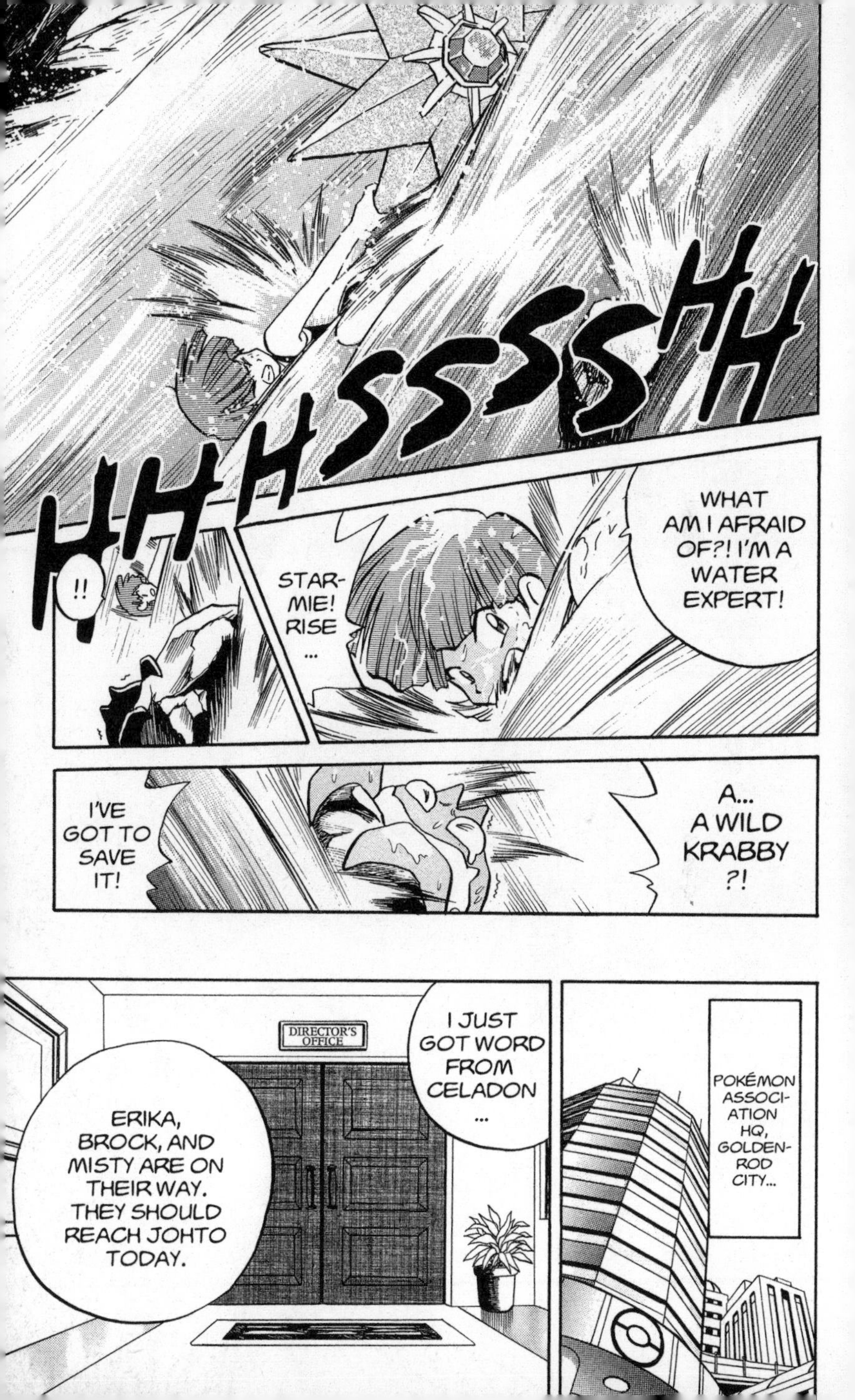
HHHHSSSSHH
WHAT AM I AFRAID OF?! I'M A WATER EXPERT!
STAR-MIE! RISE ...
!!
A... A WILD KRABBY ?!
I'VE GOT TO SAVE IT!
POKÉMON ASSOCIATION HQ, GOLDENROD CITY...
I JUST GOT WORD FROM CELADON ...
DIRECTOR'S OFFICE
ERIKA, BROCK, AND MISTY ARE ON THEIR WAY. THEY SHOULD REACH JOHTO TODAY.

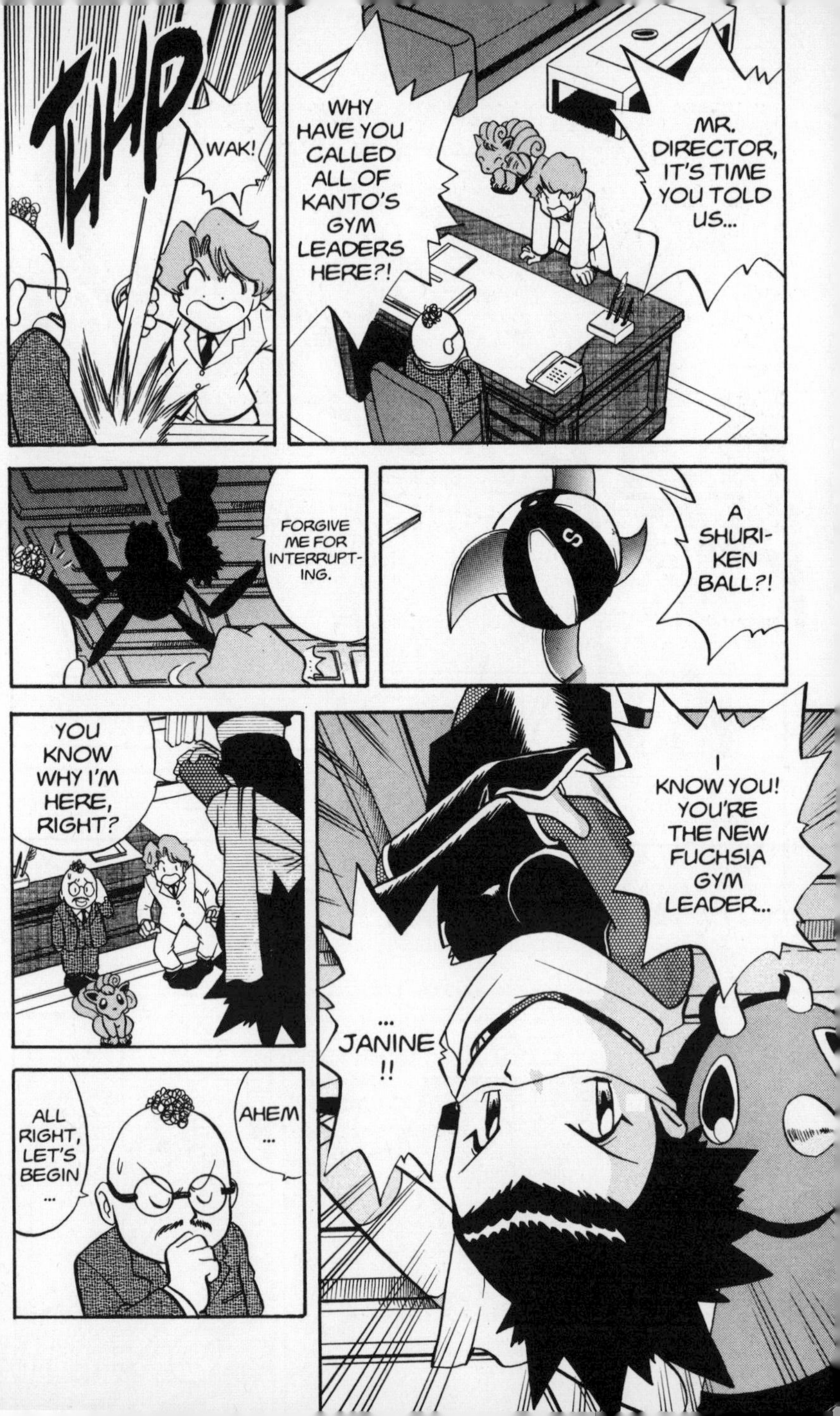
MR. DIRECTOR, IT'S TIME YOU TOLD US...
WHY HAVE YOU CALLED ALL OF KANTO'S GYM LEADERS HERE?!
THUP
WAK!
A SHURI-KEN BALL?!
FORGIVE ME FOR INTERRUPT-ING.
I KNOW YOU! YOU'RE THE NEW FUCHSIA GYM LEADER...
... JANINE !!
YOU KNOW WHY I'M HERE, RIGHT?
AHEM ...
ALL RIGHT, LET'S BEGIN ...

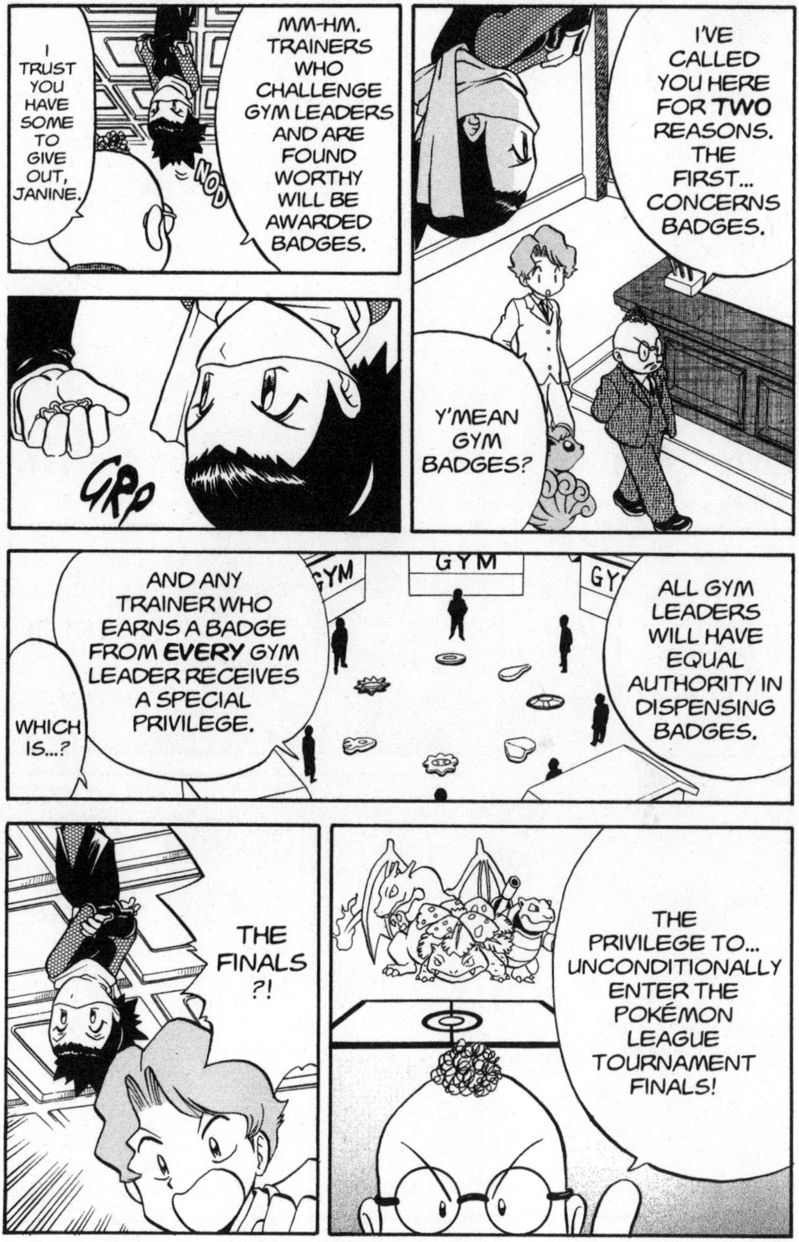
I'VE CALLED YOU HERE FOR **TWO** REASONS. THE FIRST... CONCERNS BADGES.
Y'MEAN GYM BADGES?
MM-HM. TRAINERS WHO CHALLENGE GYM LEADERS AND ARE FOUND WORTHY WILL BE AWARDED BADGES.
NOD
I TRUST YOU HAVE SOME TO GIVE OUT, JANINE.
GRP
GYM
ALL GYM LEADERS WILL HAVE EQUAL AUTHORITY IN DISPENSING BADGES.
AND ANY TRAINER WHO EARNS A BADGE FROM **EVERY** GYM LEADER RECEIVES A SPECIAL PRIVILEGE.
WHICH IS...?
THE PRIVILEGE TO... UNCONDITIONALLY ENTER THE POKÉMON LEAGUE TOURNAMENT FINALS!
THE FINALS?!

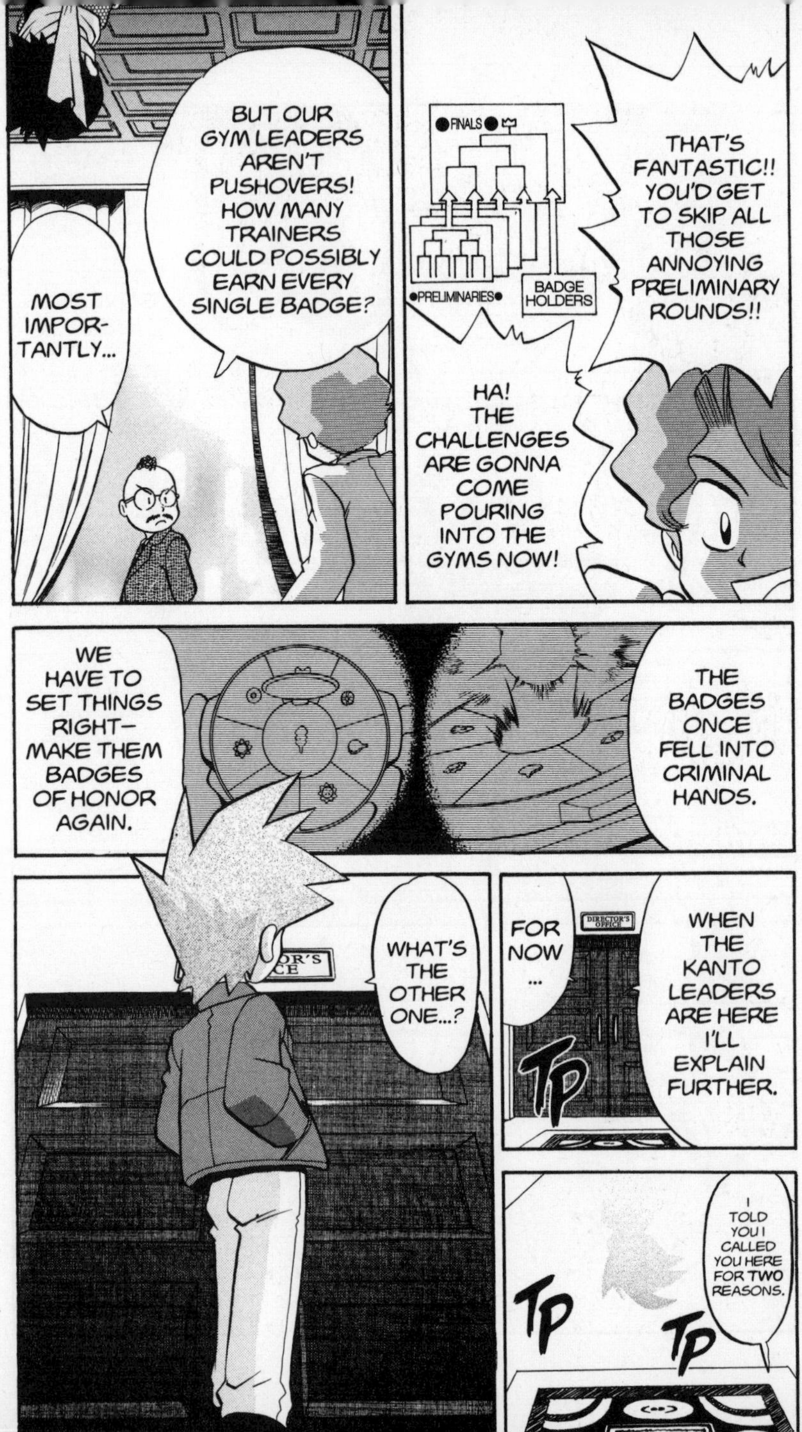
THAT'S FANTASTIC!! YOU'D GET TO SKIP ALL THOSE ANNOYING PRELIMINARY ROUNDS!!
FINALS
PRELIMINARIES
BADGE HOLDERS
HA! THE CHALLENGES ARE GONNA COME POURING INTO THE GYMS NOW!
BUT OUR GYM LEADERS AREN'T PUSHOVERS! HOW MANY TRAINERS COULD POSSIBLY EARN EVERY SINGLE BADGE?
MOST IMPOR-TANTLY...
THE BADGES ONCE FELL INTO CRIMINAL HANDS.
WE HAVE TO SET THINGS RIGHT— MAKE THEM BADGES OF HONOR AGAIN.
DIRECTOR'S OFFICE
WHEN THE KANTO LEADERS ARE HERE I'LL EXPLAIN FURTHER.
FOR NOW ...
TP
I TOLD YOU I CALLED YOU HERE FOR TWO REASONS.
TP
TP
WHAT'S THE OTHER ONE...?

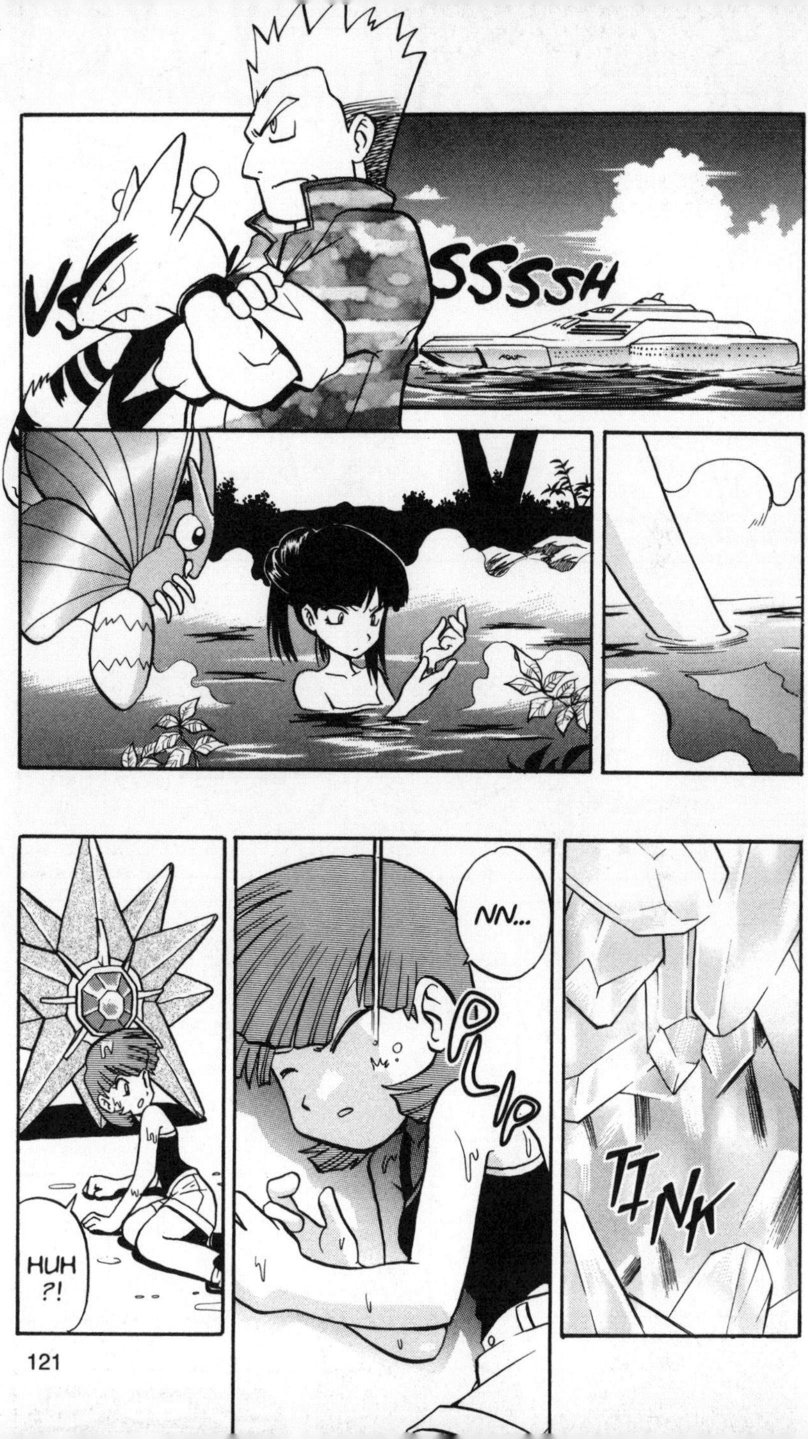
SSSSH
VS
TINK
NN...
PLIP
HUH ?!

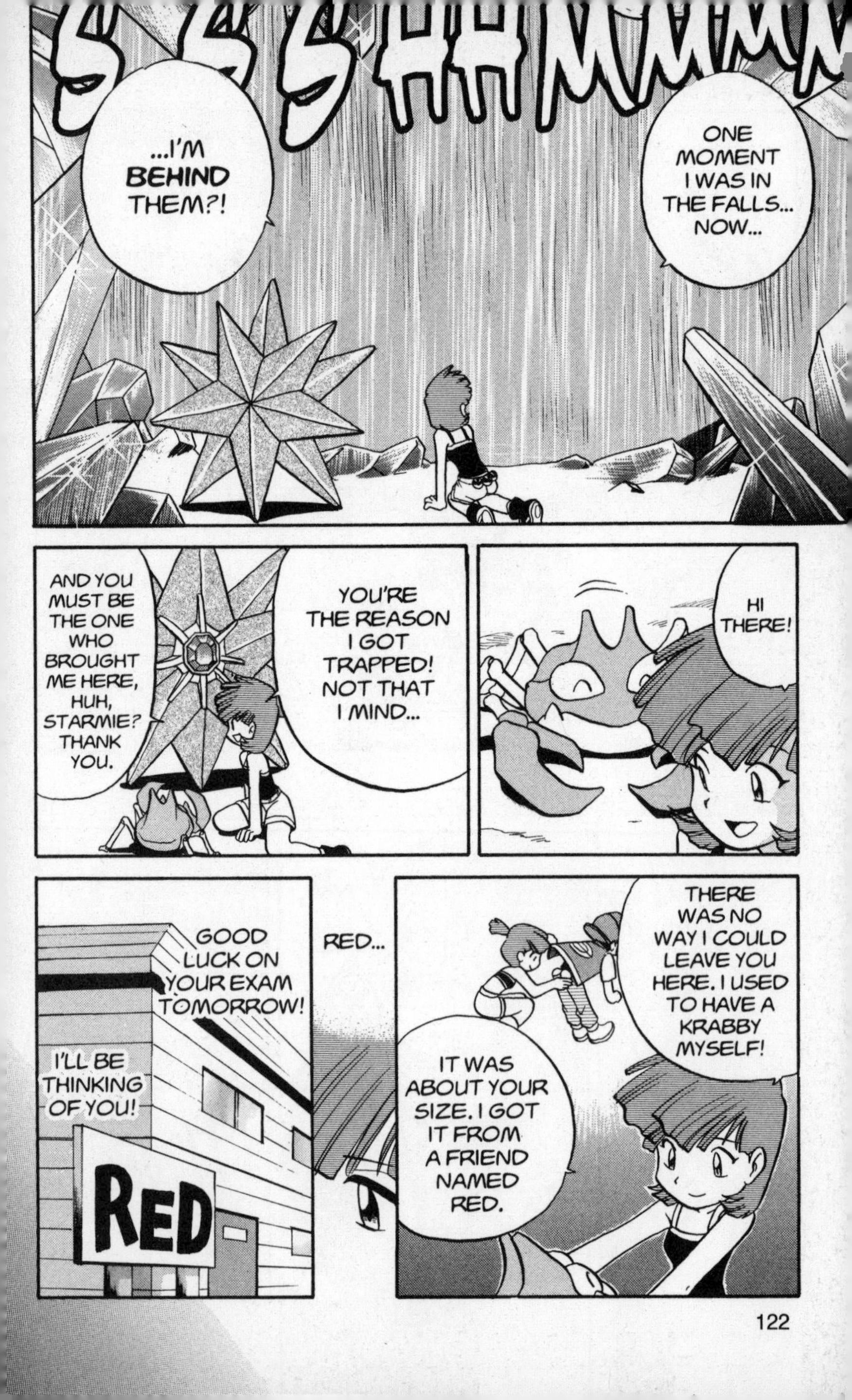
ONE MOMENT I WAS IN THE FALLS... NOW...
...I'M **BEHIND** THEM?!
HI THERE!
YOU'RE THE REASON I GOT TRAPPED! NOT THAT I MIND...
AND YOU MUST BE THE ONE WHO BROUGHT ME HERE, HUH, STARMIE? THANK YOU.
THERE WAS NO WAY I COULD LEAVE YOU HERE. I USED TO HAVE A KRABBY MYSELF!
IT WAS ABOUT YOUR SIZE. I GOT IT FROM A FRIEND NAMED RED.
RED...
GOOD LUCK ON YOUR EXAM TOMORROW!
I'LL BE THINKING OF YOU!
RED

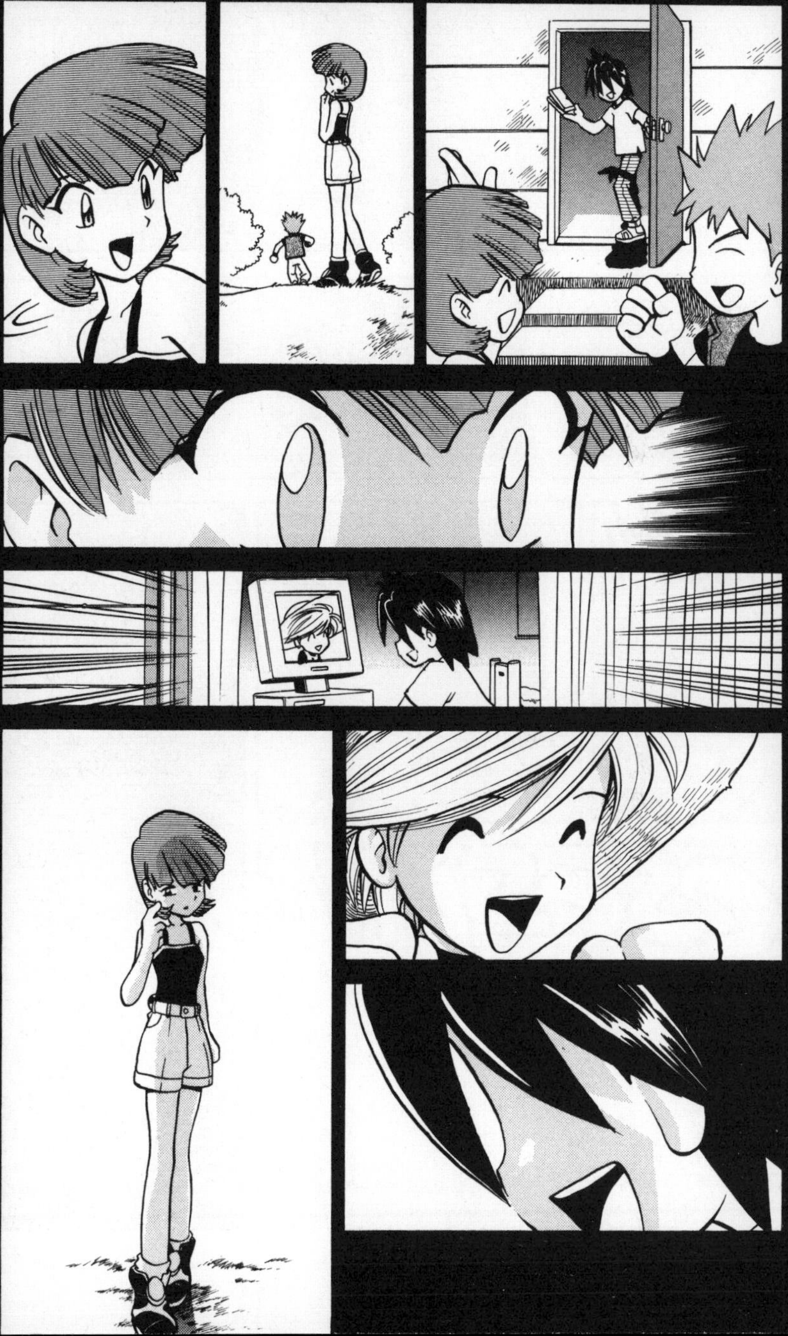

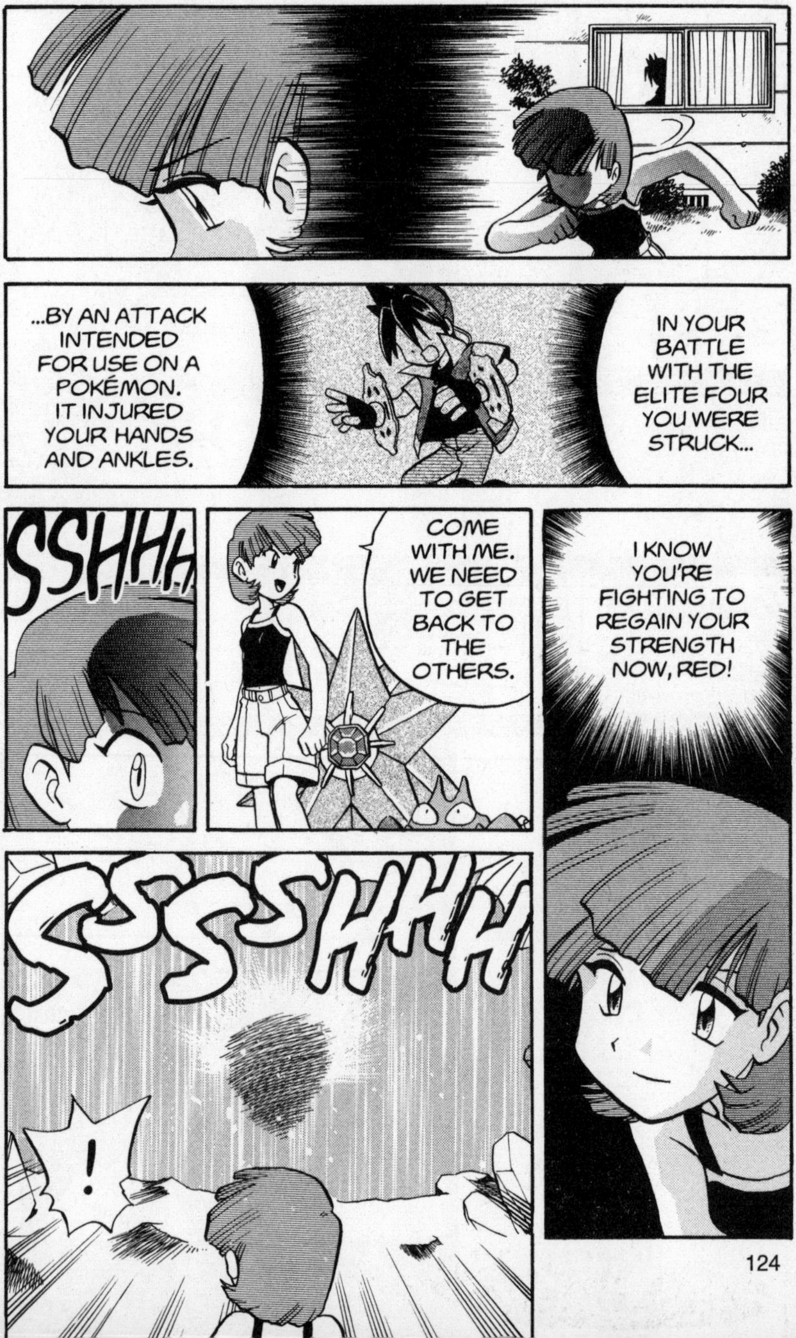
IN YOUR BATTLE WITH THE ELITE FOUR YOU WERE STRUCK...
...BY AN ATTACK INTENDED FOR USE ON A POKÉMON. IT INJURED YOUR HANDS AND ANKLES.
I KNOW YOU'RE FIGHTING TO REGAIN YOUR STRENGTH NOW, RED!
COME WITH ME. WE NEED TO GET BACK TO THE OTHERS.
SSHHH
SSSHHH
!

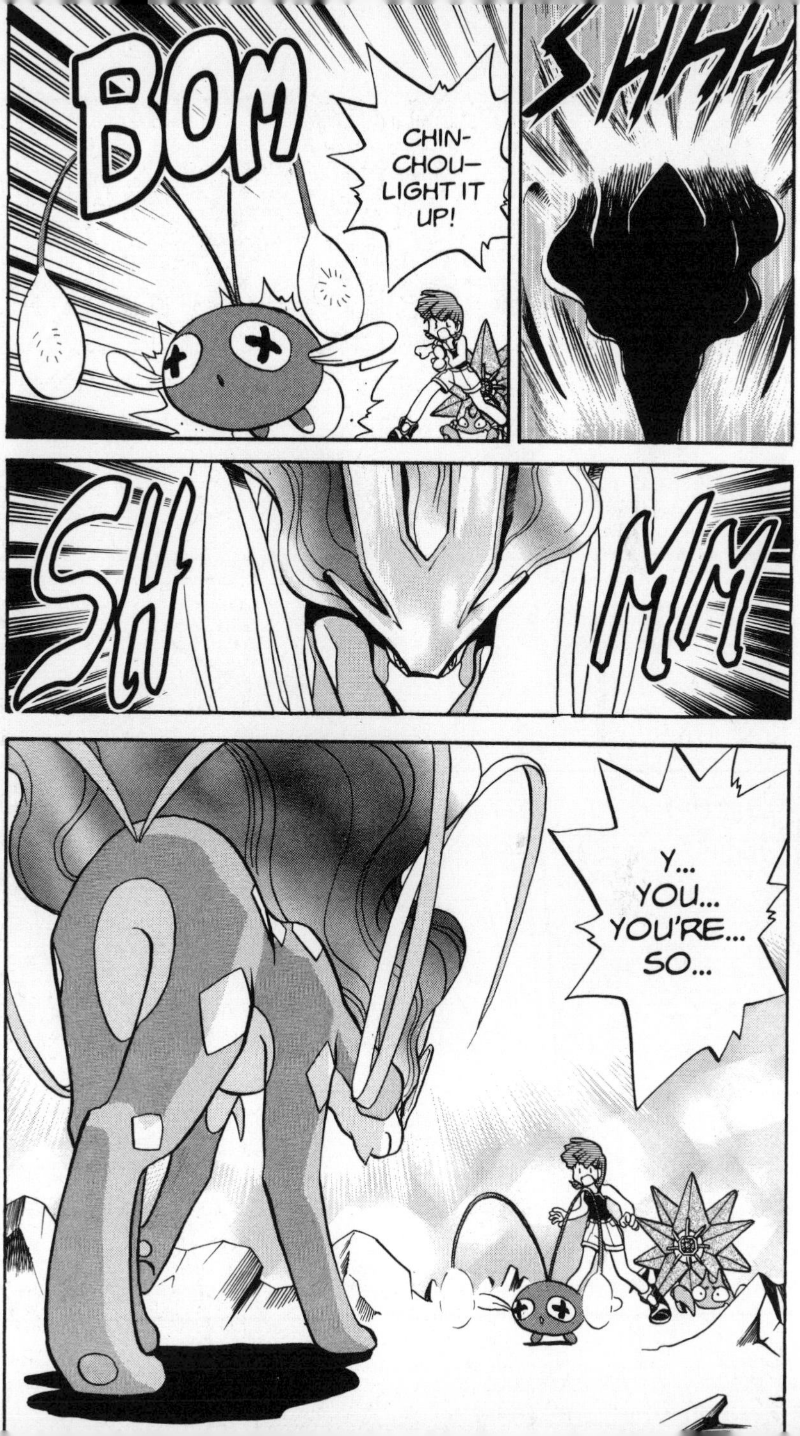
SHHH
BOM
CHIN-CHOU-LIGHT IT UP!
SH MM
Y... YOU... YOU'RE... SO...

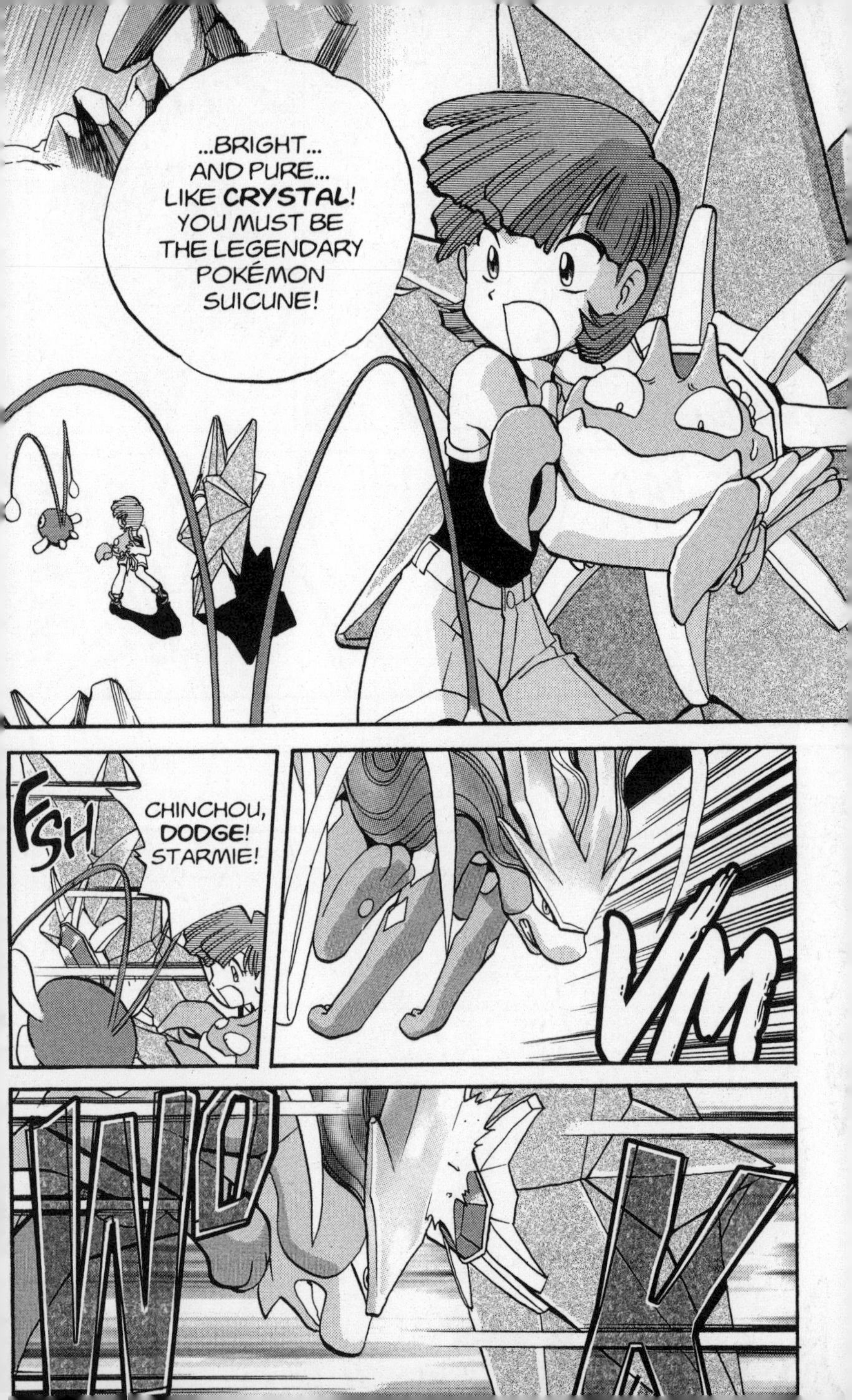
...BRIGHT...
AND PURE...
LIKE **CRYSTAL**!
YOU MUST BE
THE LEGENDARY
POKÉMON
SUICUNE!
VM
FSH
CHINCHOU,
DODGE!
STARMIE!

151 Lovely Lanturn

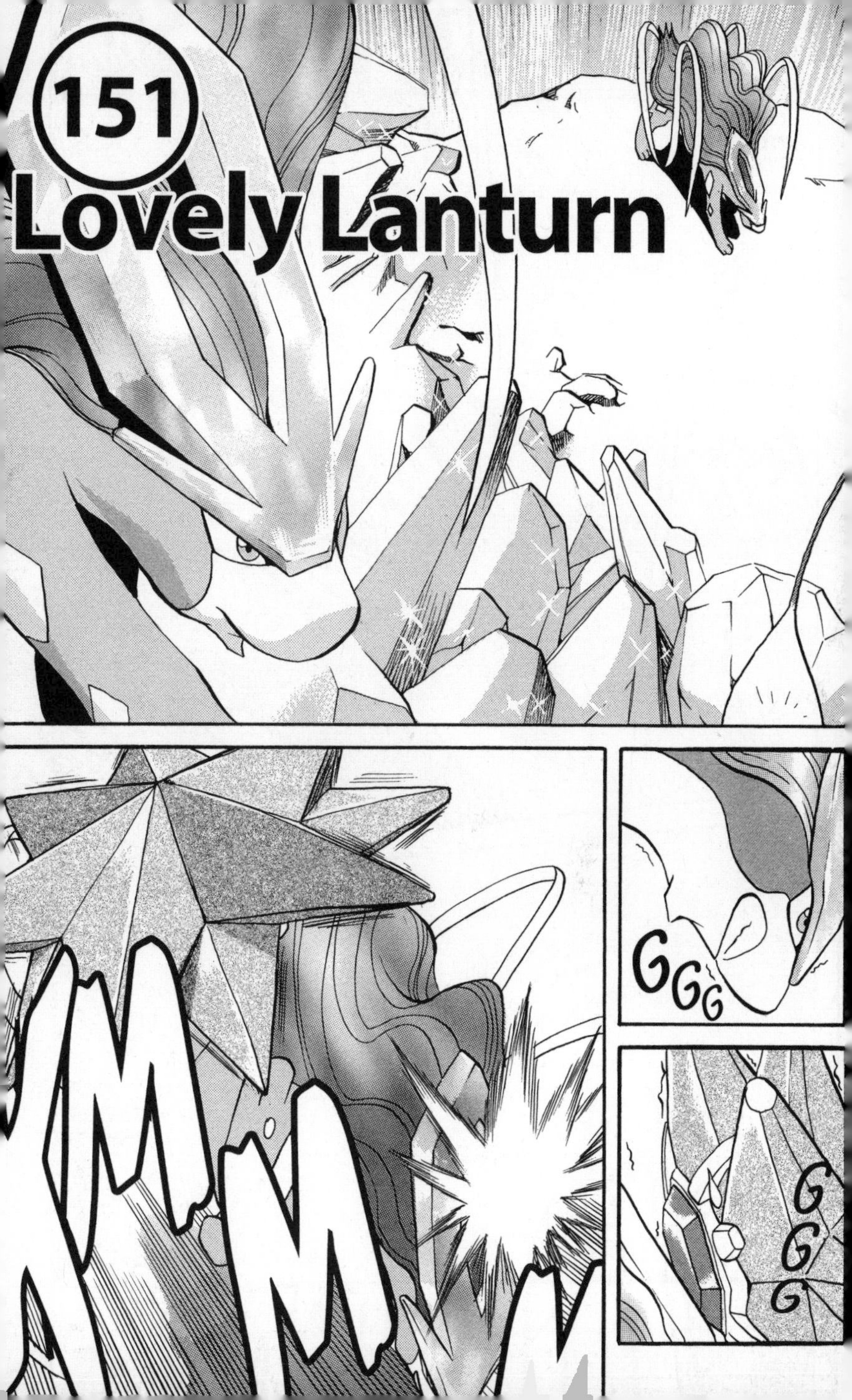
GGG
GGG

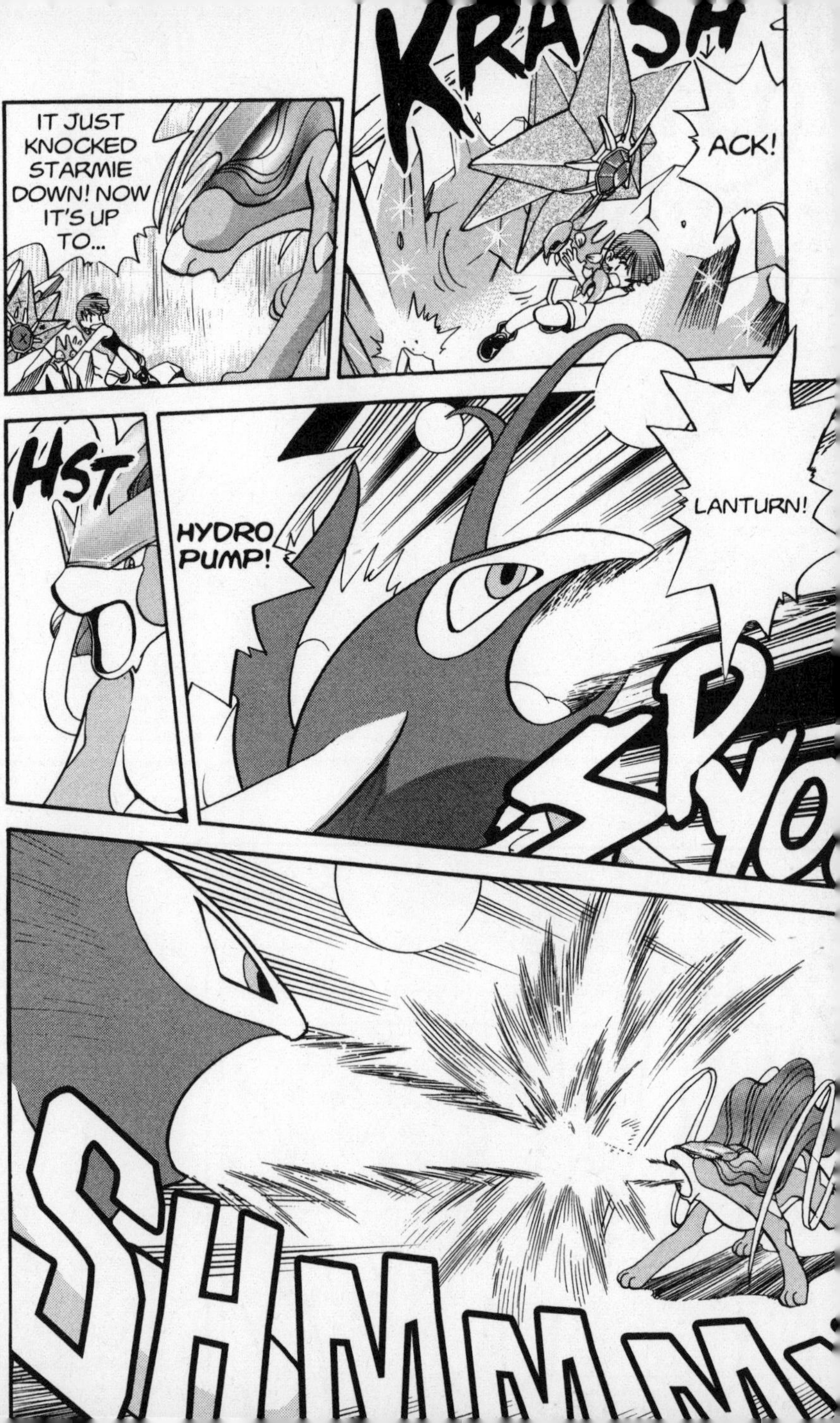

KRASH
ACK!
IT JUST KNOCKED STARMIE DOWN! NOW IT'S UP TO...
LANTURN!
HYDRO PUMP!
HST
SHMMM

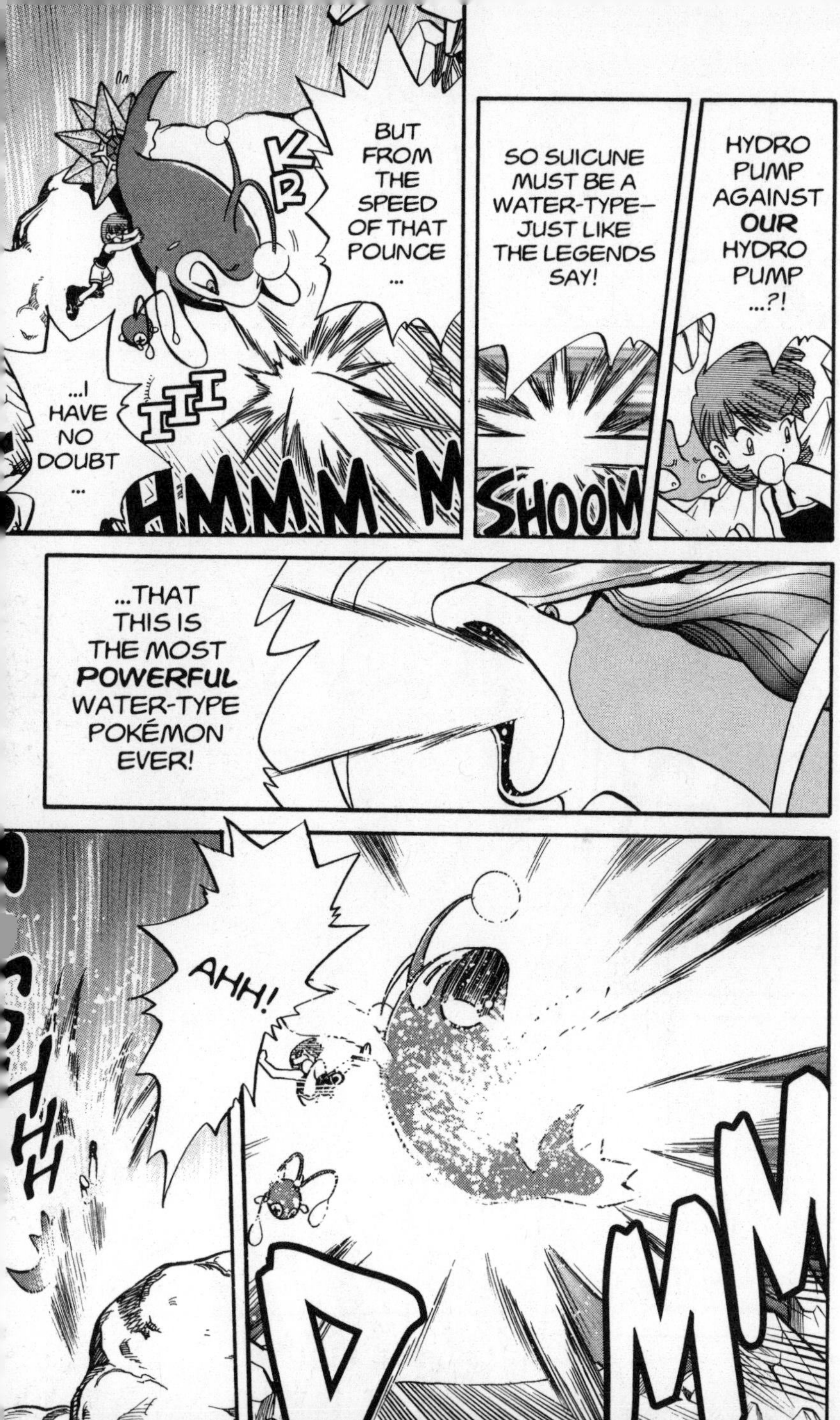
HYDRO PUMP AGAINST **OUR** HYDRO PUMP ...?!
SO SUICUNE MUST BE A WATER-TYPE— JUST LIKE THE LEGENDS SAY!
SHOOM
BUT FROM THE SPEED OF THAT POUNCE ...
KR
IIII
...I HAVE NO DOUBT ...
HMMMM M
...THAT THIS IS THE MOST **POWERFUL** WATER-TYPE POKÉMON EVER!
AHH!
D MMN

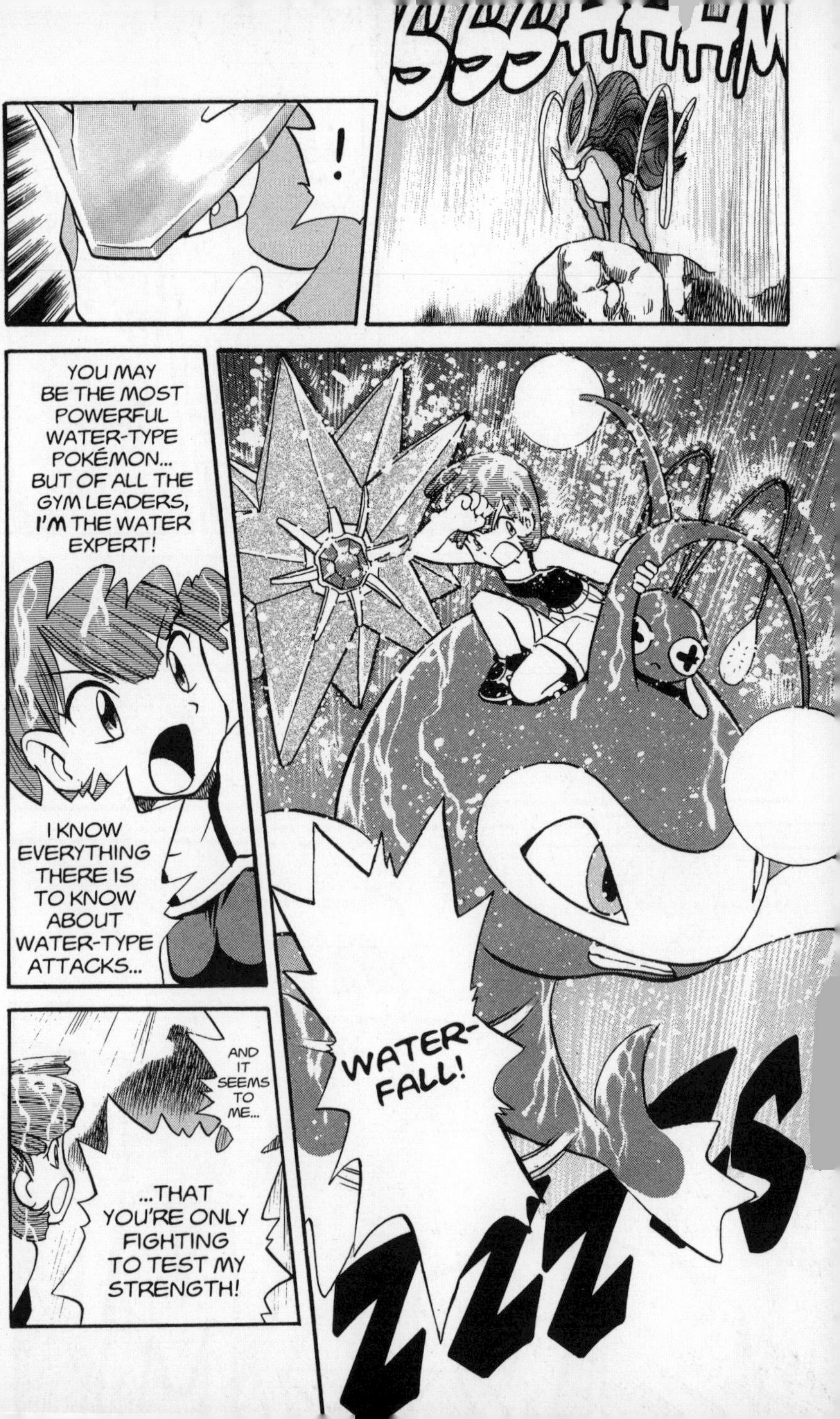
!
WATER-FALL!
ZZZSS
YOU MAY BE THE MOST POWERFUL WATER-TYPE POKÉMON... BUT OF ALL THE GYM LEADERS, I'M THE WATER EXPERT!
I KNOW EVERYTHING THERE IS TO KNOW ABOUT WATER-TYPE ATTACKS...
AND IT SEEMS TO ME...
...THAT YOU'RE ONLY FIGHTING TO TEST MY STRENGTH!

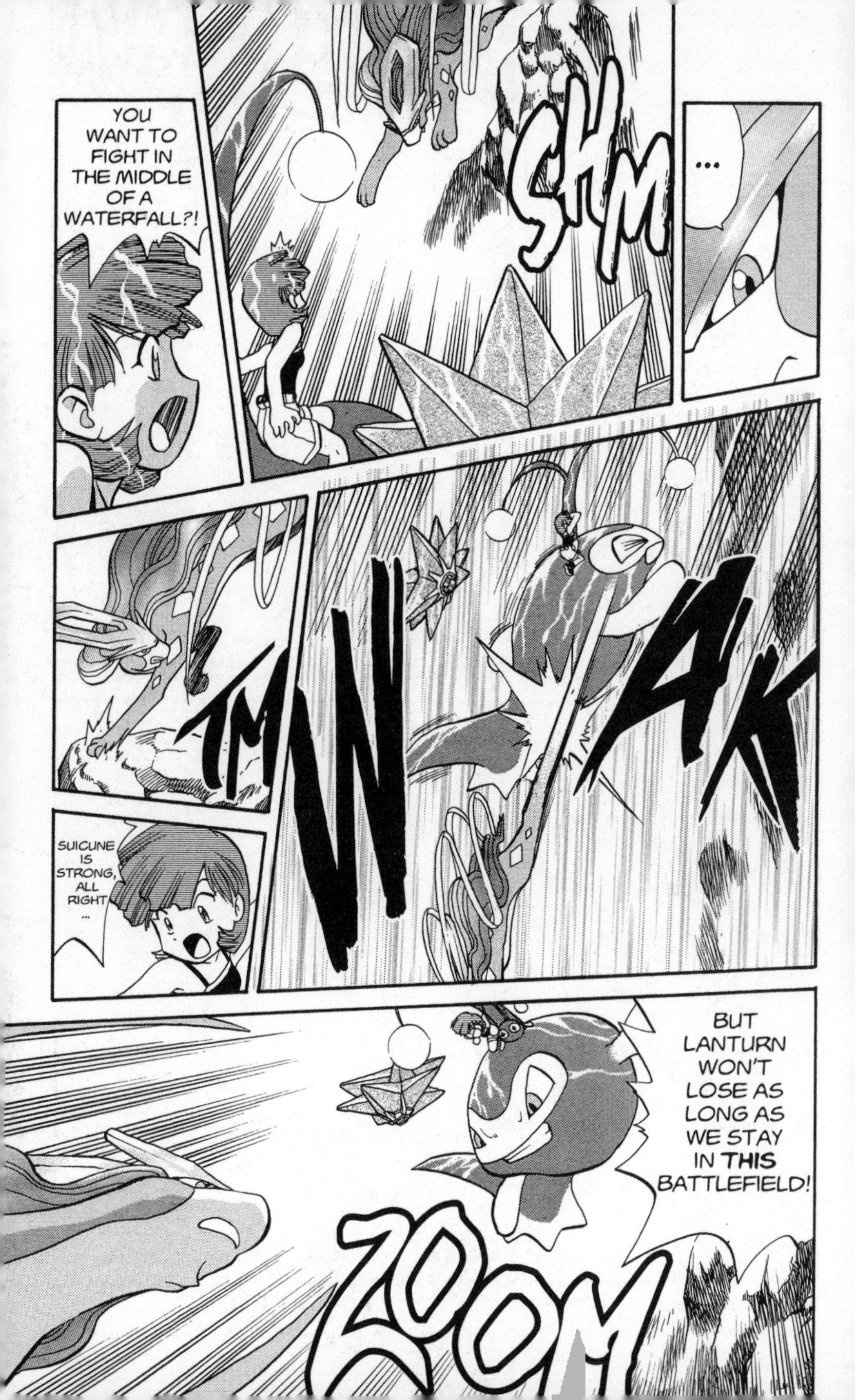
...
SHM
YOU WANT TO FIGHT IN THE MIDDLE OF A WATERFALL?!
THWAK
SUICUNE IS STRONG, ALL RIGHT...
BUT LANTURN WON'T LOSE AS LONG AS WE STAY IN **THIS** BATTLEFIELD!
ZOOM

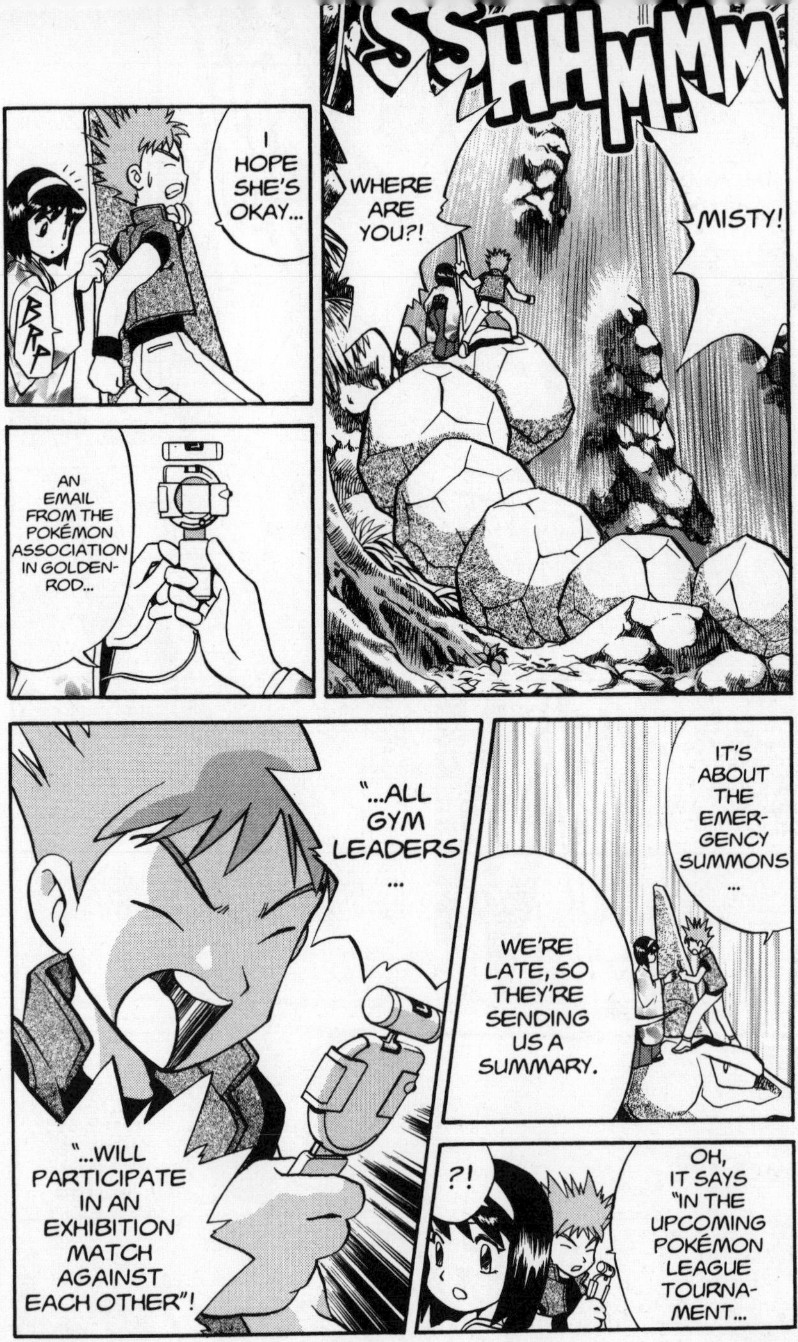
SSHHMMMM
MISTY!
WHERE ARE YOU?!
I HOPE SHE'S OKAY...
BRP
AN EMAIL FROM THE POKÉMON ASSOCIATION IN GOLDENROD...
IT'S ABOUT THE EMERGENCY SUMMONS...
WE'RE LATE, SO THEY'RE SENDING US A SUMMARY.
OH, IT SAYS "IN THE UPCOMING POKÉMON LEAGUE TOURNAMENT...
?!
"...ALL GYM LEADERS...
"...WILL PARTICIPATE IN AN EXHIBITION MATCH AGAINST EACH OTHER"!

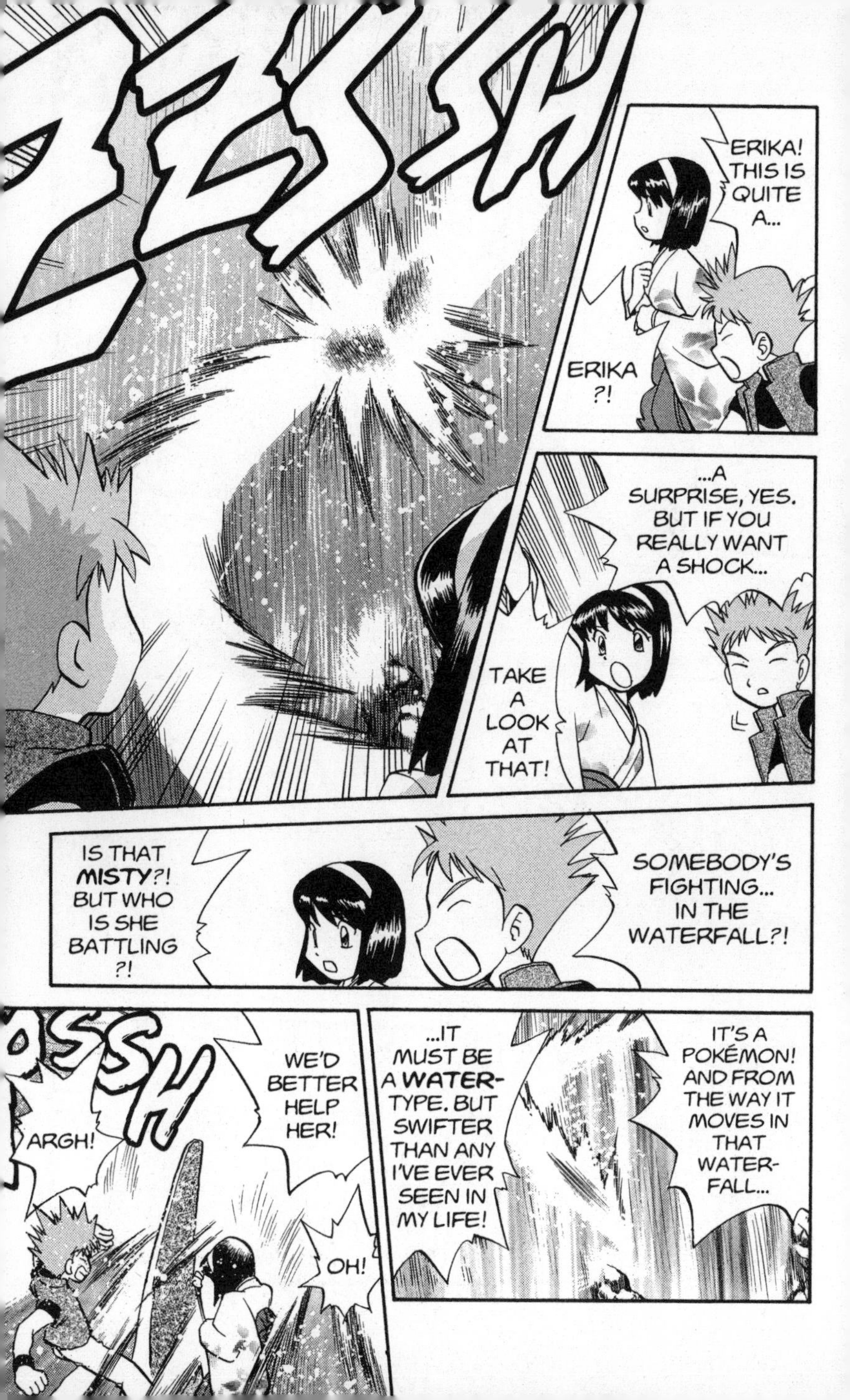
ERIKA! THIS IS QUITE A...
ERIKA ?!
...A SURPRISE, YES. BUT IF YOU REALLY WANT A SHOCK...
TAKE A LOOK AT THAT!
ZZSSH
SOMEBODY'S FIGHTING... IN THE WATERFALL?!
IS THAT **MISTY**?! BUT WHO IS SHE BATTLING ?!
IT'S A POKÉMON! AND FROM THE WAY IT MOVES IN THAT WATER-FALL...
...IT MUST BE A **WATER-**TYPE. BUT SWIFTER THAN ANY I'VE EVER SEEN IN MY LIFE!
WE'D BETTER HELP HER!
OSSH
ARGH!
OH!

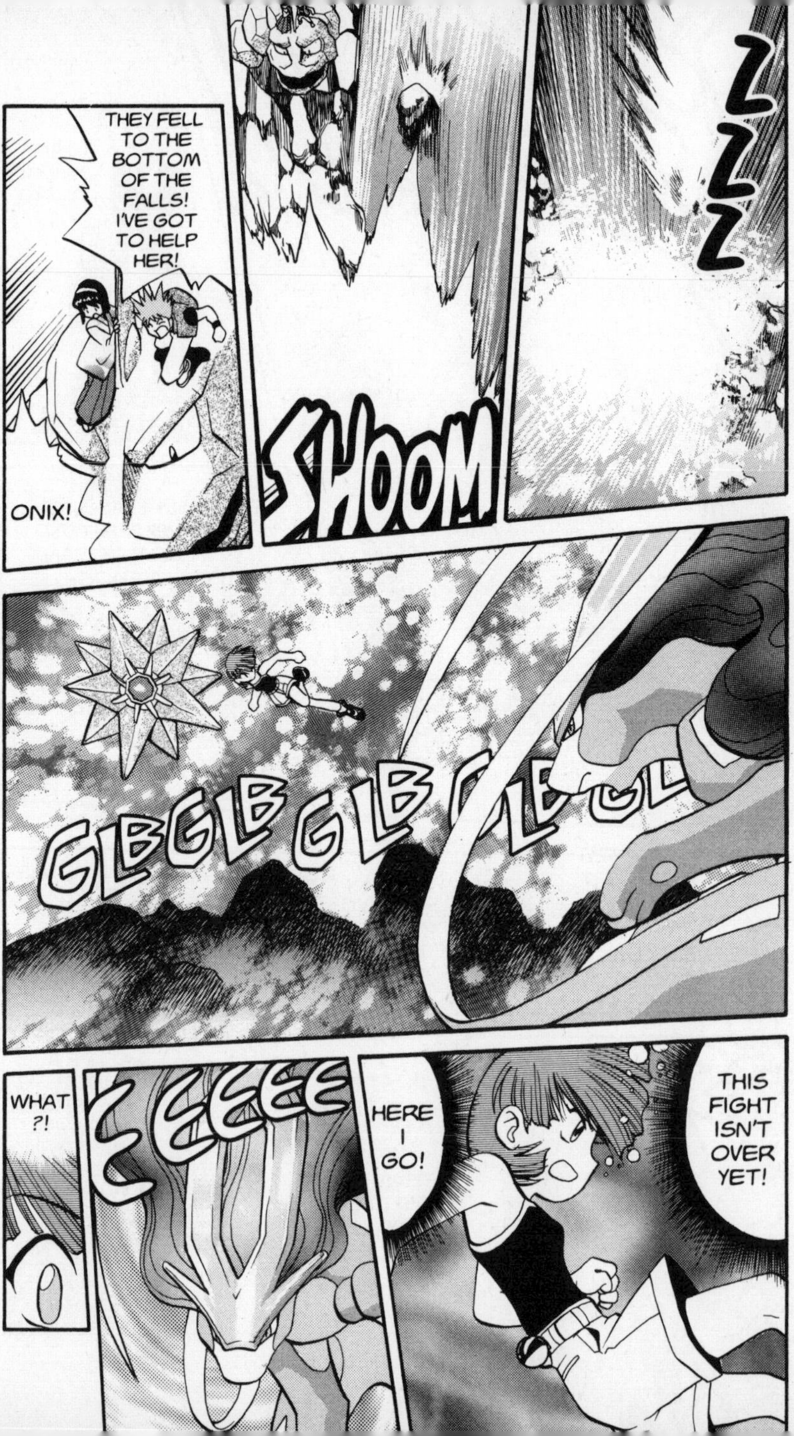
ZZZZ
SHOOM
THEY FELL TO THE BOTTOM OF THE FALLS! I'VE GOT TO HELP HER!
ONIX!
GLBGLB GLB GLB GL
THIS FIGHT ISN'T OVER YET!
HERE I GO!
EEEEE
WHAT?!

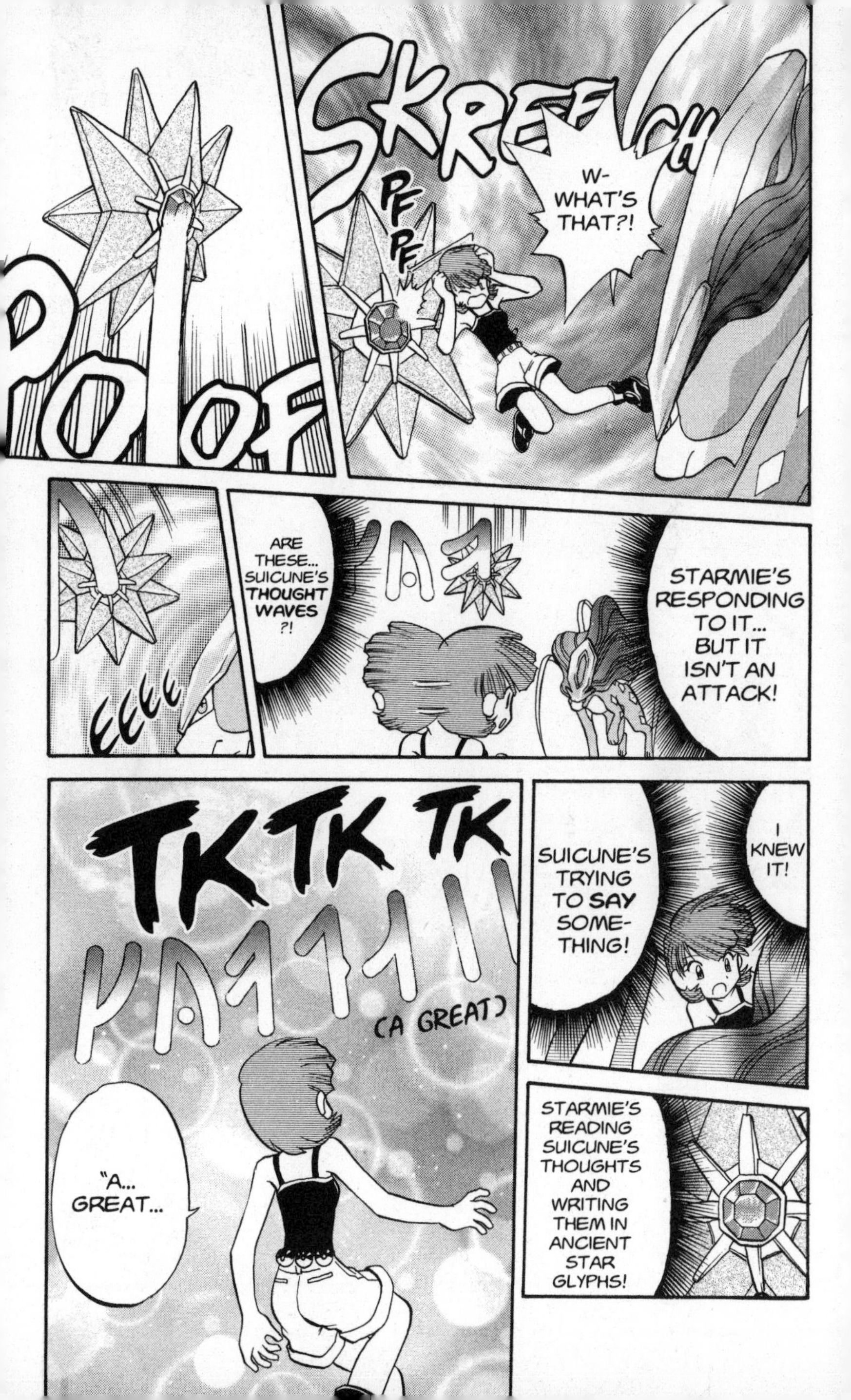
SKREEECH
PF PF
W- WHAT'S THAT?!
POOF
STARMIE'S RESPONDING TO IT... BUT IT ISN'T AN ATTACK!
ARE THESE... SUICUNE'S THOUGHT WAVES ?!
EEEE
I KNEW IT!
SUICUNE'S TRYING TO SAY SOME- THING!
STARMIE'S READING SUICUNE'S THOUGHTS AND WRITING THEM IN ANCIENT STAR GLYPHS!
TK TK TK
(A GREAT)
"A... GREAT...

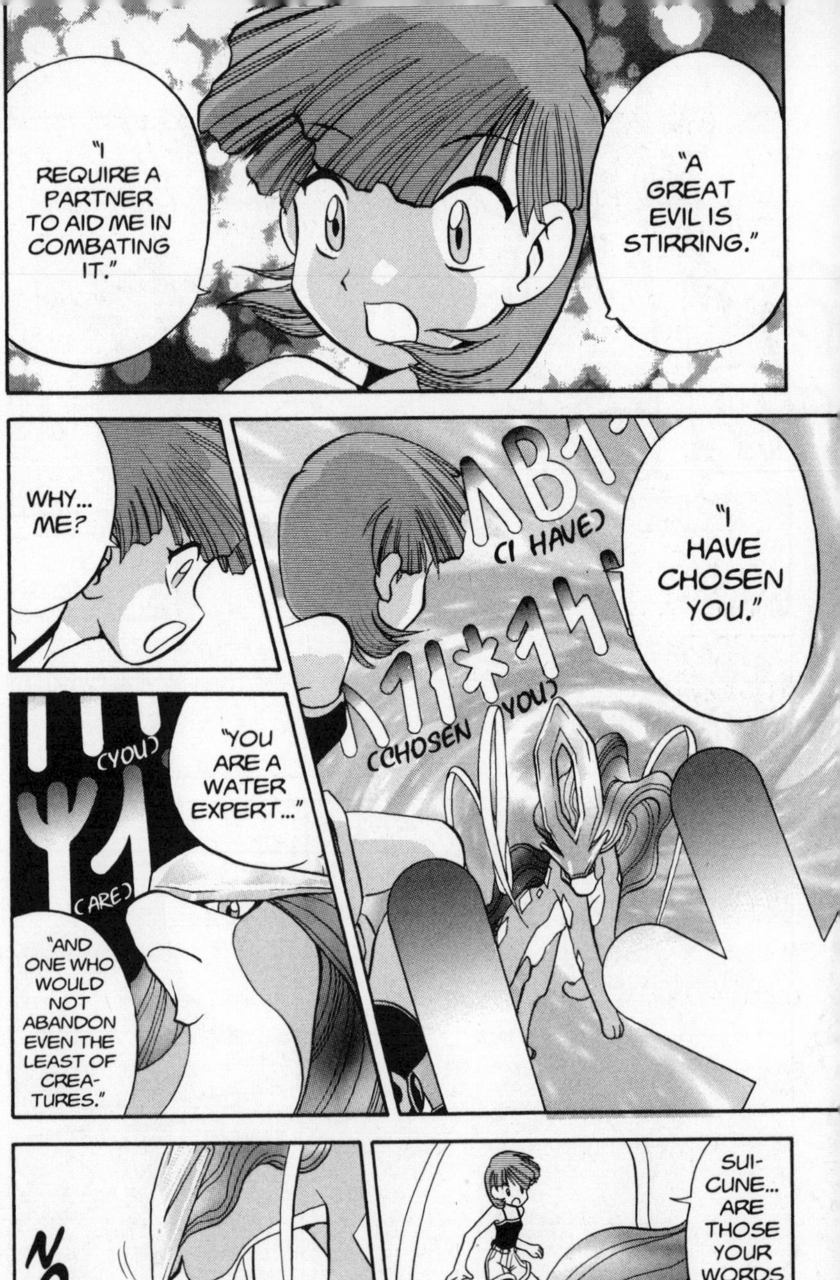
"A GREAT EVIL IS STIRRING."
"I REQUIRE A PARTNER TO AID ME IN COMBATING IT."
"I HAVE CHOSEN YOU."
(I HAVE)
(CHOSEN)
(YOU)
WHY... ME?
"YOU ARE A WATER EXPERT..."
(YOU)
(ARE)
"AND ONE WHO WOULD NOT ABANDON EVEN THE LEAST OF CREA-TURES."
SUI-CUNE... ARE THOSE YOUR WORDS?
NOD

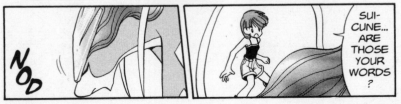

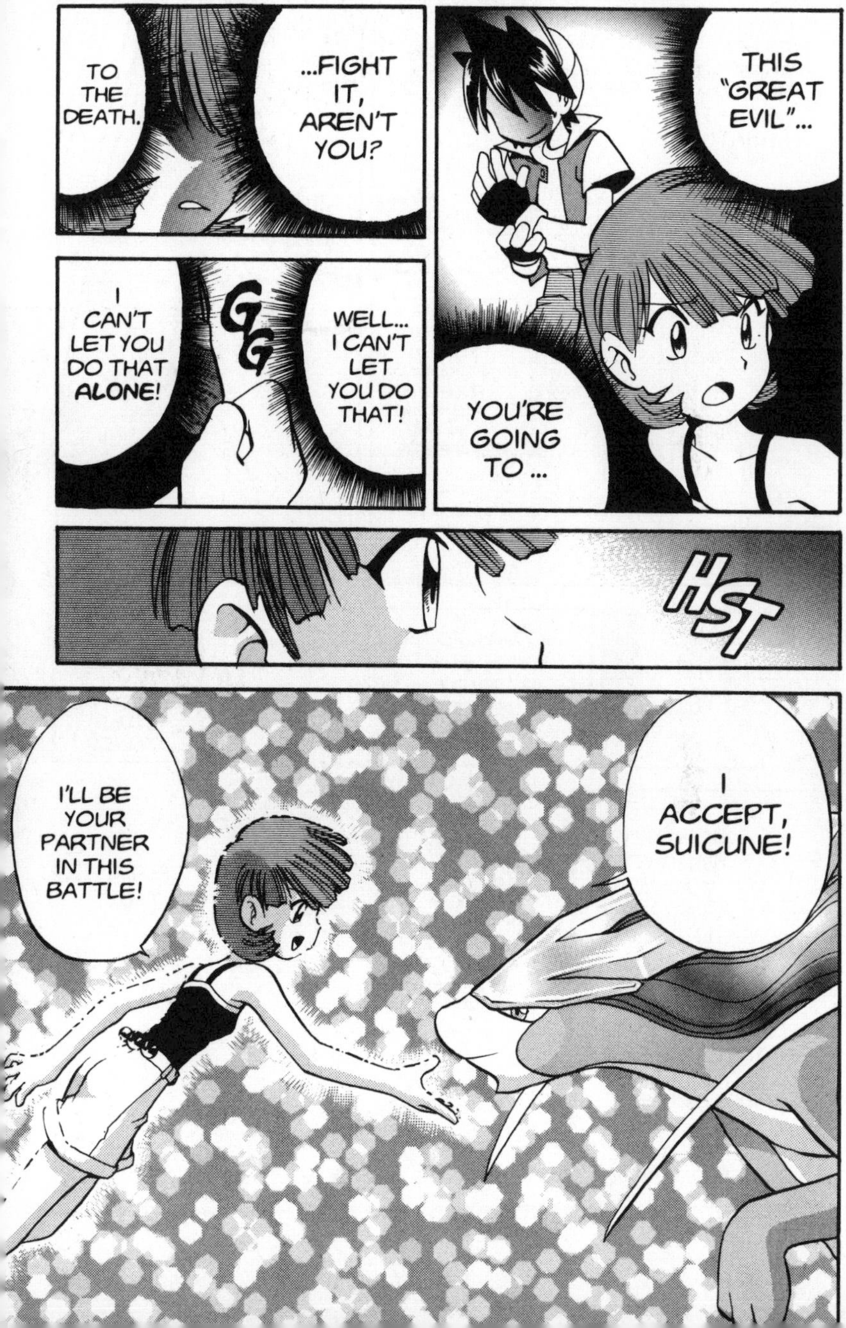
THIS "GREAT EVIL"...
YOU'RE GOING TO ...
...FIGHT IT, AREN'T YOU?
TO THE DEATH.
WELL... I CAN'T LET YOU DO THAT!
GG
I CAN'T LET YOU DO THAT ALONE!
HST
I ACCEPT, SUICUNE!
I'LL BE YOUR PARTNER IN THIS BATTLE!

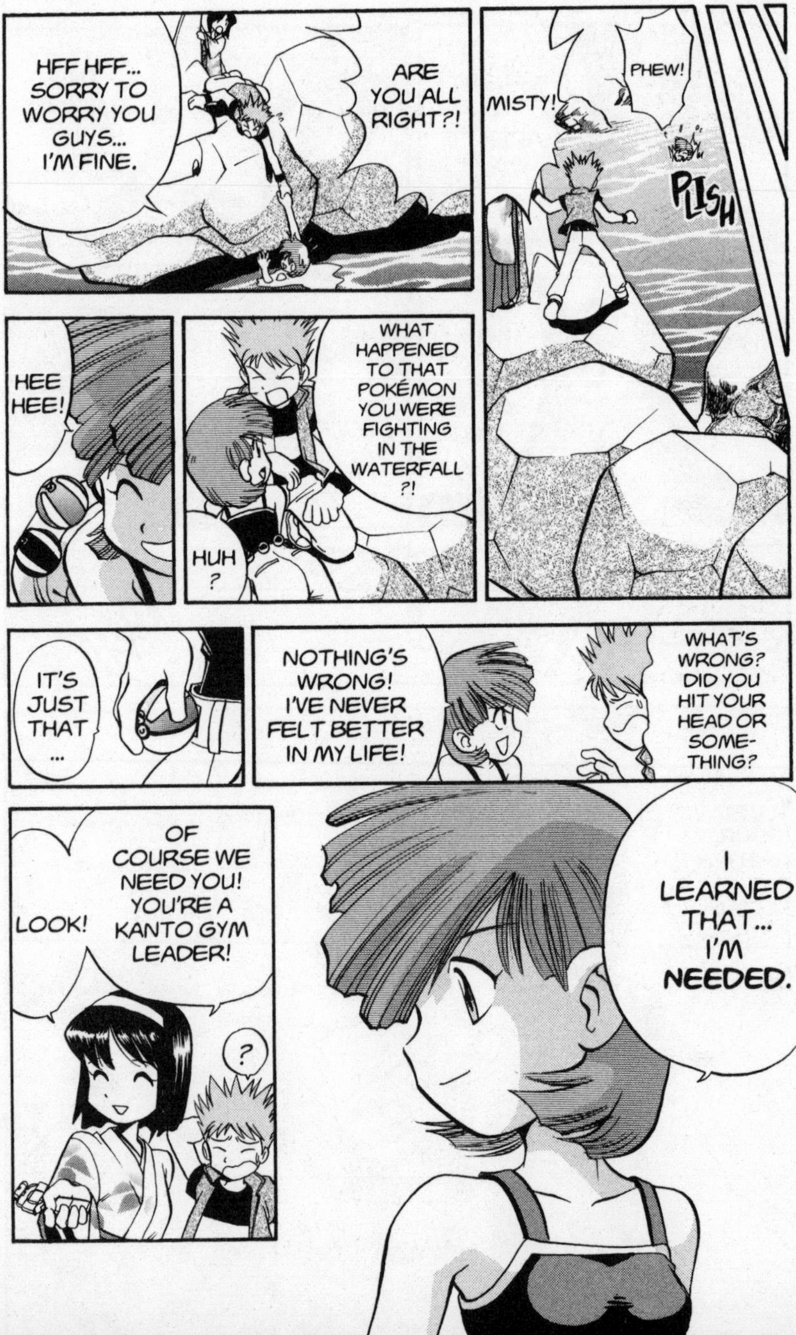
PHEW!
MISTY!
PLISH
ARE YOU ALL RIGHT?!
HFF HFF... SORRY TO WORRY YOU GUYS... I'M FINE.
WHAT HAPPENED TO THAT POKÉMON YOU WERE FIGHTING IN THE WATERFALL ?!
HUH ?
HEE HEE!
WHAT'S WRONG? DID YOU HIT YOUR HEAD OR SOME-THING?
NOTHING'S WRONG! I'VE NEVER FELT BETTER IN MY LIFE!
IT'S JUST THAT ...
I LEARNED THAT... I'M NEEDED.
OF COURSE WE NEED YOU! YOU'RE A KANTO GYM LEADER!
LOOK!
?

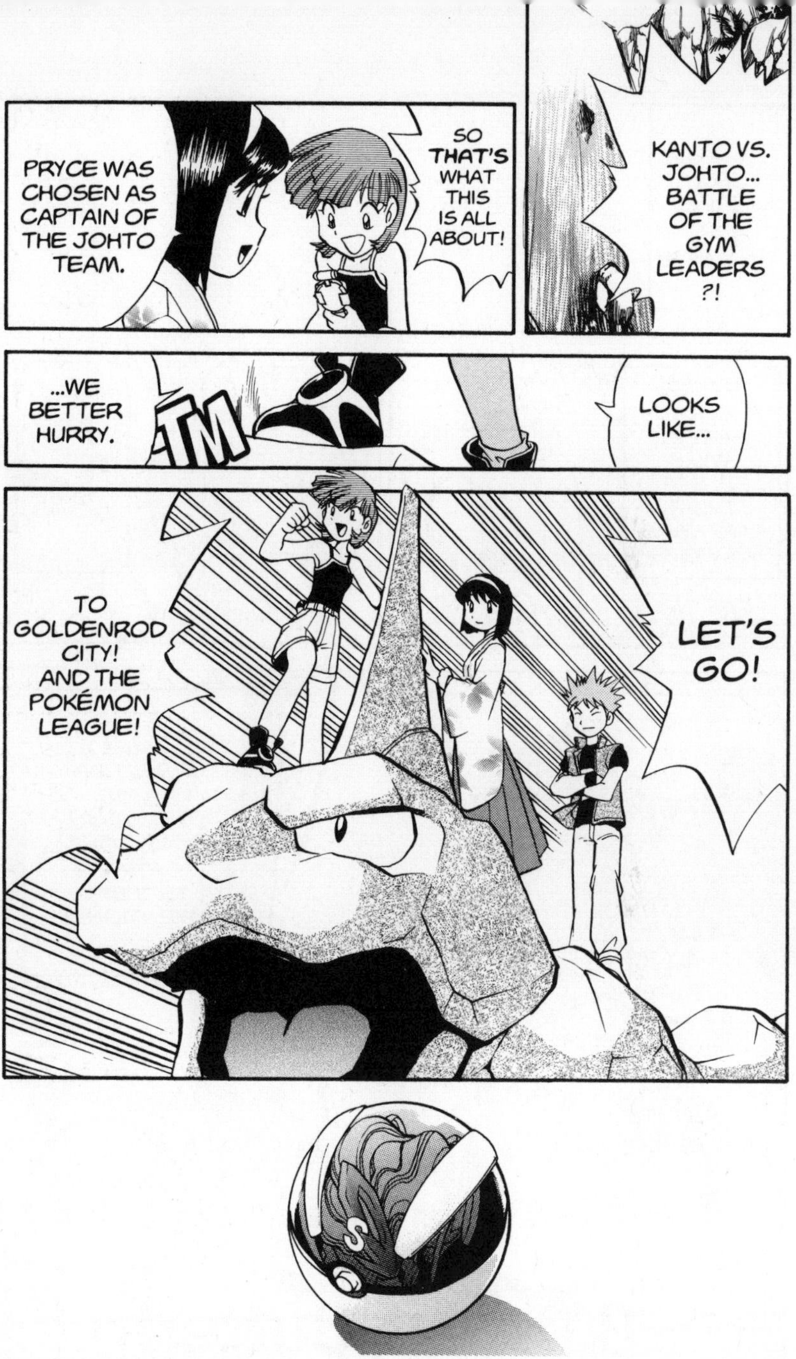
KANTO VS. JOHTO... BATTLE OF THE GYM LEADERS ?!
SO THAT'S WHAT THIS IS ALL ABOUT!
PRYCE WAS CHOSEN AS CAPTAIN OF THE JOHTO TEAM.
LOOKS LIKE...
...WE BETTER HURRY.
LET'S GO!
TO GOLDENROD CITY! AND THE POKÉMON LEAGUE!

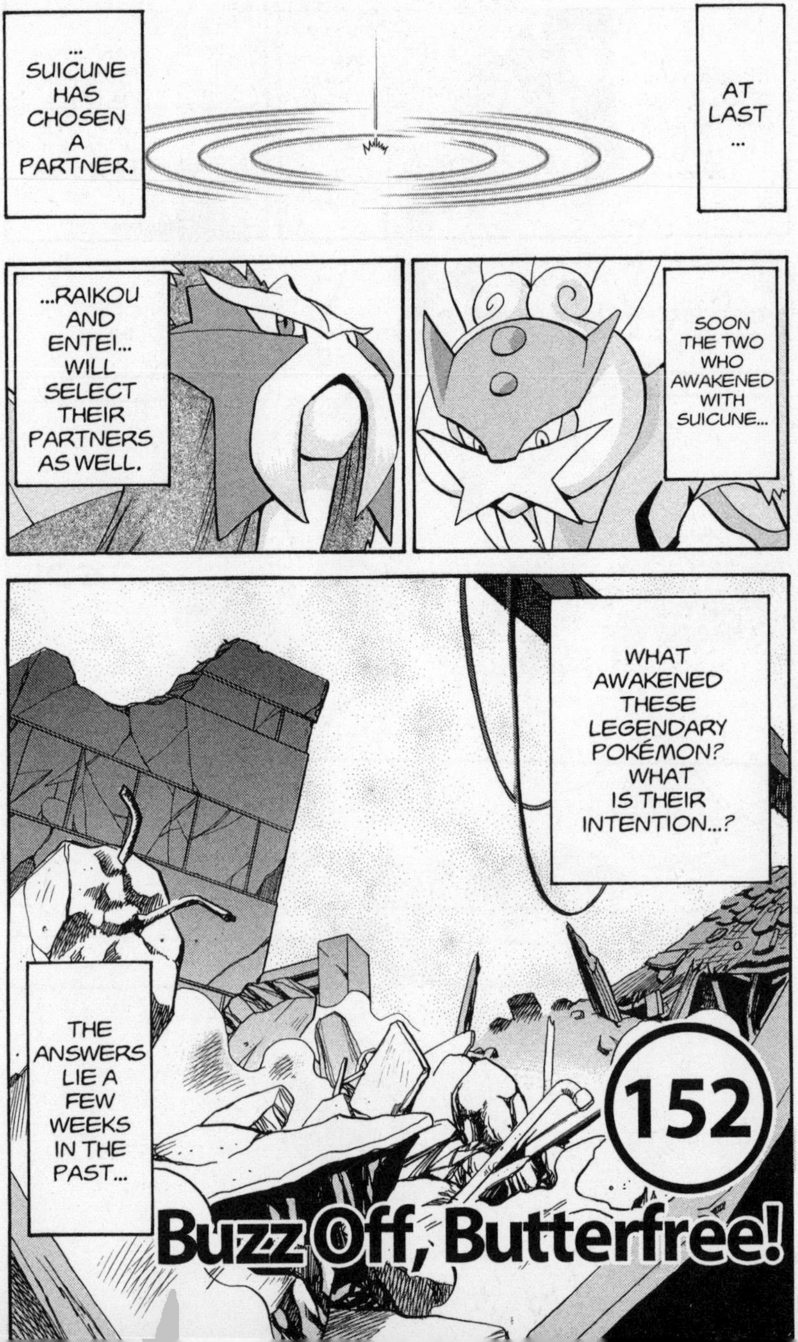
AT LAST ...
... SUICUNE HAS CHOSEN A PARTNER.
SOON THE TWO WHO AWAKENED WITH SUICUNE...
...RAIKOU AND ENTEI... WILL SELECT THEIR PARTNERS AS WELL.
WHAT AWAKENED THESE LEGENDARY POKÉMON? WHAT IS THEIR INTENTION...?
THE ANSWERS LIE A FEW WEEKS IN THE PAST...
152
Buzz Off, Butterfree!

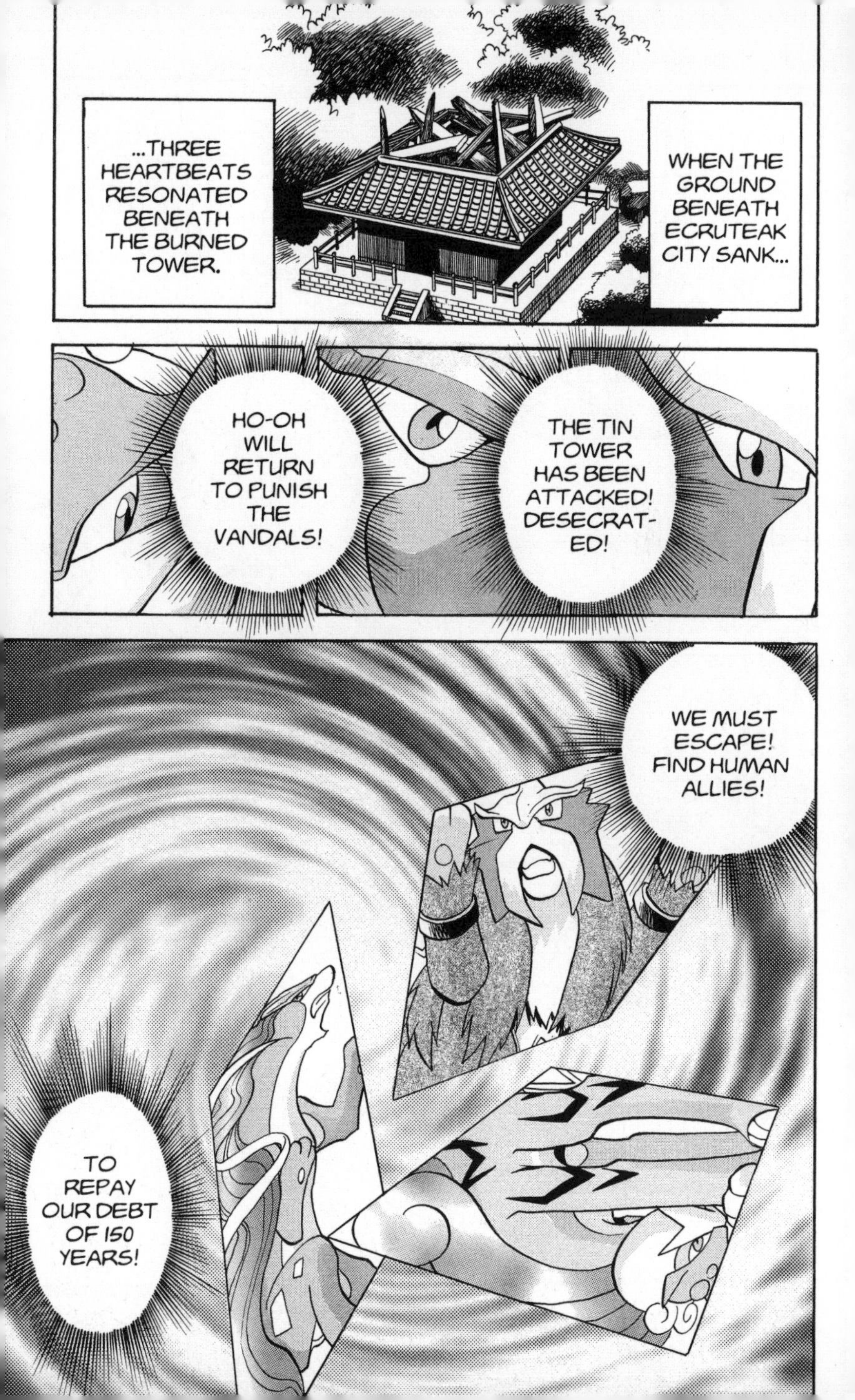
WHEN THE GROUND BENEATH ECRUTEAK CITY SANK...
...THREE HEARTBEATS RESONATED BENEATH THE BURNED TOWER.
THE TIN TOWER HAS BEEN ATTACKED! DESECRAT-ED!
HO-OH WILL RETURN TO PUNISH THE VANDALS!
WE MUST ESCAPE! FIND HUMAN ALLIES!
TO REPAY OUR DEBT OF 150 YEARS!

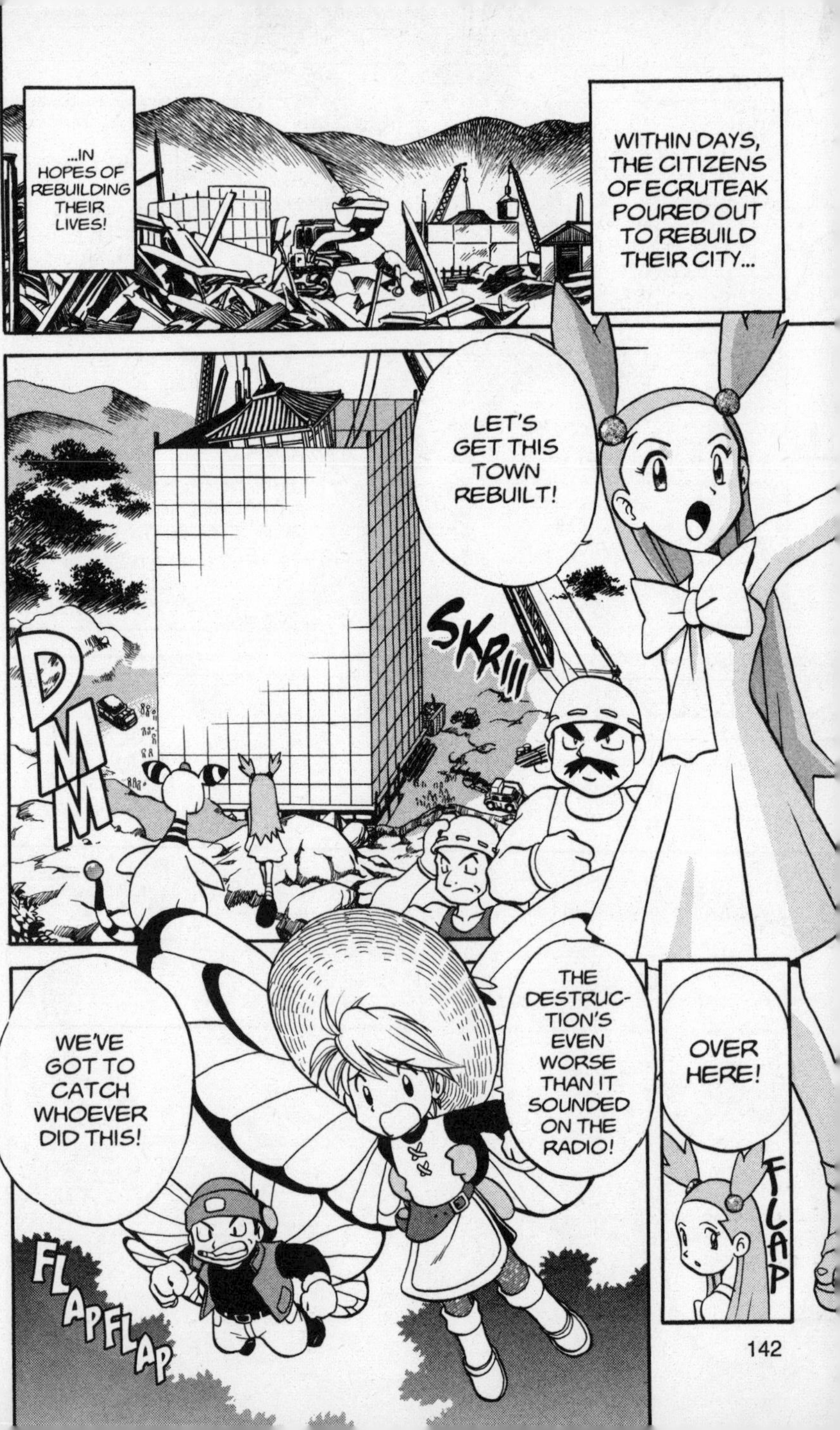
WITHIN DAYS, THE CITIZENS OF ECRUTEAK POURED OUT TO REBUILD THEIR CITY...
...IN HOPES OF REBUILDING THEIR LIVES!
LET'S GET THIS TOWN REBUILT!
SKRIII
DMM
OVER HERE!
FLAP
THE DESTRUC-TION'S EVEN WORSE THAN IT SOUNDED ON THE RADIO!
WE'VE GOT TO CATCH WHOEVER DID THIS!
FLAPFLAP

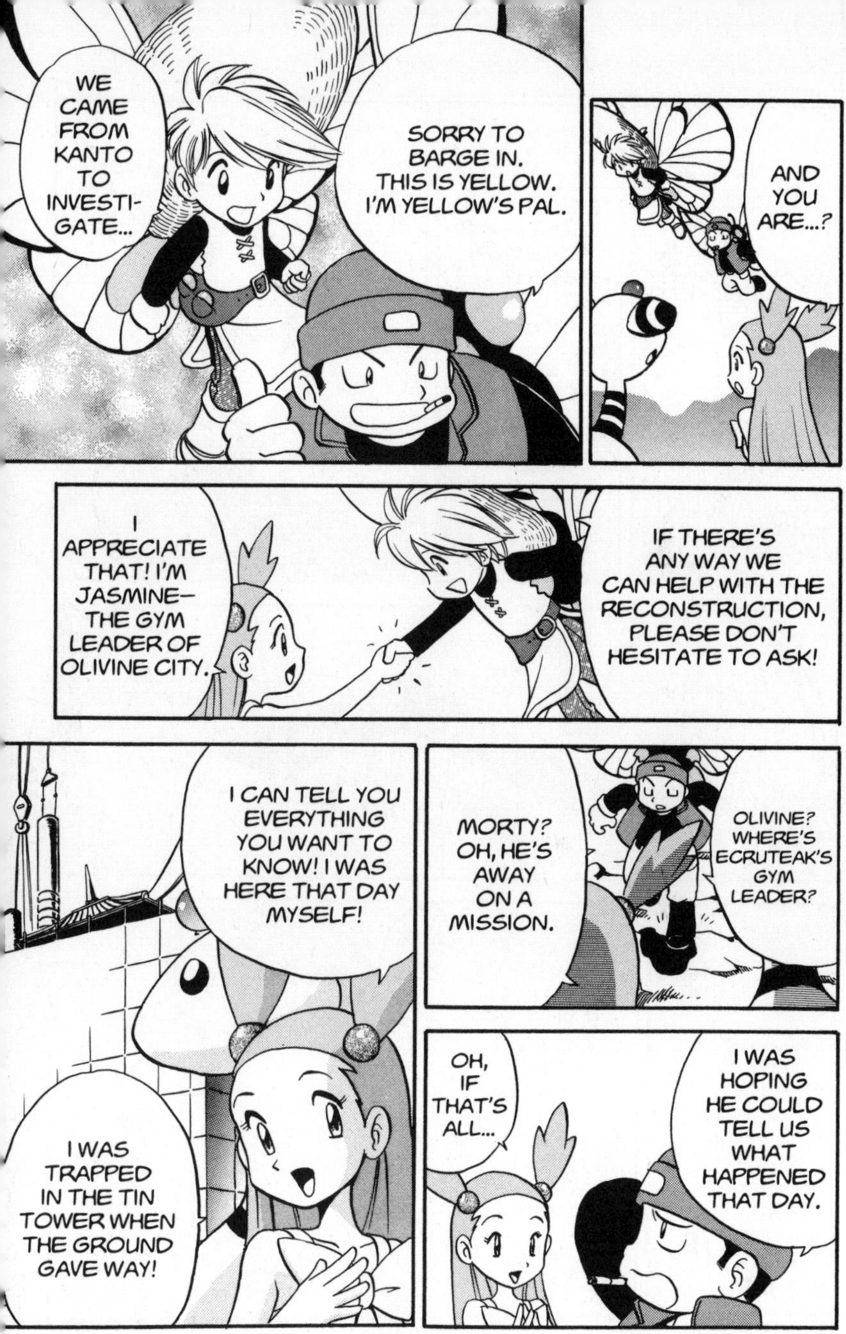
AND YOU ARE...?
SORRY TO BARGE IN. THIS IS YELLOW. I'M YELLOW'S PAL.
WE CAME FROM KANTO TO INVESTI-GATE...
IF THERE'S ANY WAY WE CAN HELP WITH THE RECONSTRUCTION, PLEASE DON'T HESITATE TO ASK!
I APPRECIATE THAT! I'M JASMINE—THE GYM LEADER OF OLIVINE CITY.
OLIVINE? WHERE'S ECRUTEAK'S GYM LEADER?
MORTY? OH, HE'S AWAY ON A MISSION.
I WAS HOPING HE COULD TELL US WHAT HAPPENED THAT DAY.
OH, IF THAT'S ALL...
I CAN TELL YOU EVERYTHING YOU WANT TO KNOW! I WAS HERE THAT DAY MYSELF!
I WAS TRAPPED IN THE TIN TOWER WHEN THE GROUND GAVE WAY!

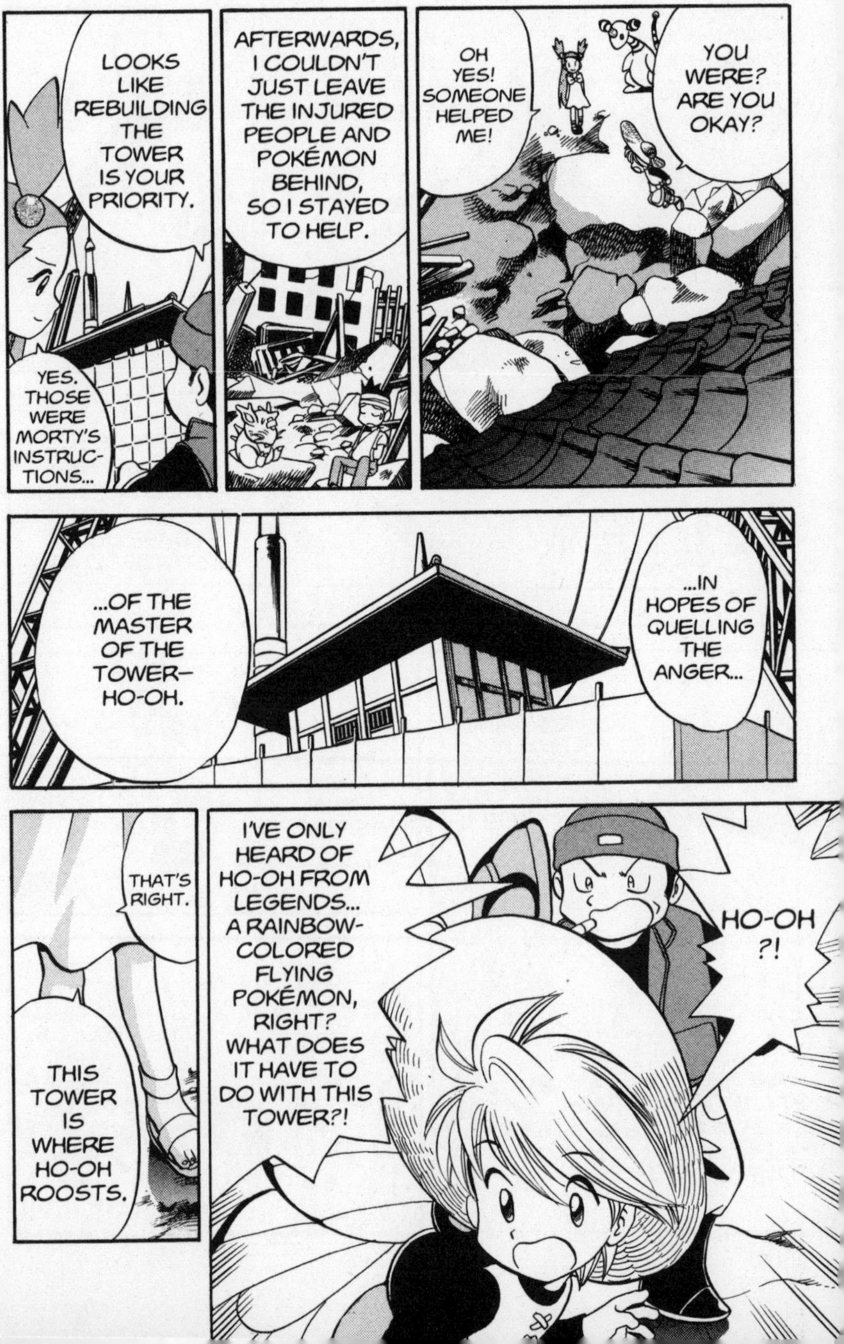
YOU WERE? ARE YOU OKAY?
OH YES! SOMEONE HELPED ME!
AFTERWARDS, I COULDN'T JUST LEAVE THE INJURED PEOPLE AND POKÉMON BEHIND, SO I STAYED TO HELP.
LOOKS LIKE REBUILDING THE TOWER IS YOUR PRIORITY.
YES. THOSE WERE MORTY'S INSTRUCTIONS...
...IN HOPES OF QUELLING THE ANGER...
...OF THE MASTER OF THE TOWER— HO-OH.
HO-OH ?!
I'VE ONLY HEARD OF HO-OH FROM LEGENDS... A RAINBOW-COLORED FLYING POKÉMON, RIGHT? WHAT DOES IT HAVE TO DO WITH THIS TOWER?!
THAT'S RIGHT.
THIS TOWER IS WHERE HO-OH ROOSTS.

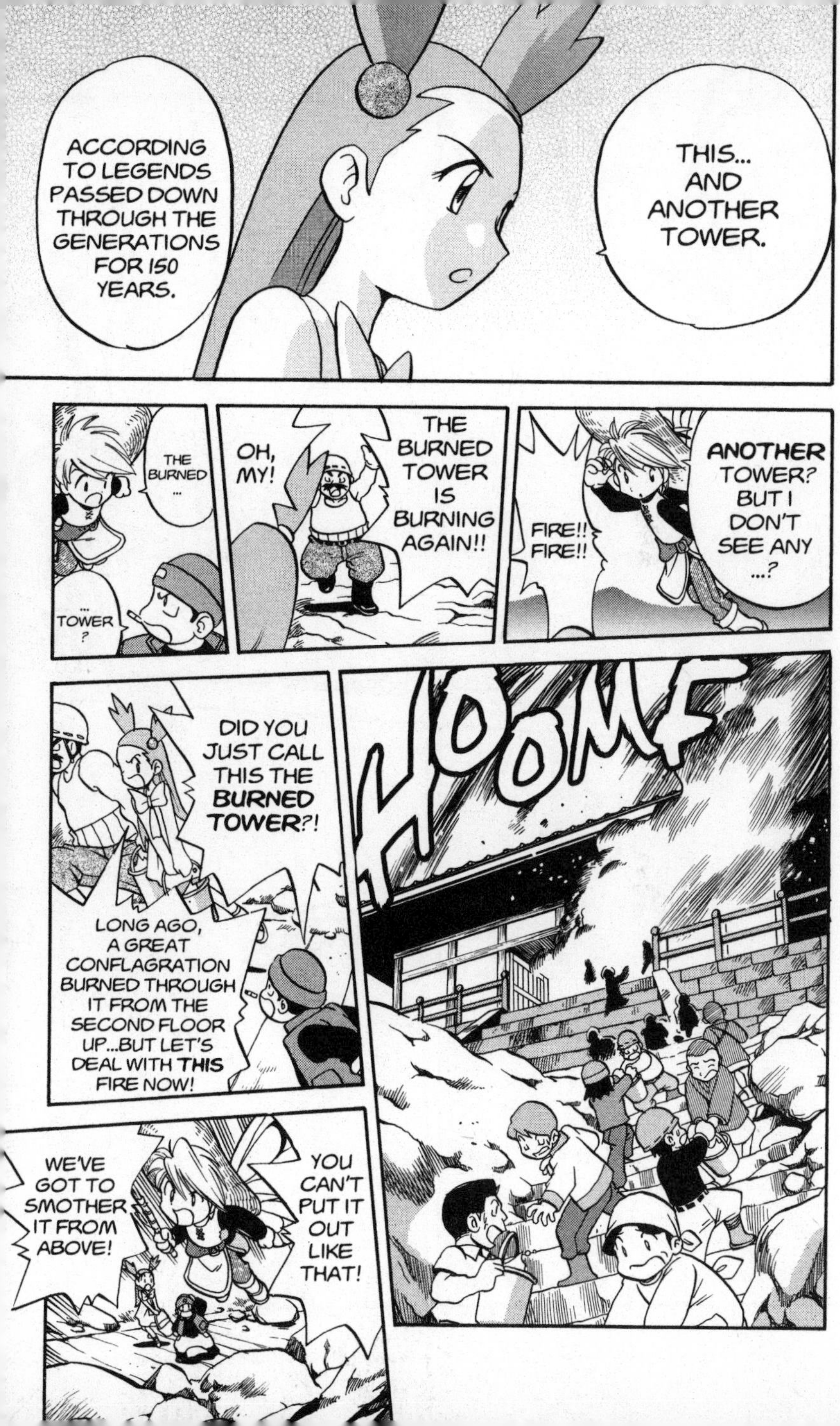
ACCORDING TO LEGENDS PASSED DOWN THROUGH THE GENERATIONS FOR 150 YEARS.
THIS... AND ANOTHER TOWER.
THE BURNED ...
... TOWER ?
OH, MY!
THE BURNED TOWER IS BURNING AGAIN!!
FIRE!! FIRE!!
ANOTHER TOWER? BUT I DON'T SEE ANY ...?
DID YOU JUST CALL THIS THE BURNED TOWER?!
LONG AGO, A GREAT CONFLAGRATION BURNED THROUGH IT FROM THE SECOND FLOOR UP...BUT LET'S DEAL WITH THIS FIRE NOW!
WHOOMF
WE'VE GOT TO SMOTHER IT FROM ABOVE!
YOU CAN'T PUT IT OUT LIKE THAT!

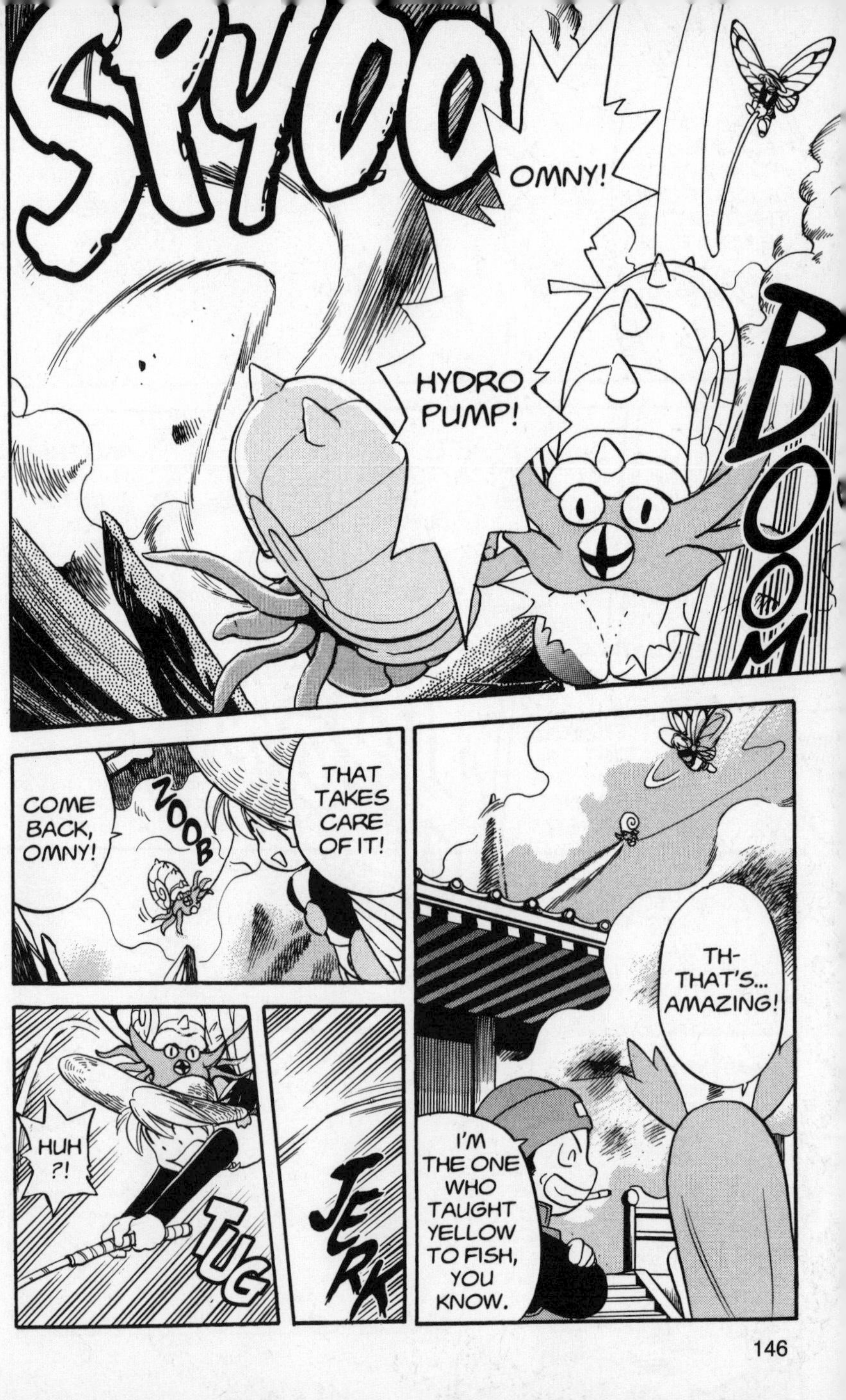
SPYOO
OMNY!
BOOM
HYDRO PUMP!
TH- THAT'S... AMAZING!
I'M THE ONE WHO TAUGHT YELLOW TO FISH, YOU KNOW.
THAT TAKES CARE OF IT!
ZOOB
COME BACK, OMNY!
JERK
HUH ?!
TUG

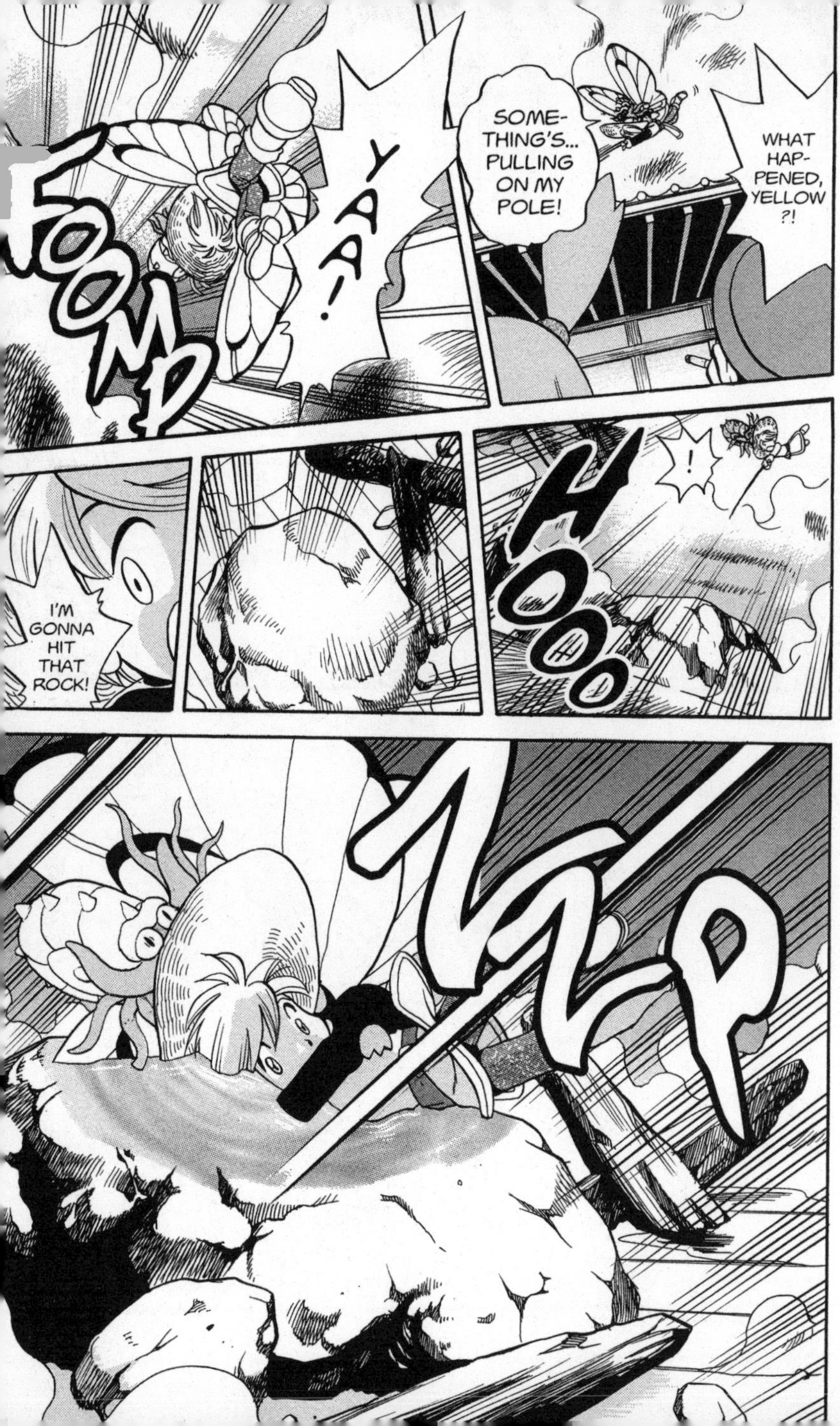
WHAT HAPPENED, YELLOW?!
SOMETHING'S... PULLING ON MY POLE!
YAA!
FOOMP
!
HOOO
I'M GONNA HIT THAT ROCK!

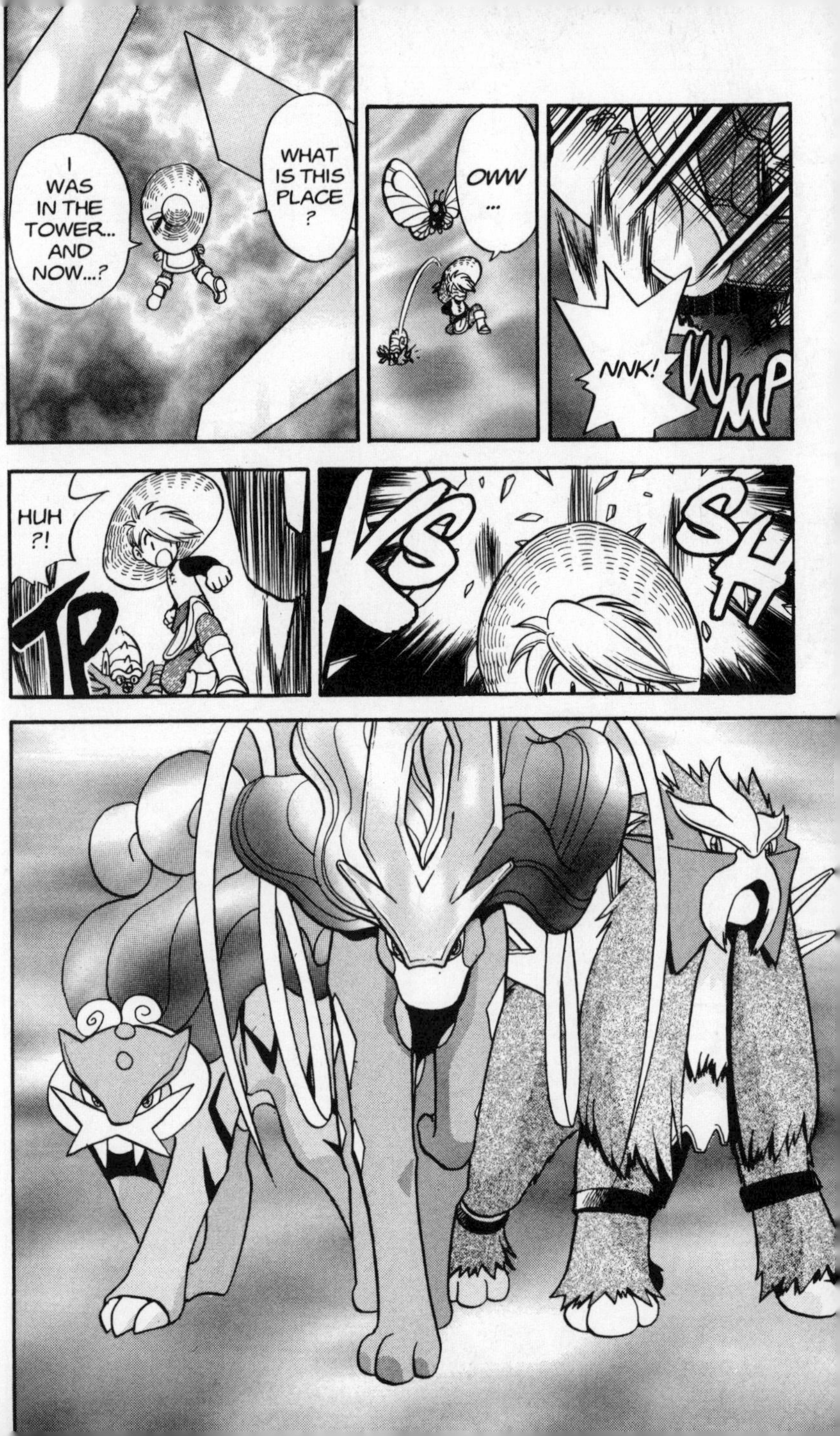
WMP
NNK!
OWW ...
WHAT IS THIS PLACE ?
I WAS IN THE TOWER.. AND NOW...?
KS
SH
HUH ?!
TP

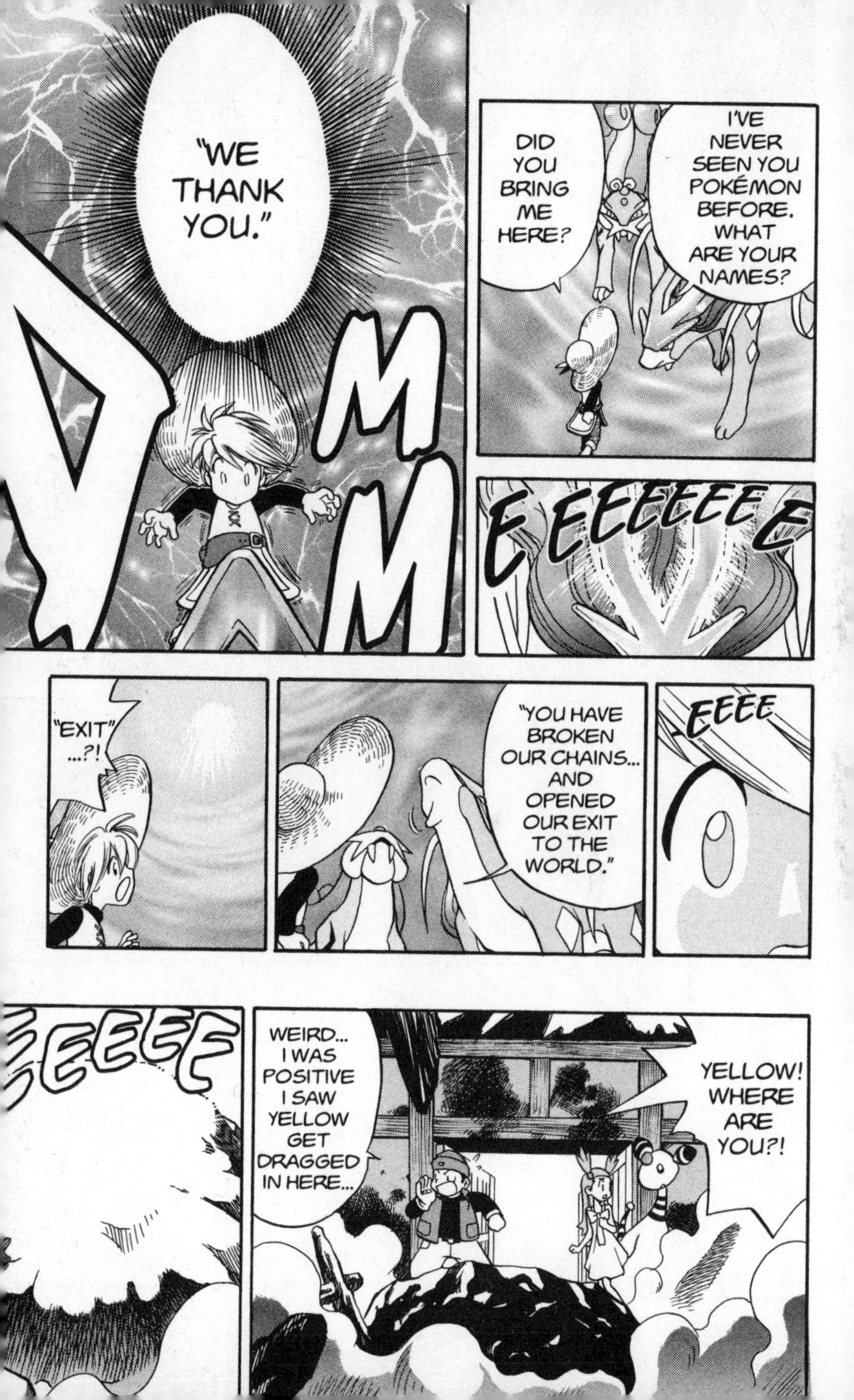

I'VE NEVER SEEN YOU POKÉMON BEFORE. WHAT ARE YOUR NAMES?
DID YOU BRING ME HERE?
EEEEEEEEE
"WE THANK YOU."
MMMM
EEEE
"YOU HAVE BROKEN OUR CHAINS... AND OPENED OUR EXIT TO THE WORLD."
"EXIT" ...?!
YELLOW! WHERE ARE YOU?!
WEIRD... I WAS POSITIVE I SAW YELLOW GET DRAGGED IN HERE...
EEEEE

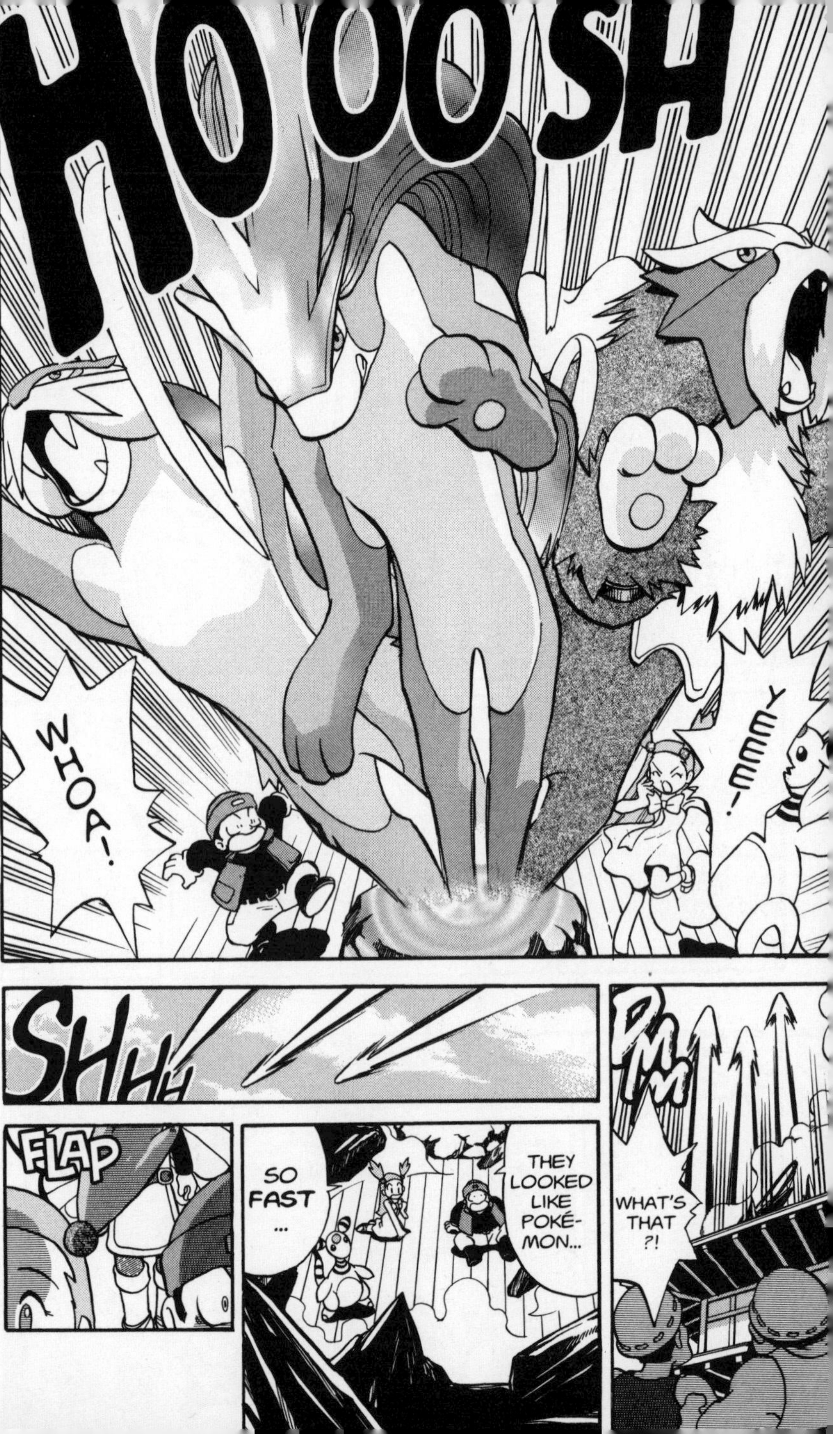
HOOOSH
YEEEE-!
WHOA!
DMM
SHHH
WHAT'S THAT ?!
THEY LOOKED LIKE POKÉ-MON...
SO FAST ...
FLAP

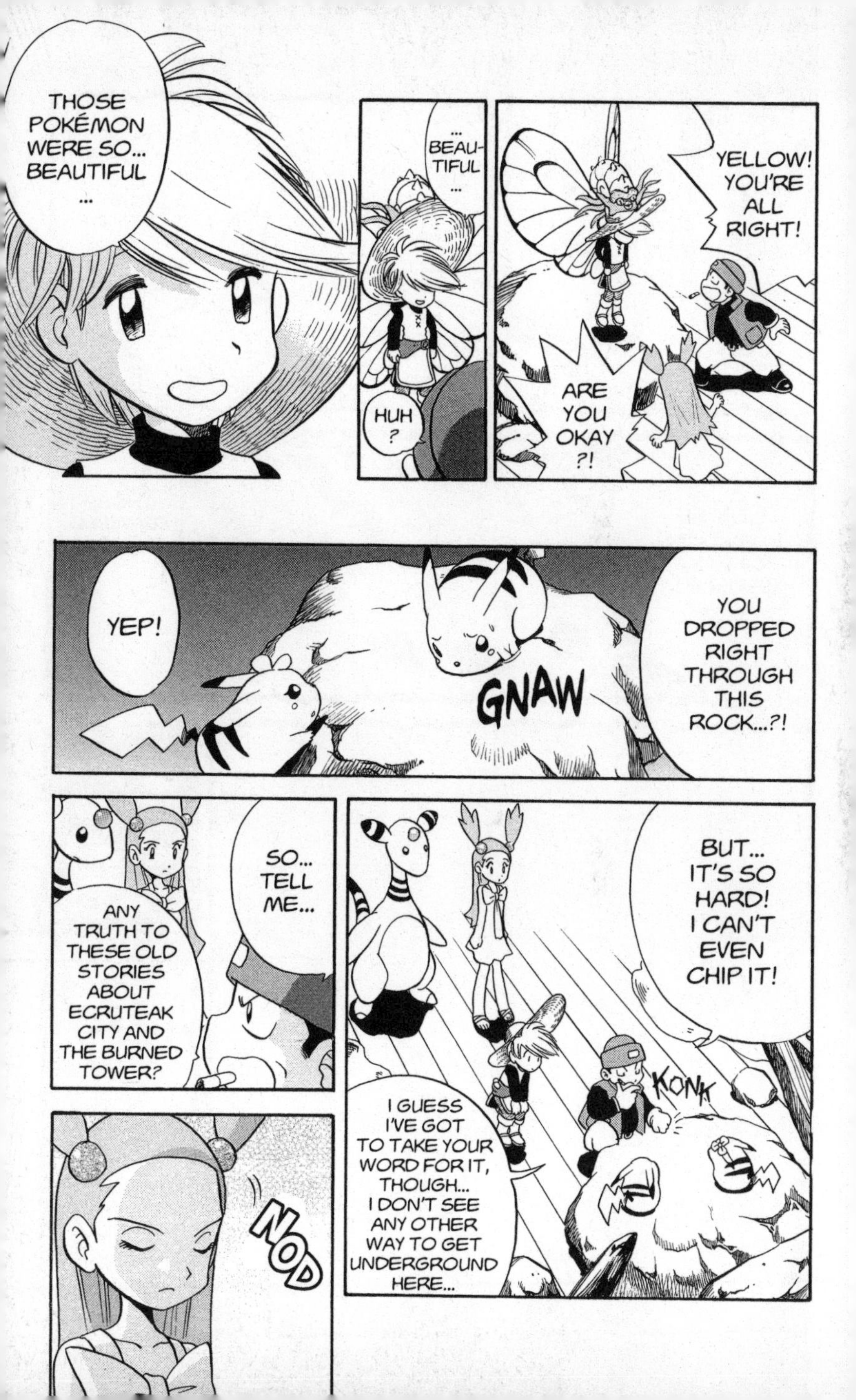
YELLOW! YOU'RE ALL RIGHT!
ARE YOU OKAY?!
... BEAUTIFUL ...
HUH?
THOSE POKÉMON WERE SO... BEAUTIFUL ...
YOU DROPPED RIGHT THROUGH THIS ROCK...?!
GNAW
YEP!
BUT... IT'S SO HARD! I CAN'T EVEN CHIP IT!
KONK
I GUESS I'VE GOT TO TAKE YOUR WORD FOR IT, THOUGH... I DON'T SEE ANY OTHER WAY TO GET UNDERGROUND HERE...
SO... TELL ME...
ANY TRUTH TO THESE OLD STORIES ABOUT ECRUTEAK CITY AND THE BURNED TOWER?
NOD

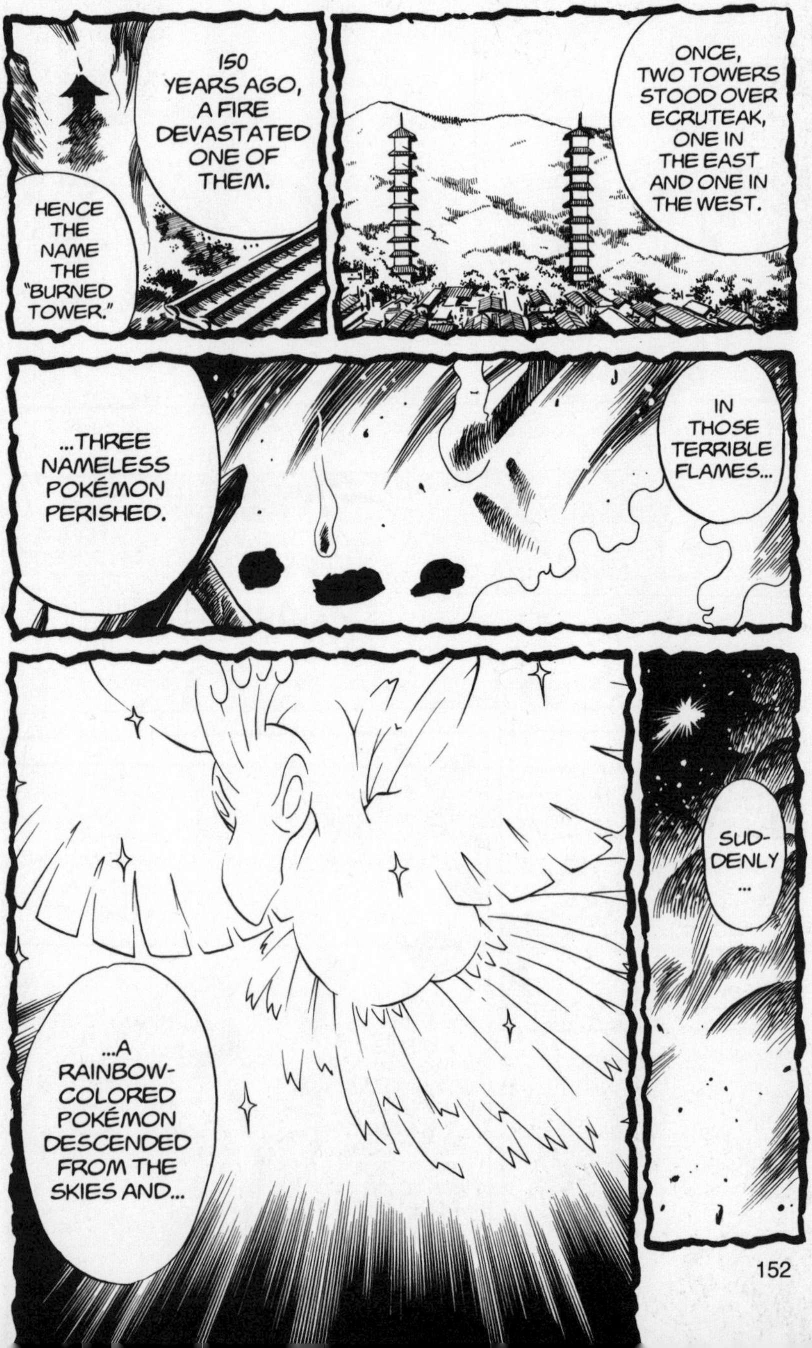
ONCE, TWO TOWERS STOOD OVER ECRUTEAK, ONE IN THE EAST AND ONE IN THE WEST.
150 YEARS AGO, A FIRE DEVASTATED ONE OF THEM.
HENCE THE NAME THE "BURNED TOWER."
IN THOSE TERRIBLE FLAMES...
...THREE NAMELESS POKÉMON PERISHED.
SUD-DENLY...
...A RAINBOW-COLORED POKÉMON DESCENDED FROM THE SKIES AND...

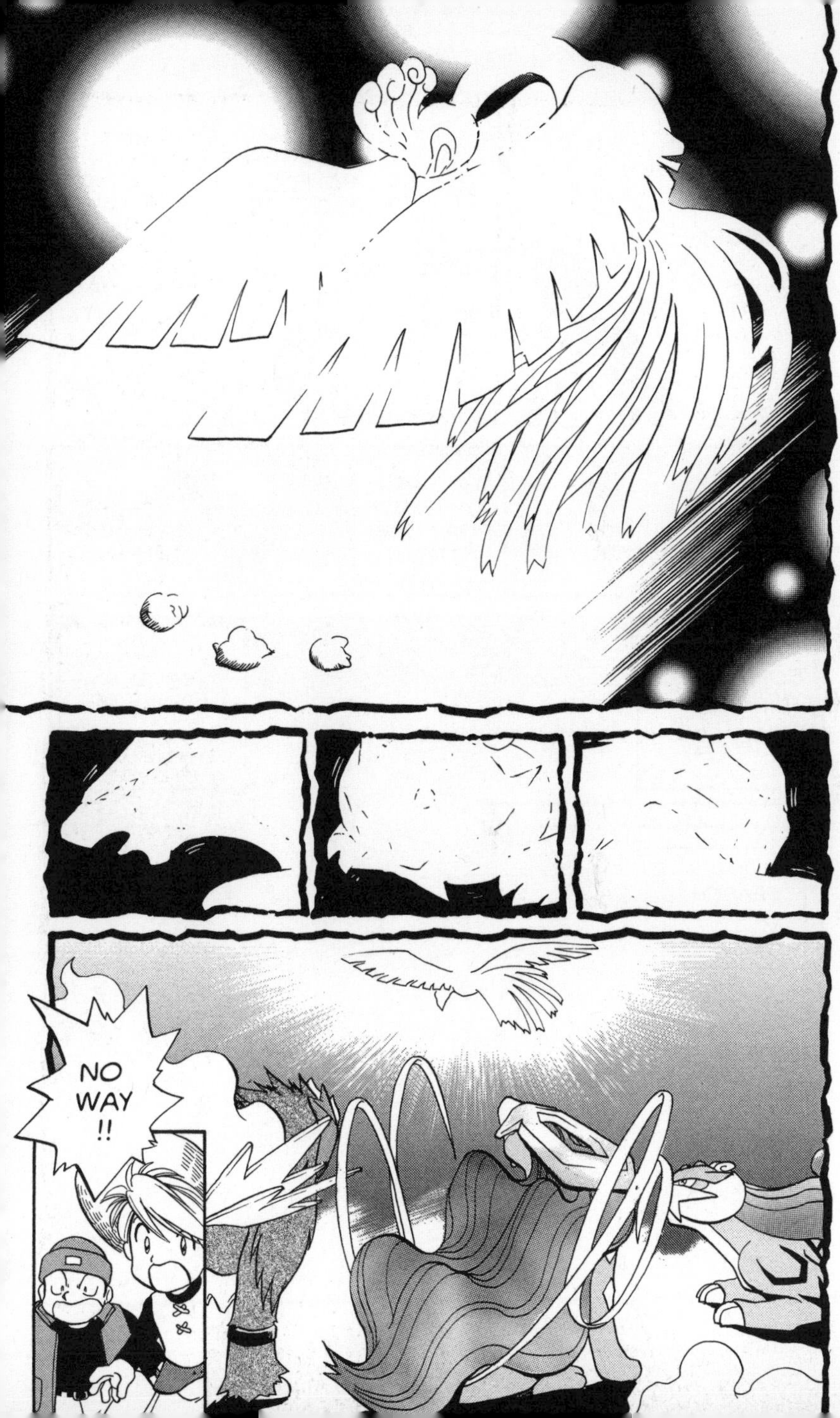
NO WAY !!

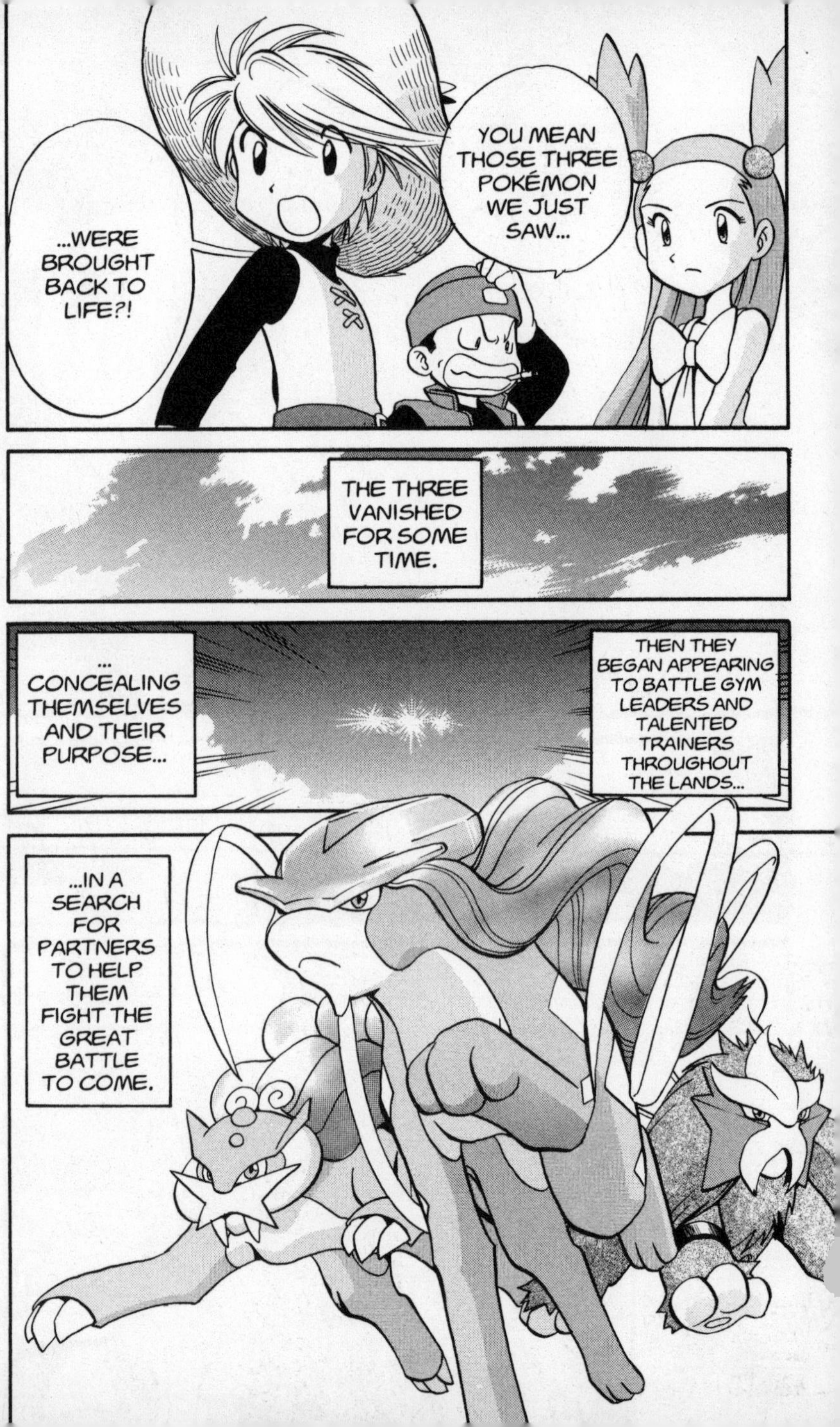
YOU MEAN THOSE THREE POKÉMON WE JUST SAW...
...WERE BROUGHT BACK TO LIFE?!
THE THREE VANISHED FOR SOME TIME.
THEN THEY BEGAN APPEARING TO BATTLE GYM LEADERS AND TALENTED TRAINERS THROUGHOUT THE LANDS...
...CONCEALING THEMSELVES AND THEIR PURPOSE...
...IN A SEARCH FOR PARTNERS TO HELP THEM FIGHT THE GREAT BATTLE TO COME.

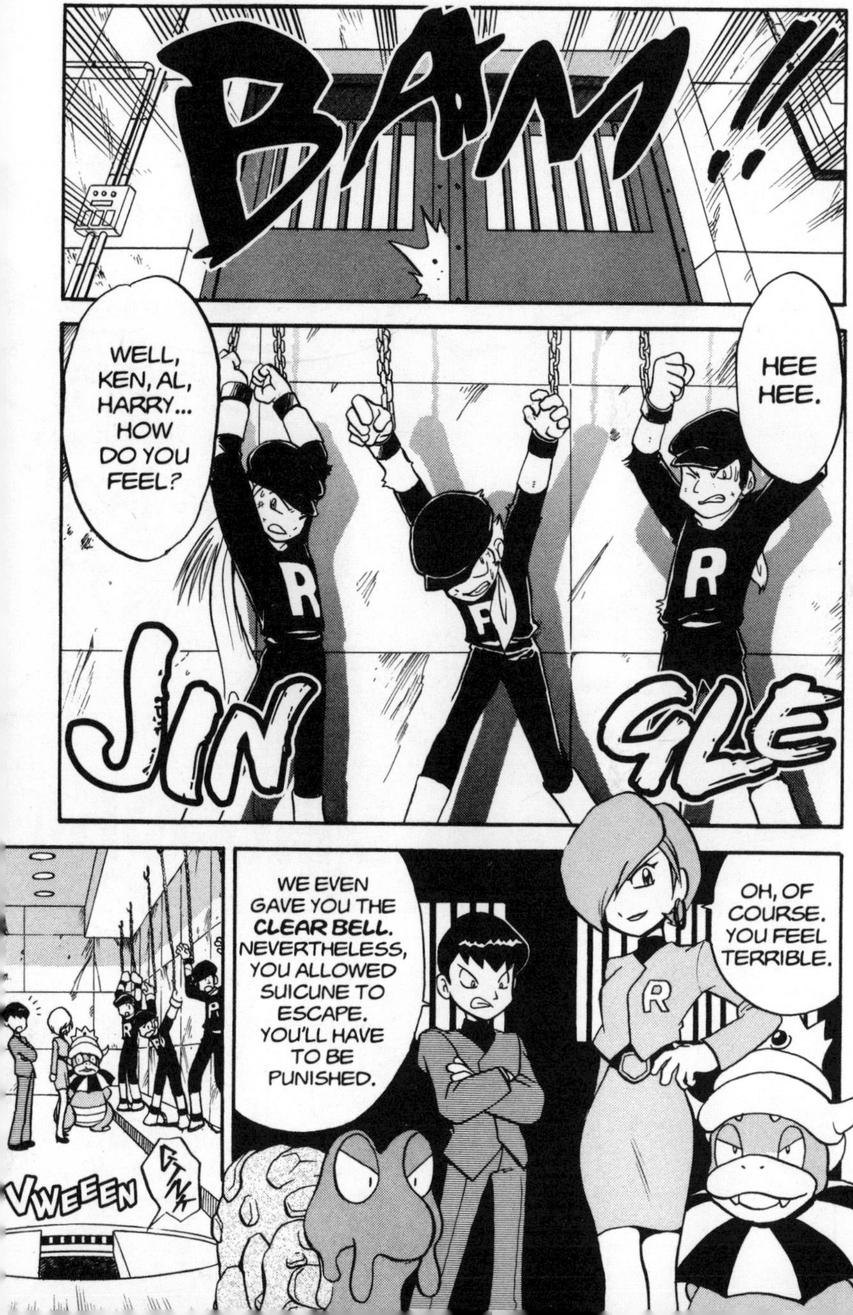
BAM!!
HEE HEE.
WELL, KEN, AL, HARRY... HOW DO YOU FEEL?
JINGLE
OH, OF COURSE. YOU FEEL TERRIBLE.
WE EVEN GAVE YOU THE **CLEAR BELL.** NEVERTHELESS, YOU ALLOWED SUICUNE TO ESCAPE. YOU'LL HAVE TO BE PUNISHED.
GTNK
VWEEEN

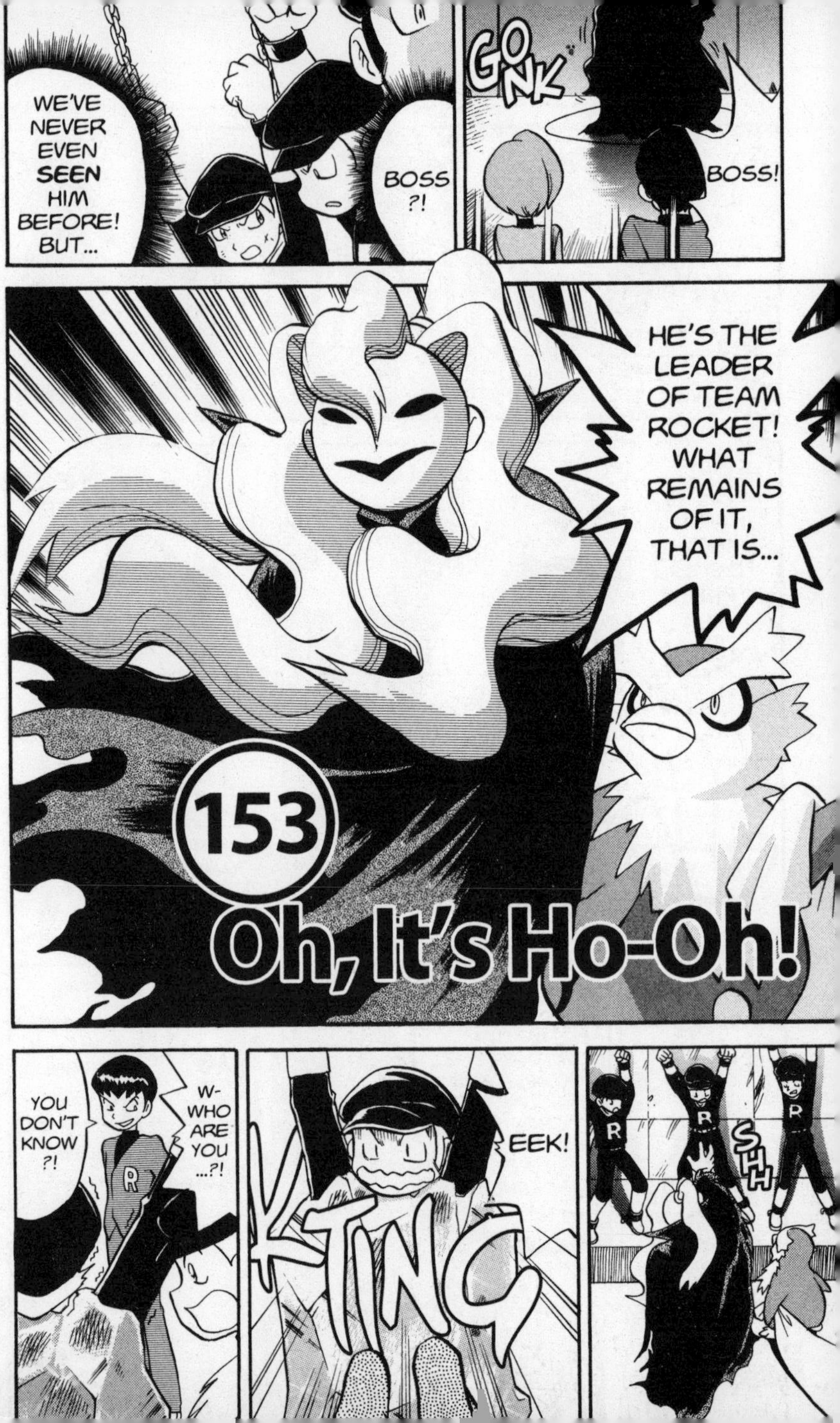
GONK
BOSS!
BOSS ?!
WE'VE NEVER EVEN SEEN HIM BEFORE! BUT...
HE'S THE LEADER OF TEAM ROCKET! WHAT REMAINS OF IT, THAT IS...
153
Oh, It's Ho-Oh!
SHH
EEK!
KTING
W-WHO ARE YOU ...?!
YOU DON'T KNOW ?!

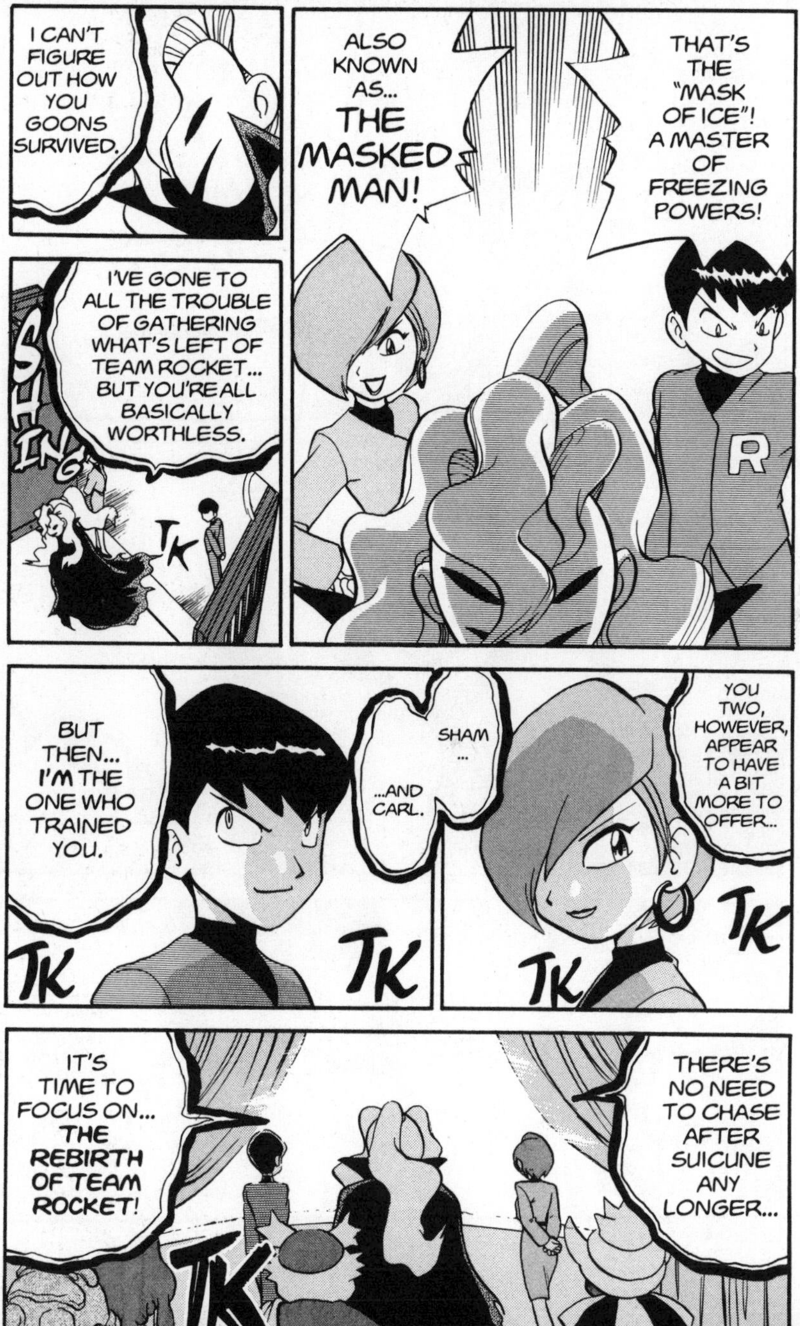
THAT'S THE "MASK OF ICE"! A MASTER OF FREEZING POWERS!
ALSO KNOWN AS... THE MASKED MAN!
I CAN'T FIGURE OUT HOW YOU GOONS SURVIVED.
I'VE GONE TO ALL THE TROUBLE OF GATHERING WHAT'S LEFT OF TEAM ROCKET... BUT YOU'RE ALL BASICALLY WORTHLESS.
SHING
TK
YOU TWO, HOWEVER, APPEAR TO HAVE A BIT MORE TO OFFER...
TK
TK
SHAM...
...AND CARL.
BUT THEN... I'M THE ONE WHO TRAINED YOU.
TK
TK
THERE'S NO NEED TO CHASE AFTER SUICUNE ANY LONGER...
IT'S TIME TO FOCUS ON... THE REBIRTH OF TEAM ROCKET!
TK

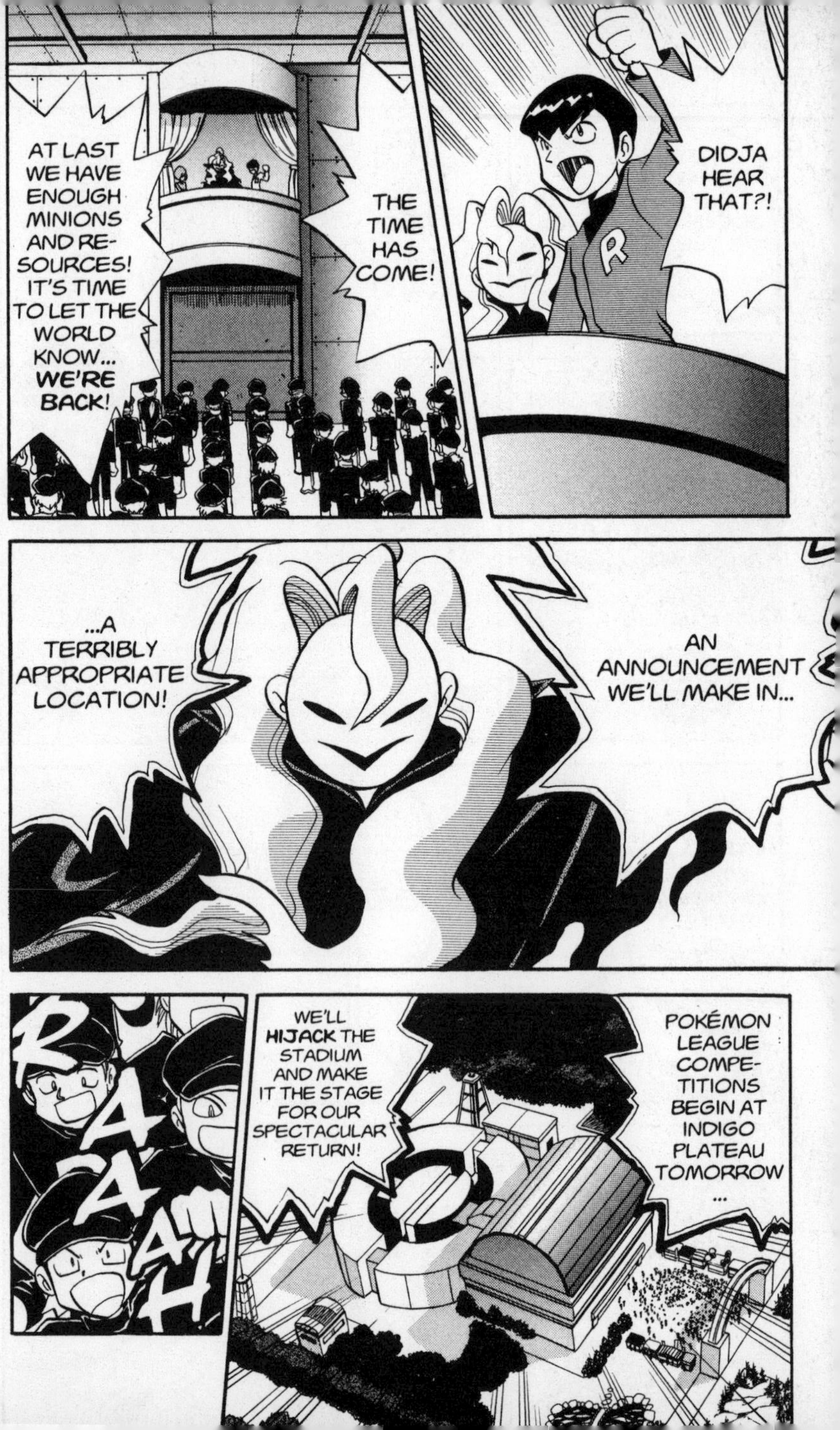
DIDJA HEAR THAT?!
THE TIME HAS COME!
AT LAST WE HAVE ENOUGH MINIONS AND RE-SOURCES! IT'S TIME TO LET THE WORLD KNOW... **WE'RE BACK!**
AN ANNOUNCEMENT WE'LL MAKE IN...
...A TERRIBLY APPROPRIATE LOCATION!
POKÉMON LEAGUE COMPETITIONS BEGIN AT INDIGO PLATEAU TOMORROW...
WE'LL **HIJACK** THE STADIUM AND MAKE IT THE STAGE FOR OUR SPECTACULAR RETURN!
RAAAH

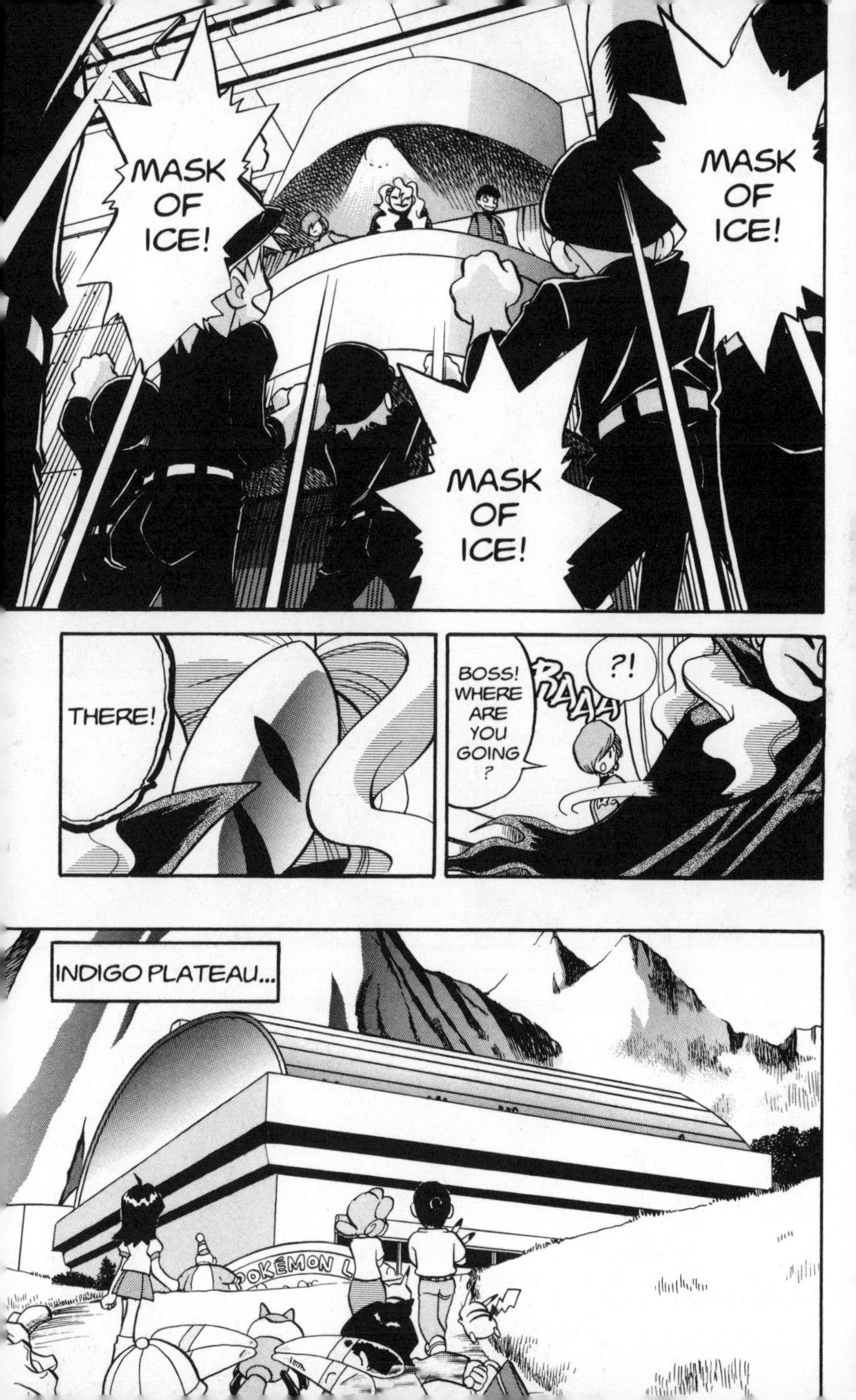
MASK OF ICE!
MASK OF ICE!
MASK OF ICE!
?!
RAAA
BOSS! WHERE ARE YOU GOING?
THERE!
INDIGO PLATEAU...
POKÉMON L

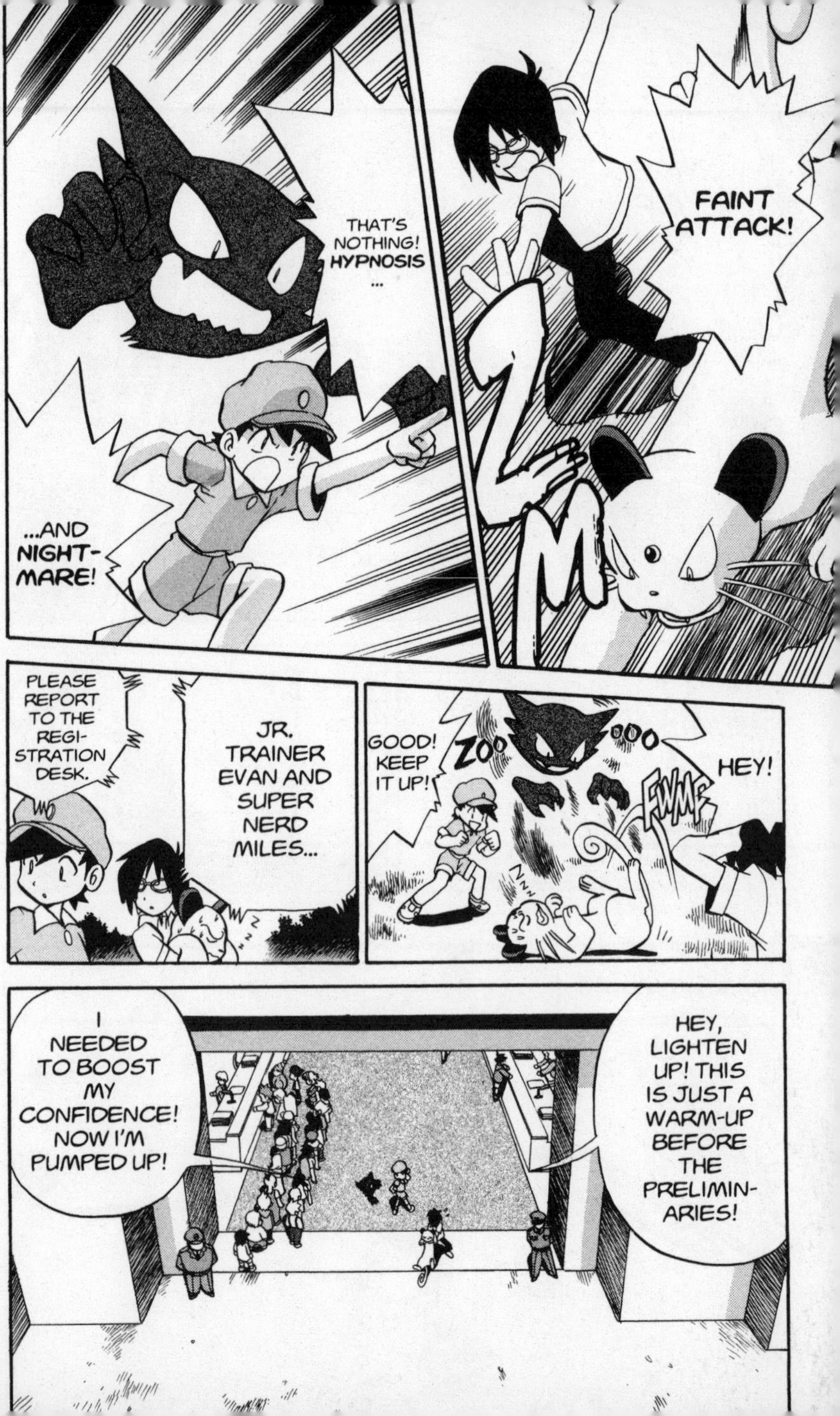
FAINT ATTACK!
ZM
THAT'S NOTHING! HYPNOSIS ...
...AND NIGHT-MARE!
HEY!
ZOOOOO
GOOD! KEEP IT UP!
JR. TRAINER EVAN AND SUPER NERD MILES...
PLEASE REPORT TO THE REGI-STRATION DESK.
HEY, LIGHTEN UP! THIS IS JUST A WARM-UP BEFORE THE PRELIMIN-ARIES!
I NEEDED TO BOOST MY CONFIDENCE! NOW I'M PUMPED UP!

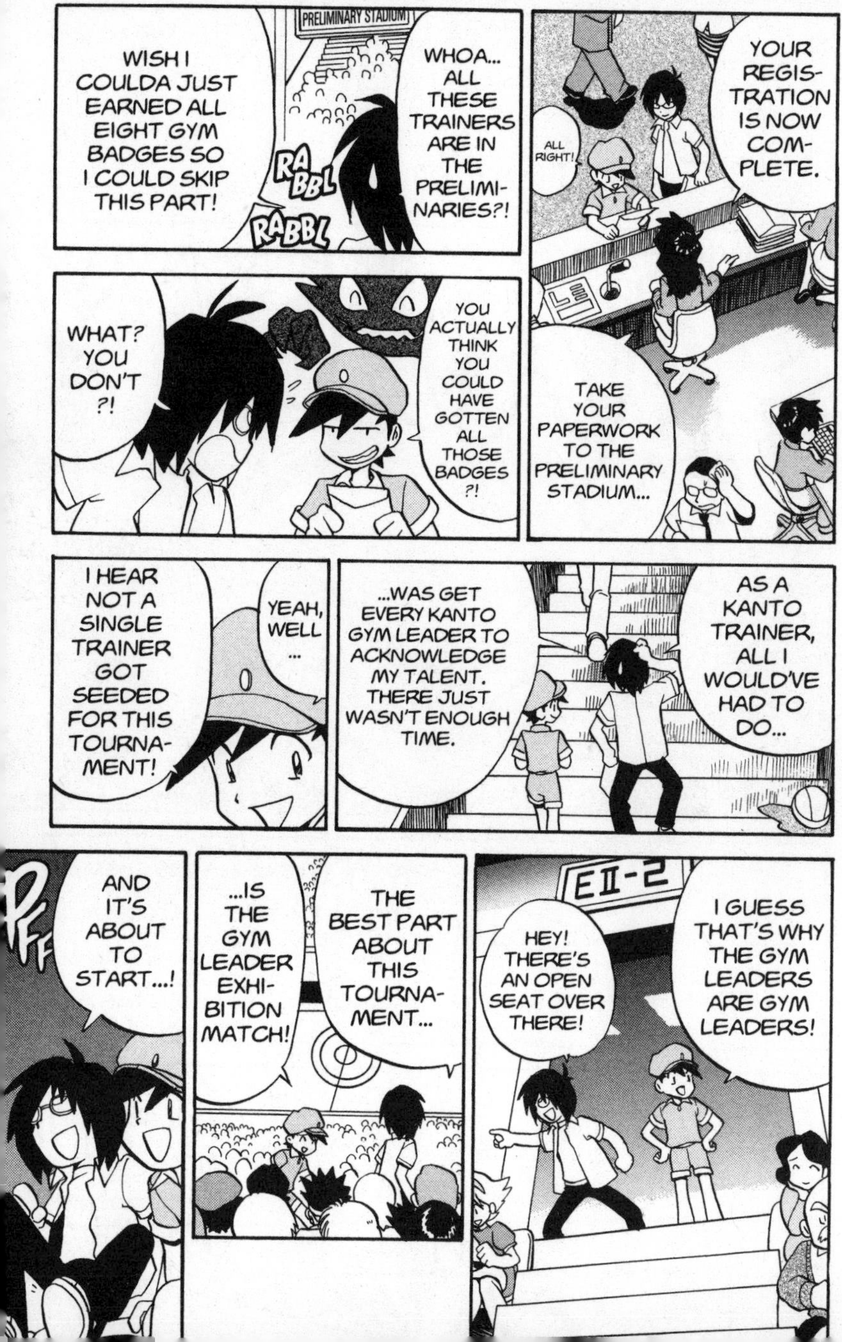
YOUR REGISTRATION IS NOW COMPLETE.
ALL RIGHT!
TAKE YOUR PAPERWORK TO THE PRELIMINARY STADIUM...
PRELIMINARY STADIUM
WHOA... ALL THESE TRAINERS ARE IN THE PRELIMINARIES?!
RABBL
RABBL
WISH I COULDA JUST EARNED ALL EIGHT GYM BADGES SO I COULD SKIP THIS PART!
YOU ACTUALLY THINK YOU COULD HAVE GOTTEN ALL THOSE BADGES ?!
WHAT? YOU DON'T ?!
AS A KANTO TRAINER, ALL I WOULD'VE HAD TO DO...
...WAS GET EVERY KANTO GYM LEADER TO ACKNOWLEDGE MY TALENT. THERE JUST WASN'T ENOUGH TIME.
YEAH, WELL ...
I HEAR NOT A SINGLE TRAINER GOT SEEDED FOR THIS TOURNAMENT!
EII-2
I GUESS THAT'S WHY THE GYM LEADERS ARE GYM LEADERS!
HEY! THERE'S AN OPEN SEAT OVER THERE!
THE BEST PART ABOUT THIS TOURNAMENT...
...IS THE GYM LEADER EXHIBITION MATCH!
AND IT'S ABOUT TO START...!

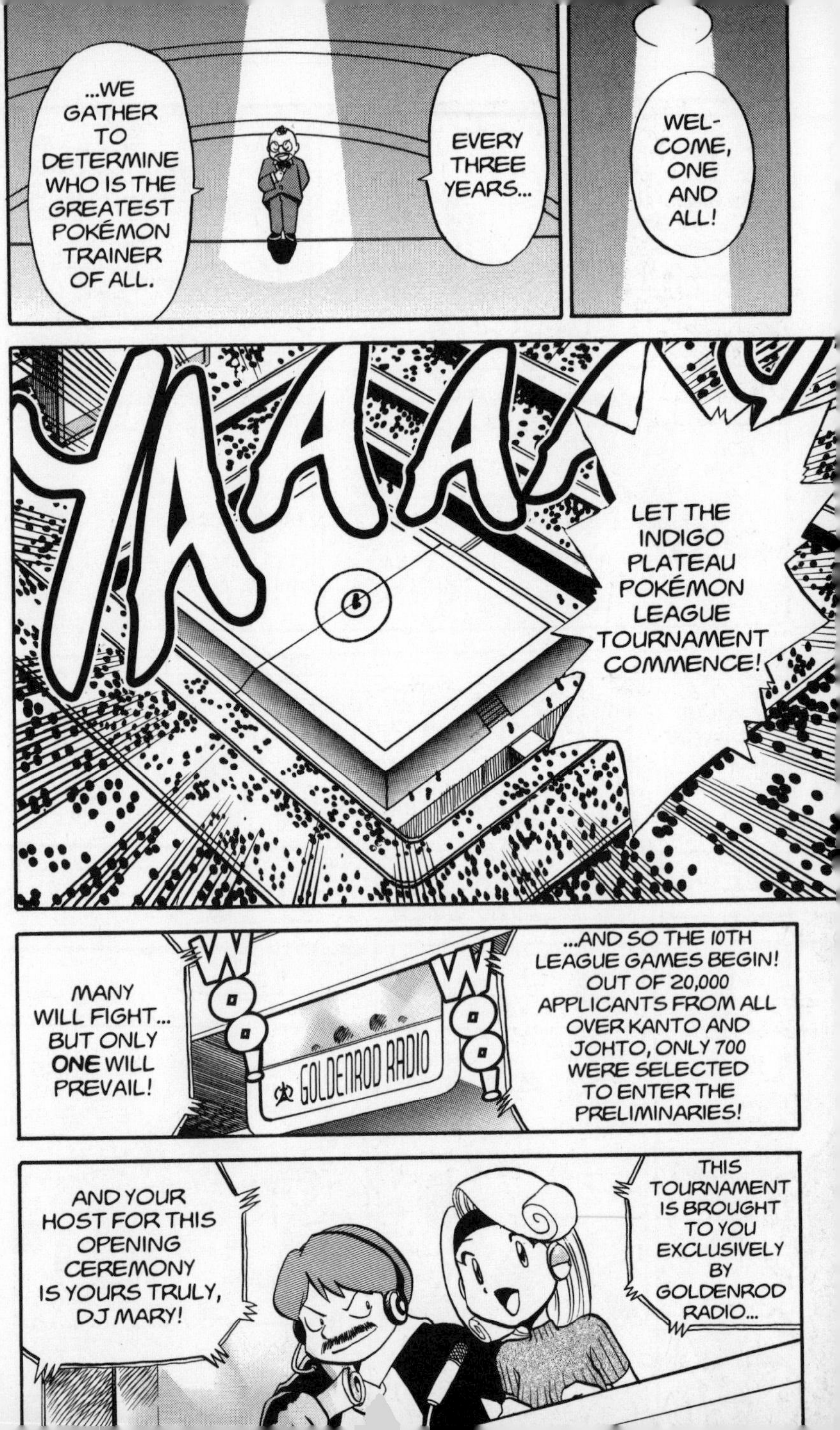
WEL-COME, ONE AND ALL!
EVERY THREE YEARS...
...WE GATHER TO DETERMINE WHO IS THE GREATEST POKÉMON TRAINER OF ALL.
YAAA
LET THE INDIGO PLATEAU POKÉMON LEAGUE TOURNAMENT COMMENCE!
...AND SO THE 10TH LEAGUE GAMES BEGIN! OUT OF 20,000 APPLICANTS FROM ALL OVER KANTO AND JOHTO, ONLY 700 WERE SELECTED TO ENTER THE PRELIMINARIES!
WOO!
WOO!
GOLDENROD RADIO
MANY WILL FIGHT... BUT ONLY **ONE** WILL PREVAIL!
THIS TOURNAMENT IS BROUGHT TO YOU EXCLUSIVELY BY GOLDENROD RADIO...
AND YOUR HOST FOR THIS OPENING CEREMONY IS YOURS TRULY, DJ MARY!

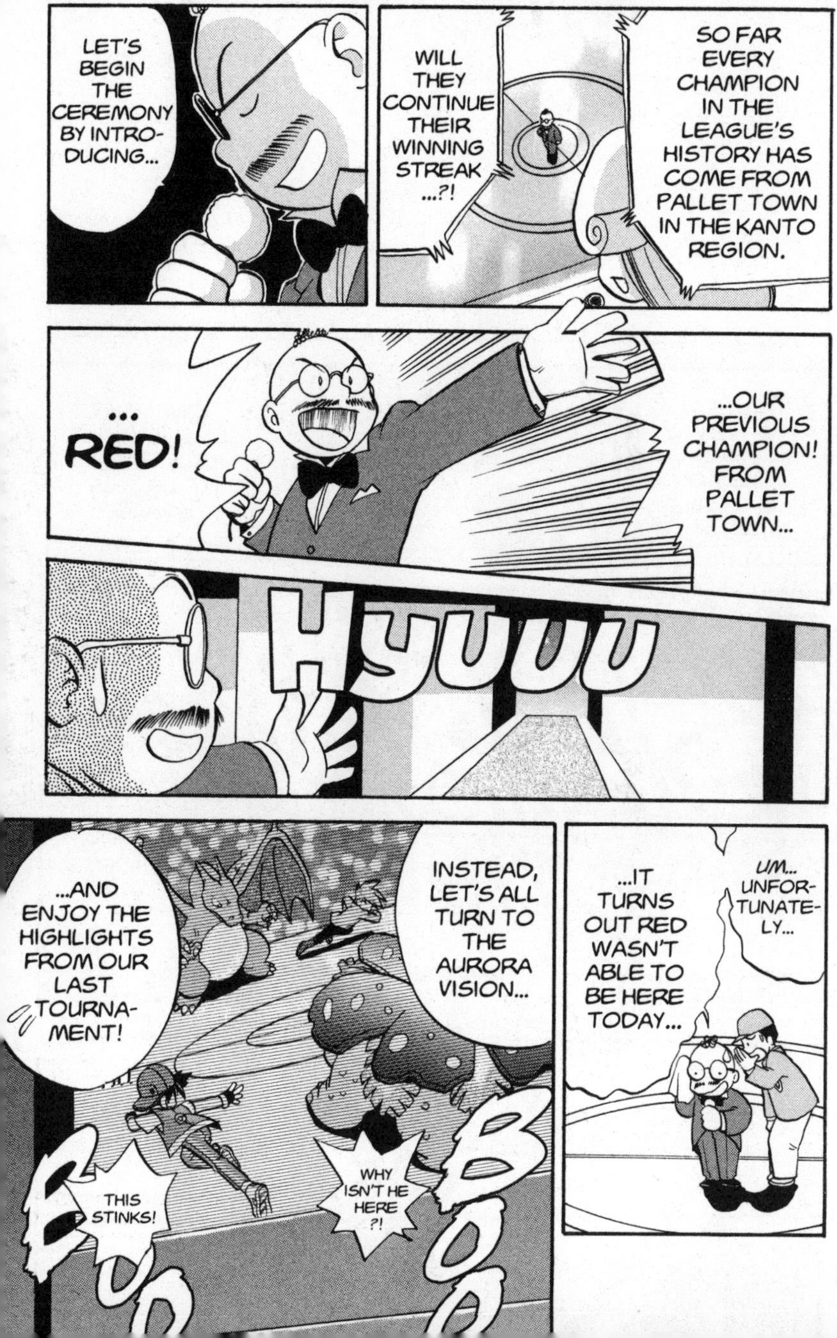
SO FAR EVERY CHAMPION IN THE LEAGUE'S HISTORY HAS COME FROM PALLET TOWN IN THE KANTO REGION.
WILL THEY CONTINUE THEIR WINNING STREAK ...?!
LET'S BEGIN THE CEREMONY BY INTRO-DUCING...
...OUR PREVIOUS CHAMPION! FROM PALLET TOWN...
...RED!
HYUUU
UM... UNFOR-TUNATE-LY...
...IT TURNS OUT RED WASN'T ABLE TO BE HERE TODAY...
INSTEAD, LET'S ALL TURN TO THE AURORA VISION...
...AND ENJOY THE HIGHLIGHTS FROM OUR LAST TOURNA-MENT!
BOO
WHY ISN'T HE HERE ?!
THIS STINKS!
BOO

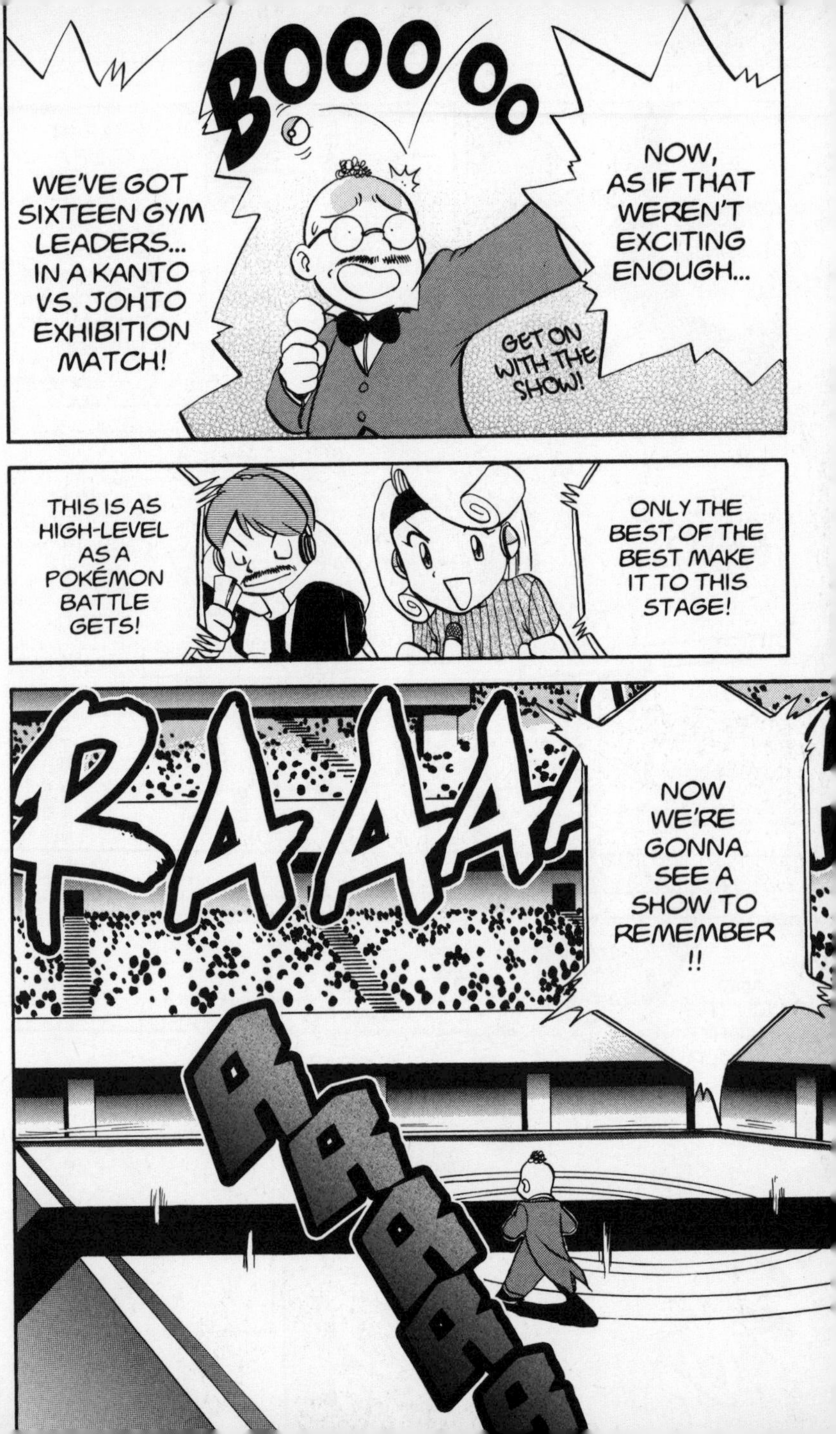
BOOO OO
NOW, AS IF THAT WEREN'T EXCITING ENOUGH...
WE'VE GOT SIXTEEN GYM LEADERS... IN A KANTO VS. JOHTO EXHIBITION MATCH!
GET ON WITH THE SHOW!
ONLY THE BEST OF THE BEST MAKE IT TO THIS STAGE!
THIS IS AS HIGH-LEVEL AS A POKÉMON BATTLE GETS!
RAAAA
NOW WE'RE GONNA SEE A SHOW TO REMEMBER !!
RRRR

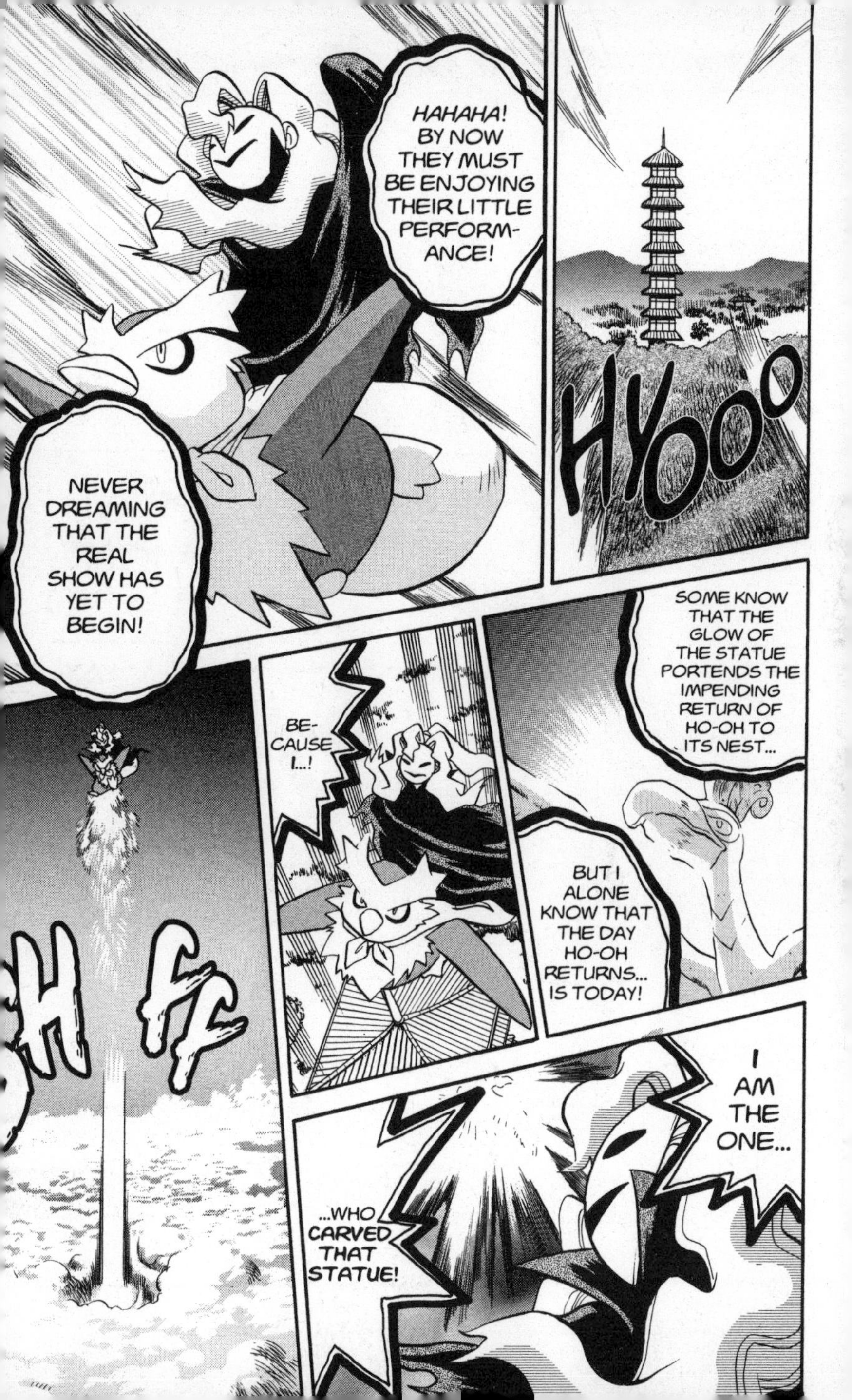
HYOOO
HAHAHA! BY NOW THEY MUST BE ENJOYING THEIR LITTLE PERFORM-ANCE!
NEVER DREAMING THAT THE REAL SHOW HAS YET TO BEGIN!
SOME KNOW THAT THE GLOW OF THE STATUE PORTENDS THE IMPENDING RETURN OF HO-OH TO ITS NEST...
BUT I ALONE KNOW THAT THE DAY HO-OH RETURNS... IS TODAY!
BE-CAUSE I...!
I AM THE ONE...
...WHO CARVED THAT STATUE!
SH FF

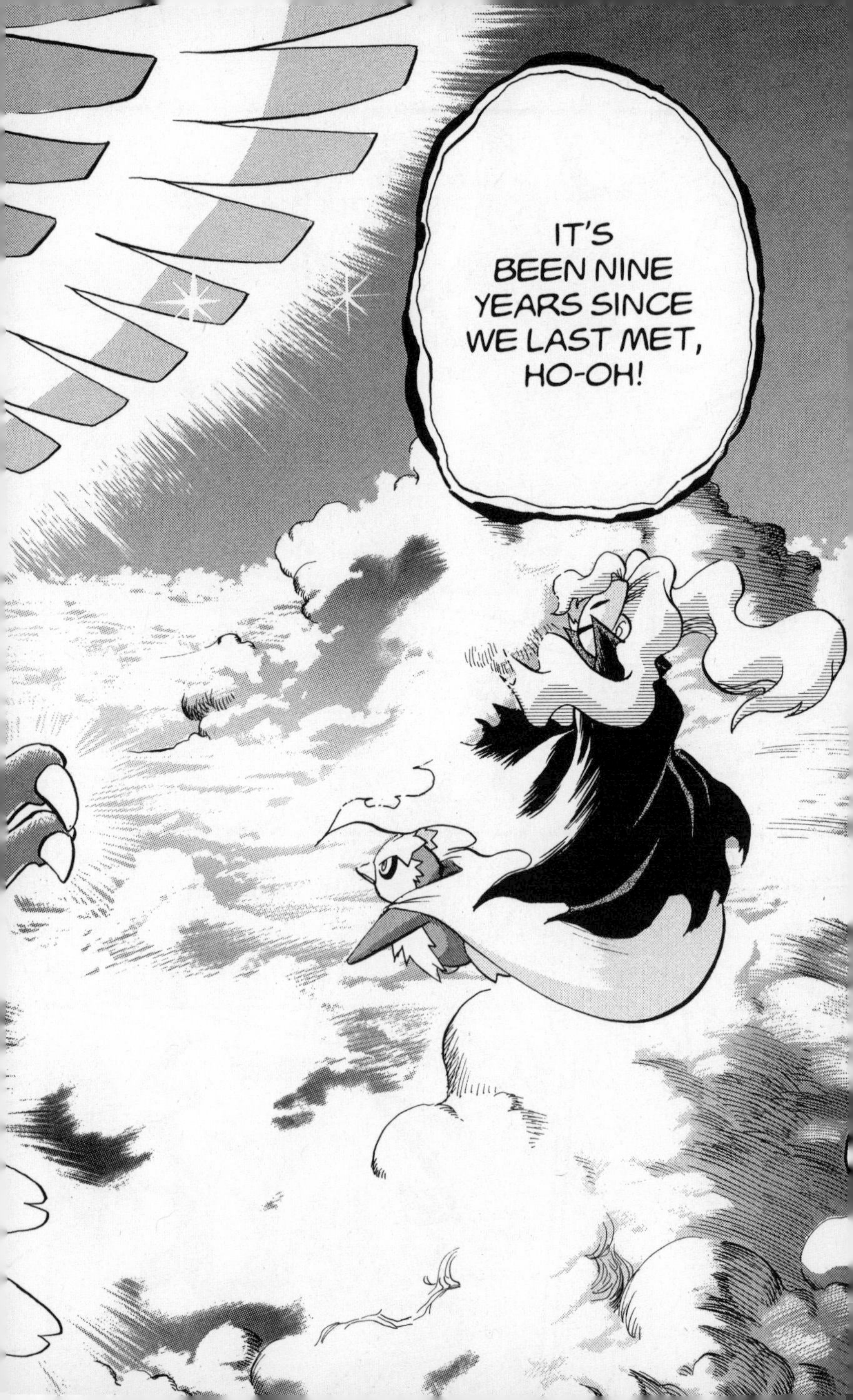
IT'S BEEN NINE YEARS SINCE WE LAST MET, HO-OH!

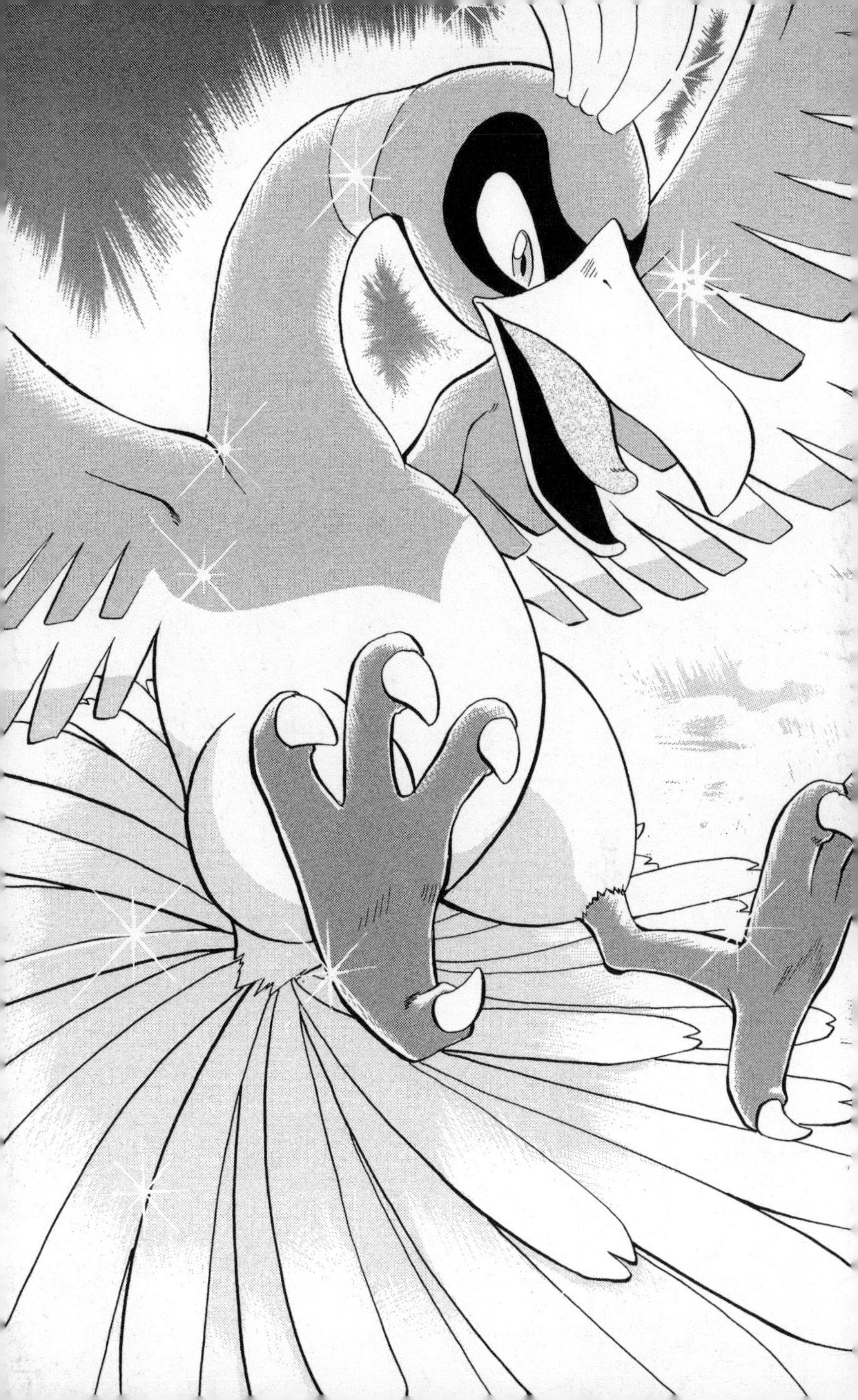

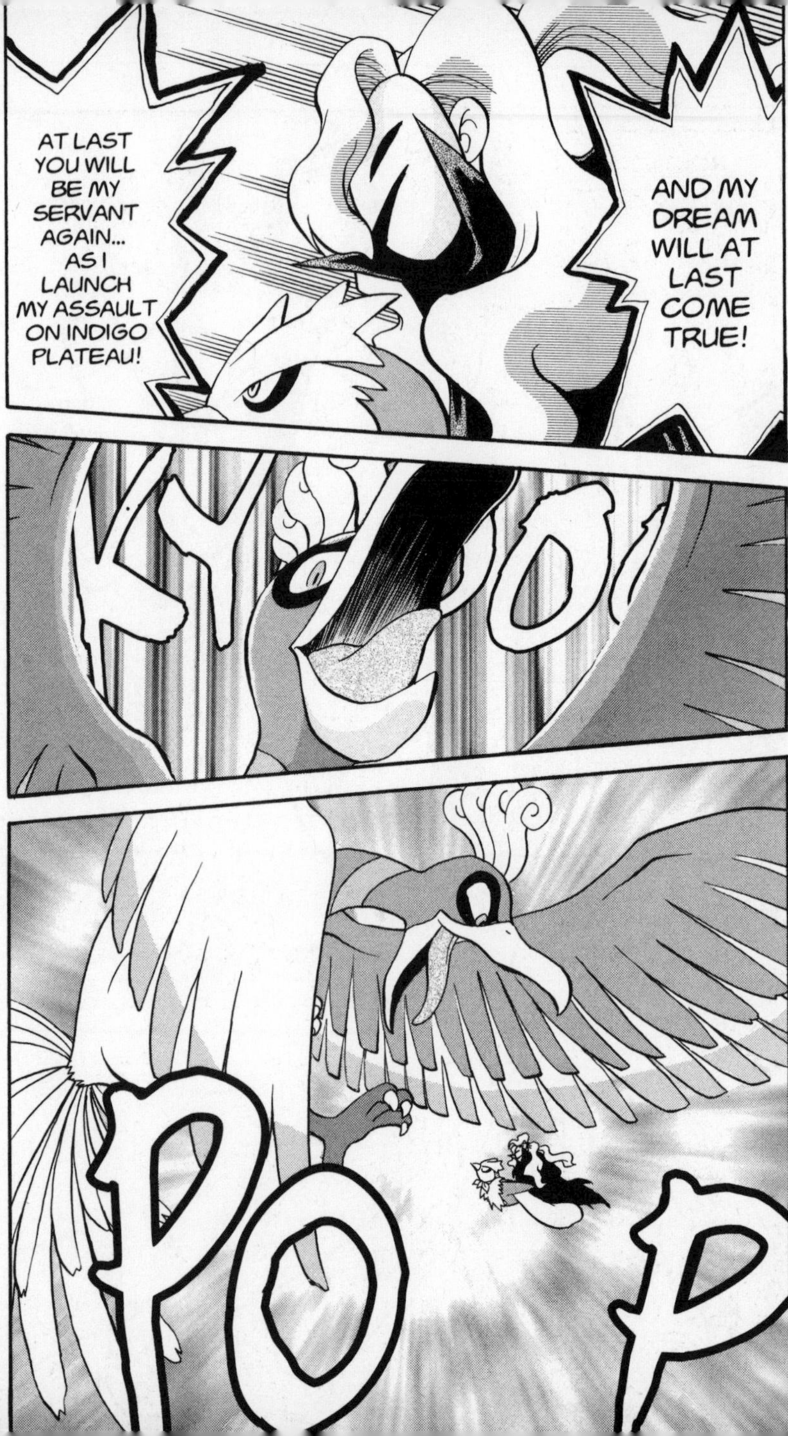
AT LAST YOU WILL BE MY SERVANT AGAIN... AS I LAUNCH MY ASSAULT ON INDIGO PLATEAU!
AND MY DREAM WILL AT LAST COME TRUE!
KYOO
POP

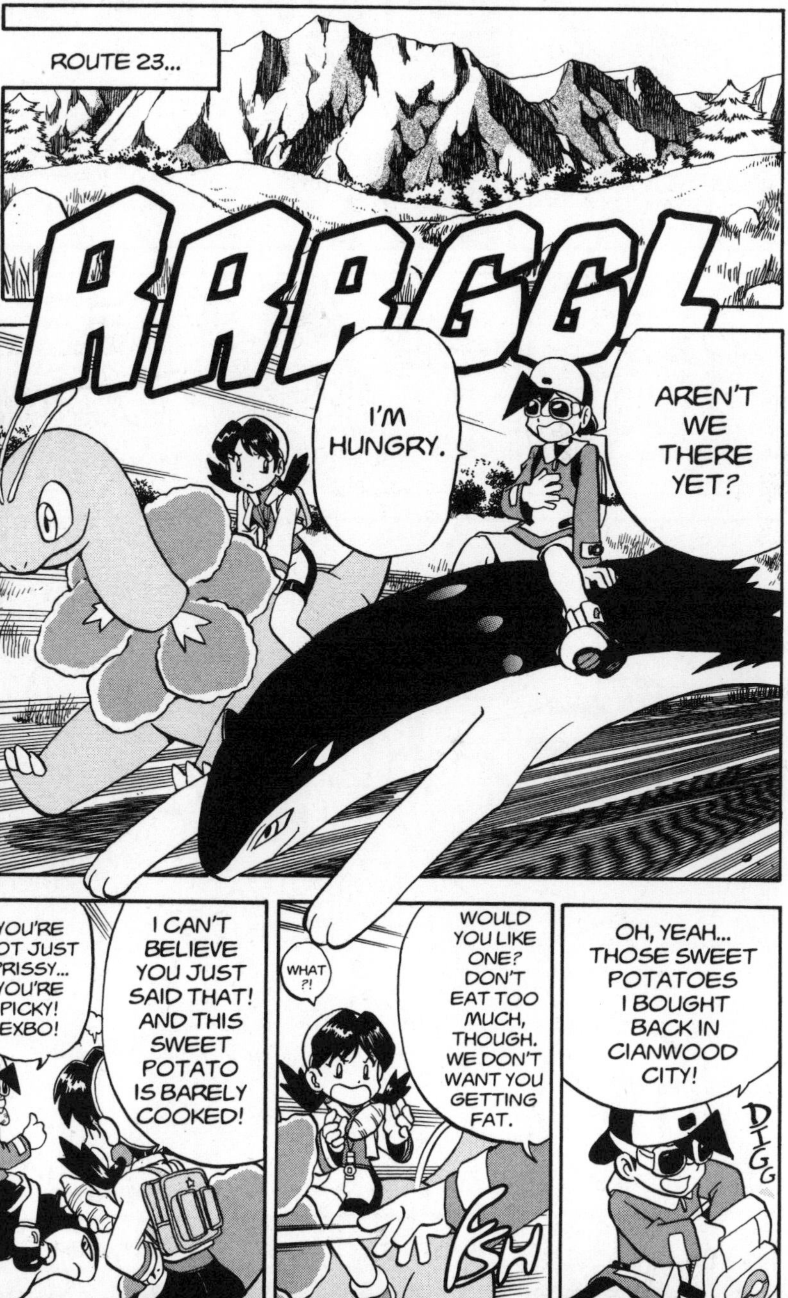

ROUTE 23...
RRRGL
AREN'T WE THERE YET?
I'M HUNGRY.
OH, YEAH... THOSE SWEET POTATOES I BOUGHT BACK IN CIANWOOD CITY!
DIGG
WOULD YOU LIKE ONE? DON'T EAT TOO MUCH, THOUGH. WE DON'T WANT YOU GETTING FAT.
WHAT ?!
FSH
I CAN'T BELIEVE YOU JUST SAID THAT! AND THIS SWEET POTATO IS BARELY COOKED!
YOU'RE NOT JUST PRISSY... YOU'RE PICKY! EXBO!

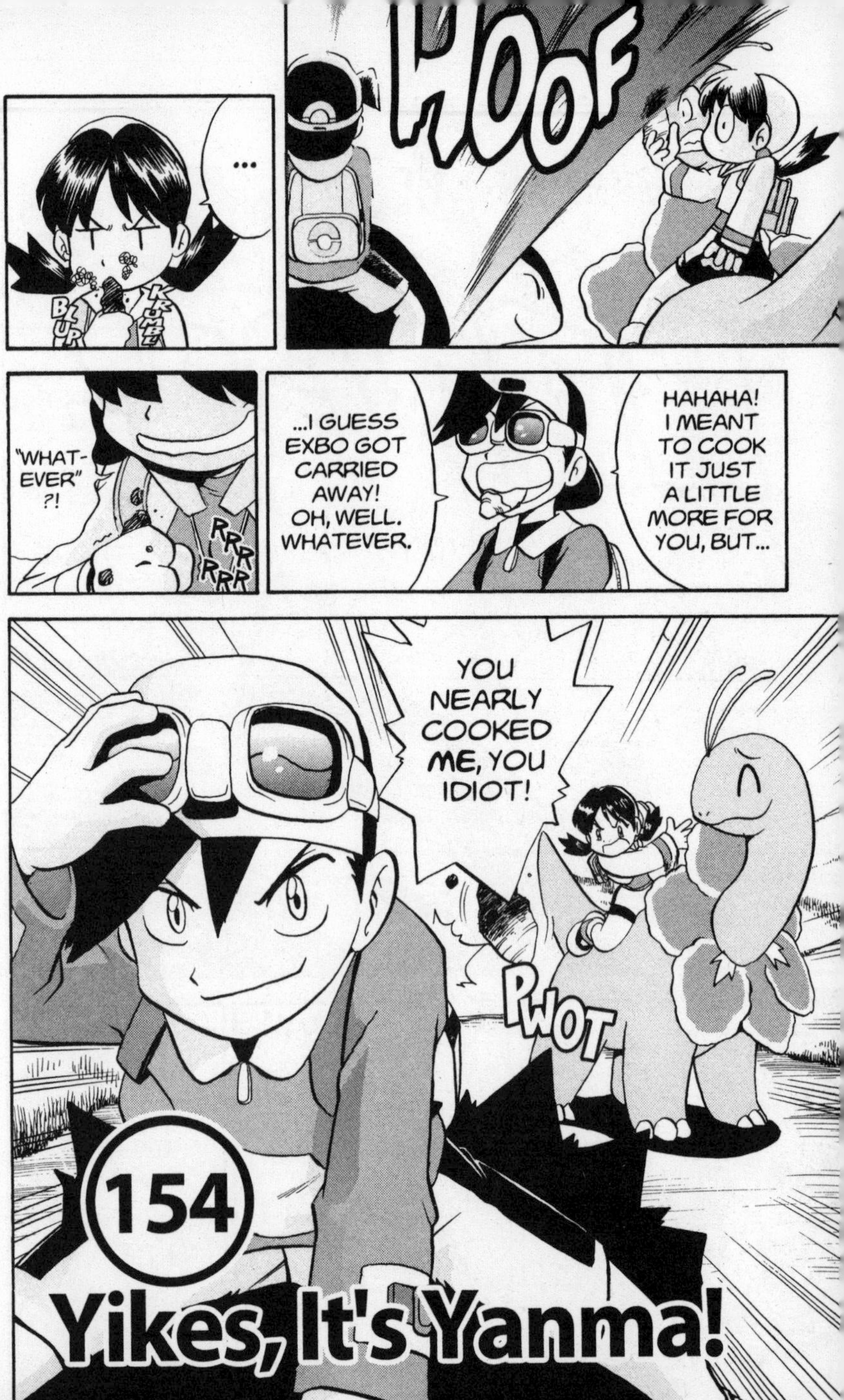
HOOF
...
BLUP
KRUMBL
HAHAHA! I MEANT TO COOK IT JUST A LITTLE MORE FOR YOU, BUT...
...I GUESS EXBO GOT CARRIED AWAY! OH, WELL. WHATEVER.
"WHAT-EVER" ?!
RRRRRR
YOU NEARLY COOKED ME, YOU IDIOT!
PWOT
154
Yikes, It's Yanma!

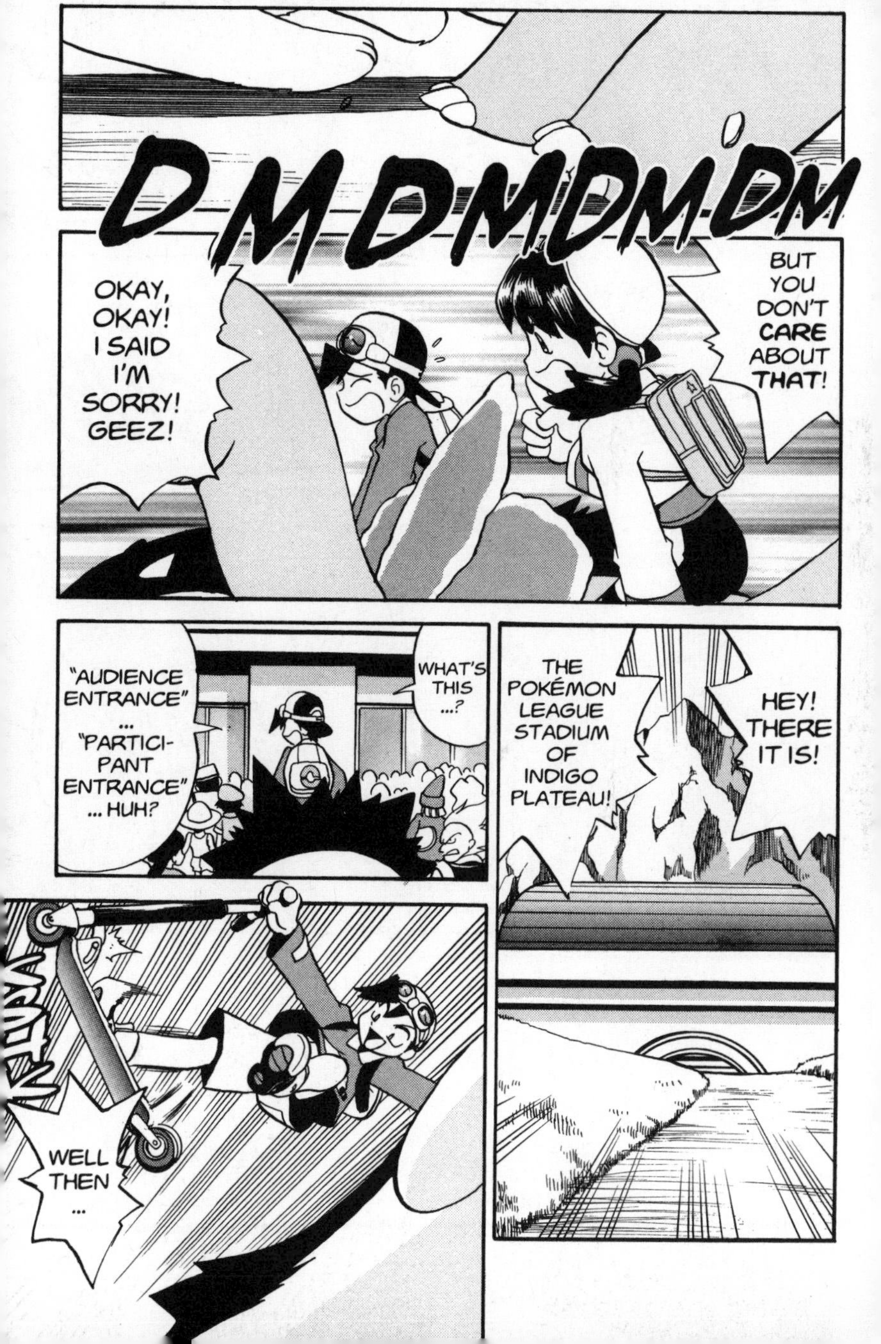
DMDMDMDM
BUT YOU DON'T CARE ABOUT THAT!
OKAY, OKAY! I SAID I'M SORRY! GEEZ!
HEY! THERE IT IS!
THE POKÉMON LEAGUE STADIUM OF INDIGO PLATEAU!
WHAT'S THIS ...?
"AUDIENCE ENTRANCE" ... "PARTICIPANT ENTRANCE" ... HUH?
WELL THEN ...

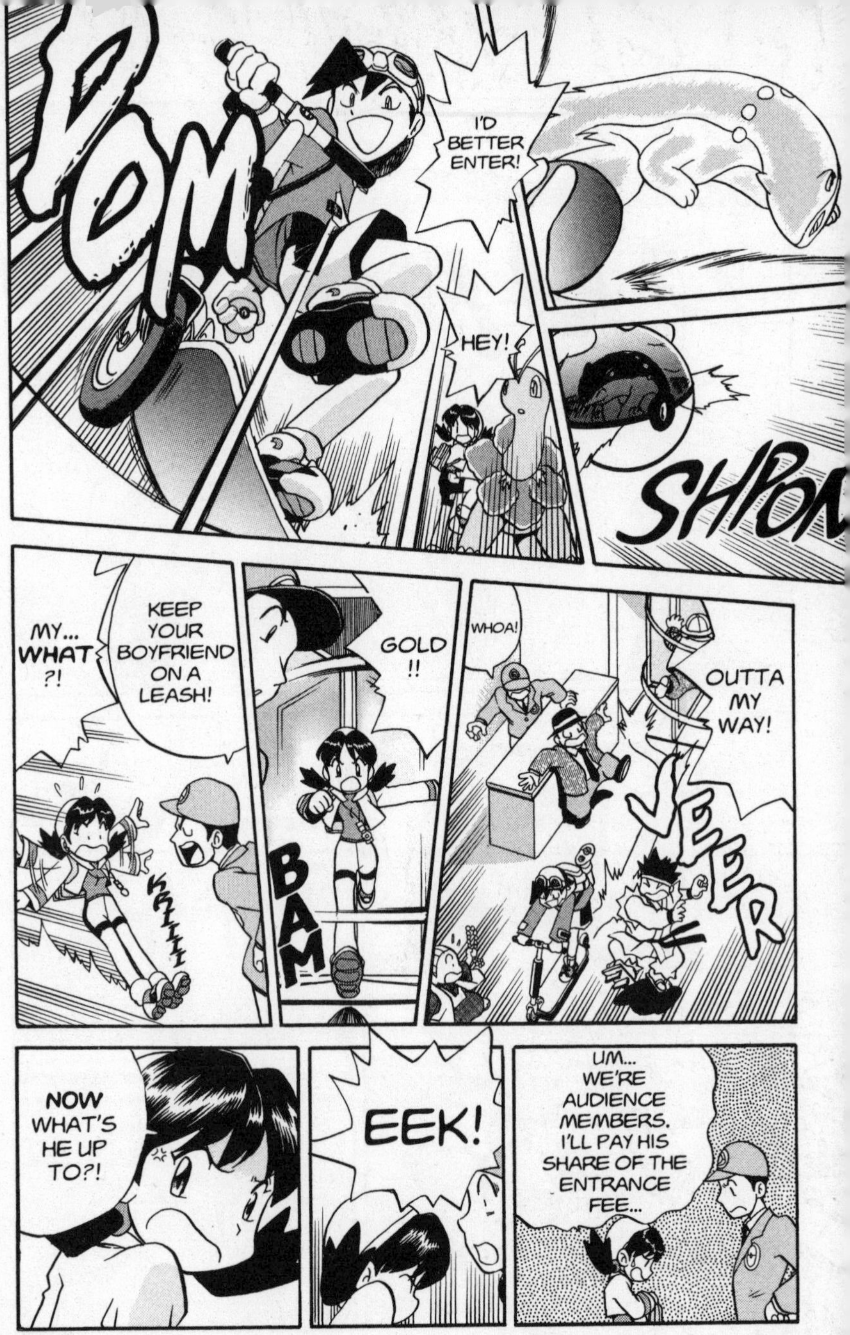
I'D BETTER ENTER!
HEY!
SHPOM
BOOM
WHOA!
OUTTA MY WAY!
VEER
GOLD!!
BAM
KEEP YOUR BOYFRIEND ON A LEASH!
MY... WHAT?!
KRIIII
UM... WE'RE AUDIENCE MEMBERS. I'LL PAY HIS SHARE OF THE ENTRANCE FEE...
EEK!
NOW WHAT'S HE UP TO?!

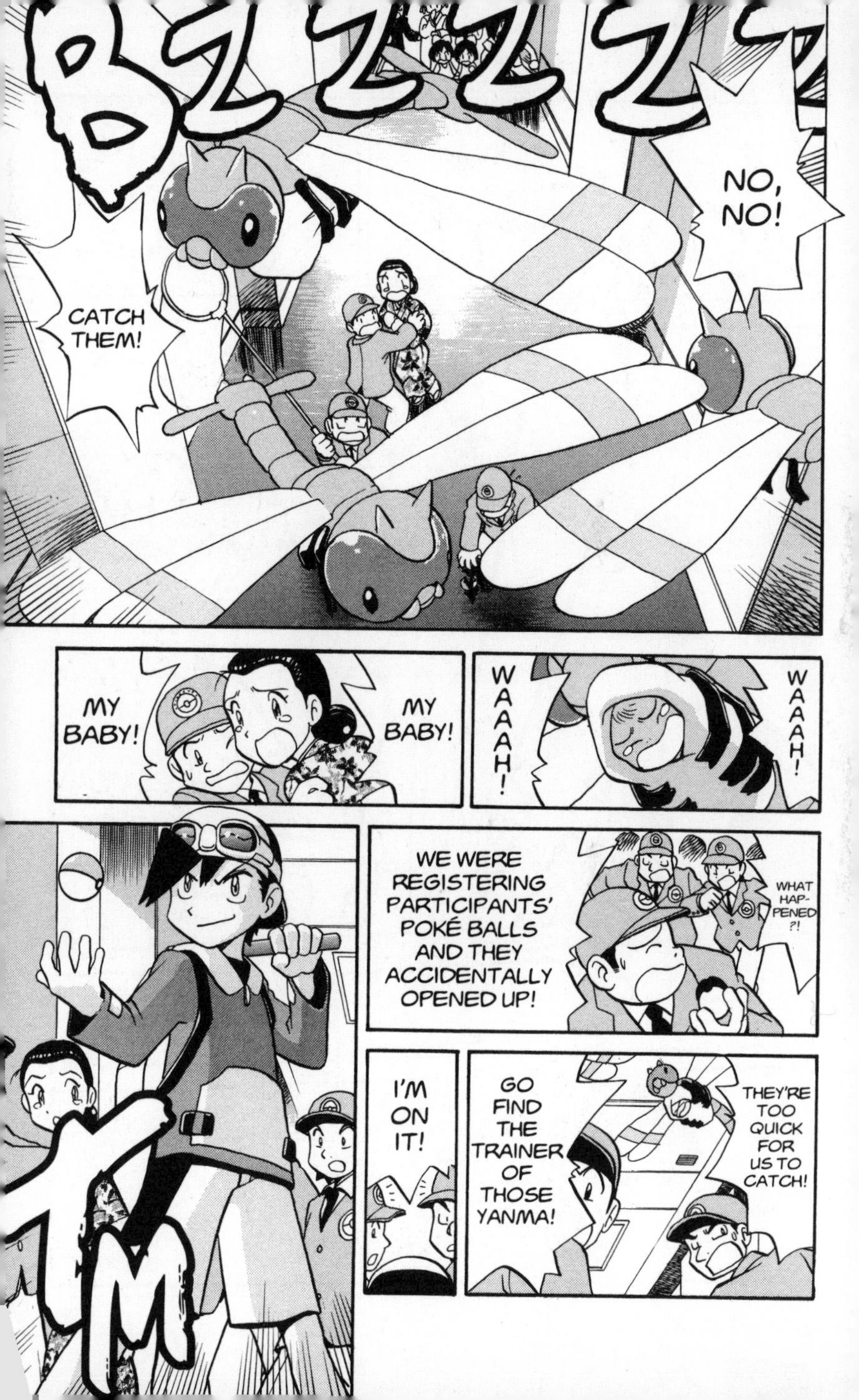
BZZZZ
NO, NO!
CATCH THEM!
WAAAAH!
WAAAAH!
MY BABY!
MY BABY!
WHAT HAPPENED?!
WE WERE REGISTERING PARTICIPANTS' POKÉ BALLS AND THEY ACCIDENTALLY OPENED UP!
THEY'RE TOO QUICK FOR US TO CATCH!
GO FIND THE TRAINER OF THOSE YANMA!
I'M ON IT!
TM

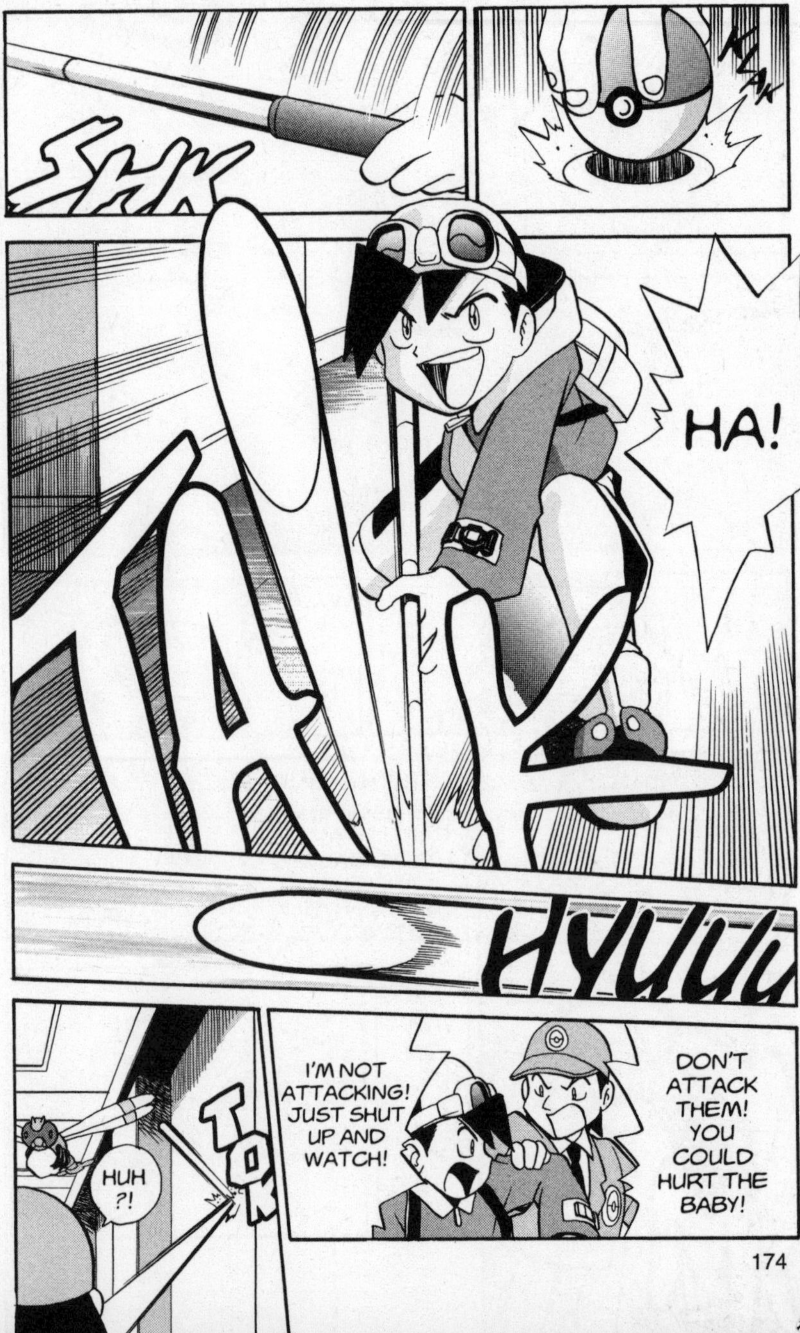
KLAK
SHK
HA!
HYUUU
DON'T ATTACK THEM! YOU COULD HURT THE BABY!
I'M NOT ATTACKING! JUST SHUT UP AND WATCH!
TOK
HUH ?!

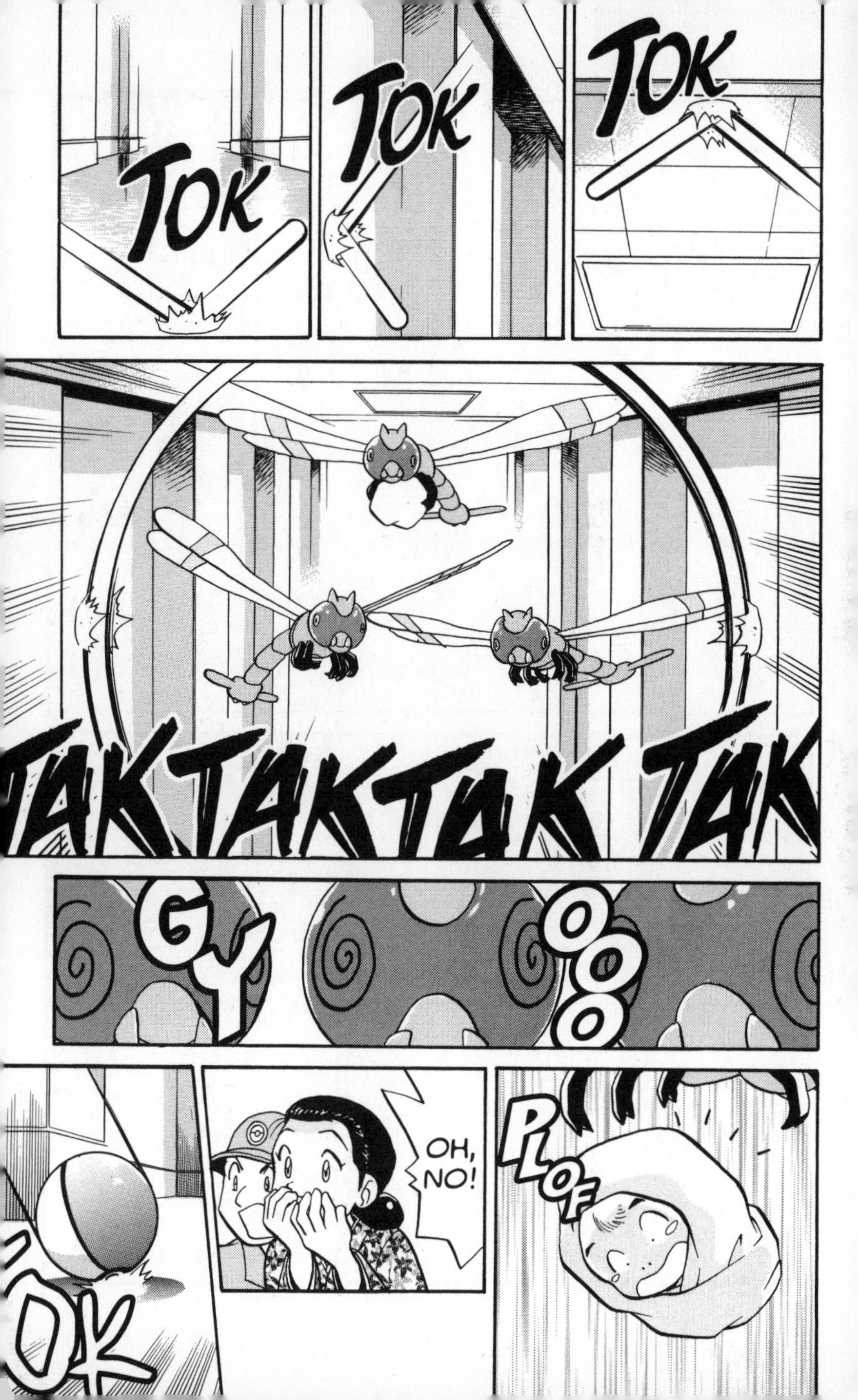
TOK
TOK
TOK
TAK TAK TAK TAK
GYOOO
PLOF
OH, NO!
OK

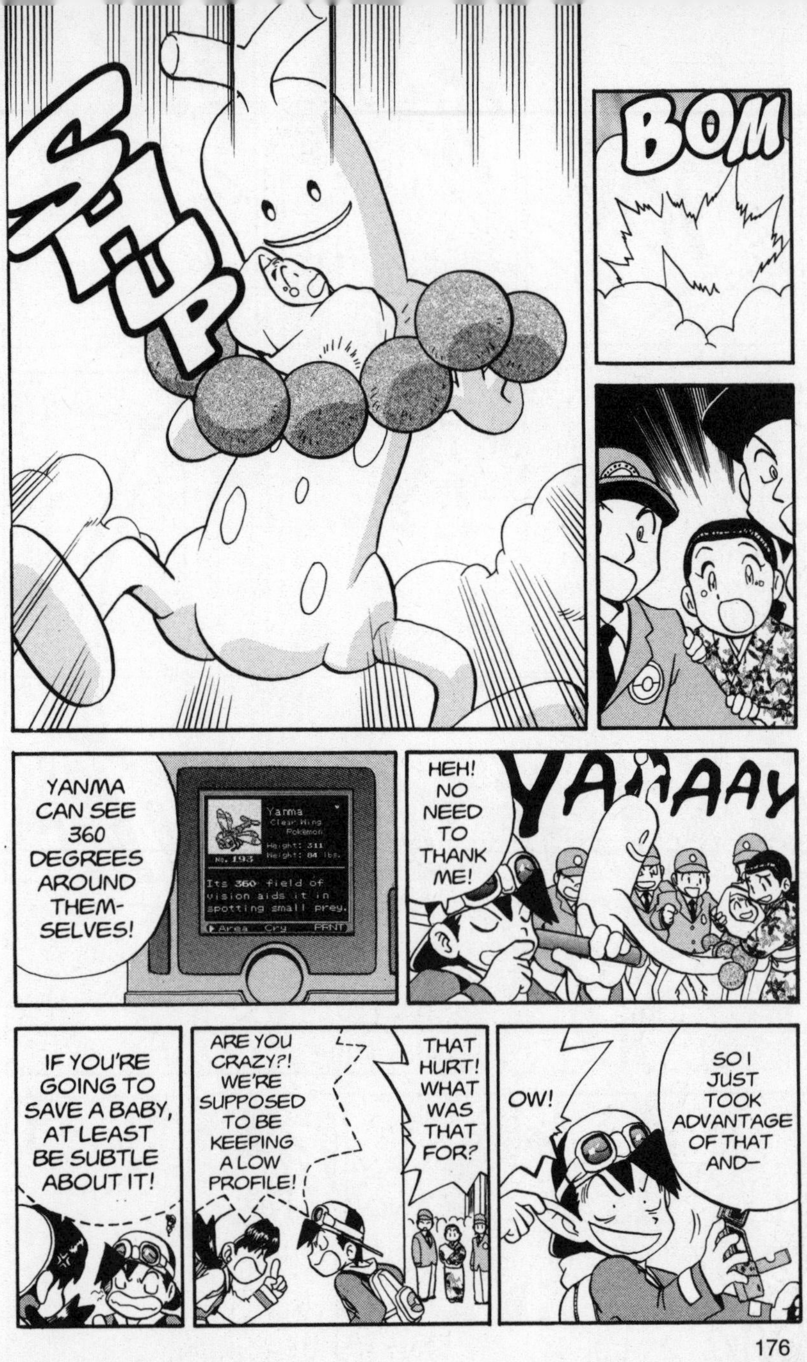
BOM
SHUP
YAAAAY
HEH! NO NEED TO THANK ME!
YANMA CAN SEE 360 DEGREES AROUND THEM-SELVES!
Yanma
Clear Wing Pokemon
Height: 3'11
Weight: 84 lbs.
No. 193
Its 360 field of vision aids it in spotting small prey.
Area Cry PRNT
SO I JUST TOOK ADVANTAGE OF THAT AND—
OW!
THAT HURT! WHAT WAS THAT FOR?
ARE YOU CRAZY?! WE'RE SUPPOSED TO BE KEEPING A LOW PROFILE!
IF YOU'RE GOING TO SAVE A BABY, AT LEAST BE SUBTLE ABOUT IT!

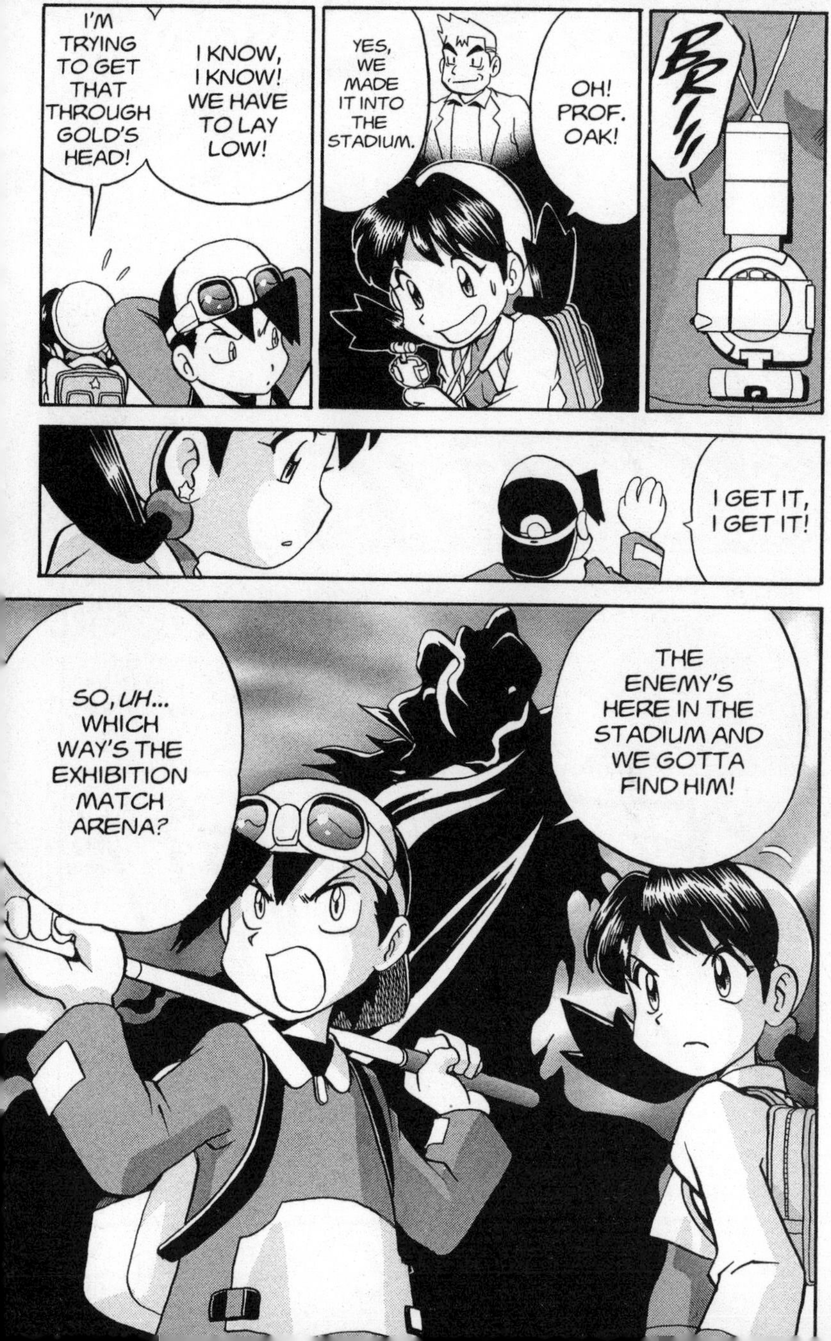
OH! PROF. OAK!
YES, WE MADE IT INTO THE STADIUM.
I KNOW, I KNOW! WE HAVE TO LAY LOW!
I'M TRYING TO GET THAT THROUGH GOLD'S HEAD!
I GET IT, I GET IT!
THE ENEMY'S HERE IN THE STADIUM AND WE GOTTA FIND HIM!
SO, UH... WHICH WAY'S THE EXHIBITION MATCH ARENA?

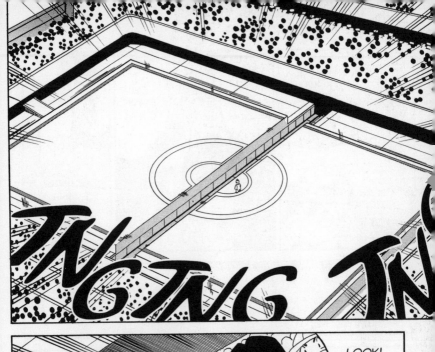

LOOK! THE BATTLE-FIELD'S OPENING UP!

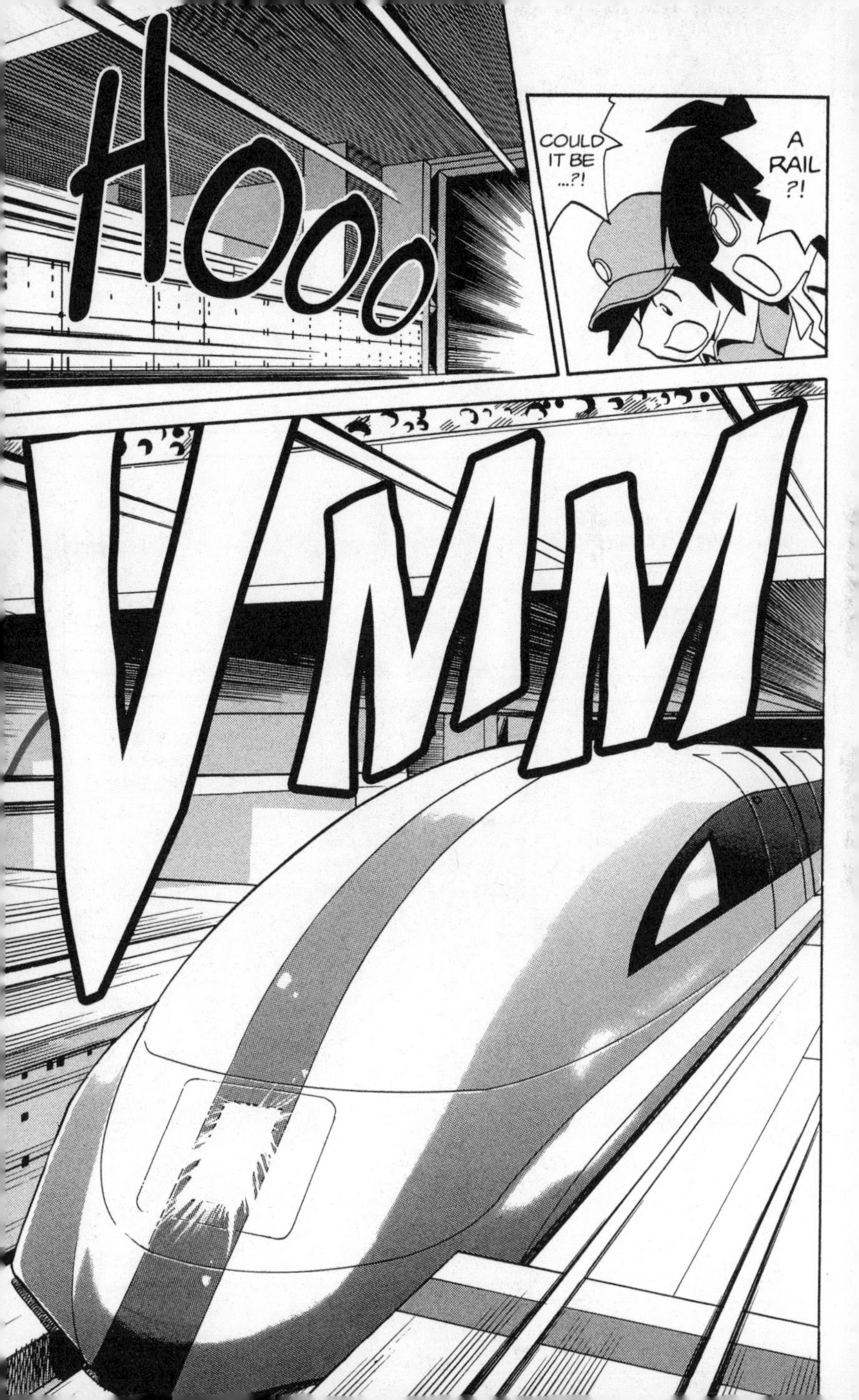
A RAIL ?!
COULD IT BE ...?!
HOOOO
VMM

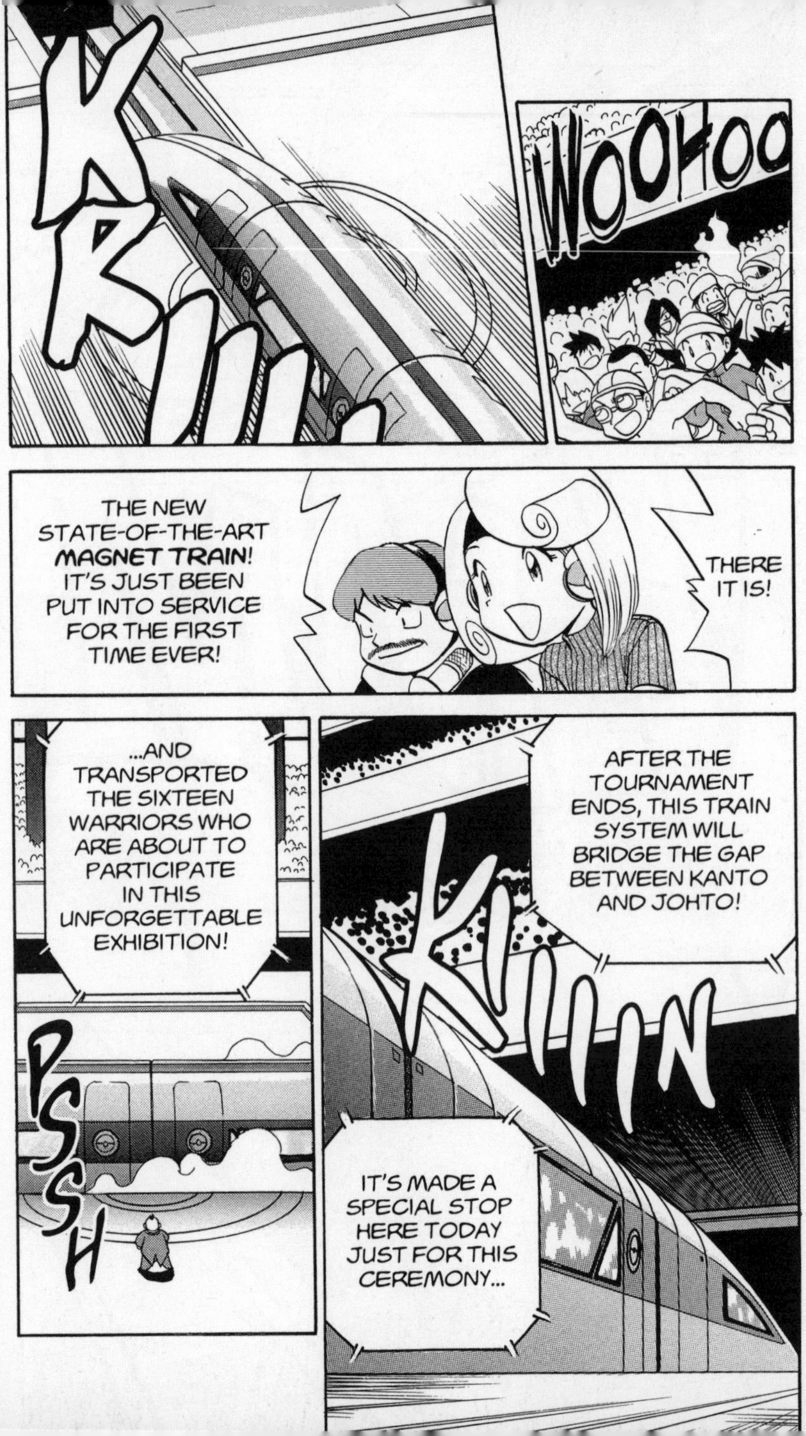
WOOHOO
KRIIII
THERE IT IS!
THE NEW STATE-OF-THE-ART **MAGNET TRAIN**! IT'S JUST BEEN PUT INTO SERVICE FOR THE FIRST TIME EVER!
AFTER THE TOURNAMENT ENDS, THIS TRAIN SYSTEM WILL BRIDGE THE GAP BETWEEN KANTO AND JOHTO!
KIIIIN
IT'S MADE A SPECIAL STOP HERE TODAY JUST FOR THIS CEREMONY...
...AND TRANSPORTED THE SIXTEEN WARRIORS WHO ARE ABOUT TO PARTICIPATE IN THIS UNFORGETTABLE EXHIBITION!
PSSH

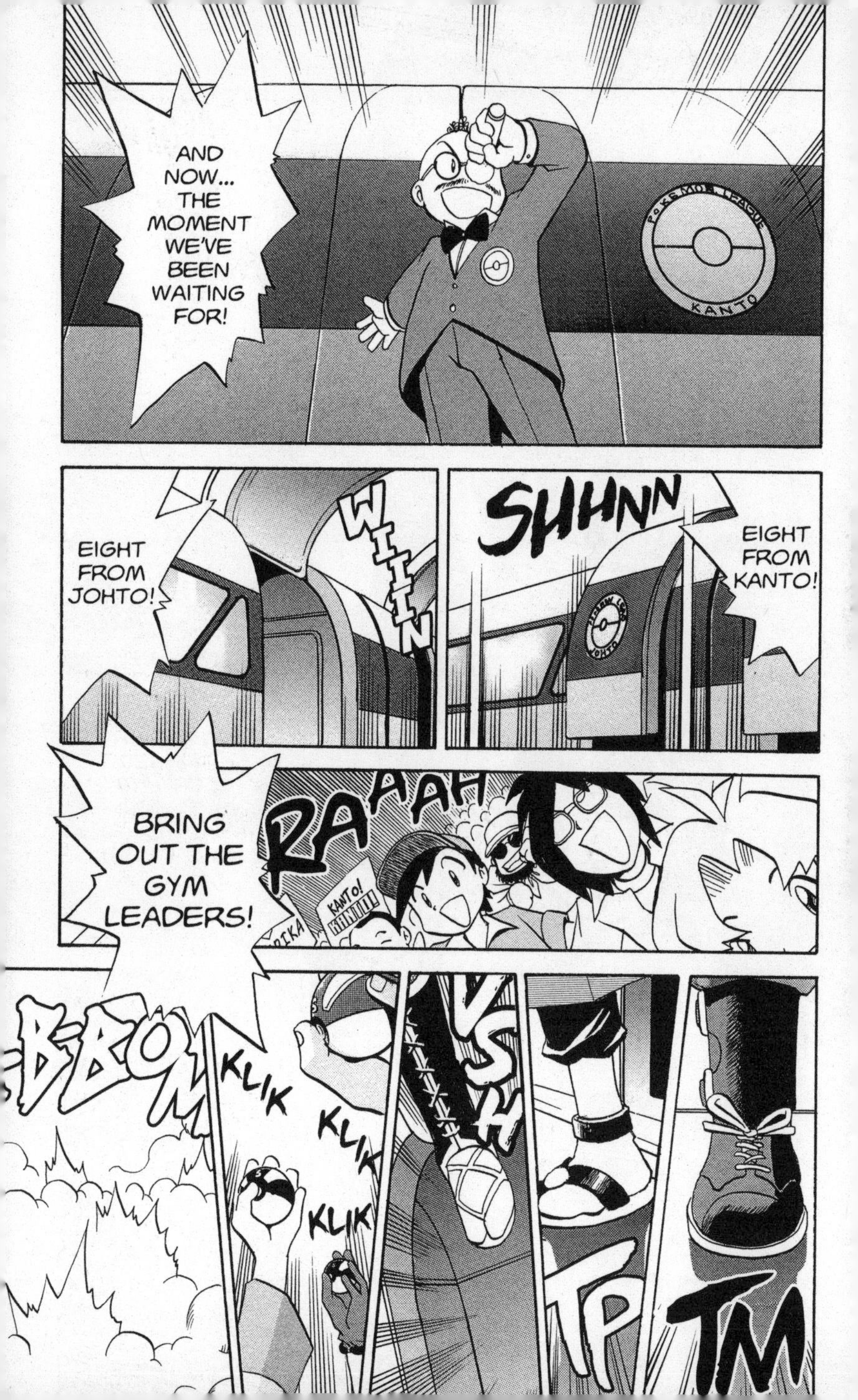

AND NOW... THE MOMENT WE'VE BEEN WAITING FOR!
SHHNN
EIGHT FROM KANTO!
EIGHT FROM JOHTO!
WIIIIN
BRING OUT THE GYM LEADERS!
RAAAH
KANTO!
TM
TP
VSH
KLIK
KLIK
KLIK
B-BOM

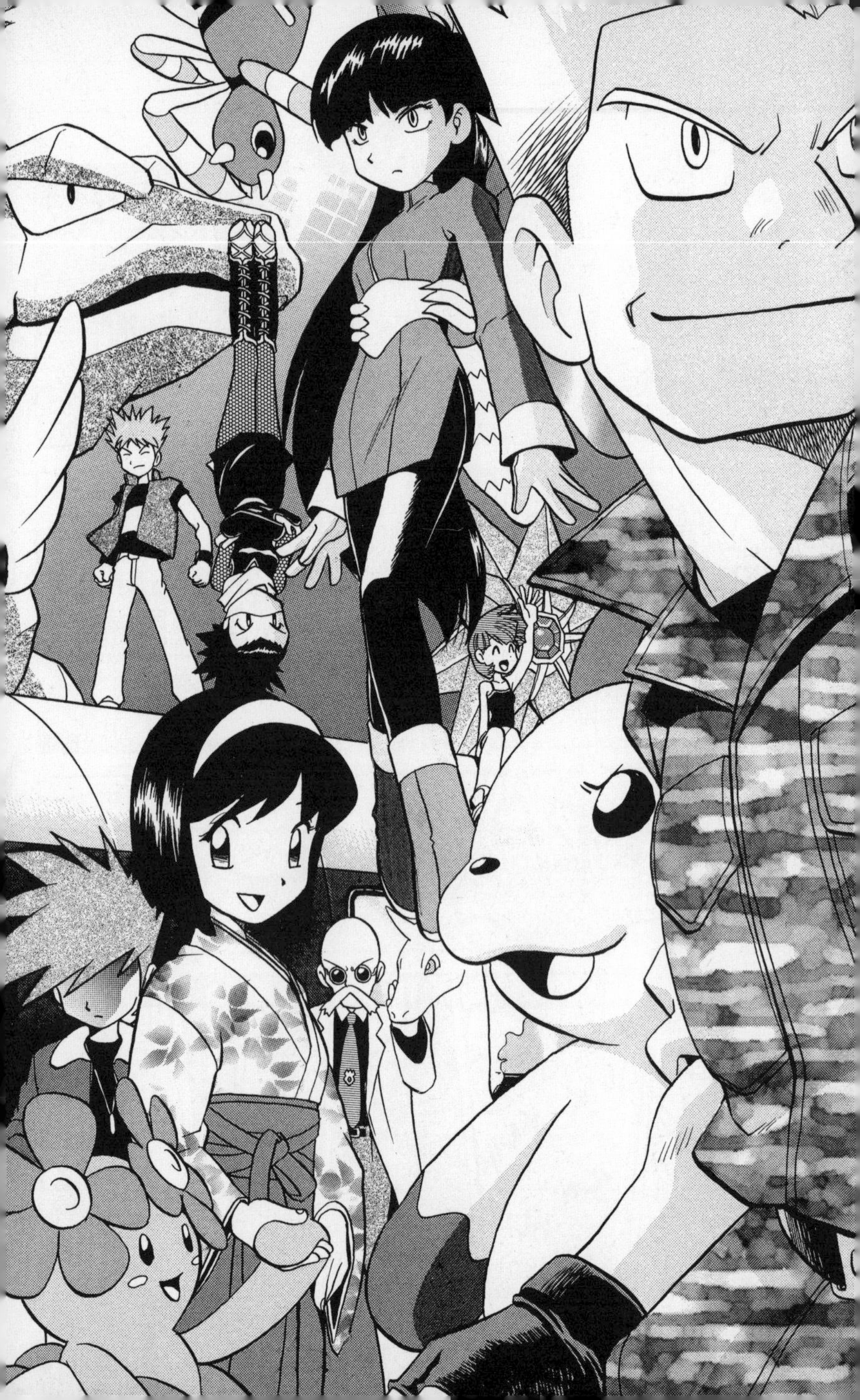

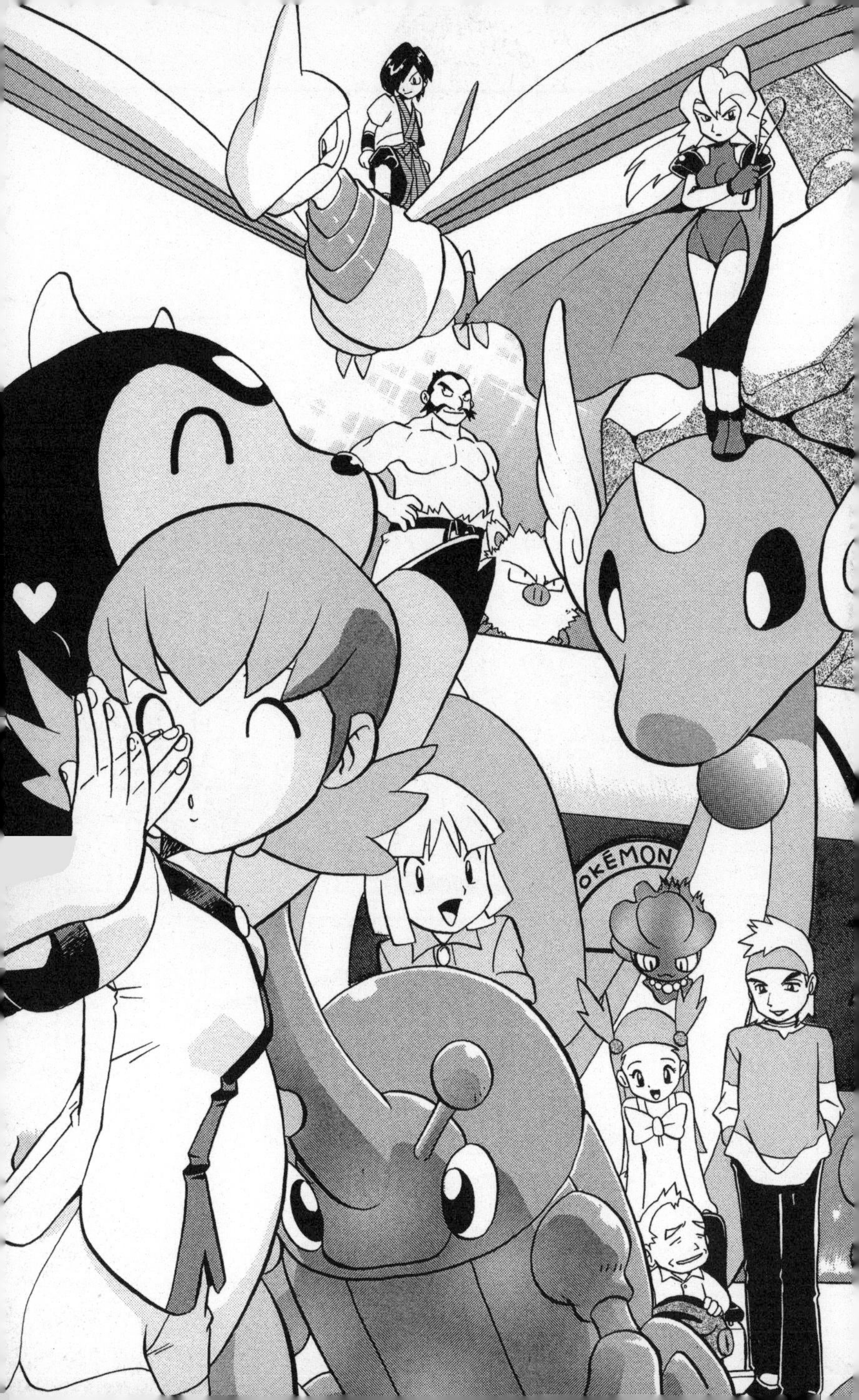

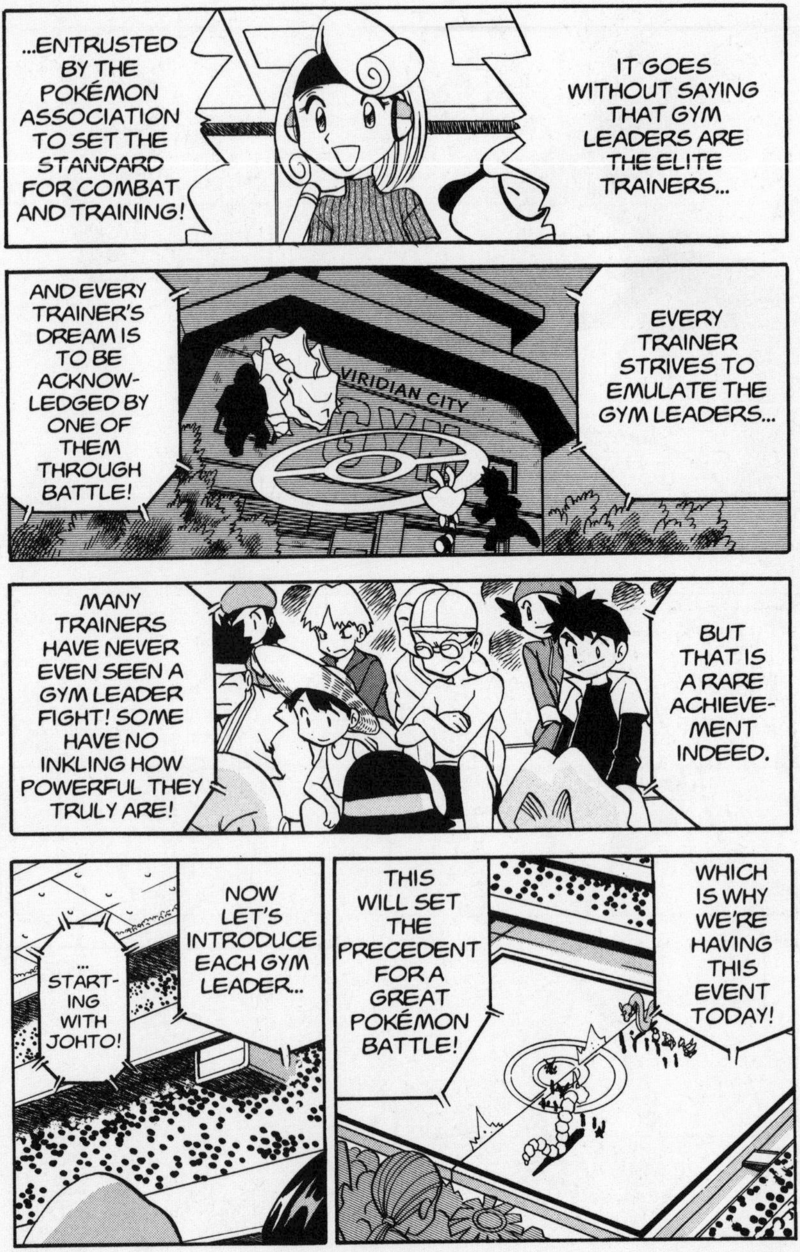
IT GOES WITHOUT SAYING THAT GYM LEADERS ARE THE ELITE TRAINERS...
...ENTRUSTED BY THE POKÉMON ASSOCIATION TO SET THE STANDARD FOR COMBAT AND TRAINING!
EVERY TRAINER STRIVES TO EMULATE THE GYM LEADERS...
VIRIDIAN CITY
AND EVERY TRAINER'S DREAM IS TO BE ACKNOW-LEDGED BY ONE OF THEM THROUGH BATTLE!
BUT THAT IS A RARE ACHIEVE-MENT INDEED.
MANY TRAINERS HAVE NEVER EVEN SEEN A GYM LEADER FIGHT! SOME HAVE NO INKLING HOW POWERFUL THEY TRULY ARE!
WHICH IS WHY WE'RE HAVING THIS EVENT TODAY!
THIS WILL SET THE PRECEDENT FOR A GREAT POKÉMON BATTLE!
NOW LET'S INTRODUCE EACH GYM LEADER...
...START-ING WITH JOHTO!

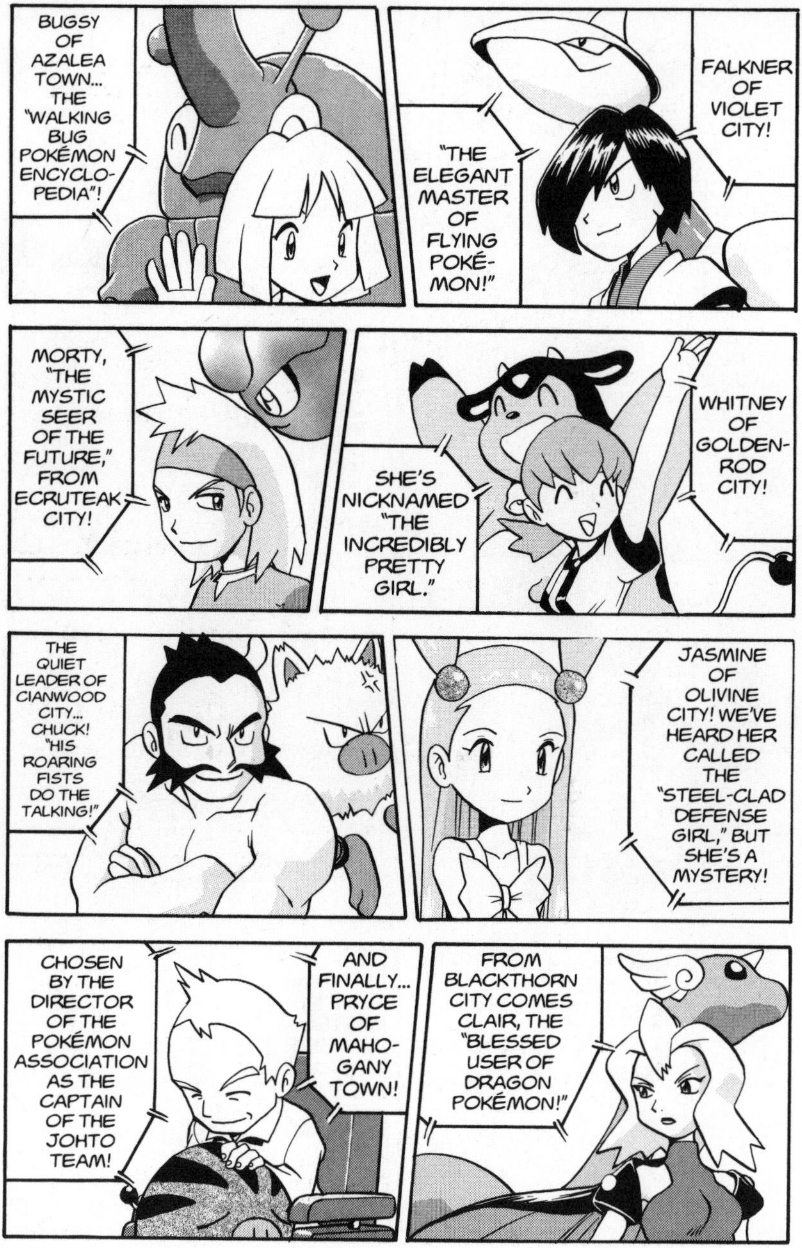
FALKNER OF VIOLET CITY!
"THE ELEGANT MASTER OF FLYING POKÉMON!"
BUGSY OF AZALEA TOWN... THE "WALKING BUG POKÉMON ENCYCLOPEDIA"!
WHITNEY OF GOLDENROD CITY!
SHE'S NICKNAMED "THE INCREDIBLY PRETTY GIRL."
MORTY, "THE MYSTIC SEER OF THE FUTURE," FROM ECRUTEAK CITY!
JASMINE OF OLIVINE CITY! WE'VE HEARD HER CALLED THE "STEEL-CLAD DEFENSE GIRL," BUT SHE'S A MYSTERY!
THE QUIET LEADER OF CIANWOOD CITY... CHUCK! "HIS ROARING FISTS DO THE TALKING!"
FROM BLACKTHORN CITY COMES CLAIR, THE "BLESSED USER OF DRAGON POKÉMON!"
AND FINALLY... PRYCE OF MAHOGANY TOWN!
CHOSEN BY THE DIRECTOR OF THE POKÉMON ASSOCIATION AS THE CAPTAIN OF THE JOHTO TEAM!

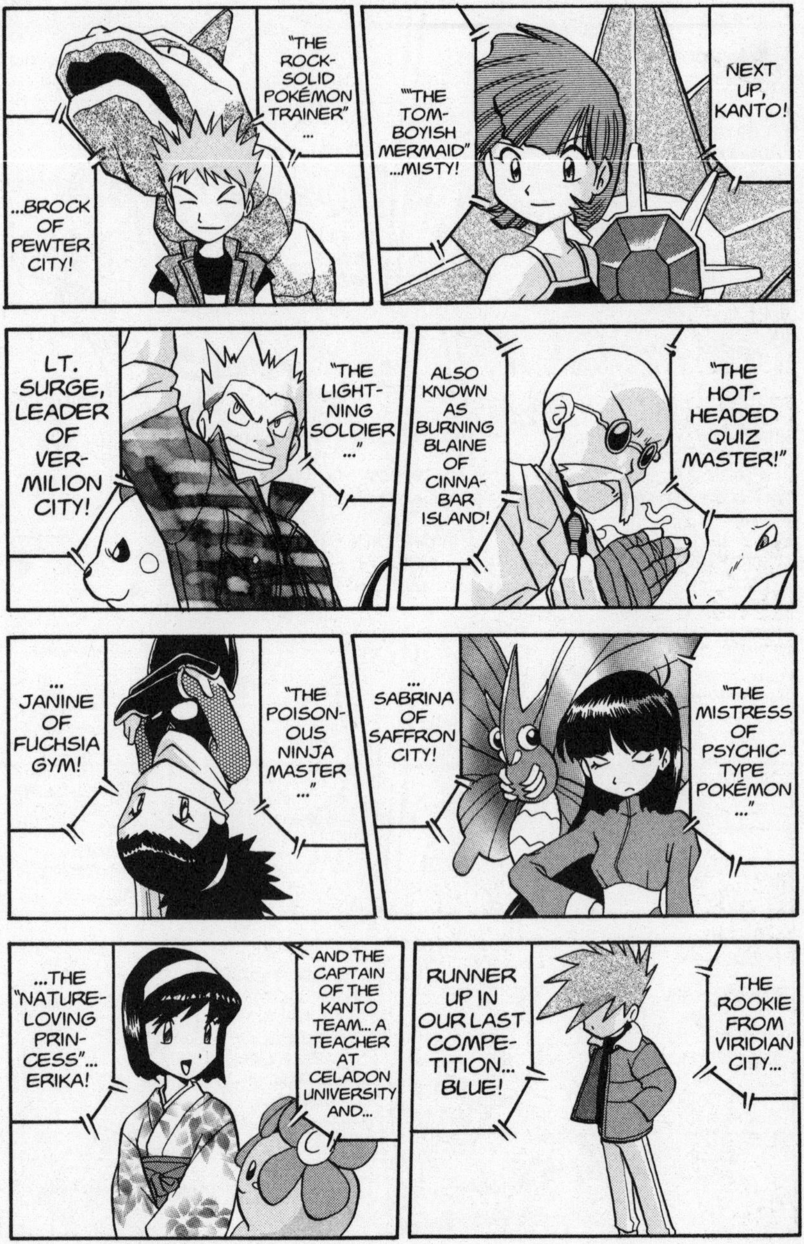
NEXT UP, KANTO!
""THE TOMBOYISH MERMAID" ...MISTY!
"THE ROCK-SOLID POKÉMON TRAINER" ...
...BROCK OF PEWTER CITY!
"THE HOT-HEADED QUIZ MASTER!"
ALSO KNOWN AS BURNING BLAINE OF CINNABAR ISLAND!
"THE LIGHTNING SOLDIER..."
LT. SURGE, LEADER OF VERMILION CITY!
"THE MISTRESS OF PSYCHIC-TYPE POKÉMON..."
...SABRINA OF SAFFRON CITY!
"THE POISONOUS NINJA MASTER..."
...JANINE OF FUCHSIA GYM!
THE ROOKIE FROM VIRIDIAN CITY...
RUNNER UP IN OUR LAST COMPETITION... BLUE!
AND THE CAPTAIN OF THE KANTO TEAM... A TEACHER AT CELADON UNIVERSITY AND...
...THE "NATURE-LOVING PRINCESS"... ERIKA!

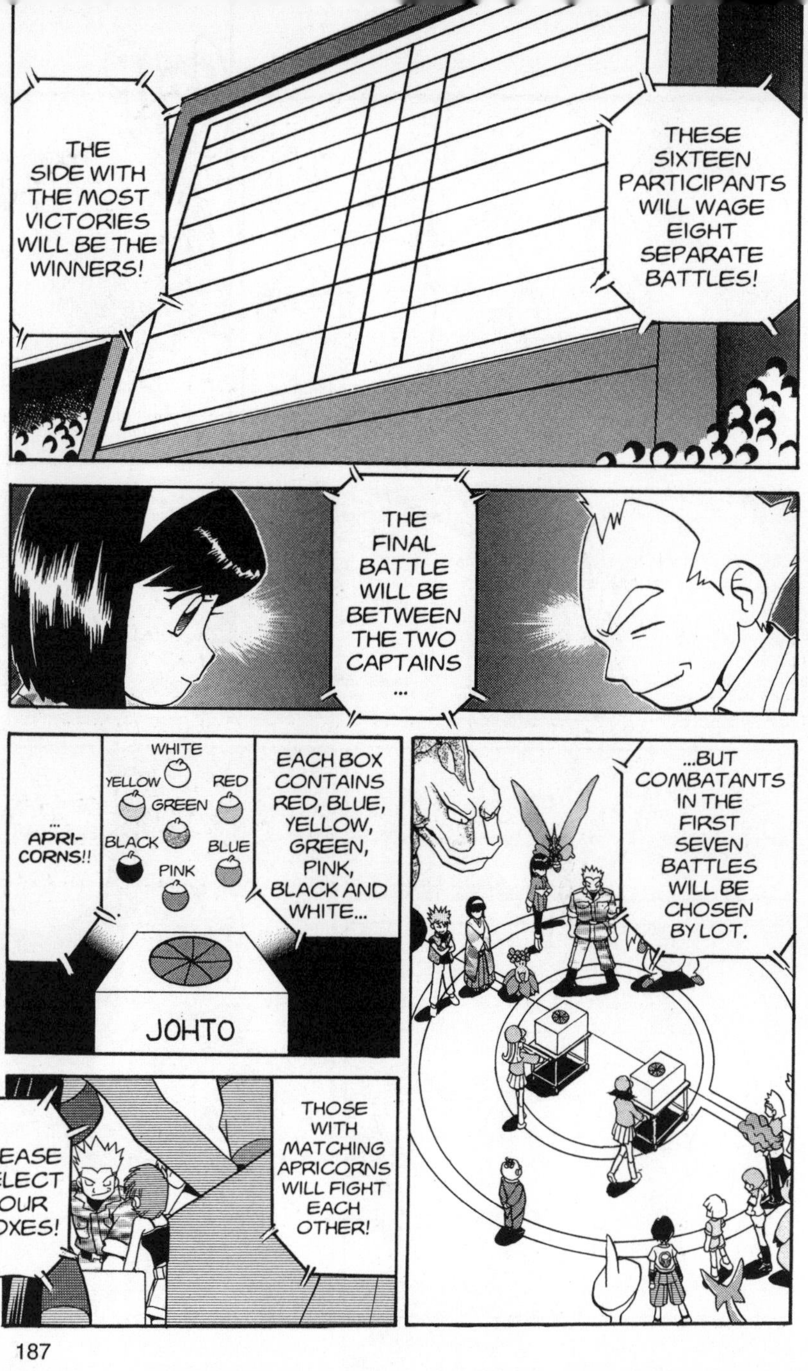
THESE SIXTEEN PARTICIPANTS WILL WAGE EIGHT SEPARATE BATTLES!
THE SIDE WITH THE MOST VICTORIES WILL BE THE WINNERS!
THE FINAL BATTLE WILL BE BETWEEN THE TWO CAPTAINS ...
...BUT COMBATANTS IN THE FIRST SEVEN BATTLES WILL BE CHOSEN BY LOT.
EACH BOX CONTAINS RED, BLUE, YELLOW, GREEN, PINK, BLACK AND WHITE...
WHITE
RED
YELLOW
GREEN
BLUE
BLACK
PINK
... APRI-CORNS!!
JOHTO
THOSE WITH MATCHING APRICORNS WILL FIGHT EACH OTHER!
PLEASE SELECT YOUR BOXES!

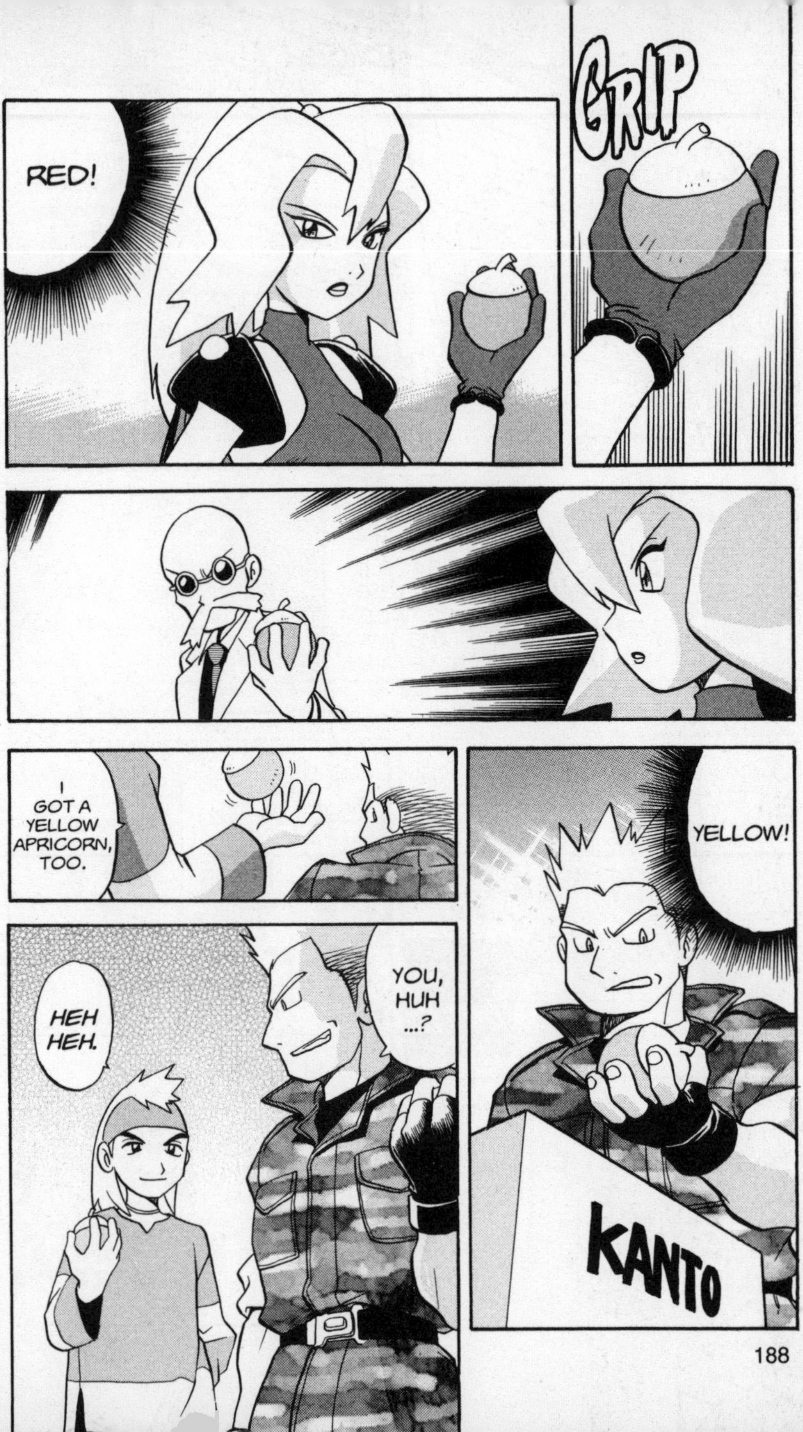
GRIP
RED!
YELLOW!
KANTO
I GOT A YELLOW APRICORN, TOO.
YOU, HUH ...?
HEH HEH.

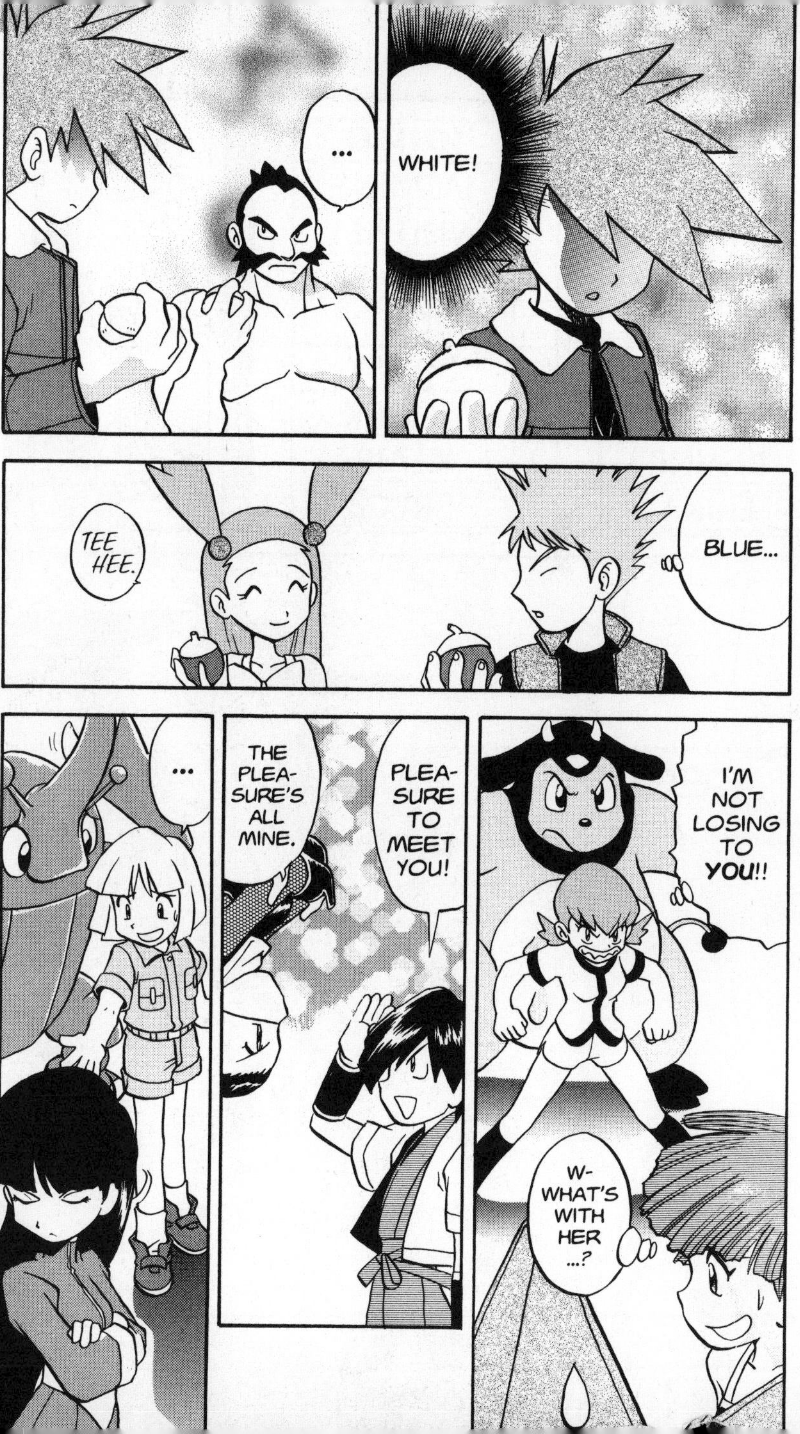
WHITE!
...
BLUE...
TEE HEE.
I'M NOT LOSING TO **YOU**!!
W-WHAT'S WITH HER ...?
PLEA-SURE TO MEET YOU!
THE PLEA-SURE'S ALL MINE.
...

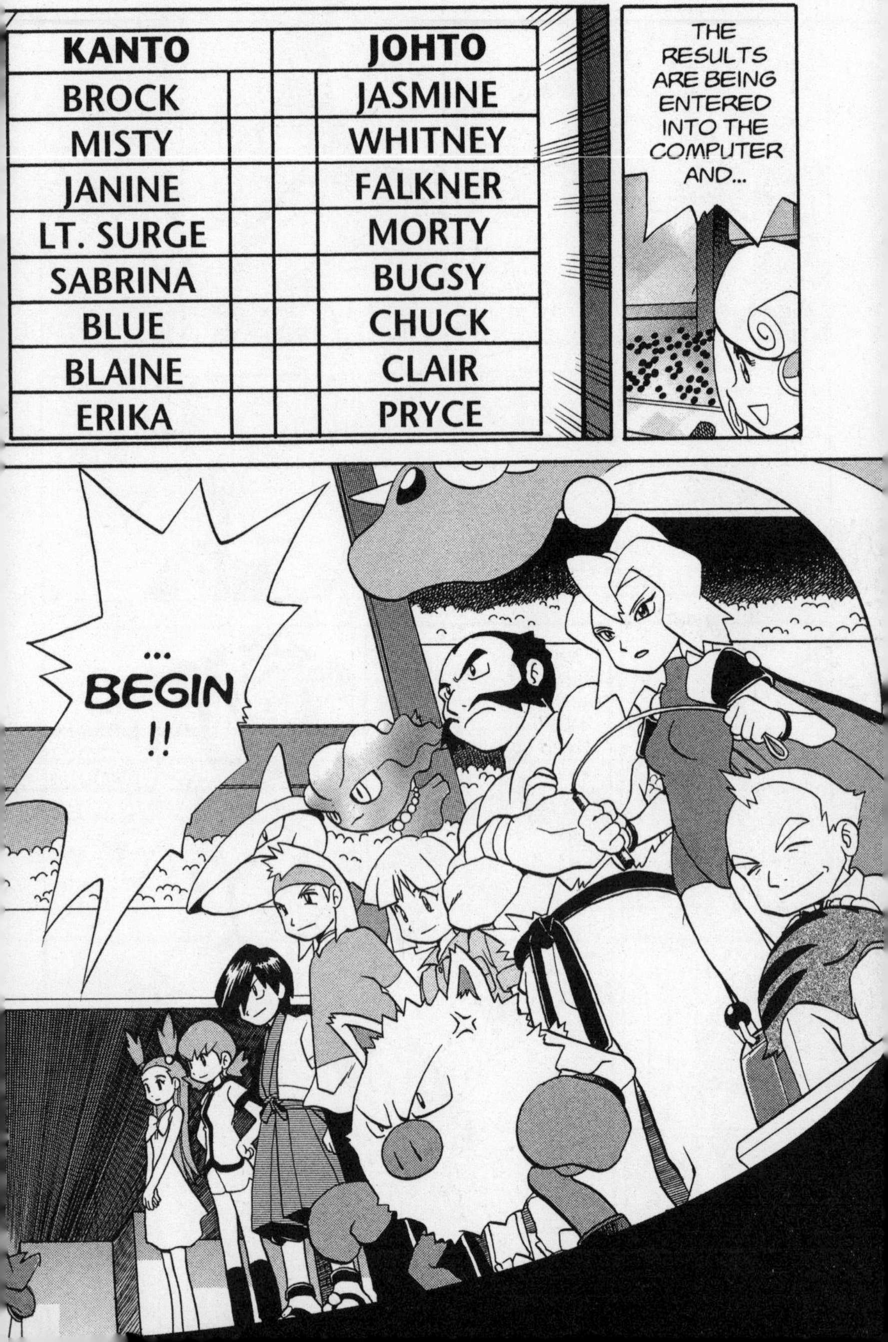
THE RESULTS ARE BEING ENTERED INTO THE COMPUTER AND...
KANTO
BROCK
MISTY
JANINE
LT. SURGE
SABRINA
BLUE
BLAINE
ERIKA
JOHTO
JASMINE
WHITNEY
FALKNER
MORTY
BUGSY
CHUCK
CLAIR
PRYCE
... BEGIN !!

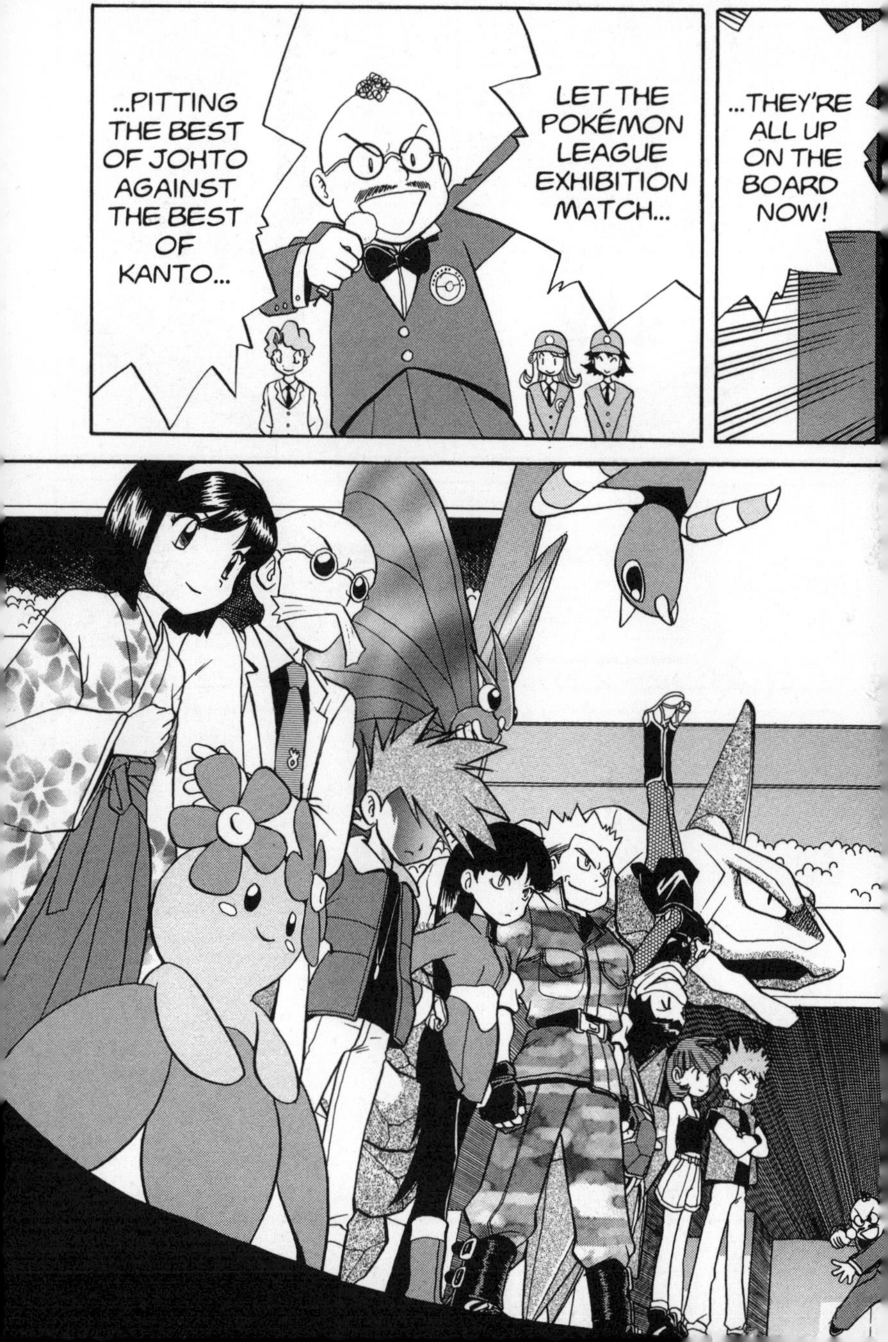
LET THE POKÉMON LEAGUE EXHIBITION MATCH...
...PITTING THE BEST OF JOHTO AGAINST THE BEST OF KANTO...
...THEY'RE ALL UP ON THE BOARD NOW!

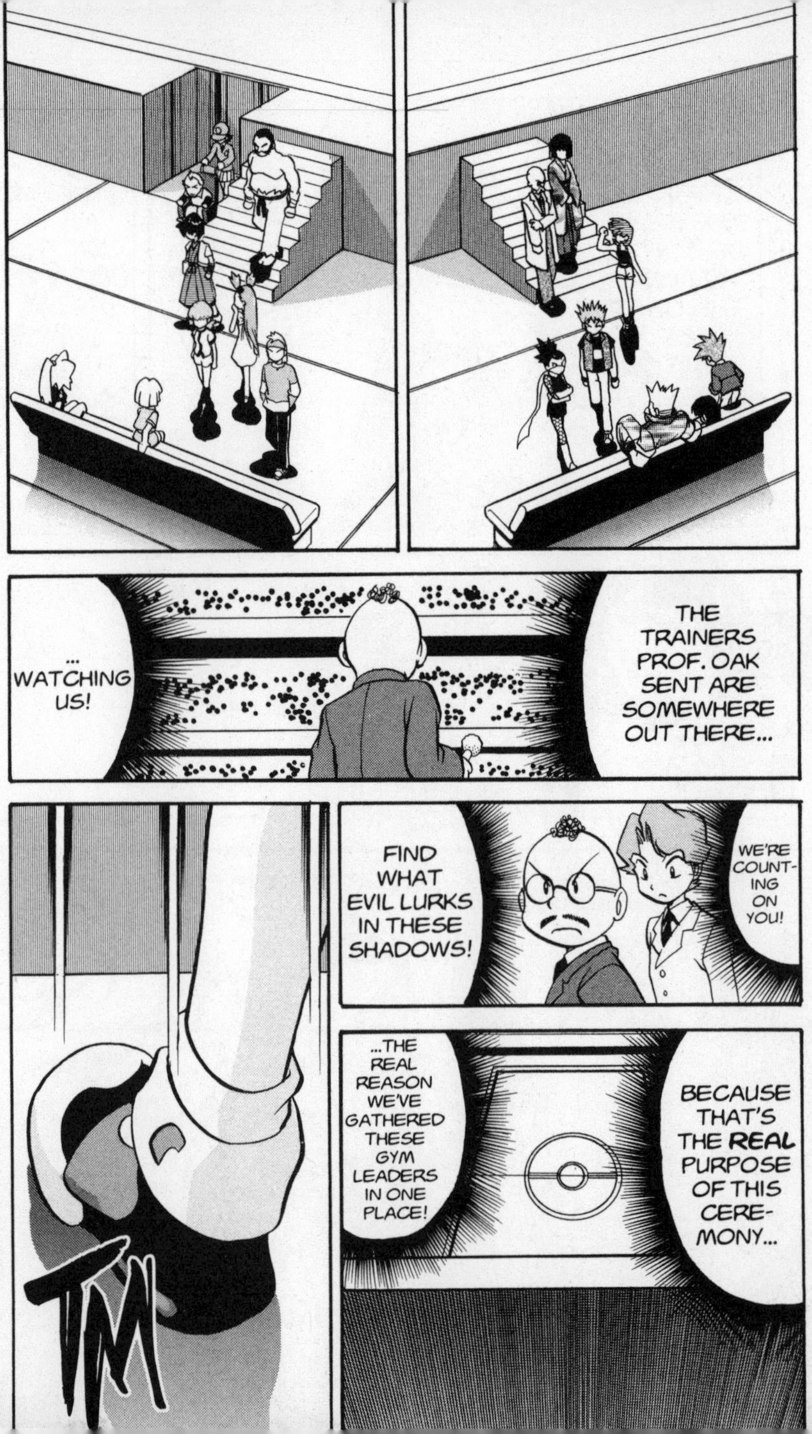
THE TRAINERS PROF. OAK SENT ARE SOMEWHERE OUT THERE...
... WATCHING US!
WE'RE COUNTING ON YOU!
FIND WHAT EVIL LURKS IN THESE SHADOWS!
BECAUSE THAT'S THE **REAL** PURPOSE OF THIS CEREMONY...
...THE REAL REASON WE'VE GATHERED THESE GYM LEADERS IN ONE PLACE!
TM

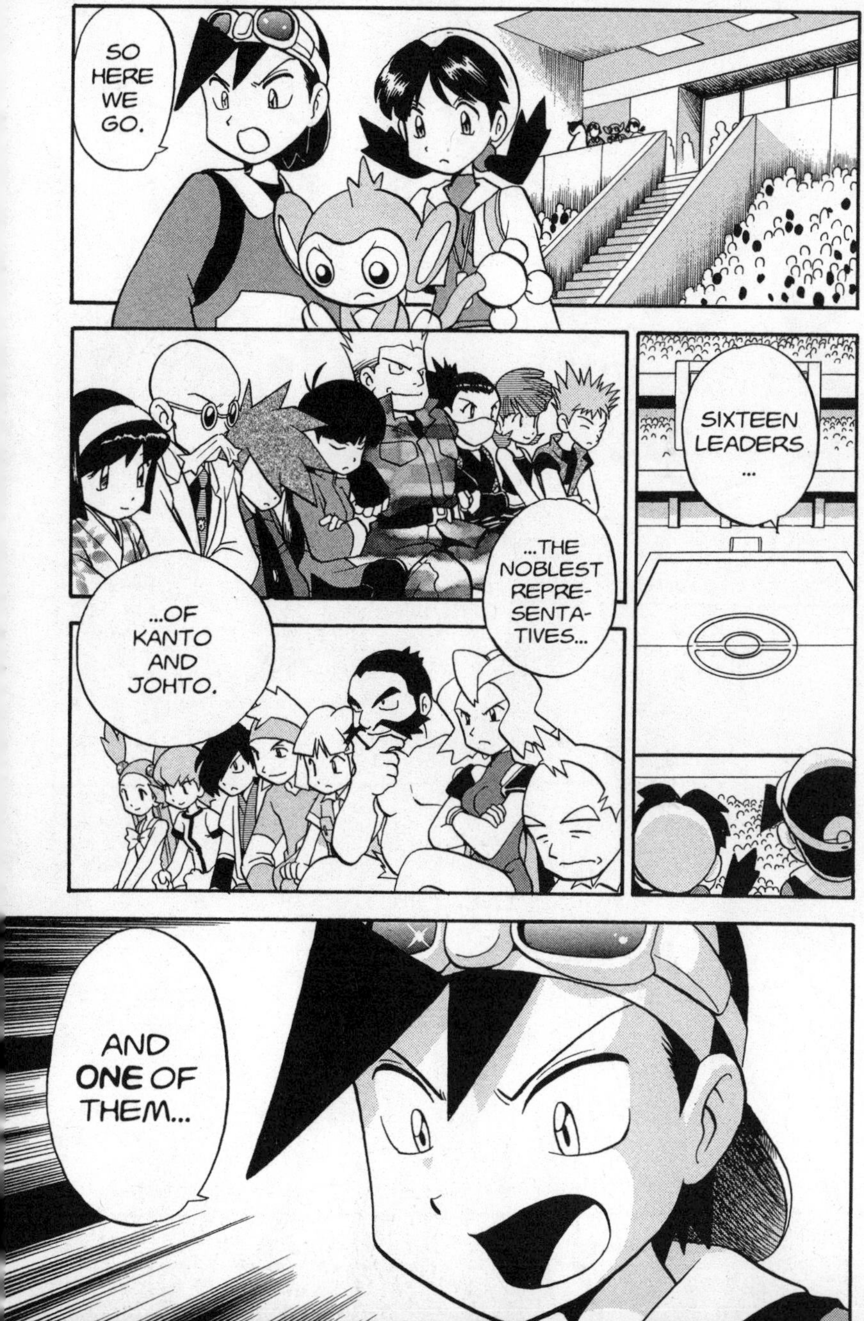
SO HERE WE GO.
SIXTEEN LEADERS...
...THE NOBLEST REPRESENTATIVES...
...OF KANTO AND JOHTO.
AND ONE OF THEM...

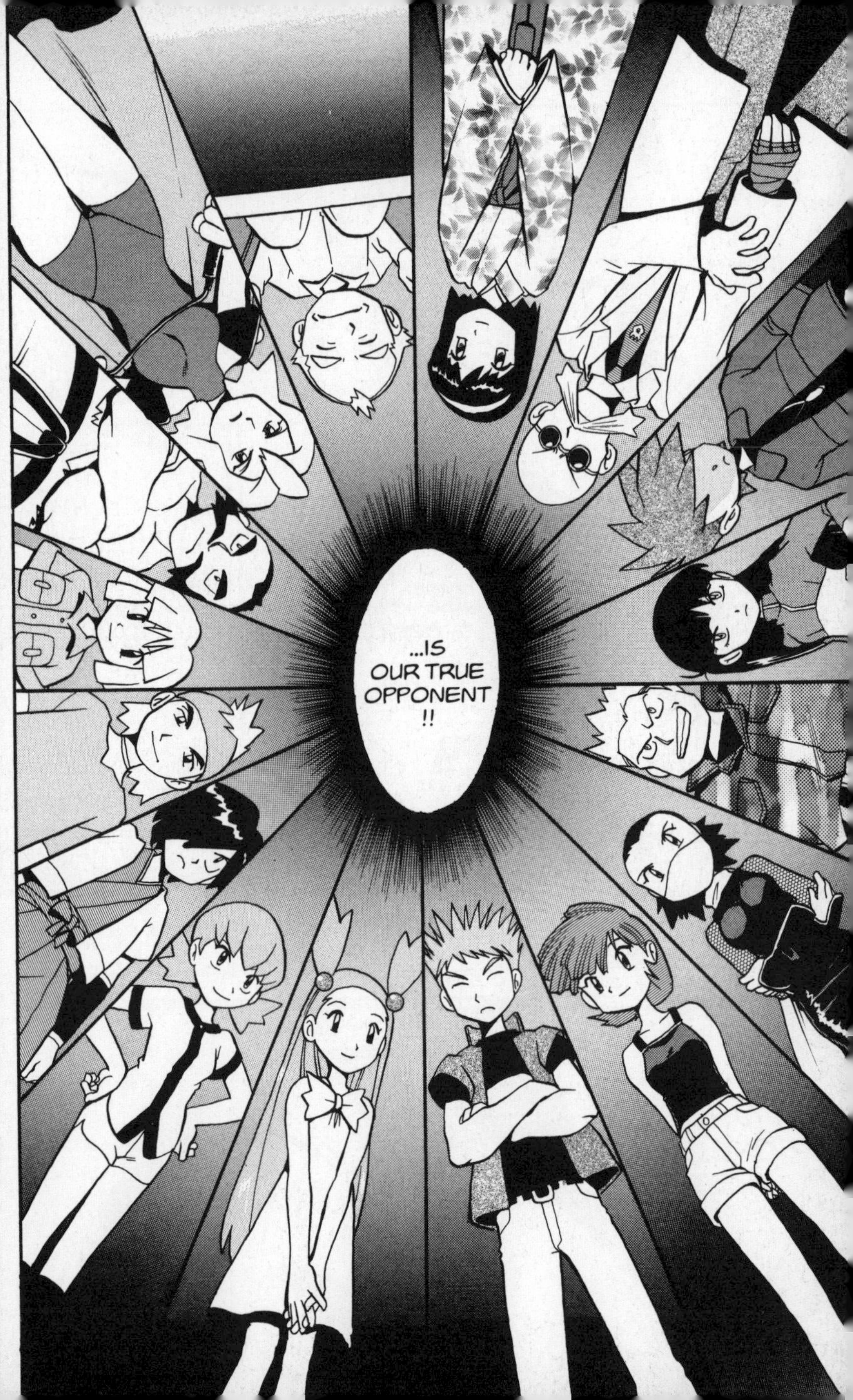
...IS OUR TRUE OPPONENT !!

TO BE CONTINUED

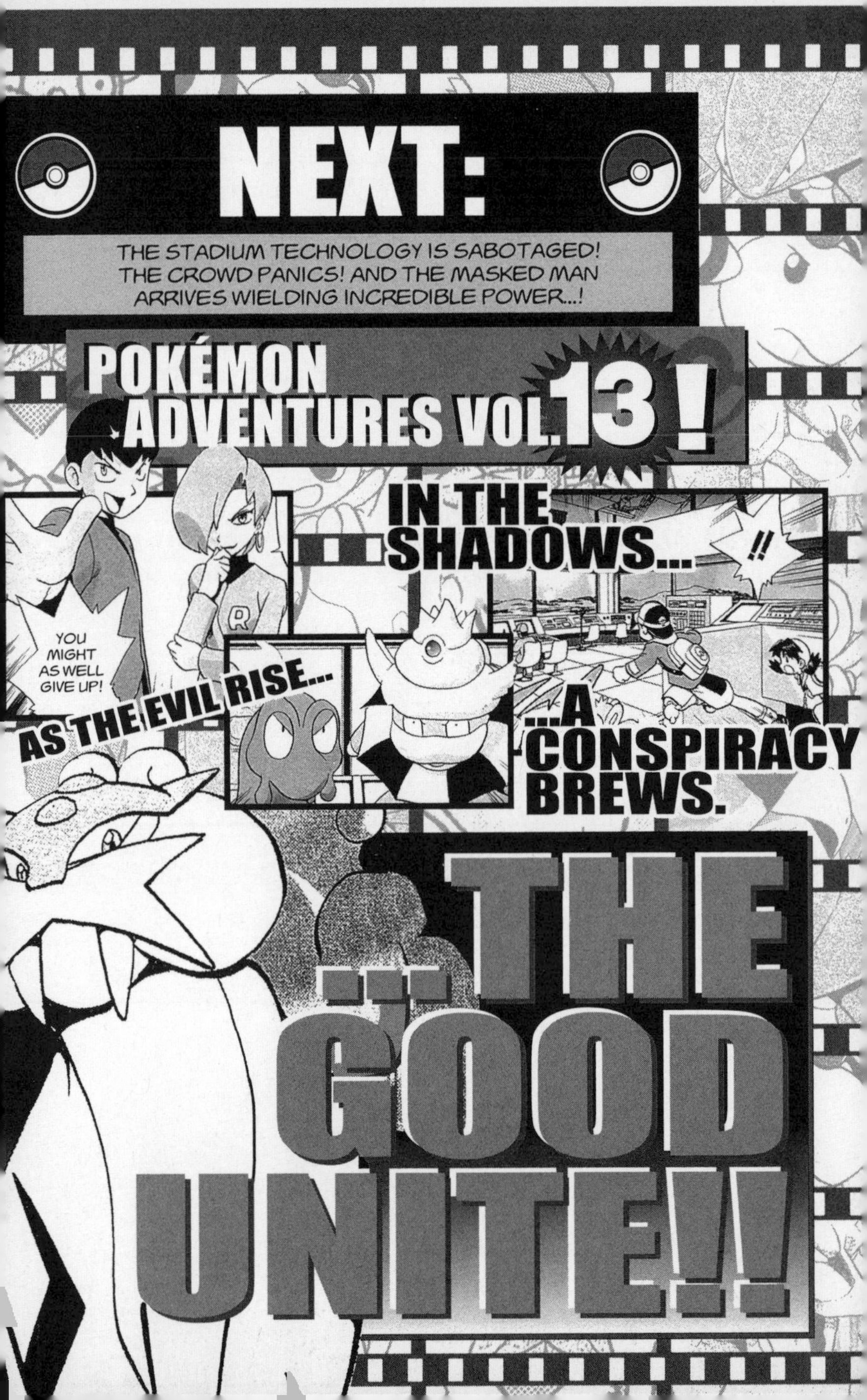
NEXT:
THE STADIUM TECHNOLOGY IS SABOTAGED! THE CROWD PANICS! AND THE MASKED MAN ARRIVES WIELDING INCREDIBLE POWER...!
POKÉMON ADVENTURES VOL. 13!
IN THE SHADOWS...
!!
...A CONSPIRACY BREWS.
AS THE EVIL RISE...
YOU MIGHT AS WELL GIVE UP!
...THE GOOD UNITE!!

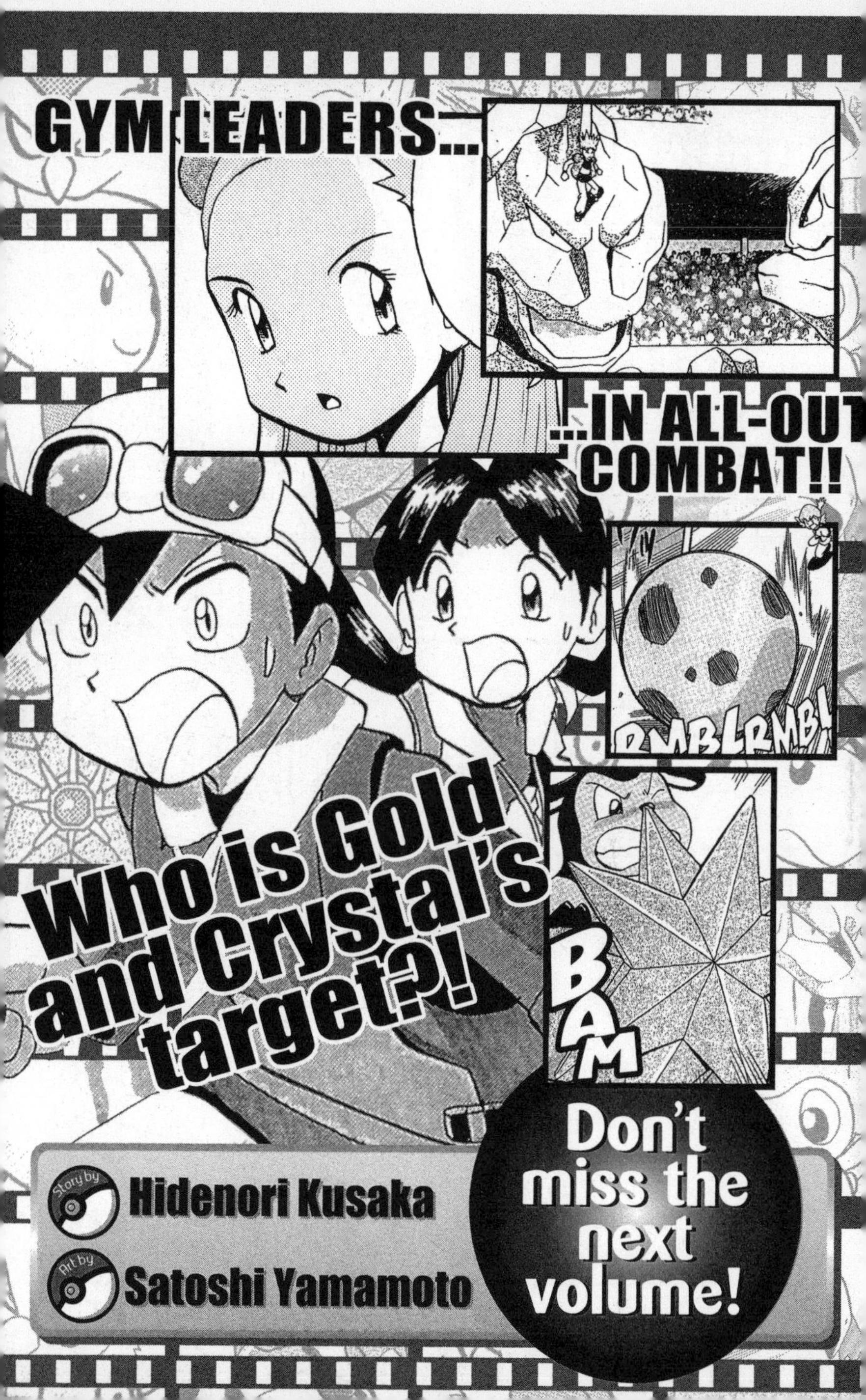
GYM LEADERS...
...IN ALL-OUT COMBAT!!
Who is Gold and Crystal's target?!
BAM
Don't miss the next volume!
Story by Hidenori Kusaka
Art by Satoshi Yamamoto

ADVENTURE ROUTE MAP 12

TRACK THE EVENTS IN THE MANGA ON THIS MAP!

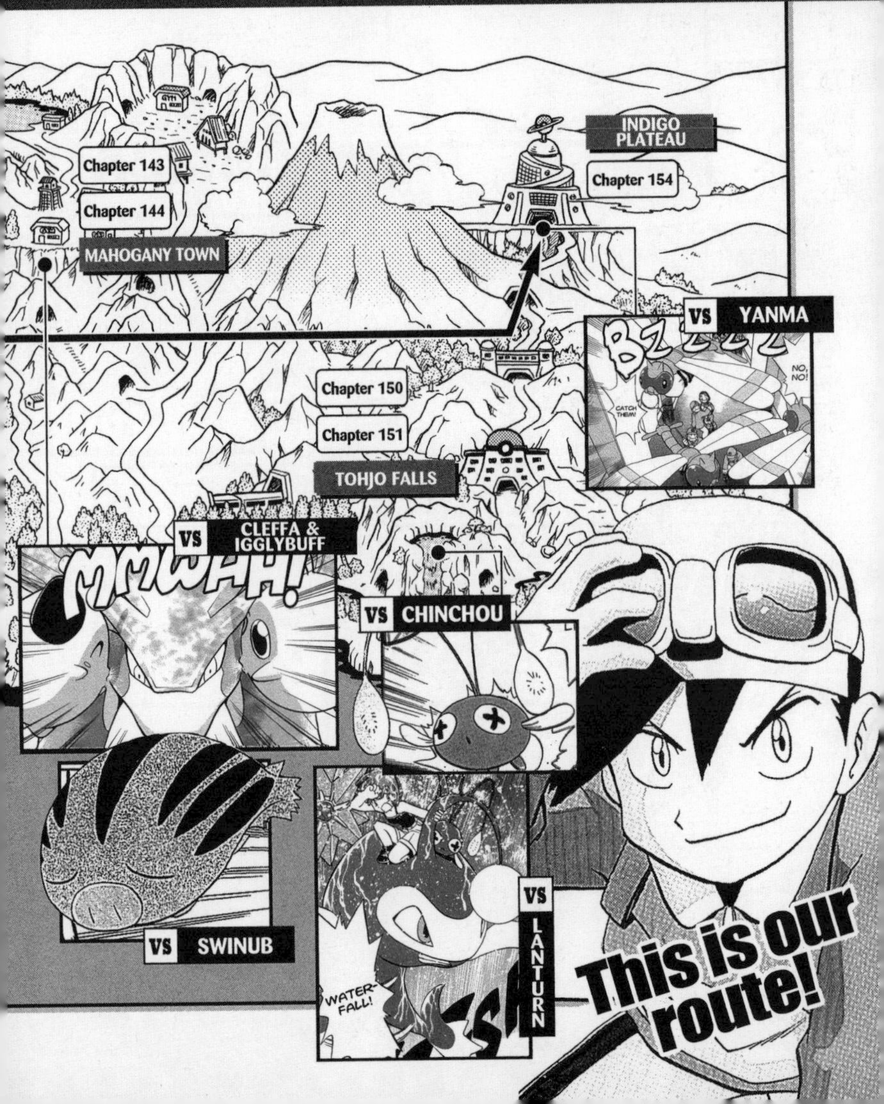
INDIGO PLATEAU
Chapter 154
Chapter 143
Chapter 144
MAHOGANY TOWN
VS YANMA
BZZZZ
NO, NO!
CATCH THEM!
Chapter 150
Chapter 151
TOHJO FALLS
VS CLEFFA & IGGLYBUFF
MMWAH!
VS CHINCHOU
This is our route!
VS LANTURN
WATER-FALL!
VS SWINUB

"GOTTA CATCH 'EM ALL!!"

ADVENTURE ROUTE MAP 12

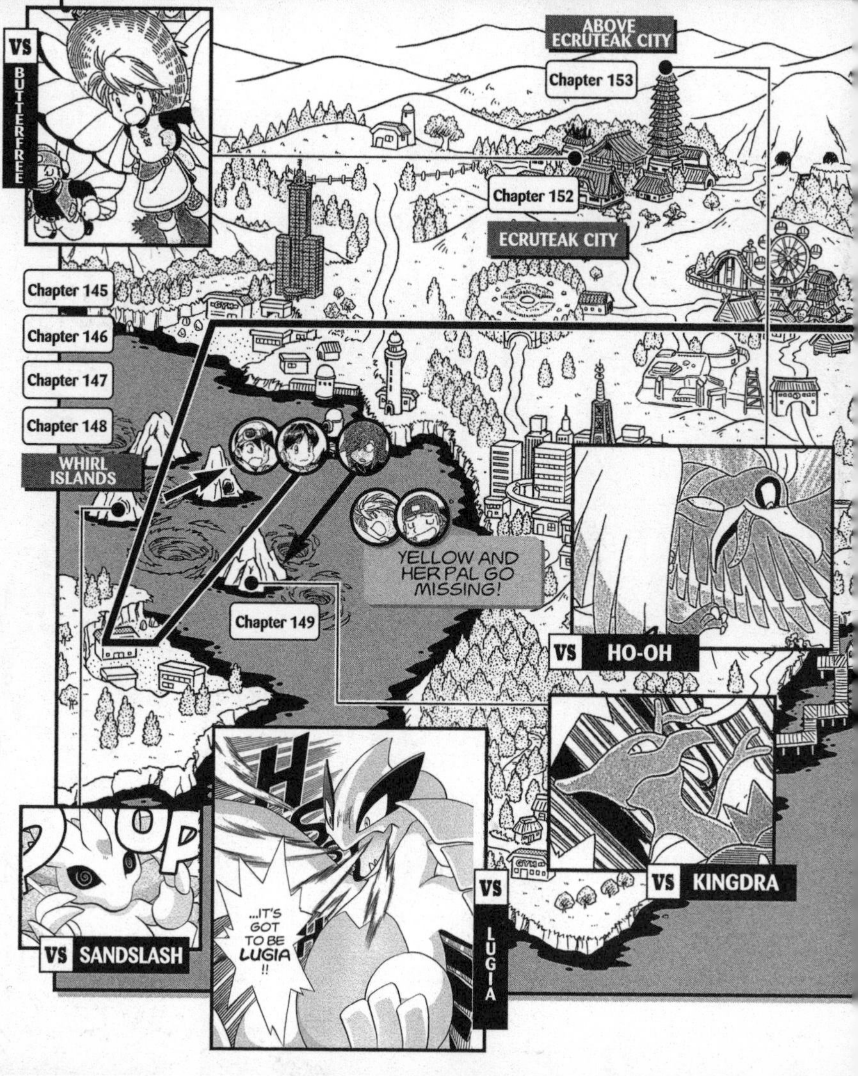
ABOVE ECRUTEAK CITY
Chapter 153
Chapter 152
ECRUTEAK CITY
VS BUTTERFREE
Chapter 145
Chapter 146
Chapter 147
Chapter 148
WHIRL ISLANDS
YELLOW AND HER PAL GO MISSING!
Chapter 149
VS HO-OH
VS KINGDRA
VS LUGIA
...IT'S GOT TO BE LUGIA!!
VS SANDSLASH

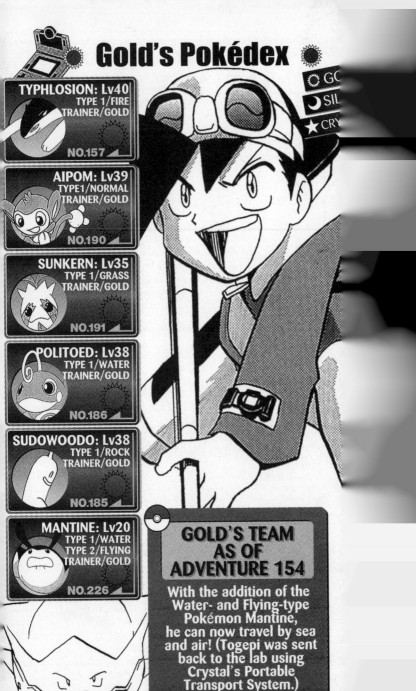

Gold's Pokédex

GO
SIL
CRY

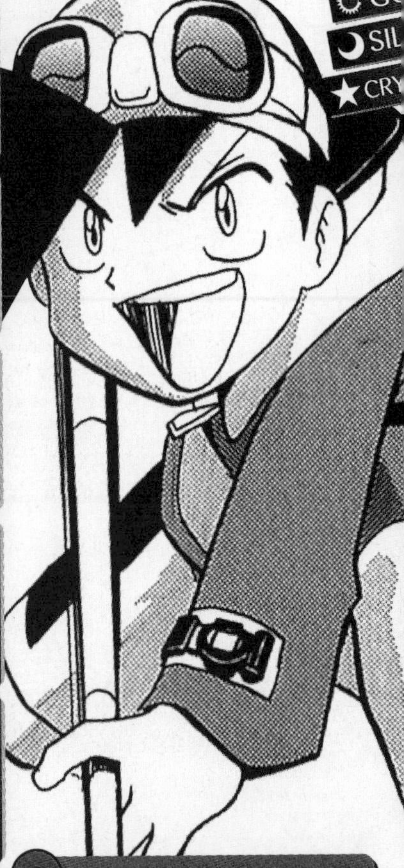

TYPHLOSION: Lv40
TYPE 1/FIRE
TRAINER/GOLD
NO.157

AIPOM: Lv39
TYPE1/NORMAL
TRAINER/GOLD
NO.190

SUNKERN: Lv35
TYPE 1/GRASS
TRAINER/GOLD
NO.191

POLITOED: Lv38
TYPE 1/WATER
TRAINER/GOLD
NO.186

SUDOWOODO: Lv38
TYPE 1/ROCK
TRAINER/GOLD
NO.185

MANTINE: Lv20
TYPE 1/WATER
TYPE 2/FLYING
TRAINER/GOLD
NO.226

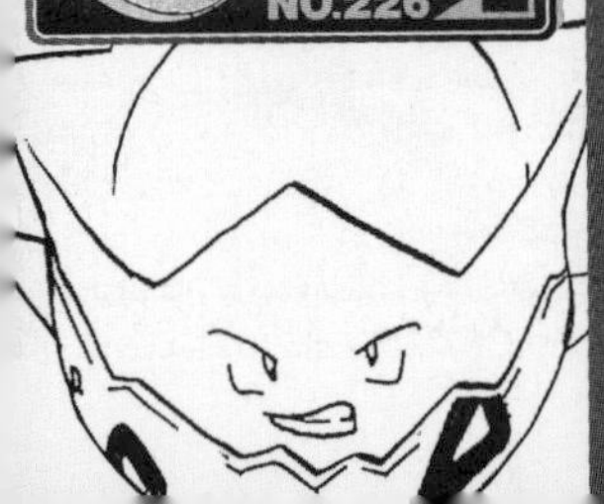

GOLD'S TEAM AS OF ADVENTURE 154

With the addition of the Water- and Flying-type Pokémon Mantine, he can now travel by sea and air! (Togepi was sent back to the lab using Crystal's Portable Transport System.)

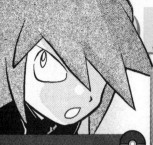

Silver's Pokédex

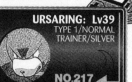

FERALIGATR: Lv40
TYPE 1/WATER
TRAINER/SILVER
NO.160

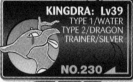

URSARING: Lv39
TYPE 1/NORMAL
TRAINER/SILVER
NO.217

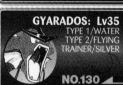

GYARADOS: Lv35
TYPE 1/WATER
TYPE 2/FLYING
TRAINER/SILVER
NO.130

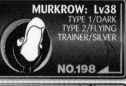

MURKROW: Lv38
TYPE 1/DARK
TYPE 2/FLYING
TRAINER/SILVER
NO.198

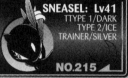

SNEASEL: Lv41
TTYPE 1/DARK
TYPE 2/ICE
TRAINER/SILVER
NO.215

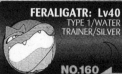

KINGDRA: Lv39
TYPE 1/WATER
TYPE 2/DRAGON
TRAINER/SILVER
NO.230

SILVER'S TEAM AS OF ADVENTURE 154

Croconaw evolved into a Feraligatr, making Silver's team even more powerful!

★ Crystal's Pokédex ★

NATU: Lv43
TYPE 1/PSYCHIC
TYPE 2/FLYING
TRAINER/CRYSTAL
NO.177

MEGANIUM: Lv39
TTYPE 1/GRASS
TRAINER/CRYSTAL
NO.154

ARCANINE: Lv52
TYPE 1/FIRE
TRAINER/CRYSTAL
NO.059

CUBONE: Lv47
TYPE1 / GROUND
TRAINER / CRYSTAL
NO.104

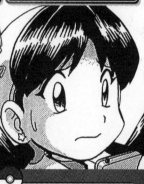

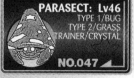

PARASECT: Lv46
TYPE 1/BUG
TYPE 2/GRASS
TRAINER/CRYSTAL
NO.047

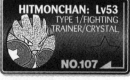

HITMONCHAN: Lv53
TYPE 1/FIGHTING
TRAINER/CRYSTAL
NO.107

FOUND	CAUGHT
164	152

CRYSTAL'S TEAM AS OF ADVENTURE 154

She's behind on her captures, due to getting caught up in a huge battle after she met Gold and Silver But one of her Pokémo evolved into its final form.

Inside the Gym Leader System!

GYM LEADERS PERFECT DATA

~Complete Guide, Part 7~

THE POKÉMON ASSOCIATION MANAGES THE SYSTEM OF GYM LEADERS. HERE IS SOME DATA ABOUT THE SIXTEEN MEMBERS.

DIRECTOR OF THE POKÉMON ASSOCIATION AND ITS HIGHEST AUTHORITY

GYM LEADERS PERFECT DATA

Basic Organization

01 What is the role of a Gym Leader?

GYM LEADERS ARE MASTER TRAINERS SELECTED BY THE ASSOCIATION TO ADVANCE THE ART OF RAISING AND BATTLING POKÉMON.

EACH IS SELECTED TO LEAD ONE TOWN'S GYM. THEIR DUTIES INCLUDE MEDIATION AND RESOLVING PROBLEMS IN THEIR AREA (SEE ADV. 151 AMONG OTHERS). MOST ARE ALSO LEADING EXPERTS IN A SPECIFIC FIELD.

▼ EVERY ONE IS AN ACCOMPLISHED TRAINER, FIGHTER AND SPECIALIST...

VIRIDIAN CITY
GYM

I KNOW EVERYTHING THERE IS TO KNOW ABOUT WATER ATTACKS...

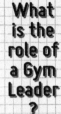

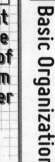

...AND HOPEFULLY AN INSPIRING LEADER AS WELL. ◀

02 How do Trainers challenge them?

WHEN A TRAINER IS CONFIDENT ENOUGH TO GIVE HIS OR HER SKILLS A REAL TEST, THEY HEAD FOR A GYM... BUT THAT DOESN'T GUARANTEE THEM A BATTLE WITH THE LEADER. IT'S ENTIRELY UP TO THE LEADER WHETHER OR NOT TO ACCEPT A CHALLENGE (SEE ADVS. 4 AND 19).

CALLING ALL FIGHTERS!!
PEWTER CITY GYM LEADER BROCK WILL TAKE ON ALL CHALLENGERS!
DATES & TIMES
CHALLENGER REQUIREMENTS
PEWTER CITY

▲ SOME LEADERS ARE EAGER TO ACCEPT CHALLENGES.

▼ THOSE WHOSE TALENTS ARE ACKNOWLEDGED BY THE GYM LEADER RECEIVE A BADGE. SO FAR, ONLY A FEW BADGES ARE GIVEN OUT, AS ONLY A FEW TRAINERS ARE WORTHY OF THEM.

FWAP

03 Kanto and Johto Gym Leader Personal Data

1. Gym 2. Expert type 3. Type of badge 4. Occupation

BADGES AND SPECIALTIES DIFFER FROM LEADER TO LEADER.

CLAIR
1. Blackthorn Gym
2. Dragon
3. Rising Badge
4. None

PRYCE
1. Mahogany Gym
2. Ice
3. Glacier Badge
4. Sculptor

ERIKA
1. Celadon Gym
2. Grass
3. Rainbow Badge
4. University Lecturer

BLAINE
1. Cinnabar Gym
2. Fire
3. Volcano Badge
4. Pokémon Ecology Researcher

CHUCK
1. Cianwood Gym
2. Fighting
3. Storm Badge
4. Dojo Manager

BLUE
1. Viridian Gym
2. ?
3. Earth Badge
4. None

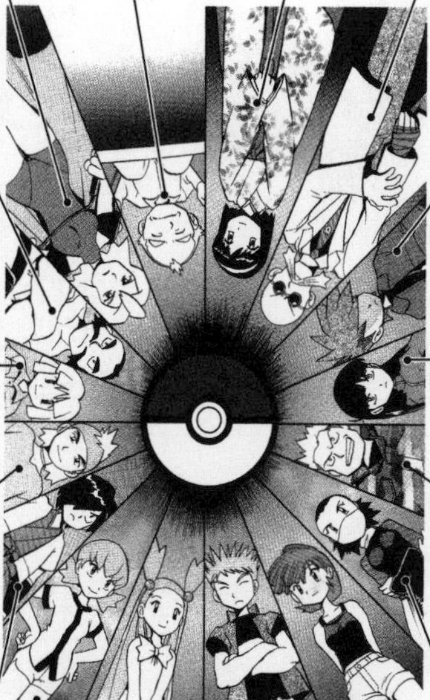

BUGSY
1. Azalea Gym
2. Bug
3. Hive Badge
4. Ruins Investigator

SABRINA
1. Saffron Gym
2. Psychic
3. Marsh Badge
4. None

MORTY
1. Ecruteak Gym
2. Ghost
3. Fog Badge
4. Finder

LT. SURGE
1. Vermilion Gym
2. Electric
3. Thunder Badge
4. Captain, SS Aqua

FALKNER
1. Violet Gym
2. Flying
3. Zephyr Badge
4. Police Officer

JANINE
1. Fuchsia Gym
2. Poison
3. Soul Badge
4. Freelance Agent

WHITNEY
1. Goldenrod Gym
2. Normal
3. Plain Badge
4. Celebrity

JASMINE
1. Olivine Gym
2. ?
3. Mineral Badge
4. Lighthouse Keeper

BROCK
1. Pewter Gym
2. Rock
3. Boulder Badge
4. Museum Security Guard

MISTY
1. Cerulean Gym
2. Water
3. Cascade Badge
4. None

Special System

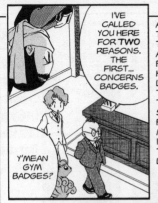

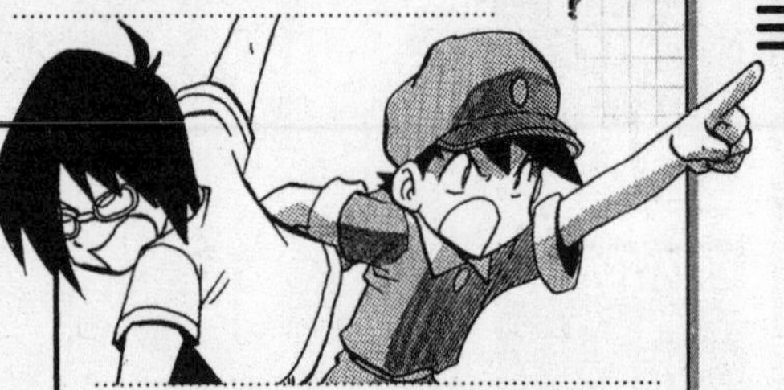

04 How do badges permit participation in the League tournament?

ALL LEADERS HAVE THE RIGHT TO DISTRIBUTE BADGES AS THEY SEE FIT...WHICH IS WHY THE ASSOCIATION GIVES SPECIAL PRIVILEGES TO TRAINERS WHO HAVE THE APPROVAL OF ALL THE LEADERS. THAT PRIVILEGE IS THE RIGHT TO PARTICIPATE IN THE TOURNAMENT FINALS. THIS SYSTEM IS NEW TO THE 10TH POKÉMON LEAGUE TOURNAMENT (THE CURRENT ONE). THIS IS ALREADY INSPIRING MORE TRAINERS TO CHALLENGE GYM LEADERS (SEE ADV. 150).

I'VE CALLED YOU HERE FOR TWO REASONS. THE FIRST... CONCERNS BADGES.
Y'MEAN GYM BADGES?

▲ TRAINERS FROM KANTO MUST EARN BADGES FROM THE EIGHT KANTO LEADERS, WHILE JOHTO TRAINERS MUST EARN BADGES FROM THE EIGHT JOHTO LEADERS.

●FINALS●
●PRELIMINARIES●
BADGE HOLDERS

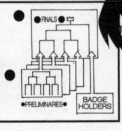

EIGHT ▶ BADGES ENTITLE TRAINERS TO SKIP THE PRELIMINARY ROUNDS.

BADGE ENERGY BOOSTER

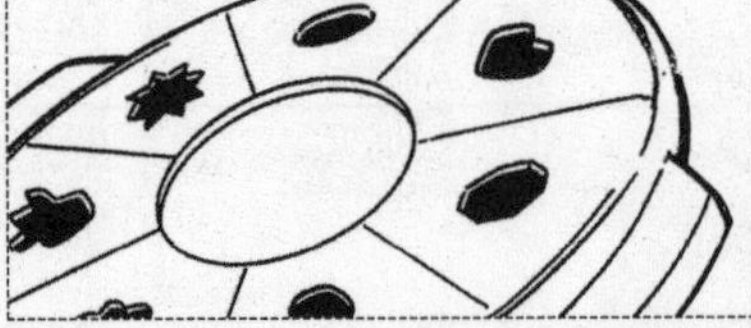

A DEVICE THAT TEAM ROCKET AND THE KANTO ELITE FOUR USED TO ALTER THE ENERGY EMITTED FROM THE BADGES. THE POKÉMON ASSOCIATION IS ENDEAVORING TO RESTORE THE IMAGE OF THE BADGE AS A SYMBOL OF THE OWNER'S PROWESS...HENCE THE NEW SPECIAL PRIVILEGES.

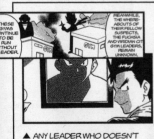

05 What is the appointment exam?

EACH LEADER IS SELECTED AND APPOINTED BY THE ASSOCIATION. TO GAIN THAT RIGHT, THEY MUST FIRST PASS TESTS IN THE FIELDS OF COMBAT, KNOWLEDGE, AND PERSONAL CHARACTER (SEE ADV. 115).

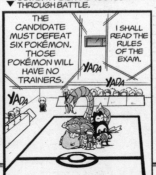

▼ COMBAT ABILITY IS TESTED THROUGH BATTLE.

I SHALL READ THE RULES OF THE EXAM.
THE CANDIDATE MUST DEFEAT SIX POKÉMON. THOSE POKÉMON WILL HAVE NO TRAINERS.
YADA
YADA
YADA

MEANWHILE, THE WHEREABOUTS OF THEIR FELLOW SUSPECTS, THE FUCHSIA AND VIRIDIAN CIT GYM LEADERS, REMAIN UNKNOWN.
GYM
GYM

▲ ANY LEADER WHO DOESN'T FULFILL HIS DUTIES OVER A LONG PERIOD OF TIME MAY BE REMOVED FROM THE POST (SEE ADV. 99).

06 What is the Gym Leader's source of income?

REMUNERATION FOR THE LEADERS ARRIVES IN THE FORM OF "GYM OPERATING COSTS" FROM THE ASSOCIATION. BUT THAT DOESN'T MEAN THEY ARE FORBIDDEN FROM OTHER OCCUPATIONS. MOST LEADERS KEEP THE JOBS THEY HAD BEFORE THEY WERE APPOINTED (SEE PERSONAL DATA SECTION). THUS, GYM LEADERS ARE OFTEN ENCOUNTERED OUTSIDE OF THEIR GYMS (SEE ADVS. 125 & 136).

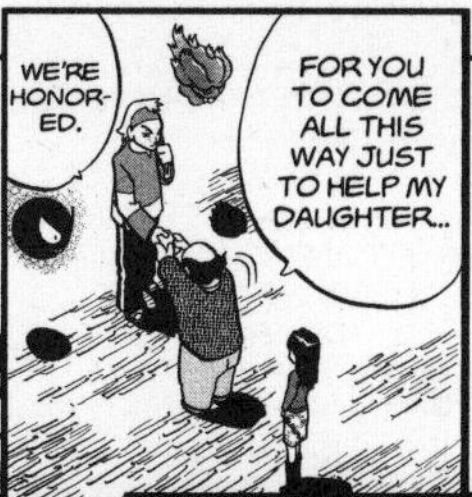
FOR YOU TO COME ALL THIS WAY JUST TO HELP MY DAUGHTER...
WE'RE HONORED.

◀▼ MANY HOLD OCCUPATIONS IN KEEPING WITH THEIR SPECIAL ABILITIES.

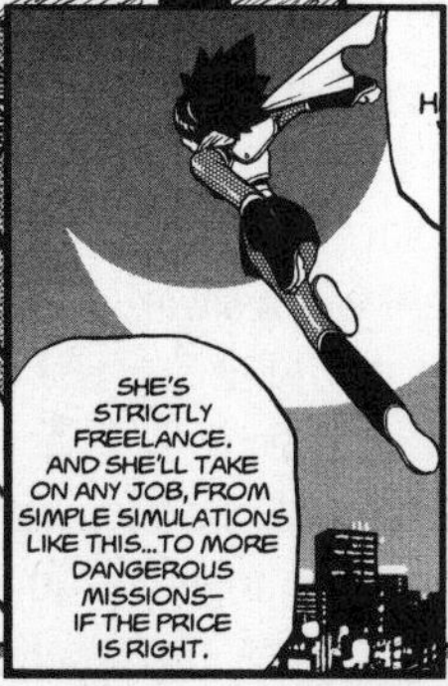
SHE'S STRICTLY FREELANCE. AND SHE'LL TAKE ON ANY JOB, FROM SIMPLE SIMULATIONS LIKE THIS...TO MORE DANGEROUS MISSIONS—IF THE PRICE IS RIGHT.

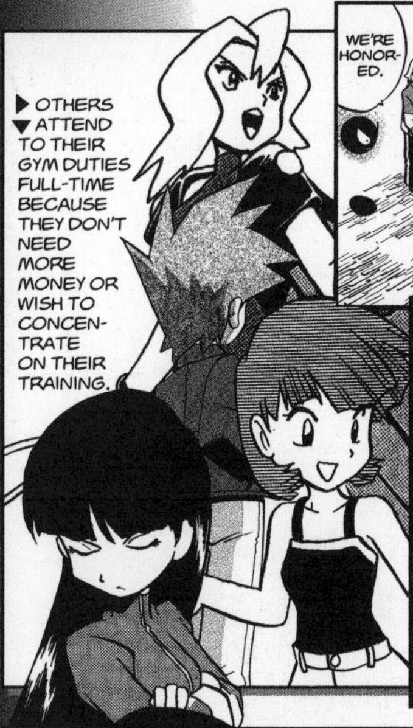

▶▼ OTHERS ATTEND TO THEIR GYM DUTIES FULL-TIME BECAUSE THEY DON'T NEED MORE MONEY OR WISH TO CONCENTRATE ON THEIR TRAINING.

07 What is the Gym Leader Exhibition Match?

MOST TRAINERS DON'T HAVE THE OPPORTUNITY TO SEE GYM LEADERS IN ACTION, SO THE ASSOCIATION PLANNED THIS EVENT TO MODEL QUALITY POKÉMON BATTLES. IT'S A HIGHLY ANTICIPATED EVENT (SEE ADV. 154).

▼ AFTER FIRST-HAND OBSERVATION OF HIS SKILLS, THE DIRECTOR OF THE ASSOCIATION RECOMMENDED PRYCE FOR CAPTAIN OF THE JOHTO TEAM.

JOHTO CAPTAIN, **PRYCE**

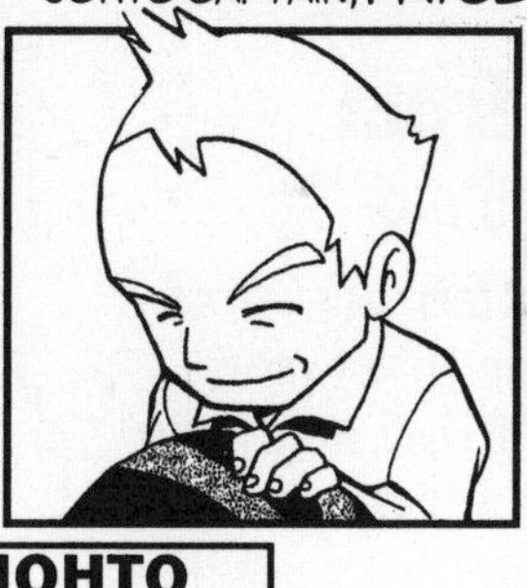

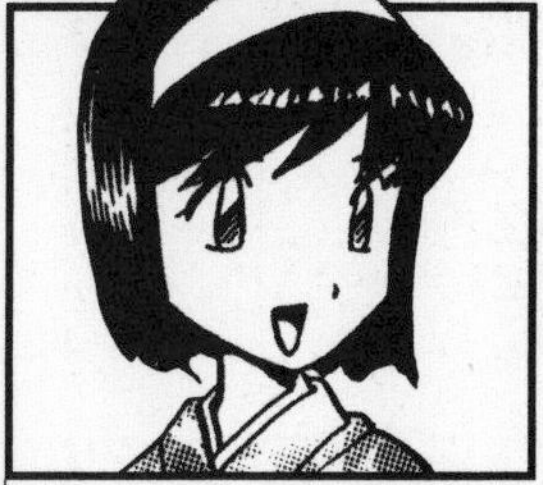

KANTO CAPTAIN, **ERIKA**

▲ THE KANTO LEADERS CHOSE ERIKA FOR THEIR CAPTAIN.

KANTO		JOHTO
BROCK		JASMINE
MISTY		WHITNEY
JANINE		FALKNER
LT. SURGE		MORTY
SABRINA		BUGSY
BLUE		CHUCK
BLAINE		CLAIR
ERIKA		PRYCE

◀ EIGHT MATCHES INVOLVING SIXTEEN LEADERS... AND THE TEAM WITH THE MOST VICTORIES WINS!

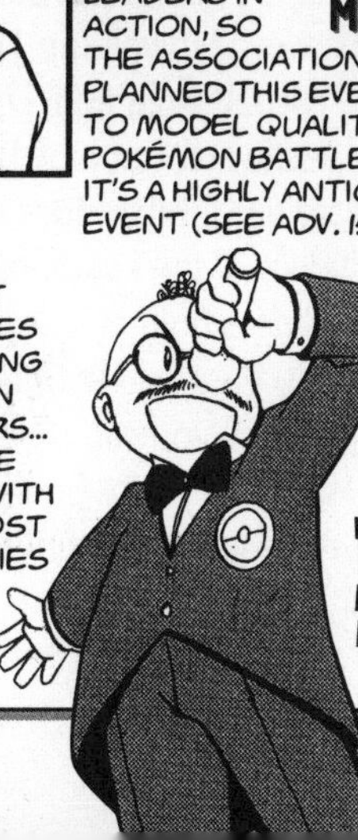

We hope you're watching the Gym Leaders' battles!

Message from
Hidenori Kusaka

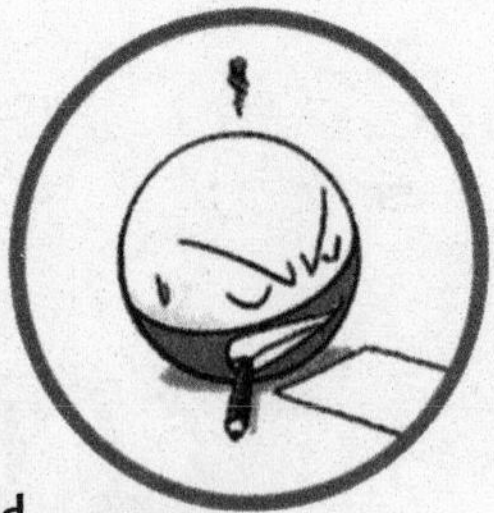

In this special volume, all sixteen gym leaders from Kanto and Johto assemble in one place! And don't miss the excitement when silver-winged Lugia goes *wild*! But the best part probably is the return of Gold and Silver. Add in Crystal and you have our three main characters back in action together. To all my English-speaking readers out there, please enjoy this volume!

Message from
Satoshi Yamamoto

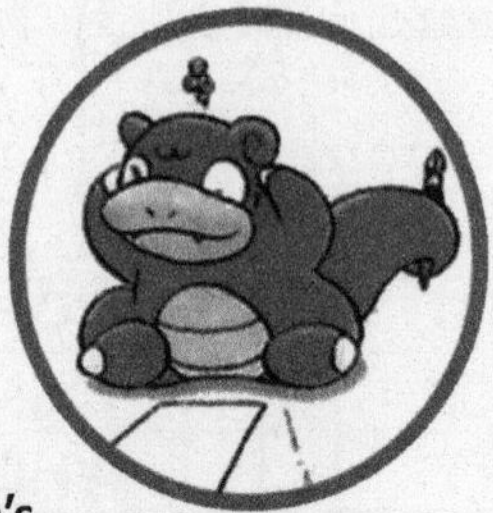

Have you noticed this issue's front cover...? In volume 11, not-yet-rescued Gold and Silver were facing backward, but now they're facing forward. What does that signify?! Also, all the Pokémon League gym leaders hold an exhibition match. At last, they are destined to meet... There's no way you can read this volume cover to cover while standing in the bookstore (ha ha)! So just buy the graphic novel already, hunker down and savor every page!!

More Adventures Coming Soon...

The Pokémon Gym Leader Exhibition matches have begun. Meanwhile, the Masked Man is plotting to invade the stadium with Team Rocket. The powers of good and evil are about to clash.

Will the Trainers be able to join forces, or will Team Rocket finally have their victory?

AVAILABLE NOW!

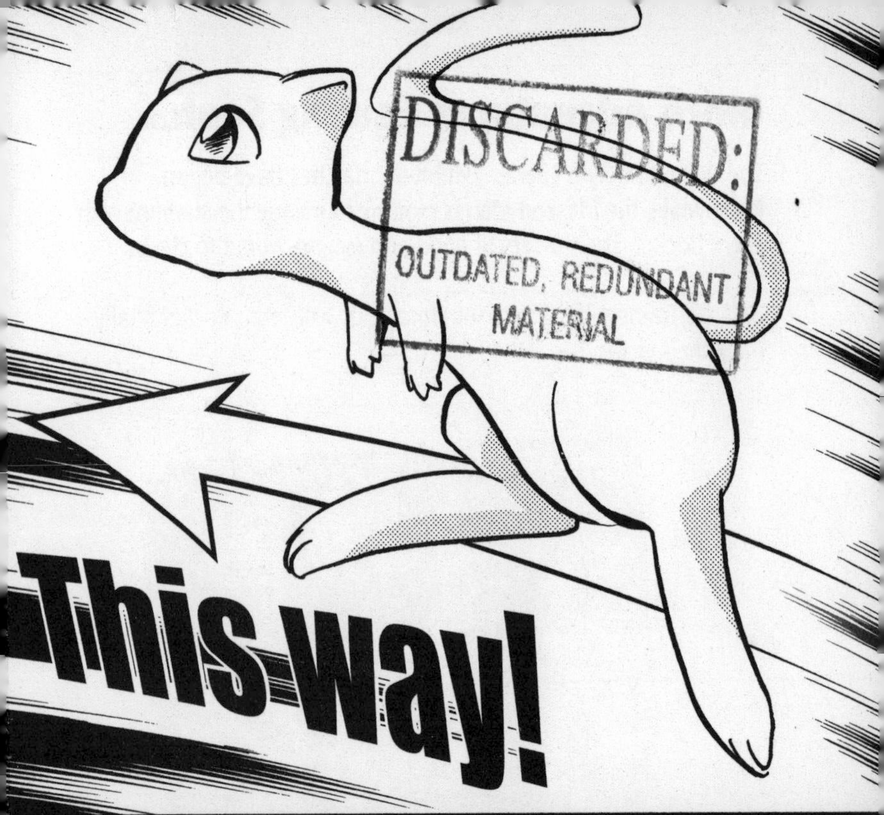
This way!

THIS IS THE END OF THIS GRAPHIC NOVEL!

To properly enjoy this VIZ Media graphic novel, please turn it around and begin reading from right to left.

This book has been printed in the original Japanese format in order to preserve the orientation of the original artwork. Have fun with it!

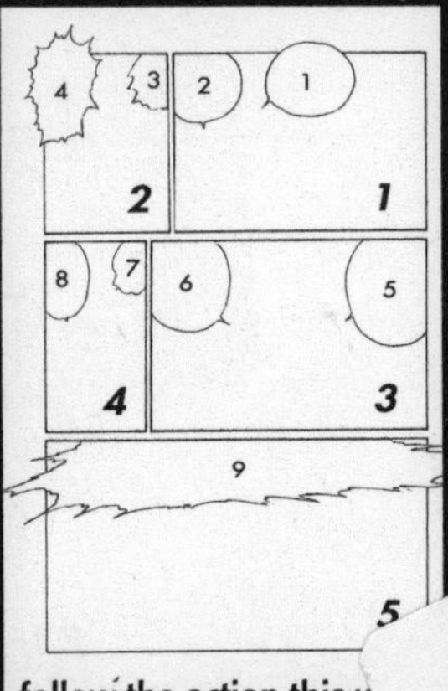
1
2
3
4
5
6
7
8
9
1
2
3
4
5

follow the action this w